Las[illegible] Night

First published in Great Britain in 2012

This edition published 2012

A CIP catalogue record for this title is available from the British Library.

ISBN 978-0-9565446-8-1

Published by Armadillo ~ Northampton

To Claude and Marjorie and to Frank and Phyllis

Many thanks to all the musicians and associates who contributed
to make our book Have Guitars.......Will Travel a best seller
and whose stories and recollections provided inspiration
in the plotting of this our first novel.

Thank you Marie Bevan, Kathleen Carnie and Paul Eales for their
candour and guidance whilst reviewing the final draft; as well
as to them, Stuart Taylor, Alan & Elaine Stanley for sharing
their insights on an early draft.

Special thanks go to Christine Booton for the loan of a writing
retreat on the South Coast, which helped us enormously
to focus on getting the early draft completed.

Thanks to Johnny (Chester) Dowling for his specialised
advice on the early 1960s.

Gerry Goffin and Carole King for 'Will You Love Me Tomorrow'.

Marty Wilde for 'Bad Boy'.

With grateful thanks to John Cox and Adrian Armishaw
for their dedication and tenacity in transforming last night's
dream into this morning's glory.

ENDORSEMENTS

'Catches the spirit of '63. Rouses our senses, serious fun and a joy to read.'

Ian Hunter, English Singer-Songwriter and Rock Legend

'In *LAST NIGHT*, Martin Thompson delivers all the sugar-rush of early 1960s culture as experienced in the provincial towns that are the greater part of England. A sincere and heartfelt watercolour of long-since evaporated moods and aspirations, painted in the pastel palette of the day, this book is an authentic taste of vanished weekends as evocative as beehive hairdos, drinks-on-sticks, Ford Anglias or the Easybeats. A tome to set the toes of memory tapping.'

Alan Moore
Writer and Publisher

'*LAST NIGHT* is a wonderful insight into the world of my parents' coming-of-age during the early 60s music revolution in Northampton.'

Jo Whiley
TV and Radio Presenter and Disc Jockey

'A gentle story of lives, aspirations and emotions to which many of us can relate. Beautiful narrative which keeps you wanting to read on. A thoughtful, well-observed novel about relationships, which can help us understand the human side of the character behind the victim.'

Saqib Mirza
Writer and General Practitioner

PROLOGUE

LAST NIGHT is about energy, fun and freedom-freedom to live, freedom to think and freedom to join in.

It is 1963. In Northampton, a small Midlands market town, the top local beat group, Kenny Waters and the Waders embrace the Mersey Beat led uprising sweeping the country.

But this is not only a music revolution; this is also unknowingly a cultural revolution of attitudes, fashion, morals and lifestyle, led by a rebellious Youth; an uprising to break away from post-war 1950s austerity and shake off parental, educational and Establishment chains.

Ken is the lead singer:	More inclined to follow his dream than settle for something good.
Gary is the lead guitarist:	Talented, practical, loyal team-player, with a girlfriend to die for.
Roger is the rhythm guitarist:	PC280, an orphan with institutional scars deep in his psyche.
Colin is the bass guitarist:	Struggling hard amid a dysfunctional family.
Dave is the drummer:	Polio as a child, bullied but not beaten.
Val is Ken's girlfriend:	Girl-next-door, reserved, wife to be, or just one of many in a long line.
Linda is Gary's girlfriend:	Feisty, mover and shaker, hot and sexy.

Colin, Roger, Dave, Ken & Val, Gary and Linda are lovers and fighters. They personify our innermost hopes, fears, and expectations.

Will they survive? Will they flourish, grow rich and famous or will they just ride off into the sunset to oblivion?

It is August 31st 1963 and it's all happening. You wanna be there? You are. Get it on!

PART ONE

AUGUST 31 1963

SATURDAY NIGHT OUT

Chapter One

5.00pm

As Ken starts to cross Abington Street, the horn of an old white van is blasted. The rusty banger screeches to a gravelly halt slap bang across his chosen path. The driver leans across, squeakily winding down his mucky window as far as it will go without the handle breaking off in his hand. Ken recognises the driver as Mick James, drummer with the Dominators, one of the best semi-pro beat groups in the East Midlands. Mick struggles to push open the sticking passenger door and beckons Ken on board.

'Hey, Ken, the very bloke I want to talk to. Climb in!'

After a split-second's hesitation, Ken eases himself onto the passenger seat and Mick drives off to Dychurch Lane, where it is safe and legal to pull in and chat for five minutes or so. 'There's a change of plan, Ken. We're leaving for Hamburg tomorrow!'

'Tomorrow? What do you mean, tomorrow? As soon as that?' Ken looks amazed, asking the question in such an agitated way that Mick could be forgiven for thinking that he is hoping that the whole project would crawl away under a stone and die.

'Yes, we're leaving Northampton tomorrow at noon. Your passport's been returned with the work visa. All the paperwork's sorted out. So there you go. C'mon, Ken, make your mind up! Are you in or are you out?'

'Has your own singer definitely counted himself out, then?' Ken appears to half-hope that the Dominators' regular vocalist has changed his mind.

'I've told you ten times that he's out. He's only seventeen. He's too young to get a work visa. Anyway, when he asked his parents they said 'No'. He's gutted! If you don't come with us, Ken, you'll regret it for the rest of your life!'

'And if I do come,' utters Ken, as his dilemma reaches its peak, 'I might also regret it for the rest of my life! You don't know my dad! He's the stumbling block! I'm hesitating because I don't know how to tell him and I'm dreading his reaction! Once I've bitten the bullet, I'm as free as a bird. Help me, Mick. Convince me!'

Mick is getting more and more irritated with Ken's attitude but for the first time is relieved to hear him talk with passion. He remains intent on making Ken his front man. 'Because you're a great vocalist, because we're great musicians and because Hamburg's the launch pad to stardom! We've everything going for us, Ken. Together, we can be as big as the Beatles! We'll become millionaires - stars of TV and radio: 'Ready Steady Go', 'Thank Your Lucky Stars', 'Saturday Club'!'

'Mick, have you broken it to your parents that you're going?'

'I told them it'll only be for six months. I'm certain it'll be longer, though. Assuming we make it really big, who knows when we'll come back?'

'What did they say?'

'Well, they weren't particularly happy. We had a bit of a row, but they've sort of accepted it. They've given me their blessing, anyway. It was a near thing, though!'

'Val will really miss me. She'll be shattered!'

Mick interrupts. 'Yeah, and before you say any more, you won't miss her. Hamburg has hundreds of girls like her and they're all waiting arms wide open for a good-looking guy like you. She'll get over it soon enough. Someone'll pick her up before long, don't you worry.'

'Can't she come with us?'

'No way, mate. Sorry. Get real, Ken. She'd hold you back. You'll need to keep a clear mind and stay totally focussed, not to be always worrying about her.'

As Mick begins to convince himself that his protégé is never going to make a decision, he is flabbergasted and delighted when Ken comes out with, 'Ok, I've decided. I've definitely made up my mind. Count me in!'

Chapter Two

6. 45 pm

'You're a bit of alright, Linda! Fabulous! Sexy!'

Gary showers his long-time girlfriend with raunchy superlatives even though she has kept him waiting on the doorstep for ages in the early evening drizzle. Easing open the front door her golden locks peep into view ahead of her shapely body. She lingers tantalisingly in a flimsy, white, sheer silk blouse and black swing skirt.

'Have a good time, you two,' her mum calls from somewhere amid the weekly ironing pile. 'Make sure you've got your key. No doubt you'll be late, as usual. Have a great time and don't wake me up!'

Linda drops the latch, closes the front door and twirls provocatively with a 'Ta dah … what do you think, Gary?'

She flings her arms alluringly in the air and glances up and down the street in the hope that net curtains will twitch and tongues will wag. She fruitlessly peers up towards the busy main road and longingly opines, 'Romeo, Romeo, wherefore art thou, Romeo?'

'Come on then, Juliet, or Marilyn, or Mata Hari…' Gary beckons Linda, or whichever femme fatale she is playing today. He clasps his Robert Mitchum palms around her Jayne Mansfield waist, encouraging the wannabe sex goddess to take a leap of faith from her Hollywood doorstep-balcony into his Tony Curtis arms.

Like a perfect gentleman, Gary escorts his girlfriend around the front of his cherished Triumph Herald to the passenger door. He unlocks it. Pulling it open, he takes her left arm and helps her to slip in. As she snuggles into the seat, her skirt slides up seductively and her fragrant peachy perfume makes him swoon.

Linda pins her dainty knees together and holds her waist to the left with her legs slightly to the right. Her posture is one she has learned from studying her screen-idol, Diana Dors. It is a position that Gary will have to gently ease her out of if he is going to get anywhere near his gear stick.

'You lucky sod!' Gary whispers to himself.

'Keep your eyes on the road and your plectrum in your pocket,' warns the lovely Linda, yearning for him to look and pluck anywhere but… !

*

Two streets away and round about the same time, Ken pulls up outside the little front garden of his girlfriend, Val. Having left the engine of his Ford Anglia running, he opens her gate. The front door is flung open and out comes the apple of his eye.

'Sorry I'm late, Val. Glad you're ready. Let's get going.'

'Oh Ken, you look fantastic. I love your new suede jacket.' Val only has eyes for her handsome boyfriend and for nobody else in the whole wide world.

'I've a show to do and an audience to wow. Can't wait!' Ken tells her distractedly, missing her compliment by a mile.

Val's mum comes to the door to see them off. She wishes Ken all the best for the show and reminds Val to be home at a reasonable time. 'You be careful, Valerie. You know how much I worry on your Saturday nights out.'

'Well don't, Mum. We've always come back in one piece,' Val reassures her, though slightly self-consciously as she glances down nervously and adjusts the lovely black and white pleated dress she has spent her wages on in order to impress her boyfriend.

Val's mum compliments her cherished daughter on how beautiful she looks in her new outfit. But Ken is in a hurry to get to the concert and turns away to the car. With Val being preoccupied by flicking off a piece of thread, she is caught out when the gate swings back due to Ken letting it slip through his fingers. As it hits her knee, Val gives a slight yelp which her boyfriend doesn't hear. He is blissfully unaware that the gate even exists.

Jumping into his car, he starts to rev up. Val, after dodging a passing cyclist, walks round to the passenger door, which is still locked. She taps on the car window, pleading to be let in by the man she adores. It has started to rain hard and this delay impresses neither Val, her outfit, her hair nor her make-up.

'Come on, Val. Look smart!' Ken calls when he has leant over to release the catch. 'Give the door a good slam. Let's go!'

Ken zips through first gear; before he has changed up from second he brings the car to 30mph. He tries to remember the words to the encore-songs he has been struggling with, even though they are classic numbers. He appears to have become totally distracted so that he can hardly raise to his lips the simplest of lyrics. Each time Val glances across at him his thoughts appear to be hundreds of miles away.

'Ken, can I ask you something?' Val butts in after a couple of minutes' uneasy silence, nervously breaking Ken's concentration, but anxious to raise a subject about which she feels slightly embarrassed.

'Well, bang goes my train of thought! So yeah, go on. What is it?' Ken asks, rather thoughtlessly and somewhat abruptly.

'Everyone seems to have been hassling me today about getting engaged or getting married. You know... Jenny Wilson at work, Mum, Linda. It's really unsettled me. I know we had a wonderful time at Butlin's and we both remember what we did together for the first time. Well, if we get engaged it will cement our relationship and kind of make it official. Do you know what I'm trying to say?'

This takes Ken totally by surprise and he squirms as he listens. For him, the timing could not be worse. He will be in Hamburg this time tomorrow and Val will be hundreds of miles from his thoughts. Moreover, he has lines in his encores to remember.

'Look, Val, we're only young. What happened at Butlin's was amazing for both of us but why should that change anything? Val, this is all about you and me, not your mum and Linda - least of all Jenny, whoever she is! They should keep their thoughts to themselves.'

Val glances down and rubs her sore knee. Although Ken may be a faithful boyfriend and a thoroughly decent lad, Val can see by the look on his face and feel by the rising emotional temperature in the car, that she has irritated him. He is still grumbling about other people not minding their own business as they reach their destination. As Val gazes down sadly at the unappreciated folds of her beautiful dress, tears well in her eyes as she wishes she had never raised the subject of tying the knot in the first place.

*

Meanwhile, as they make their way to the concert, Gary and Linda engage in a different style of similar conversation.

'We might be living together soon,' predicts Gary as he gently slides Linda's right knee away from the gear stick for the umpteenth time, a move carefully predicted by Linda, who knows exactly what she is doing!

As he smoothly glides through the gears with Linda fixing her make-up in the courtesy mirror, she agrees with him that indeed they might. 'If you're really as lucky as you seem to think you are, you might also be jumping into bed again with me soon!'

Gary's pounding heart skips a giant beat. 'Can't wait!' he sighs.

'So how did you get on earlier with our mothers, Gary?'

'I told your mum about us considering moving into a flat together. I made it sound expensive and grim, like we agreed. Then I slipped it in about whether there is any chance of me having your spare room.'

'And?'

'She didn't say 'No'; she'll sleep on it. I spun my mum the line that me and my brother sharing a room isn't working out now that we're both getting older. I told her that he's worried that his exam results might be affected unless we can find a solution. I said that he needs somewhere quiet to do his homework and somewhere peaceful to sleep. Good story, eh?

'I told her that you've an idea about me moving into your spare room, and that your home is only five minutes away. I said that I could still pop in and see her each day. I was about to tell her that it would solve Alan's problem when she butted in with, 'So who says that Linda's mother wants you round there?'

'All she said was that she would talk to Dad and let me know. She asked me what would happen if coming round to you didn't work out, and would I expect to come scurrying back home with my tail between my legs?'

'You're tail between your legs… ooh, yes please,' giggled Linda. 'Let me have a quick feel, lover boy!'

'Lin, I'm having enough trouble negotiating these bollards!' shouts Gary, as the touch of her fingers makes him momentarily lose control of his steering wheel.

'Well, I'm not!' teases Linda as Gary applies all of his limited driving skills into steering the car through the Town Centre in one piece.'Aha, so you really are pleased to see me!' she discovers with a smile, as she lets her right hand linger firmly where she has cunningly plonked it.

'Lin, stop it!' he unconvincingly pleads. 'So your mum is thinking about it and my mum is thinking about it.'

'And I'm definitely thinking about it!' she chuckles, as her unrepentant grip becomes vice-like and she does a bit of steering of her own!

The Ford Anglia screams to a halt and the Triumph Herald gently crawls up nearby. They park their cars fifty yards apart, half a street away from St Mary's Hall. As twilight falls, Ken and Val stride hastily hand in hand to the concert whilst Gary and Linda sit as motionless as they possibly can under the prevailing circumstances, chatting about domestic options and taking sexual liberties.

Ken taps the window briskly as he and Val pass the Triumph, summoning Gary and Linda to jump out and get a move on… much to the relief of Linda's right wrist and of Gary's aching virility.

Chapter Three

7.30pm

The support group is already drumming up a storm as Val, Ken, Linda and Gary approach the entrance. Linda surreptitiously hooks Ken's arm and asks him how he is getting on; Gary tells Val that he thinks her new dress is fabulous. With the entrance fee being raised to 4/6d after eight o'clock, most of the regulars are queuing early. Big Frank, the doorman, patrols around the cash desk, checking-out the punters and keeping them in order whilst his girlfriend takes the entrance fees.

Ken and Gary dip into their pockets for the reduced admission cost of two and five pence halfpenny each for the two girls. 'Gary, mate,' says Ken as he rootles around in his pocket, 'you'll never believe this but I'm a tanner short. How're you fixed for a sub?'

'It's about time you got a job and earned some money, Ken.'

'Don't you start! I get enough of that from my dad,' replies Ken, not seeing the funny side of Gary's remark. 'I'll pay you back later, as soon as we get tonight's cash for the gig!'

Ken matches Gary's three bob with his two bob and isn't even taken aback when Gary offers him the penny change. He thanks Gary and pockets the coin, the irony completely escaping him.

Big Frank is broad and well-built. He was a good amateur rugby player in his day - a powerhouse prop forward. As a bouncer there is none finer in the business. He is the top man for deciding whether or not to let in potential troublemakers in the first place or sort out any fighting later.

Once at a village hop, Frank ended up covered in blood with his brand new jacket torn in half down the back seam and his tie knotted hard around the back of his neck - talismans of a winner, his three assailants dumped unceremoniously in a heap of blood and urine in the car park amongst a pile of empty Inde Coope beer barrels.

Inside the hall, the single blokes in their Windsor knots, polo necks, jean jackets, winkle-pickers and Beatle boots are standing in small groups down one side of the hall, pop bottles frothing in one hand, roll-up cigarettes in the other.

The single girls in a mix of tight skirts, swing skirts, high heels and this afternoon's new hair-do's are sitting down the other side. Love-struck couples mingle in the central area where a large space is left clear for dancing, which usually picks up later when the lads have plucked up sufficient courage.

The aroma of cheap perfume, pungent aftershave and cigarette smoke permeates the air. The lads are on the pull, with many of the girls who are being egged-on looking shyly away. This is Saturday night and the mating game is in full swing.

Linda and Val squeeze through to the refreshments counter with Ken and Gary. Ken offers to be in the chair, ordering two Cokes, two Fantas and a couple of packets of crisps. Realising he has no money left, he glances across to Gary, who is already holding up a ten-bob note. He again thanks his mate for bailing him out, promising again that he will cough up next time (if there's to be a next time).

The four of them have arrived this early as it gives them an hour or more to soak up the atmosphere, loosen up, get in the mood, chat, dance and have a laugh. They find out all about who's kissing and cuddling whom, how the Town got on at City, the day's gossip from the barbers and hairdressers, who's been arrested for what, who's seen which film at which cinema and the odd case of who's wearing whose engagement ring or band of gold.

On stage, the Spitfires are doing a fabulous job both as support act and in competing with the chatter. They seem to be red-hot this evening, having gained a raw edge to their performance, maybe benefiting from their spell somewhere abroad.

It looks like it is going to be a full house. At half past eight the Spitfires complete their encores and wind up their spot. As Val and Linda sit and chat, and Gary starts to get a few butterflies in his stomach, Ken ambles across nonchalantly to have a chinwag with their lead singer, Jim Bishop. They know each other by sight and reputation but this is the first time they will have met. Ken knows that the Spitfires are recently back from Europe, so during the break he strikes up a conversation about a subject in which he now has much more than a passing interest.

'How was Europe, Jim? Why are you back so soon?' Ken ushers Jim away to a relatively quiet place in the front corner of the hall where the walls may have less ears.

'Watcha, Ken. Good to meet you. We're big fans of you lot. Between you and me, the German border guards wouldn't let us enter because we only held temporary holiday passports. We were forced to retreat into a lodging house in Belgium, barely surviving on two day-old, jaw-breaking baguettes and stinking Camembert, which we swilled down with an endless supply of cheap, red plonk.'

No! This is not what Ken wants to hear!

'We were soon skint. None of us spoke French or Flemish. We decided to travel to Paris, where we eventually did a few gigs through a Clichy-based booking agent for the US servicemen's clubs.

'We lodged at l'Hotel de Milieu. It was cheap and cheerful; no wonder really, as it turned out to be a knocking-shop. As such it did the trick, located as it was with a captive audience on a main street off Pigalle near the Moulin Rouge.'

Ken is speechless! The news is coming too thick and fast for his equanimity to be retained and for his thoughts to re-group. So much for the best laid plans of mice and men!

'We checked in and they gave us a welcome pack: a towel, a bar of soap and half a dozen condoms! We asked the concierge whether that was six condoms for the duration or six for each day. She told us that if we met her that night with the change and put our money where our mouths would like to be, she would tell us the answer. As we were skint, we didn't rise to the bait.

'Eric, our drummer, thought it would be greater fun to fill the condoms with water and fling them out of the window. We laughed our heads off as we watched the concierge's dream of a torrid night explode all over the unsuspecting customers creeping out of the brothel's side door; 'Johnny bombs,' Eric called them.'

Ken saw Val beckoning him from near the stage curtain: 'We're not here today and gone tomorrow, we're here today and gone tonight!' Ken could see Val mouthing his dad's favourite catchphrase as in his mind he saw Johnny bombs exploding all across Pigalle and the lights going out in the Moulin Rouge!

'The agency found us a blues trio whose drummer was forever suffering from the effects of boozing. They also needed a bass player.

Two of the Spitfires got the vacancies and filled in at a USAF NCO's club east of Verdun.

'Alfie, him over there, the lead-guitarist and me were unemployed hangers-on. We learnt a lot and became brothers-in-arms, a bit like you and Gary. We spent night after night practising routines in our room. Yeah, Alfie and me stuck together through all this crap. I think they'll be wheeling us out in a twin coffin; we're like born-again Siamese twins.'

Ken's ears at last prick up. 'Like Gary and me, eh Jim? Is that really what you're saying?'

'Our contract soon ran out. The rhythm guitarist got homesick, and left. The bass player and the drummer stayed on with the re-vamped blues group. Alfie and me, joined at the hip, stayed on to perform with an American modern jazz group: drummer, double bass, tenor sax, Alfie on guitar and me as vocalist. In a small town west of Metz, where we had a café residency for a month, I got known as 'Le Maestro du Bistro'.

'On our nights off we guested at another USAF club, 'Chez Simone', in Les Trois Fontaines. It was an ammunition depot receiving supplies daily by train. One night, amid a ferocious thunderstorm, the base shut off all power for fear of static blowing everybody up. Professional to the last, we re-named ourselves the 'Johnny Bombs' and the show went on.

'We unplugged, and in candlelight we gave a magnificent acoustic performance. We also got to snog a couple of stunning waitresses, Magda and Barbora, university students from Prague who were working their way around the world and looking for a good time.'

'A little light romance on a good night out, eh, Jim?' chipped in Ken, at last hearing some good news.

'I wish, Ken! It ended up a bloody nightmare for me and Alfie. The joint got busted, we ended up in the slammer and the girls were sent packing on a wish and a promise. The French authorities were petitioning for all work on bases to be done by local residents. All four of us had been grassed up by the jealous natives, and that was that. You know what they say... 'Every silver lining has a cloud!'

'We were released and sent home, but without our kit. Me and Alfie were penniless and thumbed it. We were picked up by another pop group from Shrewsbury who'd scraped together enough centimes for the fuel. For them, Europe had proved to be an abject disaster. But me and Alfie... we'd salvaged something and are now the proud owners of a couple of saucy phone numbers in Prague.'

Not for the first time, Ken is doing his Charm School bit. Although this sometimes irritates the others, it keeps the group tight-knit and in the limelight. The audience is swigging down, noshing up and congregating around the stage, on the dance floor and at the side tables. Expectation is mouth-watering; the atmosphere is building and if Kenny doesn't get his mind in gear he's going to be late on stage for the first number.

'The main issue is that we never did reach Germany. Who knows how big we could have become? I bet your Gary's glad he never joined us!'

'You what? Sorry? Never joined you? Gary? Our Gary? Gary Hall?'

'Erhm yes, didn't he tell you?' Jim realises he has put his foot in it right up to the waist and stumbles for his words as he digs his grave deeper in front of the bemused Ken. 'We approached Gary six months ago to see if he'd like to join us for our European adventure.'

Ken is too much of a gentleman to deck Jim. Moreover, he is shocked to the core to learn that there had even been any discussion that could have broken his brotherly bond with Gary. How dare anyone think about taking away his right-hand man and leaving the Waders in the lurch?

'Alfie had been jamming around with a Farfisa organ. We could see all sorts of opportunities for new arrangements and would've needed a new lead guitarist. He'd poached many riffs from Gary so it would've been a real coup to take your mate on tour, Ken. I'm amazed Gary didn't tell you. I guess we should've let you in on it but time was tight and we couldn't see anything wrong with the offer.'

All Ken could stutter was, 'W - what did he say?'

'Hey, Ken. I'm sorry about this. I assumed you'd have heard by now. Gary was really interested. Dead keen. Loved the idea of linking with Alfie. We assured him it would only be for six months, summer to autumn. Nothing lasts forever. He asked me to let him have a couple of days to think about it but when he came back to me he turned the offer down, making his decision at the eleventh hour.'

Ken is relieved to hear that Gary's distraction was short-lived. He trusts Gary with his life and knows deep down that he would never pull the plug on the group. He and Kenny are an item and Gary's decision not to go would have been based on the developing affinity between the two Waders. Confident that he knows that this would have been Gary's answer, Ken nevertheless asks what reason Gary gave for turning down the Spitfires.

'Usual stuff, Ken. Got a good job. A fabulous bird in Linda. A mum and dad he is close to and who encouraged him to stay as he was. The best lead guitar and singer in the business... Gary and Ken. He said he'd never do the dirty on you and we respected that. We accepted his answer at face value. I'm only sorry that you've found out this way. You should be glad to know that you've a loyal and trusted compadre in Gary. We didn't try to persuade him, Ken. We're not like that.'

Chapter Four

8.30pm

During the intermission the twist competition starts and it is time for the Waders to think about getting back-stage to the changing room. Gary takes the initiative here, ably assisted by Roger. He knows how crucial it is to tune the guitars to perfection.

When Gary nips off, Linda and Val make their obligatory trip to the Ladies. Linda needs to touch up her make-up so that she can continue to look breathtaking. As ever, many of the local girls are jealous of the two of them - their good looks, their association with the band, their clothes and their legs. It is a truth that girls go to the Ladies in twos (safety in numbers) and Val and Linda are no exception. However, where there are queues, there is trouble: up the Town football ground, at the jukebox in Lynn's Café, outside the cinema and yes, in St Mary's church hall toilets!

Val and Linda are well acquainted with the phrase 'When a glance becomes a stare... ' so they keep their heads down, avoid making conversation and never make eye contact. This is the only way to survive torrents of verbal abuse and threats of getting duffed up. This is Far Cotton's hallowed ground, a top venue for a sing-song, a snog and a scrap. Thus Val and Linda have to run the gauntlet: 'Dunno what he sees in her!' 'Stuck-up bitch!' 'Prossie!' 'Slut!' 'Posh cow!' 'Gutter snipe!'

Both girls enter the cubicles to a terrifying cacophony of thumped doors, foul screams and hurled aniseed balls. In the corner of sink-row, under the towel-roller in a forlorn crumpled heap, lies a splendid grey and white gingham oval-shaped handbag. Its two maroon handles lay open, either as an abject apology or in a cry for help! It is arrayed with the most impressive range of neat pop idol cut-outs pasted all over its sides. It is the victim of some other girl's war, having been cut to ribbons with nail scissors and soaked through with urine. The problem is that warm urine doesn't mix very well with cold paste, making the numerous cut-outs of quiffed and dreamy pop-stars kiss-curl their way off the material, their only comfort being eventual relief from the immediate pungent smell.

Linda calls to Val to get out quick. She slams back her bolt out of its keep and scarpers. But Val stays seated, taking a breather for a while. The last time she was in this cubicle was with Linda a year ago. Taking full advantage of the brilliant acoustics and echo, they belted out a stunning double-tracked 'Will You Love Me Tomorrow?' by the Shirelles, one of Ken's routine encores - an astonishingly brave or stupid thing to do, with the baying mob outside howling with derision.

Linda escapes to Ken and Jim. Regardless of her freshly-applied lipstick, she gives the newly-introduced Jim a reckless peck on the cheek. At the split-second that Val re-emerges, too scared to linger longer in the lavatory, Linda flings her arms around Ken and plonks him a whopping smacker, leaving a cherry red floret right in the middle of his forehead!

Gary sets about tuning up Colin's bass guitar in the way his father had initially taught him. His guitar tutor had also shown him some alternative techniques. At the early venues, Gary used pitch pipes but now his ear is so astute he can get the tuning-up done without aides.

Meanwhile, Dave sets up his drum kit to suit this evening's hall and feisty atmosphere. Then Colin and Roger arrange and wire up the amplifiers, speakers and PA system ready for Gary to plug in the tuned guitars for the levels to be set. He tunes his own guitar last and after coming up onto stage for the final sound checks they each give thumbs up that all is well.

It is Ken's responsibility to collect the Waders' appearance fee from Big Frank, whilst the others are setting up. After taking their cut (and, if he remembers, settling his debt to Gary from his share) he will pass on the money to his father tomorrow so that Mr Waterfield can make an HP payment on the equipment from Gary's dad's firm, Hall's Music.

When all is set, they change into their stage-wear, sleek back their hair, pose in the mirror, comment to each other on how they look, pick up their individual copies of the set lists, wish each other good luck, unite in a bonding hug and move onto the stage.

Ken, as usual, waits in the wings for the first number, ready for his grand entrance. As a safeguard, Gary always wears his guitar lower than is normal. Ever since the zip in his fly split when they were on stage at a local talent contest back in their formative days of 1961, Gary has been very careful to opt for prudence! Discretion is the better part of valour!

Gary counts in their first number,'FBI', and soon their signature start instrumental is rocking. The audience stops chattering and snogging and everyone turns to the stage. Gary starts strutting around and twanging out the lead, the others in close support. Like his hero, Hank B. Marvin, his smile erupts. They all love this tune, but none more than Gary, who now takes centre stage.

'FBI' always sends shivers down his spine, more-so tonight. He is rocking with attitude. It feels almost as good as sex and he is relieved that his guitar strap is stretched to the limits and hiding his pleasure at seeing Linda as he points the neck of the instrument her way and looks straight into her yearning eyes. With adrenaline exploding through his defenceless body, he has morphed into some mystical being. The onlookers are mesmerised by his performance. Whereas an impartial observer might say 'Good' an enthusiastic music paper reporter might enthuse 'Fabulous! Cool! The Man!'

Soon the three guitarists - Gary, Colin and Roger - line up, shoulder-to-shoulder, centre stage. The crowd knows what's coming. With driving guitars, they synchronise their chisel-toed, Cuban-heeled, brass-buckled dancing feet, ignite their blazing instruments and explode their taught bodies.

Gary leads them off in measured time, in perfect unison, in their well-practised triple-step routine... the Waders very own adaptation of the 'Shadows' Walk'. They brilliantly perform a 60 - 60 - 60 degree formation with a reverse right-heel back-kick and gyrating can-can finale: segue 'Shazam'! Pandemonium!

Their gyrating routine has the perfect rhythm and raunchiness of sexual foreplay. The girls react and dizzy themselves up; the lads join them in step whilst air-plucking their very own dream guitars. Many hours of dedication unravelled over two years' committed practising unleashes itself into one mighty crescendo which brings the house down.

At the very heart of this frenzied applause comes a big cheer from Linda, ecstatic at the turn-on part she has contributed to this orgasmic eruption. Gary takes the mike:'Thank you so much for that fantastic St Mary's Hall welcome. It's great to be back and we're going to rebel up a rousing Far Cotton riot here this evening!'

Right on cue, Dave thumps a few beats of his favourite Sandy Nelson intro, 'Teen Beat', as the crowd whistles and whoops at this pronouncement.

'And now ladies and gentlemen, boys and girls, lovers and fighters... this is the moment you've all been waiting for! Announcing two falls, two submissions or a knockout to decide the winner. Here in the blue corner we are proud to present, at enormous expense, Far Cotton's very own prodigal son... ' Gary breaks off from his fisticuff allegory amidst the pugilistic laughter and mock sparring of the gleeful crowd.

As Kenny wets his lips and rubs his hands, pacing up and down and chuckling to himself in the wings, they are enjoying the slick wrestling repartee gleaned directly from the fortnightly grunt 'n' groan wrestling extravaganzas up the Drill Hall, typically featuring Les Kellet, Billy Two Rivers and the turbulent, purple-gowned Lord of the Manor, Alan Garfield. Some of the lads in the audience try out a few half-Nelsons and exotic sleeper-holds on their mates.

Roger believes Gary would have been better advised not to have gone for a few cheap laughs. Colin gets a little edgy as he relives some of the day's events in his own life where he would have loved to land a few swift uppercuts and forearm smashes. Dave gets disconcerted as there are tensions in his life that he doesn't want alluding to on his night out. No, this is probably not the best move Gary has made, and he seems to realise it.

'Only joking, grapple fans,' he chuckles. 'Come on now, put each other down because you don't know where they've been. Please give a barn-storming Far Cotton welcome to our very own, your very own, everybody's very own vocalist, here at enormous expense, star of stage, screen and Wood Hill urinals, wait for it... the one and only, Mr Kenny Waters!'

There is polite applause as cries of 'Get on with it!' subside and the jostling abates, except from the ecstatic Linda who screams out, 'Go Ken!' and an unusually subdued Val, who, with her pallor and demeanour, is clearly not getting into the swing of things.

'Thank you, Kent Walton, I mean Gary Hall, and good evening, everybody. So c'mon everybody, let's get the show on the road with a little number from Eddie Cochran. Gary, if you please... '

Gary hits those fantastic opening bars, then Dave thrashes in with a heavy snare drum as Colin starts plucking and thumping his bass guitar. 'Well c'mon everybody and let's get together tonight,' wails Kenny. 'I've got some money in my jeans... ' he continues, again missing the irony before inviting the crowd 'to Look-out Hill' where the view up there is 'sure a thrill'. In no time, nearly everyone is dancing. The beat is hard and loud, and is pounding right into their souls and through their libidos.

The trademark special camaraderie Gary and Ken have with one another is sparkling, a chemistry hot enough to achieve instant combustion. At the Drill Hall, they would make an unbeatable tag-team to rival the Royal Brothers. They are putting on a magnificent show, knowing instinctively how to spar with each other in the limelight and excite their audience. For over an hour the show rocks then rolls, then slows for a couple of ballads before taking off again.

Everyone is well-warmed up, singing along, dancing and having a ball. Musically, the five lads are in top form... a battle-hardened unit. Gary is riding his guitar like an untamed stallion, but Colin's initial burst of enthusiasm suddenly starts to wane as memories of his edgy day sap his energy and fuel his anger.

Dave can hardly hold his head up now and is becoming withdrawn and more aloof than normal, seemingly allowing distractive thoughts into his mind. Lovelorn Roger checks out the girls: those he fancies and those he don't; those who might and those who won't!

The hall is packed to bursting point. The music is hot and so is the temperature. Something has to give. Someone's going to have to pay for this. Ken exudes pent-up energy and hip-swivelling sexuality, pacing the stage with his head tilted back, teasing magnificently, wooing the audience, making each girl his playmate. The girls love his baby face and big blue eyes, and because Val knows he is so faithful to her this doesn't make her jealous. Rather, it gives her a kick: one wink from Ken and the girl on the receiving end goes wild; when the girl on the receiving end goes wild, Val gets turned on!

If only Saturday hops could be this simple and innocent forever. If only the waking to a Sunday morning nightmare could remain the wooing of a Saturday night dream forever! If only 9.30pm at St Mary's Hall could be freeze-framed in time forever! And heart, and soul, and love, forever!

If only...

If only…

Chapter Five

9.30 pm

At the back of the hall, Gary spots the young aspiring pop stars who had visited his dad's music shop that afternoon, seeking advice on how to start a successful beat group.Alongside there is an older man, a father figure, perhaps an entrepreneur with an eye to making a fortune. They stand in a little huddle absorbing the atmosphere, listening intently and looking impressed with Northampton's trend-setting scene. Gary nods to them, acknowledging their waves of greeting.

He also notices that two girls have moved down to the stage, right in front of him. One is a real cool platinum blonde stunner named Angela, about eighteen, looking dead sexy with sparkling blue eyes, figure-hugging blouse, skin-tight pink pedal-pusher pants, and heels. The other, Karen, is equally gorgeous, with jet black hair, hour-glass figure, deep ebony eyes, white sweater, swing skirt and pumps. Two cute chicks, the best in town!

Angela and Karen turn up at most Waders' gigs and often send up a note requesting a particular song. Gary mentioned their presence only once before to Linda, who merely ignored his comments and quickly changed the subject.

To quote Ken's words: 'Karen is a perfect princess and Angela is a golden goddess'. Both girls smile at Gary. He smiles back and unconsciously wiggles his hips, playfully. This makes them laugh and maybe whisper a lurid obscenity to one another, an innuendo worthy of censorship!

Colin has urged the Waders to put into their set-list 'Skid Row', that tremendous flip-side to John Barry Seven's 'The Magnificent Seven'. The apt rendition of his mean and moody bass riff is his vibrant apology for his dad's miserable fall from grace. Gary chimes in with a crazy guitar break which has changed again this evening, being much more sinister than every other time he has played it. Dave improvises a great drum solo which lasts forever, soothing his troubled mind. Sex-starved Roger's staccato Bernstein-like major bar chords run down the phallic length of his guitar neck. Teen-idol Ken takes time out for a towel-down and a quick kiss and cuddle with the love of his life, the vivacious Val, who always anticipates the snogging-moment and hangs around right on cue at the side of the stage.

Gary invariably feels achingly jealous when this happens and secretly hates it because he feels that Kenny is taking advantage of opportunities which never occur in-concert for him. The lead guitarist never has the chance to take a few minutes out with his Linda, even during Dave's lengthy drum solos because he never knows when the drummer, given his physical disability, is likely to run out of puff.

Gary has to settle for a little long-distance flirting, envious that Kenny and Val can get down to the real thing. Particularly on this sex-charged evening, this affects Linda greatly. Her liberated views of highly spontaneous sexual freedom are thwarted by Gary being continually plugged into the amp rather than into her.

Val is a one-man girl, so these sexual nuances by and large escape her. She is dedicated to the one she adores and lovers' rituals have passed her by. All of the Waders get on great with Val and Linda, and vice versa. In their way, Colin, Dave and especially Roger all admire, nay lust over, these two visions of beauty. But Val and Linda are taken, so dream on, boys!

The evening builds to its crescendo. Ken launches into 'Somethin' Else', another Eddie Cochran hit from some four years ago. As he gets to the hook, 'She's sure fine-lookin', man, she's somethin' else', he points sequentially to Val, Linda, Angela and Karen. For flirting and turning girls on, Ken is a virtuoso.

Roger is clearly ogling Angela and Karen again. Colin can tell that Roger, who is three years older than the rest of them, is daydreaming about cradle-snatching the younger girls. When the group begins to lose its inhibitions as the gig builds to its crescendo, Colin cocks a snook at Roger and winks at Dave. Nods and winks and cocks and snooks are the stuff of schoolroom-mayhem and bike-shed brawls. As the rhythm trio take their eyes off the ball, they do not notice what storm cloud has attracted Gary's vigilant eye.

Whilst these looks and smiles are in full flow on the right side of the hall, Gary can see from mid-instrumental interlude what is brewing up on Colin's side. Northampton's very own dastardly duo have appeared on the scene - the Trasler twins: Heather and Florence.

Known in down-town alleyways and pub yards as 'Ebb' ('Ebb' because Flo is short-tongued and calls her 'Heth', which everyone else mishears) and 'Flo', these tomboys are beginning to push and shove in order to get a good view, grunting and groaning a little themselves.

Ebb has an auburn-haired ponytail and wears dark-red lipstick and crimson nail varnish, chunky mock-silver bracelets and rings, green blouse, orange and purple flared hoop skirt, multi-coloured net petticoat, a waspy belt and stilettos.

Flo has jet-black hair and also sports the same dark-red lipstick and crimson nail-varnish as Ebb. She wears powder-blue jeans, red polka-dot blouse, flat pale-pink pumps and mock-pearl necklace. Sorry Gary and Ken, it is this pair of showgirls who are the best tag-team in the business, not you!

This deceptively attractive pair of back-street pugilists (whose grandmother was once seen stripped to the waist down by Castle Station wearing a leather apron and smeared base to apex with goose grease, taking on all-comers for purses of tanners, winner takes all) seem to have sledgehammer crushes on each member of the Waders, Colin in particular. They have offered their services as personal bodyguards, always get their autographs on their entrance tickets and will snaffle up their nibbled apple cores, used drinks glasses, sweet papers, drum sticks, plectrums, set lists, broken guitar strings and any other Waders' detritus they can lay their mitts on.

When Ebb and Flo offer to mop up their heroes' sweaty brows with their imitation lace handkerchiefs, the Waders turn them down graciously. The desperate Roger has zero interest in these two sex bombs. Colin doesn't think they are too bad, and in a way feels sorry for them. They are dedicated groupies and Colin respects that, even though he is well aware that wherever the Trasler twins go, violence and mayhem are never a million miles away.

Colin is placatory to the pair of them, seeing them always as innocent bystanders - naive victims of their own reputations. As he was treating them to a cup of tea before they were kicked out after a fracas at last weekend's dance, where they caused a riot by Flo performing a striptease on a bar billiard table after Ebb had fixed the 'spin-the-bottle' with a cotton thread so that it would point to her, he presented them with complimentary tickets for this evening's show. Now the group is in full flow, Ebb waves these very tickets at Colin, calling out for him to sign them at close of show and offering to show him a trick or two with a bar-billiard mushroom she had secreted about her person as a trophy from last week's rumpus.

Adrenaline is pulsing, sweat is dripping, energy is breeding and gaskets are about to be blown as the volume reaches decibel warp factor ten.A crashing finale is assured. Kenny has St Mary's Hall in the palm of his hand; there is nowhere else in the world he would rather be... or is there?

Then, at the back of the hall, raised voices and a little scuffle occur where some louts have appeared beside the sugar daddy of the rookie Johnny and the Boomerangs, dampening the wannabes' ardour and giving their mentor's funding-optimism a steep learning curve downwards.They are soon to discover that a scuffle can easily become a melee at the thump of a chin, and the pleasure of a light romantic night out can easily become a macabre nightmare before the audience's very own eyes: two falls, two submissions or a knockout to decide the winner!

In garish tee-shirts and heavy jeans with big turn-ups and carrying pint-pots half full with beer, the three intruders shove forward, scattering throngs of dancers and on-lookers like skittles. Within seemingly seconds, Gary can see coming in at the side door, Mick Miller and Johnny Archer, the two Teddy boy acquaintances of the group, draped-up, back from the pub and looking magnificently menacing.

Big Frank has effected his insurance policy. His mates, the Teddy boys, are in the building, so someone had better watch out! Big Frank and the Northampton Teddy boy brotherhood have a pact: if troublemakers force their way in, then Teds are invited in free of charge to force them out.All these righteous tough-guys have brains as well as brawn and Big Frank will always leave them a few pints in the can to seal the deal.

The tee-shirted ruffians barge their way to the edge of the stage, invading the personal space of Angela and Karen.They make the girls cringe by leering at them as though they are the scum of the earth. They wink at them and continue to look threatening. One of the three, the one with the wildest eyes and the attitude to match, moves over to Angela and grabs her roughly by the wrist as if to drag her away and have his way with her.The evening has reached its tipping point.

The lout is unsteady on his feet, the worse for wear of a skinful of ale. Angela resists, yelping with pain as the aggressor assaults her with a Chinese burn to her captive wrist. He swears at her, whispers a filthy proposition and tries again to yank her away. She resists, then catching him momentarily off guard shoves him away. He stumbles off-balance into one of his other mates who falls across the third, their beer flying all over the place.

Ebb can't resist sticking her oar in and not being the most linguistically-endowed articulator, launches into a hasty verbal attack in classic Anglo-Saxon vernacular: 'Wanker!'

Not taking kindly to this, one of the tearaways waves his left fist in front of Ebb's face. 'Who you callin' a wanker, you fat prossie?' he enquires.

Stumped for a polite reply, Ebb stamps with all her might onto her antagonist's right foot. She swivels a full three hundred and sixty degrees so that her razor-sharp stiletto heel slices clean through his green suede shoe. It buries itself deep between the metatarsals in his innocent foot. Flo then slams her imitation leopard-skin handbag hard on top of his head. It neatly slices into his scalp with a razorblade camouflaged in its imitation-silver clasp, leaving him dazed and bloodied. Then Ebb and Flo leg it to the Ladies where they remain closeted until the coast is clear. Before long, however, they re-group and re-enter the fray.

Initially, Colin continues to pluck and slap his bass, then gains inspiration from Ebb's and Flo's bravado. Although his hands are moving precisely and powerfully over the strings, he is seething about the attack on Angela and the offence to Karen. The red mist descends! Bravado tells him that if Ebb can do it, so can he. His blood is boiling and his face has gone bright red. His jaw involuntarily clenches and his heart is pounding. Rage wells up inside him and beads of sweat fall from the tip of his twitching nose.

Colin stares-out, then points his plectrum towards and shouts at the firebrand who continues to molest Angela. Karen grabs Angela's other arm, whilst in the background, some might say in the foreground, Ebb and Flo have returned to ebb and flo the rabble-rousers on. This is too quiet a night for them in Far Cotton, so far about as dreary as anything that ever happens on Northampton's infamous 'Bunny Run'.

In an instant, Colin totally loses control, flicks away his plectrum and reacts swiftly and impetuously. 'Colin, leave it out!' yells Roger, a uniformed professional peacekeeper by day, a wily fence-squatter by night.

'Colin, no!' hollers Dave.

Too late!

Colin strips off his guitar and sends it spinning to the floor. His reaction is impulsive. His white rage is exploding into scarlet fury. He jumps off the four-foot high stage, pouncing right into the middle of the three ruffians. Fists fly. Colin launches a left-hand chop vertically under the nostrils of the toe rag furthest from Angela. It smashes into his nose with such force that the thug drops to the floor, momentarily unconscious, a dead weight, pole-axed. One down, two to go!

Angela's assailant has returned to hang on to her, so Ebb and Flo start on him. They thrash him about his head with their handbags, the blows raining in so fast that he becomes flustered and releases his prey. Colin sees his chance. He leaps in with a flying head-butt, his left hand useless, limp and trembling from his blow to the other geezer. But the lout is too quick for him. As Colin's forehead is about to land on his opponent's, up comes a clenched right fist and Colin nuts that instead. One of the oldest tricks in the book and Colin should have seen it coming a mile away. As it is, he smashes his angry face straight into the waiting fist of the tearaway.

Colin' nose cracks in two places, reverse testimony to the fact that he would have switched out the lout's lights had he connected. Cosmetic surgery would not have rearranged his face as magnificently as he has done for himself. It has become an instant patchwork quilt, his nose fused to parts of his cheekbone that it had never met before, his eyes shooting with searing pain and blood spurting Picasso-like all across his cheeks.

Colin's two front teeth have come flying out at the same hit, one lancing straight through the skin of his top lip and spinning across the floor much to the delight of Ebb who nimbly leaps on it and stuffs it in her purse - a trophy to die for. She knows a back-street abortionist who makes jewellery from spare body parts as a sideline, and is confident that Colin's incisor can be worked into a necklace if she trades a night of lust for it.

Incredibly, the band regroups and plays on whilst Colin is getting his head pummelled, testimony to the time-honoured convention that we all sing Hallelujah as the ship goes down. Mick Miller and Johnny Archer are not quite ready for action, as they have only just lit up. Smiling cheekily, they each take a few more long satisfying drags. Whilst they would like to look on a little longer and weigh up their options, they are concerned that Colin is outnumbered and are amazed that no-one else has pitched in to lend the poor lad a hand.

Mick and Johnny become Yul Bryner's Chris and Steve McQueen's Vin at the foot of boot hill, one looking at the other, the other nodding back. But there is no stagecoach for Chris to ride and no shotgun for Vin to wield, and the Teddy boys are not the Magnificent Seven, they are the St Mary's Hall Two. So they revert to Johnny and Mick, glance at each other's cigarettes, nod, smile, wink, spit and move. They are ready.

Chapter Six

10.00 pm

The two valiant Teddy boys strut their way through the panicking crowd and appear alongside lone-star Colin as the bruised and battered bass player aims, and almost connects, the sole of his left foot with venomous power to Angela's oppressor's kneecap.

Armed to the teeth, the Teds don't feel that they will have to bring much of their weaponry into play, if any. Not wanting to waste their fags, they utilise them first. The geezer who Colin has beautifully decked begins to drag himself off the floor, so Johnny thinks it is a good idea to use the lout's right cheek as an ashtray.

He screws the lighted end of his fag into it and holds it there until the skin sizzles. The sweet smell of burning flesh mingled with the pungent smell of unshaven stubble can be discerned in a sort of sweet and sour melange, and the unfortunate rascal screams for mercy. Eventually the fag extinguishes, leaving half of it un-smoked as Johnny flicks it to the floor, and the other half in the villain's cheek. A second souvenir for Ebb to scavenge, her purse becoming a trophy cabinet filled with precious mementos.

Whilst Johnny and Mick smile with approval at Colin's spirit, Colin would be pleased to do likewise; but there is very little left of his natural face to grimace with. Nevertheless, it is now three versus three, not the odds the three bullies-from-the-alley anticipated when they started this commotion.

Mick and Johnny get down to business. As the girls in the hall start to shriek, the Teds gesture to Ebb and Flo to keep out of it, indicating with calming hand movements that everything is under control. They leave Colin to deal the best he can with the irritating lout upsetting Angela and Karen, even though he is scarred and carries a distinct handicap. Mick gets stuck into the other one, who up to this point has had nothing to consider other than whether to stand by his two mates or scarper for the fire exit while the going is good. Preferring the former, it can be concluded that he isn't very good at choosing.

His next disastrous decision is to seek to ruffle Mick's velvet collar, which he soon learns is more than capable of looking after itself! He grabs the collar with a view to holding Mick steady whilst he administers a nut or two. Bad choice number two. Sewn neatly into the underside of his collar, three to the right and three to the left, are half a dozen best quality barbed fish hooks, top of the range, fit enough for the King of the Teds.

'You think you're the King of the Teds, do you?' the ruffian enquires, as he grabs Mick's collar, only to squeal like a stuck pig as two fish hooks sink deeply into the Peter Pointer and Middle Jill fingers of his right hand. One of those sewed under the right collar latches onto the Ruby Red of the yobbo's left hand. The barbs secure the three fingers as surely as though they had caught a trio of carp.

'I'm sure you'll agree, I'm still the King of the Teds,' advises Mick, before smashing a perfect head butt right between the eyes of his lamentable prey, then stubbing out his cigarette underneath his chin bone, 'and to make sure you never forget this simple fact, Sunshine, welcome to the Royal Court!'

With his fingers hooked in velvet, the poor culprit has neither hand available to soothe his ankles when Mick puts the boot in, first with his right foot and then his left. Mick has secured needles in the toes of both of his brogues, both of which snap off and lodge deep into the yobbo's legs. In total, the poor chap has accumulated no less than five shards of vicious metal (three barbed plus two vertical) one each in three of his limbs and two in the other.

As soon as Mick elicits the answer, 'Yes you are, your majesty!' to the question as to whether or not his position is vulnerable, he gives the thug a further opportunity to understand the truth of this fact by smashing into his broken face another couple of sickening head-butts followed by biting off redundant chunks of his right and left ear-lobes.

Mick happens to be the proud owner of a jewel-encrusted, nine-inch long-blade stiletto, smuggled into Grimsby on a fishing vessel, then distributed through a wet fish outlet on Northampton Market Square. He takes it out and swanks about it to his victim, who is still caught up in the fish hooks like a pair of kippers smoking on a waxy line. Ask a simple question, get a simple answer, eh, Mick?

'Do you like my present from the Dockside Gang, you bastard?'

'Oh yes, your majesty; it's lovely, thank you,' whimpers the damp squib of a firebrand, employing semi-coloned intonation, shaking and sobbing commas, urine flowing freely down his trembling legs like exclamation marks and swirling into the asterisked puddle where formerly Colin's front tooth lay.

'Would you like to see it work?'

'Oh y-y-yes p-please, your R-Royal H-Highness,' s-stutters the abject w-wreck of a hooligan in c-capital l-letters, utterly b-broken and wondering which part of his b-body would be sliced open f-first. He guesses it won't be one his ears because he isn't being made to stand against a wall with his hands cupped to catch what is left of them. He doesn't think he will have his buttocks slashed because with his fingers still caught up in his velvet collar, Mick will find it difficult to reach around his beer-belly and slice horizontally through his quivering bum-cheeks.

'If you promise to call me your lord and master whenever we meet, and if you promise to run straight away and disappear when I have shown you my knife, will that be acceptable, pal?'

'Yes sir. Thank you, sir, my lord and master!'

With that, Mick flicks open the switchblade and after threatening to slash his jugular vein drops his arm to the geezer's waistline and slices through his belt. As his jeans fall to his ankles, with an upward swish he slices through his Y-fronts, leaving his entire lower-garments in an untidy heap around his feet. The pressure these put on the implanted ankle-needles is excruciating and the villain's screams become blood-curdling.

'Run, you bastard!'

'But I can't your honour. I'm all hooked up!'

With that, Mick grabs both of his wrists and yanks them downwards, one after the other to prolong the torture. Each fish hook that comes out of the fingers rips the skin to shreds and it will be a long time before this tyrant gives any more Ch-Chinese burns.

Because the lout fails to run away as he promised, Mick brings his right fist slamming down onto the crown of his head, right at the skull's weakest point, formerly his soft spot. Thus concludes this poor fellow's entertainment for another Saturday night.

As Colin's first opponent regains his senses, Johnny, not wishing to be outdone, picks him up off the floor and batters him with a couple of swingeing haymakers. Concurrently, he offers a routine piece of advice not to mess with his ducktails, a sacrosanct house rule, one worthy of a knee to the testicles.

With Mick otherwise detained,Johnny remains reluctant to do much to help Colin, who is giving a good account of himself. Since Ebb's stiletto has already caused a shindig worthy, at last, of igniting the Bunny Run, Colin has been at it for all he is worth.

Whilst Colin is taking a terrific beating, so is the other bloke. Once Johnny and Mick have wound up their own contribution, they allow Colin one last chance to live or die for his honour and earn his badge of courage. They hold back for a little longer in the lame hope that Colin can pull it off.

But Colin has a miracle to perform. In a last desperate attempt to finish the geezer off, he pokes him in the eyes. As the lout curls up and drops his head forward, Colin's fist meets his chin with a brutal uppercut.

This is Colin's last roll of the dice; his strength is not powerful enough to break his jaw. Then, as if to confirm that enough is enough, Colin gets obliterated by another heavy right overhand flush smashing into his already broken nose. Dazzled by a constellation of midnight stars, he falls back across a table of drinks and a couple of chairs. The whole lot crash onto him as he hits the deck, yet with vestiges of broken glass all around him he is too weak to even contemplate employing a jagged piece to finish off his opponent.

Colin looks up through a curtain of blood, his senses gone, barely conscious and desperately unaware of the state of play. If he were able to think, he would now know how Don Cockell must have felt at the end of his World Heavyweight bout against Rocky Marciano in 1955, the first time he had heard a World Heavyweight fight overnight on the wireless.

He had sat there in the wee small hours on the sofa cuddled up with his dad, who loved boxing. They were both in their pyjamas, cups of tea by their side, covered by blankets as Cockell took a real beating and was done in round nine. Then the commentator's voice drifted in and out across the thousands of air-wave miles from San Francisco, as now Colin's senses drift in and out as his knees buckle under the accumulation of punches from a hardened street-fighting opponent.

Johnny and Mick have allowed Colin to attempt to win his colours, but they must now protect him. There is not much of Colin's opponent to finish off, so their flick knives, cast iron knuckledusters and bronze studded belts remain under wraps, as does Johnny's fireman's axe! Mick simply grabs the geezer's right wrist and holds his hand out for Johnny to play 'This Little Piggy went to Market', usually a bedtime children's game reserved for Enid Blyton readers' tootsies. Right on cue, at the exact moment that this little piggy ran aaaallllll the way home, with one sharp reverse yank of the final finger, Little Tom is snapped cleanly in two and that, dear farmer, is that!

Big Frank, having secured the evening's takings, now moves in. Johnny, Mick and him drag the three tearaways by their shirt collars out of the back door. They bundle them into the alley and as they lie there they are treated to one final kick to the guts, three fresh gob-fuls of warm phlegm between their eyes and a raucous Far Cotton a cappella version of 'One - Two - Three, O'Leary…'. After five minutes or so moaning and groaning under the melodic gaze of the Big Three, they skulk away like snakes-in-the-grass to lick their wounds and re-adjust their ear-drums.

Mick Miller and Johnny Archer flex their fingers, crack their knuckles, smooth down their signature velvet collars, adjust their fish-hooks, straighten their bootlace ties and thank Big Frank for the opportunity of some light exercise.

Colin could never have (and indeed doesn't) win this fight… does he? He has given a magnificent account of himself but has come too close to annihilation for comfort. He arrived on the scene, he stood strong, he took the punches, he rode the blows, he ducked and weaved and he held the line until reinforcements arrived. So in honour, he really does win, after all… doesn't he? And for the sake of honour, it needed to be done… didn't it?

In protecting Angela and Karen, Colin hopes that he will have come out of the skirmish a stronger person. 'One fight in a lifetime is one too many,' Colin thinks, then tries to rationalise that it is not win or lose that decides the winner, but how hard you fight. He tries to convince himself that it is the best message of all to have been willing to take part, but deep down he would rather have won.

With only a couple of encores remaining, the hall booking time has expired. The young wannabe musicians had crept out earlier, wondering what they would be letting themselves in for. The resident DJ calls a halt to proceedings. He requests that everyone should leave the premises quietly, makes a value judgement that they have had enough fun for one evening and would they please not upset the local residents by kicking up a racket as they walk down the street? Some hope!

A small circle of onlookers and helpers congregate around Colin, who still doesn't know whether he is on cow or horseback. He remains slumped on the floor, his back propped up by an upturned chair, his legs stretched out in front of him. Ebb and Flo offer him tissues from their handbags. Angela and Karen run to the Ladies to grab some toilet paper to stem the flow of blood and tend his wounds.

Slowly Colin regains his senses. His face is an awful mess. This is not the same face that he came in with three hours ago. Blood is everywhere. His clothes are stained and ripped and he is doubled-up with pain, especially when he tries to breathe normally. Mick Miller and Johnny Archer check him out and declare him by their rigorous standards to be Ok. They congratulate him on the effort he made against such overwhelming odds and tell him that he will always be welcome in their little corner by the jukebox in Lynn's Café.

On the grounds that Colin can see enough stars without the help of the revolving mirror ball, Big Frank hits the off switch and the flashlight shining on it cuts out. At the same time, his girlfriend flicks on the main hall lights and the stark, chilling reality of the battleground is now seen by all.

'Let's get the kit loaded on the van, lads, then I'll take Col to hospital and get him checked over.' Dave takes command of a situation for perhaps the first time in his life, clearly not knowing what he might be letting himself in for.

PART TWO

AUGUST 31 1963

EARLIER THAT SAME DAY

Chapter Seven

5.30am

Roger Edwards, Police Constable 280, turns up at headquarters at 5.30am for his briefing. He is allocated the vaunted All Saints patch. As usual, he is the first to park his bike, get the kettle on and be the fall-guy for his mess-room colleagues; echoes of his monitoring days in the children's home. The only thanks he gets for making the others a cup of tea is to be the brunt of banter about his lack of sex life and questionable parentage.

His presence as rhythm guitarist in Kenny Waters and the Waders, particularly as he is three years older than the other members, is a great asset in helping him cope. Although the younger musicians find his chivvying irritating, at least they get the sound checks done on time. Moreover, he always provides a tight and compelling rhythm section with Colin and Dave. His usefulness is his bond.

*

Roger hails from a musical background. Under a shady apple tree behind a wartime Nissen hut at RAF Goole, in the intermission of a Glen Miller 'In the Mood' evening sometime in forward-back-side-together 1940, a swift and certain spermatozoa named Tail-end Charlie boogied and syncopated eight-to-the-bar over the points at Tuxedo Junction, choo-choo'd all the way along Track 29 to Chattanooga and collided head-on with the 7.05 just leaving Pennsylvania 6-5-oh-oh-oh en route to the gal in Kalamazoo-zoo-zoo-zoooo.

Nine months later and bang on time, Roger's birth was a difficult one. For him, things never did come easy. Within months Lionel, Roger's father, left for the Second World War, soon to receive a bullet through the brain at Salerno. For poor Rachel, his mother, Roger's birth was also the beginning of the end. It started with coughing and spluttering, then wheezing and gagging. It was the commencement of a venomous attack on her body and mind which was to isolate her in an open-air hospital before her eventual demise the month before Roger's sixth birthday.

The Salvation Army took him in, then handed him over to a children's home in Doncaster along with scores of war evacuees from the East Coast ports which had been in the front line for bombs being dropped on the mainland and last line for unused bombs being unloaded when returning from raids on Coventry and Birmingham.

Every morning he was awakened by his carer, a brusque man in a dark grey suit, lovingly named 'Sir'. A slap on the backside or a flick on the bum with a slipper made him get a move on. If he didn't respond, he would be forced into a small cupboard under the stairs for five minutes. The sound of the bolt slamming into its keep confirmed his claustrophobia. Many years later, Roger, as a young copper, has an innate fear of police cells and even of locking anyone else in them.

'Barbers will be in the washroom for the boys; hairdressers for the girls in the outhouse!' barked Matron on the last Friday of each month, after their bowl of porridge and slice of toast.

Sat upright to attention at the trestle tables, their bare knees scratching on their rough undersides, they gobbled down their grub before being banished to the garden - girls to the left, boys to the right - to play out in all weathers. They wore whatever clothes they could scavenge from the sacks dumped on the dining room floor each month from the rag 'n' bone man.

By the time a monitor position came up, Roger had been slipper-thrashed into submission through years of ridicule and being kept apart from making any close friendships. Even when promoted into this authoritative position, his tenure was blighted by the reluctance of the younger children, with their stubborn nastiness, to co-operate. They couldn't take out their loathing on the staff, so they took it out on Roger.

'Roger the lodger the sod!' was his nickname, called out by the other children. This was an abbreviated version of what the house-parents called him: 'Roger the lodger, the codger, the bodger, the dodger, the sod!' When he was later on called a bastard, he had neither the confidence nor the certainty to declare that he wasn't!

'Will you be my friend?' Roger once asked Mary, a girl who was sitting alone in the day-room with her one-eared, one-eyed, one-legged teddy and a paisley cravat 'silky'.

'Yes, let's be friends, Roger,' agreed the little girl, from which gentle introduction they shared their box of broken toys, a pile of second-hand comics and their weekly confectionery ration sitting together on a rug 'cracking fleas'.

Following a rare day out at Skegness which Roger and Mary spent very happily together, a billeting officer re-located the poor little orphan to a different wing of the home, far from her ability to smile and flash her eyebrows at Roger. Who knows why, but for nothing other than fulfilling dispersal targets in keeping friendships from developing and cocooning gregarious little children within cynical bubbles of dreary isolation.

With Mary around, life had been tolerable for Roger. They would listen to bedtime stories and sometimes say 'Goodnight' to each other before they climbed their separate wooden hills to their own little Lands of Nod. For three long years these childhood sweethearts had swooned at one another from separate day-rooms and dreamed about one another from distant dormitories. The powers-that-be were never to learn of the floods of tears Roger shed from the corner of his bed, with noises of distant juvenile jollities a sinister graveyard echo.

At nineteen, Roger was called up for National Service. On his de-mob he saw a dog-eared advertisement on the NAAFI wall which proposed a career in Northampton Police Force. With the carrot dangled of cheap police accommodation, he was enticed to the town where he would soon meet up with Kenny Waters and the Waders.

At Police Training School, Roger had excelled until the role play which came to typify his future career. 'Well done, PC Edwards. We'll award you 40%, which is reasonable considering the brilliance of your mock evidence in the mock court, the only trouble being that you arrested the wrong man. In the role-play you thought that the police sergeant dressed up as a traffic warden was the thief who stole the bread from the cottage bakery, but he wasn't.

'But it was only role-play and although you were a little wide of the mark you still managed to convince the mock judge, and that was good enough for the mock examining panel. Six months simulated jail for a perfectly innocent simulated man. But no worries, you're in!'

Sergeant Jenks became his 'Father' and took him under his wing. Roger Edwards, nurtured at training school to be devoid of any critical thinking, swore his allegiance to Northampton, to crusade over the tracks into the heart of Far Cotton, to faithfully carry out his cycle patrols up in Spinney Hill, to perambulate in a north-easterly direction to the tetchy environs of Abington and to circulate amongst all bread and dripping aficionados who stroll along Birdcage Walk in their fur coats and feathered hats in sympathy with the strutting peacock. All towns have a two-tier demography, some say the puffs and the scruffs; Northampton is no exception.

It was in 1961 that Town played Rovers in a second-round match, a local derby in the cup. Hopefully to put into practice the arrest procedure he had perfected at training school, PC280 requested duty along the cinder track behind the goal, in front of the partisan and vociferous claret and white hordes.

As the British Legion band struck up Sousa's 'Hail to the Spirit of Liberty', PC 280 strolled back and forth, repartee-ing with the crowd, bantering, having fun in a money-for-old-rope sort of way, when suddenly a group of noisy, swash-buckling, misdirected Rovers' fans arrived alcohol-fuelled from the nearby pub. A melee ensued as red met claret!

'In you go, Edwards!' Sergeant Jenks bellowed. 'We're right behind you, lad!'

Roger Edwards gymnastically gate-vaulted the terrace wall, and in a Charlton Heston-esque moment commanded the crowd to part as he made his way to the back of the terracing and to the site of the ensuing tussle. Sergeant Jenks was indeed right behind him, a long way right behind him. As PC 280 moved in, the baying crowd converged and the sergeant was swallowed up in the cauldron.

There is only one thing that will unite marauding football fans from nearby towns and that is to redirect their antagonism against a common foe, in this case PC 280 Edwards. Roger went down with barely a whimper. As fists and boots rained in, no-one helped him. Onlookers cheered and howled derision. His helmet was last seen flying across the terraces and over the gate into the nearby road.

In a last-ditch bid to regain his dwindling authority, he grabbed the first person he thought he could handle - in this case, a frail fifteen year-old youth. He bundled him through the crowd, crashing him into the terrace wall then frogmarching him backwards out of the ground to the waiting police van as eighteen thousand incensed onlookers booed and hissed in united derision.

As Clifton crashed in a hat-trick for Town, PC Edwards signed off sick to the St John's Ambulance team, got patched up and brushed down and plodded home to lick his wounds. His helmet was temporarily resurrected, being kicked by two fourteen year-olds along the gutter, then in front of a double-decker bus. Edwards had survived; his helmet hadn't!

In the Magistrate's Court the following Monday, the fifteen year-old was released unconditionally as there was no evidence against him. PC Edwards' career was continuing nicely on a course of arresting the innocent.

Roger Edwards enjoyed being allocated duty in the Semilong district, where he would clip the ears of cheeky, back-chatting scoundrels, give solace to wives battered to a pulp by their husbands, and banter lustfully with ageing prostitutes standing impatiently in the neon glow outside the open-all-hours corner shops.

For turning a blind eye to their kerb-crawling customers and street-corner shenanigans he would occasionally accept kick-back hand-relief in the back room of the local taxi cab office. He thus gained a sixth-sense for the mingled aroma of cheap perfume, gin breath and stale semen that permeated the thin blue line of Northampton.

By the time PC Edwards joined Kenny Waters and the Waders, he had built a great affinity with all residents of Semilong. He empathised with everyone and, having learnt first-hand as a child, was reluctant to bang up anyone. He consistently questioned notions of right and wrong. By the time he had made up his mind, the guilty party would have walked free, an innocent bystander would have been in the nick and Roger would have ended up on a discipline charge. He was nurtured to act in haste and repent at leisure. Sometimes this philosophy worked, sometimes it didn't!

*

'It's the end of the month, lads. Keep your eyes peeled for tax discs. Never mind the fourteen-day grace. If it's expired, book 'em,' instructs Sergeant Jenks in his preliminary briefing designed to put them in the right mood to cow-tow to blind officialdom. Theirs not to reason why; theirs but to do or die!

'There are more posters in the General Office about the train robbers. Study them closely and let's lock the buggers up!'

A few 'Yes, sarges', then it is time to open pocket books and take down the local details: stolen bikes and their frame numbers, thieves on the Market Square, then today's big news printed on a circular!

'Last night at around 1.00 am, some persons as yet unknown entered the cellars of 'The Crown'. They also gained entry to the lounge bar and raided the cigarette machine. They stole several boxes of 200-pack Kensitas, Craven A, Park Drive, Senior Service and Woodbines, and many boxes, the number to be verified later, of spirits. The felons used a type of jemmy, first to snap the cellar-flap lock, then to prise open the cigarette machine. They forced open the till and stole the evening's takings.' Thus reads Circular 17/8.

'One of the cheeky bastards even crept upstairs into the landlady's boudoir and rifled all the jewellery from her poncie dressing table while the silly tart hadn't even got the sense to wake up.' Thus paraphrased an unusually sympathetic Sergeant Jenks.

'So deliver the circulars of the stolen jewellery, the booze, the fags and some cosmetics, proceeding slowly and diligently around your patches and keeping your eyes peeled. Deliver them to all pawnbrokers, jewellers, public houses, paper shops, corner shops and for you, Edwards, the market grafters. Additionally, moreover, nevertheless, Edwards, the scrap-yards are shut today, so me and you will do them on Monday.'

Roger yawns. He is already daydreaming: the story of his life! He imagines the headline: 'Local PC arrests Great Train Robber!' with an accompanying picture of himself holding up a giant bullet-ridden holdall crammed with ten-pound notes, found hidden in some shed or storeroom.

'Wakey wakey, rise and shine!' the sergeant shouts, evoking memories of Roger's formative times. 'Don't bring back any stray mongrels today, Edwards! If you're handed any, give them a kick up the arse and send the mutts on their way.'

'Yes, sir; no, sir. I mean yes, sarge; no, sarge, sir, sergeant.'

At 6.00 a.m. prompt, the keen and eager constables are dismissed. The All Saints patrol gives Roger an opportunity to enjoy the hustle and bustle of weekend life. Tantalisingly, it also gives him the opportunity to eye up the downtown tottie and maybe have a chat with some of his beat group chums as they stroll through the portico and across the square.

Had he taken his normal route rather than his favourite short cut, he would have been extremely suspicious to see his Teddy boy chums, Mick Miller and Johnny Archer, sneaking out of Wood Hill toilets. He would have been intrigued to see them make their way sheepishly up Sheep Street.

He would have been inquisitive as Mick and Johnny entered the Cross Keys public house, over their shoulders a couple of kit bags, incongruous indeed with their velvet collars and cuffs. Teddy boys would never be seen dead carrying anything other than concealed weaponry, especially at such an unearthly hour of the day. Strange! Suspicious! But Roger misses it all.

After his breakfast break at a quarter to nine, he decides to visit Rendells' pawnbrokers on Abington Street and deliver the missing jewellery list. Roger accepts a mug of coffee from Mr Rendell, the swigging of which would give him the opportunity to have a little browse through a display of goods on a little green baize card table. The articles appear to be German and include a one-litre ceramic beer stein, a wooden Nussknacker (nutcracker) in the form of a soldier and a Leica camera.

He shivers at the memory of the bullying and rigors of barrack room life in Germany and the sadness of his failure to hit it off with any of the local girls at the Bierkellers, mainly as a result of him asking potential female partners if they were 'Jungfrau' meaning 'virgin', when he thought he was asking them if they were single.

The highlight of Roger's National Service was when he was posted to Hohne, where he learned to play guitar. His mate Geoff, in the next bunk, had been a skiffler up in Ripon and had bought with him his guitar and banjo to play in the Corps dance band.

One evening, Roger and his army mates went out for a drink, to be totally amazed by the Wurlitzer jukebox which was blasting out 'My Old Man's a Dustman' by Lonnie Donegan. This made him homesick and lovesick for Mary, the childhood sweetheart he had lost.

Germany had loomed large and hostile in the formative years of the Waders' rhythm guitarist. The Second World War had taken the life of the father he never knew. German bombs had forced his evacuation from Hull, and National Service had taken him away from the dubious safety of the children's home…and from Mary.

Chapter Eight

7.30am

Is Ken dead, murdered by a thief in the night? His head is hanging half over the side of the bed. His forehead hosts small beads of perspiration. Slobber emanates from the corner of his mouth; his body is flu-like and clammy…

('I'm happily cruising along the road in my Ford Anglia with not a care in the world. Suddenly, without warning, I'm falling into a huge, silo-like hole, a gigantic swirling pit; falling faster and faster, further and further, deeper and deeper - on and on… and on…

('I can see nothing but I can feel myself out of control, dropping ever faster into the pitch black. I can hear music, pop music, in the far distance. As I fall further it gets louder, louder, like I'm passing by a huge loudspeaker. But I see nothing. It's still pitch black, then it gets more distant again and I'm still falling, falling into oblivion. I'll soon crash and be dead. They'll never find me in here. I'll be gone forever. People will say, 'Whatever happened to Ken? Here tonight and gone tomorrow!' Will they look for me? They wouldn't know where to start….')

*

Ken awakes with a jerk! 'I'm alive! Was that a nightmare? I can't shake it off!' The horror remains vivid.

A strange metallic taste pervades his mouth. Perhaps it is an overnight chemical reaction between the beer at the pub and the hastily-brushed peppermint toothpaste following his return home. Ken runs his coated-tongue around his mouth, seemingly checking that all his teeth haven't fallen out. His ears are awake first, his brain coming a close second. His eyes are struggling to open and even finish the race.

The late night fish supper he gorged in his car is now stalled some distance short of his beer-lined stomach. The extra fish cake (offered at a bargain price as the fish-and-chip shop was about to close) and the free-of-charge batter-bits are now poised to lead a contra-flow up to their origin.

Ken burps loudly, hoping this might relieve the situation. It doesn't. He is drowsing: 'Get lost! Leave me alone! Let me think of something more pleasant than this - take me back a fortnight to Butlin's!'

He turns slowly onto his back and widens his arms but there is no touch of his lovely Val on either side. He clouts his left-hand knuckles on the wall with a jarring thud. Now he is really awake! His eyes are still clamped firmly shut and will need time and coaxing to open.

'No, I'm definitely not at Butlin's. No seven o'clock trumpet fanfare through Radio Butlin's public address speakers. No 'Wakey-Wakey; good morning campers; reminder call for first-sitting breakfast at 8.15am,' from an over-enthusiastic and over-sexed Redcoat. That cheerful music they played! If I'd had some wire-clippers with me, the chalet speaker cable wouldn't have lasted more than a day.'

Ken gropes down and around with his right hand, then retrieves his absent pillow which is lying forlornly on the lino below. He gives it a hug and a kiss: 'Morning, Val.'

A quick glance at the loud-ticking Westclox alarm clock, through his one now-open but squinting eye, shows 8.15am. But what day is it? 'Yes, it's Saturday. Fantastic! I love Saturdays - as a young lad, it was football all day. Now it's dance, dance, dance the night away with my very own 'Kenny Waters & the Waders'. School's in the past, work's in the future, so it's singing with the group and out with the girls: a perfect day to savour. What shall I do?'

Music comes wafting from a distant radio. Probably his mother's in the kitchen. He strains to hear. It's not any music, not Mum-type music, but something different. Is it 'Children's Favourites'? He strains to make sense of the lyrics. He can also hear his mum humming along with the tune: 'Nellie the elephant packed her trunk and said 'Goodbye' to the circus. Off she ran with a trumpety trump...' never to be seen again.

'Oh, yeah, that's me. Gone. Slip my dad's ball and chain, and when daylight comes I'll be on my way.' Ken's hopes and wishes, however, are tinged with uncertainty. 'Another fifteen minutes in bed will do the trick, providing my bladder'll hold on.' He presses it with his fingers, crosses his legs and lets it stew. Ken begins to realise it is good to be alive. Surrounding him on his bedroom wall are posters of the Beatles, Cliff Richard and a full-size pin-up of Brigitte Bardot in a fur bikini.

'That could do with a change after two years,' he thinks, meaning replacing Brigitte with Ursula Andress, his latest pin-up, emerging from the sea in the film 'Dr No'.

Ken yawns and stretches his long frame until his thigh muscles quiver just short of spasm. He reflects on what a good night out it had been with Val, Gary and Linda. He rejoices in the fact that being eighteen he is now legally allowed to drink alcohol, having spent the last two years secretly swigging pints of beer in backstreet bars, hoping his father or some schoolmaster wouldn't catch him red-handed. This could result in the dreaded 'whack' of the headmaster's cane, or, much worse, severe rebuke and days of humiliation from his father.

Since being a celebrated choir boy, Ken has always liked singing. When he was eight, he was encouraged by his parents to make his public stage debut at a Working Men's Club in a special 'Have a Go, Joe' post-Coronation party. Dressed as Davy Crockett, King of the Wild Frontier, complete with imitation raccoon fur cap, he sang Frankie Laine's 'I Believe'. He has adopted the song title as his motto ever since.

At Butlin's two weeks ago, Ken won the weekly Talent Contest hands-down, receiving an invitation to return free of charge in a few months' time for the Grand Finals and a potential £250 first prize. Secretly he has no intention of returning, knowing even then that he has bigger fish to fry. He did, however, love the queue of young girls and Redcoats jostling for his autograph.

'I could get used to this,' he thought, 'being a star!'

Living within the same catchment area, the four pals, Ken, Gary, Val and Linda, were Barry Road mixed-infants, then juniors, until their educational paths had diverged - Gary to the Boys' Tech, the girls to the Girls' High and Ken to the Boys' Grammar. That September day was the worst moment of Ken's eleven year-old life. He was heading south and the other three were heading in totally different directions. How would he survive a whole day without them?

The Grammar school was the first goal he had ever yearned for.

When the 11-plus exam results envelope dropped through the letterbox in mid-1956, he knew beyond all shadow of doubt what it would say.

'Well done, Kenneth. Your father will be delighted. Nothing less than we expected!' His mum was jubilant: that was the problem... his father's expectations were always so high! Even when Ken succeeded (as he always did) it diluted the achievement and spoiled the celebration.

At junior school, Ken was the star pupil in the 'A' stream. He was centre forward in the football team and the three-legged race champion (with Val) at the school sports day. It was when he was paired with Val, aged ten, that they had first hit it off. He was so competitive that he demanded that they practised after school in the park by 'our bench' before dark.

'Our bench' was the special one next to the paddle-boat office which to this day has the letters 'V' and 'K' enclosed in a love-heart, carved by Val following a walk in the park with Linda. It embarrassed Ken when Val first showed him, but underneath his tough exterior he was proud that someone loved him, proud that it was Val.

Val was the first girl in whom he showed any interest. The first time he held hands with her and the first time he kissed her were amazing. He grew to like Val, then over the years to more than like her. Val idolises Ken; they seem inseparable and now stalk each other everywhere.

'Don't waste your time watching football, Kenneth. Rugby is a man's game. It will toughen you up and develop your character. It's a team game.'

Ken was not sure how one's character got developed by shoving your head between the backsides of two front row forwards while trying to obliterate your opponents in a scrum. ('Feet and on! Tackle him low!')

'Because I'm tall I have to play second row, the worst position in the team, with two wing-forwards up my backside, too. Purgatory!' he thought. ('Ball's coming in........ now! Heave!')

Why had Ken's dad changed his tune? Mr Waterfield had encouraged Ken to play football and each May invited home seemingly everybody from work and close neighbours to watch the Cup Final on the only

TV installed so far in the street. Their front room - with the thin polyester curtains closed and black-out curtains left over from the war years draped over them to keep out the strong May afternoon sunshine - would have about a dozen blokes packed in it: six on the chairs and settee, six cross-legged or stretched across the floor, all smoking.

Ken, at the front, could vaguely be seen through the blue haze, propped up between his dad's feet. Within ten minutes of the final whistle he would run upstairs, get changed into his football kit, collect his white vinyl football and head off for the park for a pre-arranged game with his best friend from the next street, Gary Hall. Ken would be Jackie Milburn, Nat Lofthouse, Bobby Smith or Peter McParland for the next hour. He wanted always to be the match-winner, the goal-scorer, the hero. 'No-one remembers a loser!' was his motto!

Ken thought his new school would be a breeze, like before. At the end of the first year, though, it was touch and go whether he would even make one of the two 'A' streams. He eventually scraped into the 'A' languages stream, putting him in the top seventy pupils of the year. From top to seventieth in one year? His dad was not amused when he returned from Parents' Evening where his three term reports were assessed and corrective actions noted.

'Could do better,' was soon changed by his dad to 'Will do better, or else!'

And better he jolly well did! 'Homework, homework, homework' This became Charles Waterfield's mantra for the next seven years. His father was very hard on him, but Ken eventually turned it around and his results got better year on year. Four years later he took six 'O' levels and passed five, only failing in Chemistry, which was a subject tagged on to make up his timetable.

His mother and father offered him no sex instruction, neither did the procreation lesson at school. Ken was too embarrassed to ask about the facts of life, so his development was in his own hands, with a little help from some mind-boggling graphic diagrams he found on the walls of public toilets.

When he was sixteen, the discovery of a paperback copy of 'Lady Chatterley's Lover' in his mum's bedside cabinet proved most educational when he sneaked it away for the odd half hour on the toilet so he could flick through to the interesting bits. But it is over the last few weeks reading the details of the Profumo affair in his dad's newspaper that he realises that the whole world seems to be at it, so why should he miss out?

Prime Minister Macmillan's slogan 'You've never had it so good' is ready to be replaced by 'You've never had it so often!' He has also built up a hot crush on Christine Keeler, the young long-legged brunette involved in the political sex scandal. Is it her sultry looks or her sexual antics that make her so attractive to Ken?

It seems that Linda is the expert on the subject of sex. She instructs Gary, who then illuminates Ken. Linda has often embarrassed Ken with the suggestion of a clandestine meeting to personally extend his sexual education. Ken has smiled and changed the subject whilst secretly admitting that Linda would be a much better proposition than the blackboard diagrams at school!

Ken switches on his record player and pulls from its sleeve his latest '45' purchase, Gerry and the Pacemakers' 'How Do You Do It?'. He grabs his hairbrush off the dressing table as a makeshift microphone and starts to duet with Gerry: 'How do you do what you do to me? I wish I knew... If I knew how you do it to me then I'd do it to you...'

'Yes, I'd do it with you, Linda; I've done it with Val!'

Along the landing he drags his gangly frame to the bathroom, clad only in his orange judo-style pyjamas tied up with a black belt, running his hands through his mop of dark hair. He grabs a shave, then brushes and combs his hair. He likes the fact that his hair is getting longer, much more rock 'n' roll. He pouts in the mirrored door of the bathroom cabinet.

Finding himself more irresistible than Billy Fury, he gets dressed and tries to memorise the words of Val's and Linda's favourite, 'Will You Love Me Tomorrow', and the one he likes best, 'Bad Boy', two great tracks he fancies as encores in tonight's show.

Ken is now eighteen, with five 'O' levels and two 'A' levels under his belt. He has achieved everything his parents had set for him but each year his father seems to increase his expectations and it is starting to grind him down.

'Each day,' he carps on, 'I'm put on the back foot and have to defend my actions, my life. I'm always obliged to prove myself to him. Why can't my father just be a little more kind, give me some encouragement? Will I never be able to please him and shut him up?'

Chapter Nine

7.45 am

Doris Roberts, in a self-made, heavily-patterned crimplene dress, courtesy of material bought from Cyril on the town market, cotton floral pinafore, slippers and hairnet, is sitting busy at the yellow formica kitchen table. She is the picture of domestic bliss with a pile of clean dishes on the drainer waiting to be put away, a bowl of dirty dishes in the sink and two greasy breakfast plates on the kitchen table. Her pinny is well-stained with a week's toil. It looks overdue to join a pale blue plastic basket of dirty washing and a box of Oxydol sited on the floor by the back door.

In front of her, on the table, is a yellow cardboard box, about twelve inches by six, with the words 'Radiance Devon Cream Toffee Made in Doncaster' in red and brown, emblazoned three times across the top, the centre two inches of which have been covered by a poorly-torn sheet of exercise book Sellotaped onto the lid with the words 'Bills' written in blue biro.

Inside the box are six tins, orange and cream in colour, each about three inches high and three inches diameter. On the side of each, in white, are the words 'Bile Beans' and in black, 'Laxative Plus'. On their lids are the words 'A reliable corrective for constipation, liver and stomach disorders'. But again, handwritten in biro on paper and Sellotaped over each lid, are the words 'Rates', 'TV', 'Phone', 'Coal', 'Electricity' and 'Gas'.

Mrs Roberts unscrews the tin marked 'Coal' and peeks hopefully inside where she sees a mix of bank notes and coins. She takes these out, lays them on the table and begins to count. By merely handling them, she has resigned herself to the fact that there is a shortfall and heaves a sigh of frustration. Four fivers, three one-pound notes, two ten-bob notes, four half crowns and a florin makes twenty four pounds twelve shillings. She calculates in her head, then confirms by taking a pencil from behind her ear and writing the amounts and her reckoned total in an old red exercise book left over from her daughter's schooldays. She knows that it is not enough and that she is going to have to rob the 'Electricity' tin yet again. She utters the words 'Damn it' under her breath.

Her concentration on money matters is unexpectedly broken as her daughter, Valerie, enters the room. She is seventeen years old, five feet two inches with long shoulder-length honey-coloured hair tied back in a pony tail, with a few long strands hanging down in front of each ear. She is wearing a thigh-length white wrap which she is just tying up around her white cotton 'Baby Doll' nightie above her shapely legs, and soft, pale blue slippers. She yawns and stretches.

Mrs Roberts greets her daughter with a smile and asks her what she wants for breakfast. Val is not at all in a breakfasting mood, still feeling a bit over-full as a result of the late night fish 'n' chips in Ken's car. She picks up one of the six tins on the kitchen table and reads the wording on its side, wondering whether 'Bile Beans' might be the answer to her digestive dilemma, not realising it only contains notes and coins.

Val reluctantly agrees, mainly to please her mother, to try one slice of toast with marmalade and a cup of tea. As the grill over the cooker is preparing the toast, Val watches her mum sit back down at the table, scratching her head and using her fingers to try to figure out how to make two and two equal more than four, more than five even. Six would be best!

But Saturday breakfast time is set aside for juggling bills, tins and wage packets, with the express priority of keeping the wolf from the door and leaving enough cash for enjoyment, especially their regular Saturday nights out. The recent installation of a telephone has pleased all three of them and has kept them up with the Jones's, whilst frustratingly leaving Doris an additional tin to set up and manage.

One mouthful of tea is all that Val can stomach; it tastes slightly strange and the marmalade is not much better. She is feeling a bit queasy, made worse when she notices a packet of ten Woodbines on the kitchen table by her father's empty breakfast plate, and a disgusting half-filled ashtray of dog-ends. She quickly, hardly daring to look, moves all three items off the table, placing the plate in the sink and emptying the ashtray in the flip-top plastic kitchen bin.

It is not often that Val is up and about the house in the morning at the same time as her father. However, when she is, she is normally treated to ten minutes of coughing, choking and generally waking everyone up in the street, whilst his nicotine and charcoal-encrusted lungs readjust and realign their operation from the horizontal to the vertical.

'Where did you go last night, duck? I heard you come in; it must have been late.'

'No, it was only about midnight, Mum.'

'Well, that's plenty late enough for a girl of seventeen.'

'Eighteen, in a fortnight, Mum.'

'Which reminds me, Valerie. What would you like your dad and me to buy for your birthday?'

'Only one thing I need, Mum. Clothes! But clothes that I choose, Mum, not you and Dad.'

'Well, why don't we go into town together one day next week and get you what you want? I'll pay for it.'

Val baulks at this proposal, stays silent, then after a few seconds suggests, 'Or I could go with Linda, Mum? Then you don't need to worry yourself.'

'No, I better come with you, love. If you ask Linda to help you there'll be no telling what you'll end up with! I don't want you looking like a common tart. Linda's a right little madam. Wears her skirts and dresses far too short for my liking, and her high heels are much too high. I don't know how she can walk in them.'

Val feels increasingly frustrated with her mother's Victorian dress sense and attitude, and stands up for her best friend - not letting her mother get away lightly with unfair criticism. 'Linda, has a good taste in clothes, Mum. Knee-length is the current fashion, so are stiletto heels. Don't forget, Linda's this year's Carnival Queen. Even you said how good she looked in her pink and white satin dress, golden sash and a rose in her hair. She even got the Waders a booking to play on the bandstand in Abington Park after the Cycle Parade ended. There was a huge crowd there, at least until the punch-up. They even got their picture in the Echo the following week.'

Doris moderates her attitude only a little. 'When she is on show and all dolled up with you helping with her make-up, she turns heads, does that one. Her mum and Gary must have been very proud of her, sat there on top of that float with her maids of honour, waving and smiling at everyone as she went past. Delusions of grandeur, if you ask me. I don't know why you didn't try for Carnival Queen. You could have given Linda a good run for her money.'

'I could, I suppose. But Linda has a way with the men, and all the judges were local dignitaries. Footballers, cricketers, councillors… all men. She knows how to attract them with the 'glad eye'. I couldn't do that.'

'Poor Gary. He'll soon wish he was with someone not quite so attractive. I bet she leads him a merry dance. You make sure that you're careful when you're out with her. Linda likes to act a lot older than she actually is. She's not the best example for you.'

The mild criticism continues. It is starting to feel like a lecture to Val. 'I hope you're careful what you drink, Valerie. I remember young fellas from my day. Ply you with drinks then try it on. 'Ply it and try it', they used to say.'

'Mum, Ken isn't like that. A Babycham or a Cherry B is all I normally have. Linda drinks vodka and lime, or Martini.'

'There you go. Proves what I was saying. Vodka! Good grief, what next?'

'I think it's perhaps time for us to go and see the doctor about you growing up, Valerie. You'll need to get yourself sorted out before it's too late. There are new medical things available to avoid unwanted pregnancy, they say. I could tell you that you must keep your legs crossed until you get married, but I understand that it's not always that simple.'

'Did you and Dad wait, Mum?'

'Well that's for us to know and you to guess!'

'I have guessed and the answer is - No!'

Mrs Roberts' cheeks go bright red, but behind the blush her eyes are reminiscing on those good old days during the war when she was Valerie's age and you lived for the day. 'The brave men who had to go off and fight for our country needed some love and affection to send them on their way and to welcome them home safe and sound.' She continues to blush as she thinks back.

'Your dad would never forgive me if I let you get pregnant at your age.'

'But it's not your responsibility, Mum, it's mine. Ken knows what he's up to.'

'Up to? Until you get married, my duck, it's mine, too.'

Val's mind returns to a fortnight ago at Butlin's. The four of them were only allowed to go together to Butlin's on the condition that the two girls and two boys would be in separate chalets. However, as dictated by Linda, it was clear that this was never going to happen, and it didn't. Ken did try it on every night, and after intense pressure, Val went all the way for the first time. She was worried that not sleeping with Ken might frustrate him and ruin their friendship. She also knew that Gary and Linda were always at it and Ken knew this, too. You could clearly hear them in the adjoining chalet. Having sex was wonderful and such a relief. She felt that she had at last grown up and thrown off the mantle of childhood. Afterwards, Ken was also flying; he must have felt the same.

The next day they stayed in bed all morning and Val missed the heats of the Beauty Queen contest, which Linda subsequently won. Both Ken and Val couldn't stop smiling, kissing and touching each other. It was a great secret - to have been in bed with the one you love: two peas in a passionate pod. Rolling on top of each other, grappling and stroking, kissing and cuddling, huffing and puffing, mumbling and fumbling, wet lips on moist and tender lips, skin on warm and naked skin, tongue on tongue, breathing the same air in and out, hearts beating in unison: a perfect harmony of two separate people into one connected being.

That night had been sublime. Such deep and passionate feelings one had for another resulting in ecstasy and fulfilment. They were baffled as to why they hadn't done it sooner! Val was certainly aware that she could get pregnant but Ken seemed to have it all under control, like she thought he would, so she wasn't concerned.

Her glorious memory is terminated by her mum's voice. 'Kenneth's a pleasant lad. He's a good catch for you, Valerie. He's from a very good family. His dad's got his own business; his mum's a bigwig at the church. You need to tie him down a bit, though. He'll have the pick of the field. You don't want to lose him and be left on the shelf, do you?'

'Mum, I'm not even eighteen! Ken and I are like Linda and Gary. You can't imagine one without the other. Morecambe without Wise? Pearl Carr without Teddy Johnson? We've known each other since we were five; that's thirteen years. We've been going steady since we were thirteen, that's five years. We go everywhere together; we do everything together.'

'There aren't many boys like Kenneth with such a good future. I bet his dad'll see him alright in the firm. He passed his 'A' levels, didn't he? Have you discussed the future with him, Valerie?'

Mrs Roberts can see it all - a big spread in the local evening newspaper with a picture of Valerie and Kenneth sitting in the garden on a bench, floribunda roses in bloom behind them, him holding her left hand which has a diamond ring on it. Mr and Mrs F. Roberts and Mr and Mrs C. Waterfield are proud to announce the engagement of Valerie with Kenneth, who plan to marry in 1966. She'll be twenty one: perfect!

'Are you out this evening, love?'

'Yes, the group's playing at Mary's Hall.'

'St Mary's… a bit of reverence, please. You be careful. There's always trouble down there. Watch out for Teddy boys else you'll end up in an alley with your throat slit.'

'Mum, please relax. I'll be with the group and Roger's a policeman. They'll not mix it with him.'

'Yes, Roger's a decent lad. It's always handy to know a policeman. You might need one yourself one day, Val. You won't remember the trouble we used to have three or four years ago with Teddy boys in their drapes and brothel creepers, carrying weapons. I don't know where they got their money from. Those suits cost a pretty penny, you know. You had to watch where you walked. They should have put them in the army; that would have sorted them out.

'I remember one day your dad and I were arm-in-arm down town, strolling outside the cinema then up by Lynn's, when three Teds came out of the café and approached us. Your dad smelled trouble 'cos he took his hands out of his pockets and got ready to protect himself. He thought he was going to be duffed up. Then one of them said, 'Hello Frank, how are you, old bean? Is this your better half?'

'After a couple of seconds your dad realised that it was a chap called Julian, who worked with him at the factory. I never saw him look so relieved. He got the shock of his life! He'd never seen Julian dressed like that. We had quite a laugh afterwards and called in to Lynn's for a hotdog and a milkshake.'

The mother-daughter chatting continues as Mrs Roberts puts the money tins back in the box and into the cupboard, although at times it becomes more like a mother lecturing her little Valerie, not the near-eighteen year-old young woman before her.

Val hurries back upstairs. Twenty minutes in the bathroom then hair, make-up, eye-shadow, black eye-liner, mascara, a bit of rouge on the cheeks and pale-pink lipstick. With her nail polish still looking good from last night, there is a complete transformation from a seventeen year-old teenage girl to more-like a twenty-two year-old modern woman. She grabs her handbag and rushes downstairs.

By one minute past nine, following a fifteen-minute crowded bus journey, Val is just moving into her position, buttoning up her white nylon Boots' smock and checking that her name badge is correctly in place as the manager opens the doors and the early-birds (checking their watches and muttering that he is over a minute late) file into the shop.

Before Val and Linda left school, Linda decreed that career courses were a waste of time. Her perspective was that by the time they were twenty one, Val would be married to Ken and she would be married to Gary. They would each have a comfortable house and the lads would have good jobs with much better wages than us women. We would have two or three kids over a ten-year period, which we would bring up until they left home in their early twenties, by which time we would be in our forties.

'So what's the point of studying for exams now for a career that we would soon have to give up? Life is for living, and the time for doing that is now.'

Chapter Ten

8.15 am

Linda Murray wipes the steamed-up window next to her with the back of her hand, not so that she can admire the view, but more importantly so that she can check out and adjust her hair and lipstick in the reflection. Sitting next to her on the double-decker bus is her mother, Janet. It is very unusual for them both to travel into the Town Centre together on a Saturday morning, but this week Linda is in sole charge of the Record Department at Adnitt's Department Store in the Drapery. She feels that she needs to be in a little earlier than normal to set a good example to the rest of the staff (one full-timer, Katie, and two fifteen year-old Saturday girls, Beverley and Wendy).

All this week Linda, although only eighteen, assumes departmental control as the manager, Mr Jones, is away on a week's holiday with his wife at a B&B in Mablethorpe. She enjoys it when she gets this added responsibility, as well as the added freedom it gives her to make decisions.

*

Janet Murray is forty years old, a war widow, with Linda her only child from a very short liaison and subsequent marriage to Horace Murray. Her good looks and friendly manner endeared her to more than one boy before she came upon Horace. He was home on leave, sitting next to her and sharing an arm-rest in the back stalls at the picture house by the Market Square. She immersed herself into Celia Johnson and Trevor Howard's 'Brief Encounter'.

Janet and Horace, exchanging glances and smiles in the ice-cream queue during the interval after the 'B' film, had a good feeling about each other. They agreed a first date and soon walked out together. They even had a weekend in Skegness before Horace had to leave again for war. 'You look after yourself, duck, and before you can say 'Jack Robinson' I'll be home.'

He was wrong; he never returned. Their own brief encounter left Janet with only one 'real' souvenir. It was a few weeks after that sad farewell that she discovered she was pregnant. Six months later a beautiful baby girl was born who she named 'Linda', now eighteen and sitting at her side. Janet still remembers every minute she spent with Horace, and will to the end of her days. It has left her with an overwhelming desire not to feel anything so deep ever again.

To be a widow with a baby daughter in the post-war years was hard, especially as Janet herself had lost first her father to diabetes, then her mother to who-knows-what, when she was a child. Janet was the youngest of a large family of four brothers and three sisters. Although none of them had much money they all pitched in to help her through the intervening years.

Apart from family help with money and hand-me-down clothes and shoes, Janet also had to live on her wits to enable her to pay her way. To this end she made friends with a man who she originally befriended during the war and who subsequently became known to Linda as 'Uncle Arthur'. He was bit older than Janet, assumed unmarried, assumed unemployed but un-assumedly had the gift of the gab.

Janet had met him in the bar at the Abington Park Hotel on a rare evening out with some of her brothers and sisters. Janet was warned of him more than once but he offered things in short supply like chocolate, cigarettes and ration coupons. He could also provide genuine luxuries like Spam and nylons (with personal free fitting service). Janet usually stained her bare legs with stewed teapot water or gravy colouring, then created a make-believe seam down the back of her legs with her eyeliner stick. Beggars couldn't be choosers!

Soon after becoming pub friends and having a good laugh together, Uncle Arthur enquired if Janet could do his washing on a strictly one-off basis, for a small payment. Then, predictably, that became regular. He stayed the occasional night in the spare room before he eventually became an official lodger and paid Janet handsomely for her domestic services.

After the war and out of the blue, he was gone without so much as a 'by your leave'. He went out one day, bright and breezy as usual, and never came back. After a few weeks the local police banged on Janet's door looking for him, following a tip-off. Apparently he was a wide-boy and a known wheeler-dealer but Janet only confirmed that he had lodged there for a few weeks before suddenly departing.

The police asked to see his room, but luckily, prior to this visit, Janet had cleared it and had found a wad of cash, and ration coupons, which she had moved to her brother's house for safe-keeping. After not hearing anything from Uncle Arthur for around two years they felt entitled to use the stash; this helped Janet feed and clothe Linda and herself. There was, of course, always the worry that one day he would knock on the door and demand his money back, but it never happened. Perhaps he had upset somebody and been bumped off: another unsolved mystery.

During the terribly severe winter of 1947, mother and daughter struggled to survive the cold, the power cuts, the food rationing and the long queues for almost anything useful. They dressed in warm layers, sometimes in all they owned. They cuddled up on the sofa and bedded down early in the evening, sometimes together in one bed so that Janet could keep Linda warm. They snoozed late and cosy and in a big part, thanks to Uncle Arthur's stash, they survived the misery of the snow and the freezing temperatures, then the damp and floods of the thaw.

Janet Murray's only treats were a 'Daily Mirror', and a 'News of the World' on Sunday, which together with her trusty radio ('Educating Archie', 'Henry Hall's Guest Night' and 'Mrs Dale's Diary') had to keep her entertained for the whole week before the newspapers were folded and torn into six inch squares for use in their outside toilet or to light the fire in front of which she sat knitting and playing with her daughter.

Janet also did some darning, ironing and dress-making for the family at the corner shop, in exchange for which she received some treats like a weekly bag of broken biscuits, and eggs or butter and cheese from under the counter, which she collected after the shop closed in the evening when it was dark outside and she was unseen by prying eyes.

As she grew older, Linda was farmed out each work day to one aunt or another while Janet secured various jobs, from shop assistant to factory worker to her present position as a clerk in the Rates Office. Without fail, Linda would sit in the bus-shelter at the end of the street and wait for her mum to come home each tea-time. Apart from Uncle

Arthur's contribution, her mother earned enough to keep them in house and home with an acceptable standard of living.

Linda never wanted for anything as a youngster, and what she never had she never missed. It is only in the last three years since she left school and got a job that she began to live a little and have spare money to buy the things that most teenage girls need, like clothes, make-up, magazines, coffee-bar refreshments, coins for the jukebox… and records.

The best thing about Linda's early years, apart from the fact that she had a loving and caring mother, was that she had a very good school where she met classmates who have now become best friends like Val, Ken, and especially her steady boyfriend, Gary.

Even though academically she wasn't the brightest, like Val and Ken, Linda was well above average and excelled particularly at the practical subjects of needlework, embroidery and housecraft. She needed a bus journey to secondary school, which she undertook either with her satchel or with her cane gondola basket on her arm containing the required ingredients for the day's cookery lesson before returning home with the completed meal which might be something like scrambled eggs, Welsh rarebit or bread and butter pudding.

Val was her first true friend and has remained her best ever girl friend, ranking second only to Gary, her first and only regular boyfriend. Val and Linda were in the same class at two different schools for over ten years. They cemented their friendship at Brownies and Guides and when they surprisingly met at private piano lessons given by Mrs Sprittlehouse in her studio near the recreation ground.

En-route to a piano lesson, riding their bicycles double-breast, Linda was busy chatting to Val when she lost her concentration and pedalled straight across a road junction. She collided with an oncoming car, splitting her head open and ripping her cheap grey Pacamac so badly that even half a roll of Sellotape subsequently failed to hold it together for more than a few weeks. Neither girl was a budding Winifred Atwell and eventually they both compromised with their mothers that they could give up piano lessons provided they started to attend Sunday School; this proved equally dull and uninviting. At least at church, then subsequently church Youth Club, they could meet many boys, although the ones they were attracted to and hung around with were the very same Ken and Gary from junior school.

*

'Mum, as I'm in charge this week I need to do the cashing-up and make sure the department is in good order ready for Mr Jones to return on Monday.'

Geoffrey Jones is the Manager of Adnitt's Record Department. He is in his mid-forties with receding, greasy, poorly cut hair and a pock-marked face. He always dresses in the same dark grey suit with shiny seat and dandruff on the collar. He wears black shoes, polished thoroughly on the uppers but never properly on the scuffed, worn-down heels. Mr Jones is married to Constance who, in Linda's eyes, is equally dull and boring, both to look at and to speak to. They have no children but they have a cat which they dote on and which is the sole subject of the limited non-business conversation that forever emanates from him. He has been manager for around three years and knows approximately nothing about popular music.

It is eight thirty-five and Mrs Murray rushes away to her work. Linda bee-lines for College Street and into Adnitt's security entrance. In the Ladies Room, Linda is the first one in from the Record Department. She exchanges pleasantries with Miss Clarke from Ladies' Underwear and Mrs Davis from Haberdashery. She slips into her nylon, lightweight, standard-issue Adnitt's overall, checks and improves upon her make-up in the mirror and heads off to the Record Department, where there is an island-counter for serving singles and extended-plays.

The singles are now 6/8d each and are displayed as dummies in the racks to avoid pilfering, especially by mischievous teenage schoolboys. They are filed in three categories in alphabetic sequence: 'Top 20'; 'Oldies'; 'Miscellaneous'. As the EP's vary little, they are individually priced with small sticky labels on the top right-hand corner of the cover: 10/9d is the normal price.

The main counter is along the wall and contains the cash register, empty LP covers in front of the counter, and the actual vinyl LPs, EPs and singles in racks along the back wall. There is a locked plastic Perspex cabinet containing styluses, cleaning liquids and cloths. On display are record cases, variously-sized singles racks and photos of current pop favourites.

There are two revolving carousel stands of budget 'Golden Guinea' LP's. To the right are two stand-up listening booths which can accommodate two people or three at a crush; to the left are two enclosed booths which can accommodate two sitting, three at a push, plus two more standing at a crush, or even more standing for a laugh!

Everything is in the same order as Linda left it on Friday evening. Like the efficient employee that she is, she checks that the float is in the till and that the till receipt paper is in order. On the wall behind the cash register is a poster advertising a concert at St Mary's Hall, Saturday August 31st at 7.30pm featuring Kenny Waters and the Waders, plus supporting group!

The performance is this evening: she can hardly wait!

Chapter Eleven

8.30 am

Whilst the Liverpudlian troubadours turn the national music scene on its greasy-quiffed head in this cataclysmic Merseybeat year, very little is changing in Northampton life. Before 'Six-Five Special' became a huge hit, and the diminutive Janice Nichols 'gave it foive' in 'Thank Your Lucky Stars', from time immemorial, ancestors of Waders' bass player Colin Harris have struggled in factories and supported one another through thick and thin.

Three generations of Harrises have lived and loved in the criss-cross, crisis-torn, terraced streets amongst the bed-sits, the lodging houses and the open-all-hours corner shops in Semilong.

'See them Harrises? Poverty-stricken and Parish-damned!' exclaims local grocer, Mrs Tarry.

'Salt of the bloomin' earth, Walt's family,' is Mr Tarry's favourite saying, down at the corner shop that he runs with his wife.

The local shoe factory has gained from the Harris' exemplary service over many years: diligent workers who could show everyone else on the shop floor a clean pair of heels; honest people who always did a fair day's work for a fair day's pay; fastidious time-keepers with meticulous punctuality; grazed-knuckle grafters whose word was their bond.

That was until Walt Harris, Colin's dad, let down this splendid family by getting mixed up with a rum lot down the bottom end of the shoe factory's clicking room and using their skulduggery for a quick fix to the financial problems into which they had plummeted.

Not very clever, Walt. Act in haste, repent at Her Majesty's leisure.

Colin had taken to heart the violent crime his dad had been suckered into with his two mates, a stunt he never would have thought of pulling had he not spent several years frittering away his wages. To his credit, Walt Harris had already taught Colin to know the difference between right and wrong and to have good family values. The shock of Walt's demise has become the talk of Semilong, and if it wasn't for his son's escapism in the twilight world of skiffle and rock 'n' roll, Colin would have driven himself mad with the courtesy stigma he harboured.

Lil, his thin-as-a-rake, uniformly hair-rollered and dressing-gowned mother, had been persistently verbally-abused by Walt, and Colin's younger, pretty, blonde-haired sister, Jeanette, sometimes unspeakably much worse. Now, under Colin's respectful Teddy boy-like leadership, his mother and sister were in much better hands than they ever could have hoped for.

It is amazing how Colin can still keep his pecker up and always be there for his nervous little sister and wayward mother, whilst carrying on his own shoulders the burden of his father's guilt.Along with Dave 'Ding Dong' Bell, the poor polio-inflicted drumming son of Archie Bell (the Rag 'n' Bone Man) and Roger Edwards (the desperately lonely rhythm guitarist) he pins down the insistent rhythms and beat that drive singer Kenny to greater heights of virtuosity, and the Waders to the brink of local beat music fame. Colin is an adequate musician, no more, and this takes him into evening flights of fancy to alleviate the daytime gloom.

He had learnt his trade down at the Boys' Brigade Headquarters, from side drum to bugle, then to whacking a tea-chest bass in the Brigade talent contests. The tea-chest bass was a work of art, constructed by Gary Hall in his school woodwork class and donated by him to the Brigade. Colin was never happier than when sticking his foot on its corner and slapping the string.

It is a regular Saturday labour of love for closet Teddy-boy Colin Harris to nip down town to go food shopping at about eight o'clock, before anyone else gets up. But not today. Colin has overslept, his tiredness and mild hangover kicking in, probably because the previous evening he had crawled his way round too many town centre pubs.

From mid-morning, he is due to be looking after Jeanette, his thirteen year-old kid sister, taking her somewhere or other, yet for them to discuss. In the evening, he will be off to St Mary's Hall to top the bill, yes, with his first love, Kenny and the boys. He had spent five years at Grammar School with young Kenneth Waterfield, the mate he called for at his privileged Abington home, to walk or bike to school together. Being out on a Saturday evening now puts the spiky cat amongst the petulant pigeons with his mum, Lil, who wants to go off to the pub, a privilege she used to enjoy on a regular basis when Walt was at home looking after Jeanette.

But Lil's chances of a Saturday night out these days are limited, and she has resigned herself to some compensatory drinking in the house and to inviting home a series of 'boyfriends' who are known as 'uncles' to her daughter, Jeanette.

No, Lil Harris is not averse to drinking indoors. There is plenty of bottled ale in the Tarry's corner shop crates, and the pennies she gets back from returning the weekly empties pays for her weekend fags.

By eight o'clock this morning, a cacophony of sound shatters the peace in the Semilong district: the tinkling door bell that announces the start of bread and milk trade at Tarry's, the early morning Birmingham express slamming through the central track under the Spencer Bridge Road signal gantry and the incessant shunting of goods wagons in Marshall's Yard, a stone's throw from his bedroom window, all collide to inform Colin that it is time to wake up. He accordingly obliges, not knowing that his peace is soon to be re-shattered by the rudest of awakenings from a most unwelcome intrusion.

The first thing that the bass-thumping, pen-pushing, trainee-manager needs after sleeping off his boozy slumbers is a dash to the bathroom toilet along the landing opposite his mother's bedroom and next to his sister Jeanette's. Colin creeps up to the grimy bathroom door, tightly clutching himself through his pyjama trousers in an effort to avoid an embarrassing accident.

He cups his plectrum finger and thumb around the dented knob, trying to turn it round without squeaking, as he would often try to do on stage in an attempt to sneak a few decibels over his sound-checked mates. Dropping his right shoulder against the door, he gently pushes. Nothing. He pushes again. It is bolted. Someone is in there, but who? He squats down cross-legged and tight-lipped on the laundry basket and waits, and waits… and waits.

He glances around him and is struck by the paucity and gloominess of the whole scene. A brown and white photograph hangs ghostly above the 'whatnot', his moustachioed grandfather standing proudly at the end of the back line, broad chest out, thin waist in, holding the regimental flag. He looks as glum before evacuating Ypres as Colin feels sitting waiting in agony to relieve himself. The ghosts of times-past define the spirit of time- forward in this hard-up household, long-term Victorian austerity prevailing over short-term 1960's hedonism.

A sad little oak bookcase, wobbly and wormy, a cast-out that Dave Bell had sold Lil Harris for a tanner, carries a small array of dog-eared books, useful to pass the time whilst sitting contemplating navels and hoping for better days ahead. There, laying on the top shelf, is yesterday evening's local 'Echo', its entertainments' page upwards, announcing the spectacular appearance of 'Wonderful Kenny Waters and the Fabulous Waders' on Saturday evening.

Paintbrush smears, ghostly shadows of previous décor and uneven plaster surfaces make the upstairs a pretty glum place in which to go to bed. It is an un-cosy nest in which to rear the late-born Jeanette, a home as grey and functional as it is cold and cheerless.

The Harris family are not the poorest in the street by any means, nor, despite everything, the most miserable. But there is never a surplus at the end of the week to put away for a rainy day, or to have a little treat now and again. Perhaps one should not have been too judgemental, then, when it came to dishing out summary justice of six years on Walt Harris for his six seconds of indiscretion.

Loathsome as it appeared, he had nevertheless tried to raise a bit of cash to take them all away for a week in order to keep his wife's mouth shut - the second holiday it would have been since he had become engaged to Lil in 1943, and the first for teenager Colin and his sister Jeanette. Sadly for them, none of them got to see the inside of a B&B at Skegness. All Walt got to see, was the inside of a prison cell for an unscheduled holiday in Bedford Gaol.

That was at the time when gambling had become something of a national epidemic: dogs, horses, treble chance, and 'Chase the Lady' with any American servicemen who had turned up in town to hang out at whichever of the two pubs they were officially allowed to visit, black or white, racially segregated and brutally marshalled by their own military police.

Although Lil was beginning to get a bit of a name for herself on the taxi rank, up the pub and in the bedroom, again one might have had some sympathy when she was stuck with bringing up Colin and Jeanette on a shoestring, hiding fearsome secrets which no doubt would one day come to light.

Colin has done well, all things considered. He has chosen a moderate career with good prospects and conditions of service, as well as making some ready cash by chasing the bass. He is rising to the challenge in the wake of his dad's demise, and it is clear to all that despite the poverty and haphazard lifestyle of the family home, and despite his shortening temper, he has got his head screwed on.

Yes, the landing is pretty bleak, as Colin sits there wondering how to keep Jeanette entertained through the day. Also running through his mind are the fretting and plucking sequences for the evening's performance. Overlaying the muffled sounds of road and rail is the deafening silence from within the bathroom. Then the hiatus is relieved.

First the chain is pulled: 'Wow, that's taken a bloomin' long time!' Then the sink taps are turned on, and Colin hears the immersion heater flare into life as water flows for the mandatory swilling of the hands. Then, a supplementary flush, clear indication that hard one-ply toilet-paper prefers to swirl around and float upwards in the lingering pan, rather than gush round the u-bend and away to the gluttonous conduits below.

The ablutions are nearly over, then comes the towelling down, a claggy gargle and an honest spit, pre-cursing a third tug of the chain. The sound of another honest expulsion of phlegm concludes the cleansing process, every orifice now evacuated. The moves have all been heavy and resonant, and it takes Colin a few seconds to snap out of his shortening patience and call out, 'Come on, hurry up! I can't hold on much longer.'

'So who is it this time?' Colin asks himself, instantly dismissing his previous courtesy to the sleeping females and thumping on the bathroom door.

'Oi, mush. Open the door and piss off. I need the bog!'

Silence!

'I know what you're up to, you bastard, you and your stinking cosmetics and cheap nylons. Get your arse out of it and get out of my house. If you don't open up now, I'll kick the door in and kick your stupid head in, too!'

Silence!

The bolt is drawn back, the door swings inwards, dragging Colin in with it. A huge hulk of a man, at least six inches taller than Colin, bundles past him, shoving him over and into the bath, slamming the door on him and stomping off down the landing to Lil's bedroom door. Flinging it open, he disappears inside. Slamming it shut, he screams at Lil: 'You fuckin' bitch!'

Silence!

Clearly there is mutual unawareness on the part of the two men in respect of each other. Colin picks himself up, dusts himself down, and with no physical harm having been done he at last manages to gain a strategic position over the stained and smelly pan.

'I hope Jeanette didn't hear any of that.' he muses, as if to convince himself that she must have been born stone deaf. After drying his hands, blowing out the intruder's scurfy hairs from his Christmas present Remington electric razor, putting the little cap on the top of his birthday present Old Spice and disinfecting the bowl with Parazone from what smells like a late night supper of sardines on toast, he creeps past his mum's bedroom door then pokes his head round Jeanette's.

Silence!

Colin slowly closes Jeannie's door, and returns to the bathroom. He frustratingly has a quick wash and brush up in a sink that stinks of some man of mystery, declines to clean his teeth in case the unwelcome non-paying non-guest has polluted his toothbrush with alien plaque and decides against shaving until he has had a chance later to completely clean up his contaminated electric razor.

He grabs the last clean hand-towel from the bathroom cabinet, dries himself down then hastens away from this unhealthy scene which has been violated by an unwelcome intruder, who has clearly been brought in off the streets by a wayward mother who has fancied a bit of company, a lot of love and a load of cash.

It would be a frustrating start to any Saturday, but today is one Colin that has been looking forward to for days. It will be one rare Saturday that, unbeknown to him, is about to go from the dire to the bolical.

Chapter Twelve

9.00am

Ken bounds down the stairs, stops with five steps to go (his record is six), slides his hands squeakily down the two hand rails and lever-jumps to the bottom landing with a thud. Back along the hall he trundles, then into the kitchen at the back. His mother greets him as she stands bent down under the sink searching for the washing-up liquid underneath the small green and white gingham curtain.

'Next time could you walk downstairs properly, please, Kenneth?'

Mrs Waterfield seamlessly changes the subject to one that she appears to be thinking about deeply: 'You are very lucky to have the friends you have, Kenneth. Valerie is a lovely girl. I hope you appreciate her.' Mrs Waterfield continues out loud a conversation she is already having with herself.

'I appreciate her more than you can imagine, Mum,' he confirms, a bit startled and unsure why this subject has arisen.

'She is a lovely girl, a bit reserved, which is not a bad thing. Good family people. I am not sure about that Linda who Gary knocks around with. She is not at all like Valerie. She is a bit forward. Always has too much to say for herself. Nice looking girl, though, don't you think?'

'Linda's absolutely fine, Mum.' he replies. 'This is more like a cross-examination by Eliot Ness!' he thinks.

'You and Gary are like brothers. I have always liked Gary. When you were younger, you and him were like 'Me and my Shadow'. If his mother bought him a new pullover then you wanted me to buy you one exactly the same. When we bought you a transistor radio, he got one the same week. Bicycles, balaclavas, fishing rods, scooters... you always wanted the same. Like brothers, you two.'

Ken walks over and gives her a hug.

'The four of you have always got on well together. Look out for each other, do you?'

'We do our best.'

Ken absorbs his mother's words but prefers to drop the subject. He is cogitating whether now is a good time to drop some hints of his Hamburg plans. He knows the 'what' and the 'where', but not the 'when'.

Ken's self-imposed initiation rite into a career of his own choice will make or break him. He might not come back if he is really successful. He has got everything going for him, so why shouldn't he make it to the top? The split-second opportunity to break the news comes and goes. He loses his nerve as speedily as the thought comes to his mind. He quickly thinks of something else to say. 'Even in those days, people were 'doing it' before they were married, weren't they?'

'Those days were not normal, darling. We missed our men-folk terribly and they missed their wives and girlfriends more than you can imagine.'

'Did you have any other boyfriends when Dad was away? I bet you did! I've seen those old sepia photos of you; you looked like a film star in those posh, feathered hats.'

She blushes but does not answer.

'I can't stand here nattering to you all morning. Your dad has gone out for a haircut. He wants to see you before you go out. Ok?'

'What's he want?'

'I think he feels it is about time you stop loafing about and start to work at the company.'

'But Mum, you said I could have the summer off if I did well in my exams, and I did!'

'You did, son. You have achieved everything we ever asked of you. We are both very proud of you, but your father thinks the summer is over and that it is now time for your next challenge. Anyway, I think that is what he wants, so do not go out until after he sees you.'

Ken finishes his breakfast, grabs his car keys from a hook on the wall behind the kitchen door, then leaves the house by the side door. His blue Ford Anglia is parked on one side of the two-car drive.

As he turns to open his car door, a dark blue Humber Super Snipe pulls in, crunching the gravel as its huge bulk moves along the short, curved drive. Charles Waterfield, accountant, business man, Masonic Grand Master, church elder, husband and father is at the wheel. He pulls up, gets out and beckons Ken with a double-waggle of his index finger.

Charles Waterfield is around forty years old, a bit short of six feet tall, a couple of stones overweight, mainly in the belly, with a moustache, dark, slightly-receding hair, freshly cut and greased that morning. He has a slight stoop, testimony to working at a desk for the past twenty years.

He is proudly wearing a new navy blue, serge blazer, its breast pocket embroidered with the crest of his wartime regiment, his lapel adorned with a brass regimental stick-pin, white collar and striped tie with tie clip, a pair of grey flannels, brown belt and brown brogues.

In his mouth, he balances an unlit pipe of St Bruno. He looks extremely important, with a sergeant-major air about him. If he speaks, then you listen! Then you act, or else! (Especially if your name is Kenneth!) He can also be very charming, especially with the ladies. Ken's mum loves him, warts and all. He considers himself a role model of success, so he demands similar accomplishment from those around him.

Charles expects Ken to work long and hard for a fair day's pay. He anticipates that his wife and son will do as he tells them! Bluebottle would call his Capitaine 'a dirty rotten swine': very apt, with his unattainable standards and myriad prejudices!

'Kenneth, I need a word before you go out, and please wash that car of yours. It is a disgrace! It needs to shine like mine. Have pride in its appearance, lad. If you do not keep it clean it will go rusty and I am not buying you another one. When you are in it, your car is your home! Would you really want to sit at home in such a mess? Treat it like you treat yourself. Ok? I told the barber that you will be coming to see him this morning. Do you hear me?'

Ken nods, crest-fallen. These never-ending snipes are winding him up and setting his nerves on edge. He feels that he cannot stand this bullying, not for even one more day!

'Ken, your school record did us all proud. You know that, because we have spoken about it already. You might guess what I am going propose. Waterfield's Accountants was established by your grandfather, my father in the nineteen thirties; it is renowned across the county.

'Your granddad built it up from nothing and when he handed it over to me a couple of years ago I was determined to keep up the good name and take it from strength to strength. My hard work and dedication have enabled us to have the standard of living we now enjoy. Money doesn't grow on trees, let me tell you, and this isn't a genie that has popped out of a bottle, you know.

'In twenty-odd years time, hopefully, the same will happen again, and I can hand over the baton to you. So, my lad, you needed to join the company yesterday, enrol for your accounting exams today, and learn how to manage the business tomorrow. Law of the jungle, son. It must happen. Meddle with Nature and Nature will always get its own back!

'On Monday, I want you to put on your best suit and clean shirt and tie. Spit-and-polish your shoes and come down to the office. I will put you in the capable hands of Jack Tyson, my office manager. He will look after your accounting education, fix you up with a desk, assign you work and so on and so forth, etcetera. You will get a good wage (at least £5 a week) and you will be on the ladder to eventually taking over the company. Any questions, son?'

'Yes, one. Do I have a choice, Dad?'

'Choice? Choice? How dare you, you ungrateful bugger! You should think yourself lucky. There are not many sons who have such a career laid out before them. All you have to do is knuckle down and work hard. You have the brains, now you need to apply them. Choice, my arse!'

Ken is beginning to feel desperately sick and giddy as he recoils from his father's aggression, but just when he thinks things could get no worse...

'Oh, and by the way. If you do not turn the volume down on that blasted record player that we bought you, I am removing it to the garage. You can play it there!'

'But, the music I listen to needs to be played loud. It's beat music. It's rock 'n' roll. I can't play it softly! No-one can!'

'You and your blasted choices, Kenneth! Well, this is the sum total of your choices: one! Loud in the garage or more quietly in the bedroom. Which reminds me. It might also be a good idea if you stop performing with that bloody pop group of yours, and I've got better things to do than cover for you. Late nights and rock 'n' roll are not conducive to becoming a top businessman. It will not do if you want to join the Masonic Lodge, and you do, believe me. So choose!'

Ken's dream has not only turned sour, it is fast becoming a nightmare of Hammer Horror proportions. What he really wants to say to his father remains unsaid. He has enough good manners and respect for that, together with a healthy dollop of fear, but the words passing through his mind cannot be halted: 'I don't want more studying or to be an accountant yet, or ever. I don't want to settle down with Val yet, maybe sometime. Clean the car, get your haircut, pack up the group, no, erhm, not pack up the group!

'He even wants me to be a mason with all the secrecy and strange initiation rituals that are entailed. By the light of the full moon, roll up your trouser legs and stand in a bucket of custard and repeat the secret code: 'Abracadabra - Open Sesame'! Dodgy hand-shakes with equally dodgy businessmen?'

Ken is flummoxed.

'How do I get out of this lot? My whole life is being organised for me, by my dad. Do I get any say in this? No! He kicks the tyre on the car, hard, in frustration! 'He's ruined my day. I'll not let him wreck my life. I need to take action and take it soon, before it's too late.'

Ken is horrified by the prospect of Waterfield's accountants. A half-dozen middle-aged married men in dark pin-striped suits, crisp perfectly-ironed white shirts, clean on each day, dark boring ties with gold tie pins, polished tie-up shoes, sit regimentally in three rows of two, all facing one way… in homage towards the boss's office.

Sign the book with the time you arrive in the morning. Sit down, take the flask and packet of sandwiches out of your briefcase and put them into your desk drawer. Change the date stamp and desktop calendar, replace the blotting paper, top up the inkwell, take out your six HB pencils and sharpen them up on the office pencil-sharpener, then line them up ready for action!

Nine o'clock, heads down, start work. Half past twelve, heads up and lunch. Half past one, heads down and work until five o'clock. Lots of shuffling of papers, stapling, licking of pencil leads, rubbing out, writing, calculating, the occasional cough but generally very quiet, like a library.

All the figures must be double entry, all the numbers must balance.

Everything must be accurate down to the last halfpenny. At lunchtime the secretary must continue to knit her husband's new grey socks, the men must read their newspapers, do the crossword and chat about their children's education.

Then when you reach sixty-five, you sign out in the book and they present you with a mantelpiece clock with your name engraved on the bottom: 'To thank Kenneth Waterfield for forty-seven years' service, 1963 - 2010.' Then you retire with a backside the shape of your office chair.

'Not for me!' he asserts to himself. 'No double entry, not even a single entry into Waterfield's Accountants!'

'Kenneth, I want what is best for you. I know what is best for you, you do not, yet. Trust me on this. In years to come you will thank me for this conversation,' says Charles Waterfield, completing his sermon.

Ken's mum has been wringing her tea towel nervously at the exchange at the front of the house. She comes out to inform her husband that there is a cup of tea poured out and going cold on the kitchen table. As Charles hastens indoors, Ken's mum hangs back and asks him how the chat with his father went.

Ken is dejected. 'He's mapped out for me the next forty years of my life! It's totally cast in concrete, no questions asked, no answers required, signed, sealed and rammed down my throat!' he sulks.

'Look, love, he is only trying to do the best for you, like his father did for him.'

'It's my life, Mum, and I want control of it. If I go into the company with Dad, then that's that. I'll have lost my freedom to do what I want. It'll be like being in a very comfortable prison! Purgatory! He wants control of not only my working life, but my private life, too. I'm sick to death of it all!'

Ken's mother makes no further comment. She sees both sides of the argument and takes no side. She is stumped! Mrs Waterfield knows her husband, knows her son - there is only going to be one winner of this debate! Irrespective of what her heart is telling her, she acknowledges her duty to back her husband while commiserating with her son. She has been dominated by her husband throughout their marriage, but love for their son is always the acid test! She always gives in to Charles. She stands her ground the best she can and on balance life is indeed very comfortable.

Ken bids farewell and jumps into his Ford Anglia. He puts the car in reverse gear but with his brain locked in overdrive, he backs out straight into the path of a passing car. The enraged driver blasts his horn, swerves to avoid a collision, then shakes his fist and shouts at Ken.

Charles Waterfield, the 'monarch of all he surveys', looks out of the front-room window and shakes his head accusingly, wondering what on earth he has done to deserve such an utterly useless moron of a son!

Chapter Thirteen

9.15 am

Back in his bedroom, Colin dons a faded black tee shirt, a snug pair of ice-blue jeans, white socks, and a pair of size-10 chisel-toed, brass-buckled, Cuban-heeled shoes. He splashes on a dash of Yardley, slicks back his hair with Brylcreem, sweeps up the sides, loops over the quiff and fixes the D/A at the back. Then, strapping on his silver bracelet watch, he patters down the uncarpeted stairs to see what he can rustle up for Jeanette's breakfast. His mum will eat later, if at all. She is clearly having a lie-in after last night's goings-on, and the rhythmic creaking and banging sounds as though her nasty client, having scored late, is now getting his money's-worth.

Colin goes to the shelf across the cellar head where the dairy products are usually kept: milk, butter, eggs, cheese.

Nothing!

He goes to the larder to search for bacon, sausages, faggots and baked beans.

Nothing!

He goes to the kitchen cupboard to see how much jam there is in the pot.

None!

Lil's housekeeping has now dropped below Ol' Mother Hubbard standards; even the doggie has left home! So it is over to Mrs Tarry's. He will have to shop with the little bit of cash he has put aside.

Colin leaps grudgingly back up to his room, where he keeps his spending money in a bedside drawer. After he grabs a pound note and stuffs it in his jeans' pocket, he eases open Jeanette's door to tell her what he is up to. She is now wide awake, sitting bolt upright in bed looking as miserable as sin and reading intensely last week's 'Bunty'. Colin tells her what is afoot and that he is off to get the breakfast from the corner shop. When he has gone, Jeanette puts aside her comic, slides down below the sheets and sobs her heart out.

*

'Morning, Mrs Tarry,' Colin mutters, as he shuffles in.

'Morning, Colin. You're up early. Don't say you've nothing in for breakfast again,' replies the shopkeeper, prophetically.

'She's doing my head in, Mrs Tarry. She's picked up another lousy rotten punter in some grotty little pub down town.'

'Who's she? The cat's mother?'

'She's my darlin' mother and she's getting worse. Sorry to be in a bad mood, Mrs Tarry.'

It is clear from his abstruse greeting that Colin isn't feeling too happy and that perhaps life could be a bit better. Ethel Tarry merely scrapes the pork dripping off her downy chin and swallows her last piece of toast before wiping her greasy fingers down her grubby pinny. Her husband, Bert, takes the fag out of the corner of his mouth, spits some soggy tobacco off his lips into the open potato sack, wipes the snot off his nicotine-stained moustache with the back of his fist and stubs out his dog-end in the upturned biscuit-tin lid balanced on the bacon-slicer.

'Colin, calm yourself. Come and sit in the kitchen. Bert, go and fetch our Colin a cup of char, will you?'

'I'd better not hang around too long, 'cos I've got Jeanette to sort out. I've got to do something with her today, poor kid. She's getting dead bored and unbelievably lonely these days. I don't know what it is. She just won't go out to play any more. She's got lots of pals who keep calling for her. Kids! She's got right clingy to me.' Colin's line of concern is valid but it is not addressing the real issue, that of his mother's falling from grace. He focuses on the child victim and fails to mention the mother perpetrator.

'That's because your dad's in the nick, Col. I know how your mum's changed so much, and what a burden she has become to you. You imagine what's going through her addled brain.'

Mrs Tarry's intuition and neighbourly concern drags the conversation back to where she wants it to be focused, but she doesn't have much success. She seizes the moment to try and make Colin aware of what she thinks of the family's degradation, in the hope of helping to stop the rot and turn the tide. But Colin doesn't bite. Then Bert Tarry puts his foot in it by referring back to Jeanette, much to Ethel's glaring displeasure.

'Do you know that your Jeannie pops in here every day on her way home from school to tell us all her troubles?' butts in Bert, fuelling Ethel's irritation in its instant deflection from her chance to tell Colin about her concerns for his mother.

'What troubles, Mr Tarry? No, she never said. What's up with her, then?' Colin asks, his ears pricking up in the hope of some new information which might throw some light on his sister's sullenness.

'It's those Dixons from Suffolk Street,' Bert Tarry exclaims, dropping one of his best customer's families in it up to their necks and getting his frustration with them off his chest at the same time.

'All seven of them, little bleeders. They're the scourge of Semilong - call themselves the 'Pram Posse'. When they ain't got little Babs in the pram, they've got dolls under the blanket with a whole load of weapons - chisels, table legs, even knuckledusters. Learnt it all from Tommy, the eldest. Right yobbo since he came out of the army.'

'Bloomin' 'eck,' says Colin. 'So that's why they push that stupid old pram all over Semilong, creating chaos. You live and learn!'

'Certainly is. It's not so bad when they go up the park, but when they come in here with that pram we don't half have to keep our eyes on them. Bars of Punch, halfpenny chews, sticks of barley sugar, slab of green soap, even corn plasters - you name it, they nick it!'

'Get to the point, Bert. He ain't got all day!'

'Well, they bully Jeannette unmercifully, calling her a blonde bastard and telling her that her dad's a dirty rotten crook. They slag off your mum, too, but it's Jeannette who gets it in the neck all the time. She tells us that's why she's not going out to play. That's the reason she's clinging to you, Colin.'

'One of the reasons, Bert. Don't forget she's also worried about her mum and she hasn't really got over what her dad's been up to.' Bert thanks Ethel for correcting him, though completely missing the point that his wife is trying to have her two penn'urth about Lil Harris.

'How do you know all this?' enquires Colin. 'You're telling me that Jeannette's in a tizzy, but you also seem to know more than I do about what's going on in my own home.'

'Bert, you go and look after the shop,' instructs the matriarch, pouring herself another cup of tea and pulling up another chair to get close to Colin. 'I know you can't stay long, Colin, but I'm glad you've called in. There's something I've been dying to tell you!

'Colin, me and your mum have been in some dire scrapes all our lives. We've lived in the same street, been thrown out of the same Sunday School, got our bums smacked together at church, scrumped apples from the same garden and snogged the same wolf cubs. When I met Bert up at the Co-op club he played darts and drank beer with your dad. I took Lilian along with me to meet Bert, and Walt was there. Well, one thing led to another and no sooner had Bert and me got married, your mum and dad tied the knot. A sort of 'rebound' type of thing.'

'I knew you were close, Mrs Tarry, but I didn't know you were that close,' Colin chips in.

'We used to rock 'n' roll together and bop and jive down the Co-op club. It was great. We were the gals of the Pink and Black Days with our toreador pants and chiffon scarves, and day-glow lipstick from the Yanks. We danced together at the club, then sometimes Bert got up and jived with me. Your dad was self-conscious. He leant against the juke-box, clicking his fingers and tapping his feet in his black suede brothel creepers,' remembers Ethel, as Colin swigs his tea and dunks his ginger nuts.

'Everything was hunky dory. Our Rose was born, then Lil had you. Our Barry came next, and the three of you got on like a house on fire. Rose was a bit of a bossy boots. She loved to bring you jam tarts in Barry's wigwam in our back garden, and she always wanted to pick sides when you were playing football in the street. Walt and Bert were good mates. They carried on playing darts and worked like mad on the club committee. Our little shop came on nicely, and your mum and dad worked with all the other Harrises over at the factory earning a good crust.

'That was until your dad let us all down, which was when everything started going pear-shaped, Colin.'

'Why did Dad do it, Mrs Tarry?' Colin asks the million-dollar question.

'The bottom-line was gambling. He got the bug after making a few quid in the factory's Grand National sweepstake. He liked the feeling of having some ready cash in his pocket for a few days, and he felt big and important by calling for drinks all round at the club.

'However, when he kept betting on nags that couldn't even have pulled the milk cart, he couldn't stand life with empty pockets so he swapped each-way bets for straight wins; he lost a bloomin' fortune. It drove Lil mad, because each week he brought home less and less housekeeping money. He'd gambled it all away on his way home each Friday. So your home got more and more run down. Then when young Jeannie was born, well, he got to the end of his tether.'

'What really happened, Mrs Tarry? I heard he just got mixed up with a couple of crooks and somehow blamed Mum,' Colin says, getting a bit panicky at the name of Jeannette, having left her with a strange bloke in the house.

'Lil was exhausted,' went on Mrs Tarry. 'You were a bit of a rebel, Jeannie needed feeding and all your dad would do was throw good money after bad, hit the bottle and smoke like a chimney. Your mum started to change. No longer would she shut up and put up. She wanted to decorate the house and get some decent furniture, even buy some nice clothes. They argued, Jeannie cried, and you got out of it nicely by rehearsing with the Waders. Jeannie kept coming over here, where she felt safe.'

Colin gulps hard. He doesn't really want to hear this, but he grits his teeth, giving Ethel the opportunity to tell all.

'We didn't see much of your dad at the shop. He went from home to work, to the bookies, to the pub and back again. I suppose he felt guilty, and certainly Bert would have given him a piece of his mind had he put one foot in here. We knew how hard we had to work to give our kids a good start, and it drove my Bert mad to see Walt leave you lot in the lurch.

'Then it happened - the bubble burst! Lil threw a fit about everyone in the street going away for a week during the factory fortnight, bar you lot, and in order to shut her up, and who knows, possibly to save the marriage, Walt got sucked in by a couple of wide-boys from the clicking room. Big lads, enjoyed kicking people's heads in but always on the scrounge - geezers you wouldn't want to cross dinner knives with in the factory canteen.

'Before Walt's gullibility prevented him from catching his breath and thinking twice, he was counted in. Stan and Joe revealed to him that the next Thursday afternoon it was wage-snatch time. They'd chosen to lurk about round the corner down the side of the police box. This would be the least likely place to lie in wait for the security van making its way down the road before pulling up in front of the factory.

'When the two guards lifted off the strongbox containing the cash for the week's wages, Stan and Joe would smash the guards over the head with the baseball bats the Yanks had smuggled out of the American Air Force Base for them. All Walt had to do would be to grab the loot and run for his life across the park to a safe house the other side of town.

'Walt bit instantly; he is easily led, you know. With their silly bats, they didn't get past first base. The two American soldiers who supplied them had shopped them because of some stupid argument in the Cross Keys over some two-timing girls from Far Cotton and Stan and Joe had been watched by the boys in blue. They had been under observation for about a month, and as they raced across to attack the security guards the CID came swooping out from every nook and cranny.

'That was that! The bullion raid of the year fizzled out without even one jugular being severed and no red alert at Accident & Emergency. The heist came in with a whimper and went out like a damp squib, and all the three crooks got for their trouble were hefty prison sentences.

'Well, there you go, Col. That's why your mum cracked up and that's why she's going down hill fast. Everyone around Semilong has taken it out on her ever since, for being a money-grabbing, insensitive bitch who was directly responsible for getting your dad banged up.

'Now, young Colin, from the moment you leave this shop, you take heed of what I've told you. Then your mum's smoking, boozing and street-walking will all make sense. She's not any old moonlight lady doing it for a lark; she's a grieving woman with a broken heart. We love your mum, Colin, and no-one coming in this shop dare say anything about her here, because they know they'll get a piece of my mind.'

'And mine,' butts in Mr Tarry. 'I put the gobby buggers right, no doubt about that!'

'Come on, Colin. Keep your pennies in your pocket. Here's some eggs and bacon, a pint of milk and half a pound of butter. Oh, and a bottle of orange juice. If you can pay up next Friday, pay. If you can't, you can have the grub anyway,' Mrs Tarry tells Colin, not for the first time putting some goods on the slate, sometimes for it to eventually be wiped clean, sometimes not.

'Thanks for everything,' Colin says, before running home to get Jeannette's day under way and to deal with the fall-out from his mum's latest flirtatious escapade. It was to be a mighty long day for Colin Harris, one that would end in chaos and change his impoverished life for ever.

Chapter Fourteen

9.30 am

Gwen Hall stands at the bottom of the stairs, an Irish linen tea towel in one hand, a big, black bakelite telephone receiver in the other. She bellows loudly enough to wake not only her son Gary, who is wanted on the phone, but his brother and sister who are undoubtedly still fast asleep upstairs.

'It's your Uncle Sid!' she barks.

Gary emerges from his bedroom. He looks like he feels - still tired and slightly the worse for wear from last night's beer. He is tying the cord of his pyjama bottoms as he staggers, yawning down the thirteen stairs.

'Ok, Sid, here he is.' She hands Gary the receiver.

Sid explains to Gary that the private job that they planned to finish today will need to be put off until tomorrow morning, as Sid has just been asked by his boss to go into work for an urgent job and therefore Gary now needs to be available tomorrow morning at about nine thirty.

Gary knows that he is playing with the group this evening followed by the usual late night warm-down at the night club, but this private job with his Uncle Sid, to make up and install some fitted wardrobes in a house up Spinney Hill, needs finishing and he can earn some good extra money and learn a lot from his uncle, a master carpenter.

'Ten o'clock alright, Uncle Sid?'

'It's worth a try,' he thinks.

'I'll pick you up at nine thirty. Be ready, Gary. I want to get it done before one o' clock as I have promised to take your auntie to the club for a drink before our Sunday roast, and they draw the tote then.'

'Ok, I'll be ready. Bye.'

Uncle Sid, Gary's dad's brother, is Gary's favourite of his five uncles. Gary is Uncle Sid's favourite nephew. Their mutual binding interest is wood-work. Uncle Sid can build seemingly anything from wood. Gary passed his school woodwork exams with top marks and is now an apprentice carpenter at White's, Northampton's biggest house builders, a job for which Uncle Sid recommended him to Joe White, the owner.

Uncle Sid often picks up small private jobs at weekends and evenings for extra money to pay the bills. As he has no children of his own, he treats Gary like a son and likes to invite him to help and expand his woodwork education. Together Sid and Gary make a great team, Sid providing the tea and sandwiches, Gary bringing his transistor radio and boundless enthusiasm.

'I'm working with Uncle Sid tomorrow now, so I'll go down town today and pop in the shop and see Dad after lunch.' he tells his mum.

The TV comes a distant third in popularity in the Hall household, after the radiogram and the radio and Gary seems to have been born with music in his blood. Les, his dad, had always wanted Gary to follow in his footsteps and become a musician. He started his son off with a small accordion, tutoring him at home with two-hour sessions.

As the skiffle craze emerged, Gary saved his pocket money and secretly sent away for a Spanish acoustic guitar that he saw advertised for £7 17s 6d in the weekly 'Tit Bits' paper. Gary then set about teaching himself to play, but was found out, hauled before his Dad and invited to play a tune for him. Les was suitably impressed, so a partnership was born: father and son; teacher and pupil.

Gary then had guitar lessons from a renowned local teacher, and his improvement was unbelievable. He learned an abundance of chords and then spent hours working out sequences, practising a tune until it was perfect.

It was a dream come true for Les when three years ago he opened the musical instrument shop in Gold Street. After the war ended, Les was an accordionist in a semi-pro local dance band, had made lots of local music contacts and with the rise of pop music, rock 'n' roll and the like, he saw an opportunity to open the type of business that the town had sadly lacked.

When Mr Hall first purchased the old second-hand furniture shop following its bankruptcy, there used to be, at the back of the property, two big storerooms, in total about forty feet by eighteen feet, which were full of rubbish and junk. After much thought and planning and a big clearance operation, where Gary helped his dad, it was decided to create one big room and use it by turning it into the first professional recording studio in the East Midlands.

Together with technical help from newly-emerging local electronics and sound buffs, and with tricks of the trade from Les's brother, Sid, on the carpentry side, the building was fire-proofed, sound-proofed, burglar-proofed and disturbance-proofed. A separate control room about twelve feet by eighteen feet was built at the end of the room, behind big windows.

Gary, who was then doing his 'O' levels, learned a lot from Sid and it was following this, his first real work experience, that Gary decided he wanted to be a carpenter when he left school rather than just helping his dad in the shop.Apart from Saturday each week there wasn't really enough work for two people, anyway.

When Gary was fourteen, he made a tea chest bass for the skiffle group with Sid's help, and even a collapsible stand for the washboard to sit on.These were his first two wood-working projects and proved that he had a real gift when working with his hands.

It was late in 1959 that Gary's dad, through contacts in the trade, got the group a five-minute audition with the Carroll Levis Discoveries TV show at the Hippodrome in Birmingham.The group members went up together by train, then changed into new costumes, each hand-sewed with hundreds of sequins by Linda's mum. They shared a dressing room with a ventriloquist, who insisted (for practice sake) in only speaking to the lads through his dummy.They shared a bag of 'gish and gips' and a 'gottle o' yinger geer', then they were ready for their performance.

Sadly, after much debate, the new costumes had to be abandoned as the TV technicians were worried that their 'fairly primitive' cameras would be affected by sequin-glare, so the lads resorted to their normal day clothes, but still to great effect. However, they were still playing skiffle and the craze had just about run its course, so although they went down very well, no contract was forthcoming, only a piece of expert advice:'If you want to succeed, go electric'.

At the Technical High School, woodwork and metalwork were Gary's forte and shortly after the Birmingham audition he plucked up courage and asked the woodwork teacher, who he liked and got on well with, if it would be possible for him to make a guitar during lessons, even volunteering to stay later after school to work on it. That home-made 'Hall' guitar is now standing in Gary's bedroom and is used for practising at home with his original old 'Elpico' amp when Mum is out of the house - much to the adjoining neighbour's annoyance, who would bang repeatedly on the wall.

The group's kit has recently been updated, thanks to Ken's dad, but that Hall guitar will remain with Gary forever. Originally he plugged the amp into the ceiling light socket but his dad put a stop to that when the house lights fused twice in one night. The guitar stands right by his dressing table, the last thing he sees at night and the first thing he sees each morning. He would have it no other way.

Capitalising on his success in making his red guitar, Gary made a bass guitar for Colin, again with the help of Uncle Sid, as by now he had left school. So by 1961 the group was electric. Skiffle had been a means to an end. The 'Abington Skiffle Group' had morphed to 'Kenny Waters and the Waders', 'Rock Island Line' had acceded to 'Shakin' All Over' and Lonnie Donegan had given way to Cliff and the Shadows.

*

Gary is now eighteen and has to share a bedroom with his younger brother, Alan, which in his eyes is no longer acceptable. But a three-bed-roomed house for a large family gives them little option. Gary knows that Linda shares his views on change. They had spoken about it at length at Butlin's. There are two obvious options: either get a flat together, or Linda's brilliant idea, hatched in the Beachcomber Bar, is for Gary to move out of his house and take the spare room at Linda's house.

Then that nasty little Alan can have his own room, Gary's sister can have her own room and everyone will be happy. Gary can get into bed with Linda whenever the mood takes, providing her mum is out. The only snag Gary could imagine is their parents: in Linda's case, her mum; in Gary's case, his mum and dad.

*

Linda had first come into Gary's life at junior school when they were awarded the leading roles of Mary and Joseph in the school Nativity in which Ken was merely a wise man from the East and Val the fifth angel from the left. That top-of-the-bill pairing seemed to give them official religious approval for their relationship, which went from strength to strength. Now, a few years later, Gary is indeed a carpenter and Linda is indeed not a virgin. Val is indeed still an angel but whether Ken is indeed a wise man remains very much to be seen.

Ken has always been Gary's best friend since they first met at infants school before moving on to the juniors. At age ten they both played in the school football team a year ahead of the other boys. Ken was the selfish centre forward and goal scorer, Gary was schemer and provider. The following year, aged eleven, Gary was particularly proud to be nominated school football captain. Ken, to this day, wonders why it was Gary and not him. 'Best team player' was how the sports teacher described Gary, not 'best player' as Ken describes himself.

When they were twelve they joined Abington Youth Club mainly for the table tennis, darts and snooker. But as Lonnie Donegan became a TV star, Gary soon set up the 'Abington Skiffle Group'. Ken became the singer and strummed a guitar to look cool, although he had no real idea how to play it properly. On accordion, they recruited Gary's dad as he had experience of playing on stage with a local dance band. On another acoustic guitar was Brian Smith (a neighbour from the same street). He was older. Then on tea chest bass they got Colin Harris (Ken and Colin were at Grammar school together). On washboard they got Dave Bell, as no-one else was interested. The group practiced at Les Hall's Gold Street shop.

They played skiffle in the Lonnie Donegan idiom, put on concerts at the youth club and occasionally at a village hall. One Sunday they were asked to do an hour across lunchtime at a summer fete. Their problem was that Brian was a milkman and he couldn't finish in time. Eventually it was decided that the youngsters would all get up about 5.00 a.m. to help Brian deliver the milk, in order to get the milk round finished in time to fulfil the booking. It was cold, it was dark, but they did it in the name of show business! What was even more amazing was that Brian delivered milk by horse and cart, not by electric float. There was no rushing the horse, who only had three speeds: slow, dead slow and stop. Dave was awarded the dual role of talking to the horse to try and speed it up and shovelling up the horse-shit, which Brian used in his garden for his roses. Dave didn't mind too much. He was used to horses - his dad had two at the yard. It was all a real laugh but whether the customers appreciated the noise and horseplay that went on at that early hour was debateable.

They were also the first group ever to play at the local Salon-de-Danse. They did a Saturday evening guest half-hour during the Jersey Cow and Pork Pie Barbecue Dance, amid protests from the James Trent Orchestra that the boys were not members of the Musicians' Union. After heated debate and threats of a walk-out, they were allowed to play and did even join the union at a later date.

The skiffle craze waned as rock 'n' roll hit Britain, but even that, Gary found was easy. The first ever record he bought and learned to play was 'Peggy Sue' by the Crickets. It had three major chords, E,A and D, as many records had in those days. He spent every bit of spare time practising these chords until he could play them as fast as the record. But with rock 'n' roll things got more technical and Gary's dad set him up with a very small eight-watt amplifier. That is when he built his red guitar. Dave the drummer's own dad acquired him a drum kit, it having fallen off the back of a lorry. Then Gary made the bass guitar for Colin. Gary's dad retired and Brian soon found out that the rock 'n' roll life doesn't mix well with horse 'n' carts and early-mornings.

An ad in the local paper, a fifteen-minute audition in Gary's bedroom and a resounding 'You're in!' from all the lads, brought Roger into the group, although once his past life was uncovered the rest of the lads agreed to omit Tony Sheridan's 'Nobody's Child' from their repertoire. The words 'No mommy's kisses, no daddy's smiles, Nobody wants me, I'm nobody's child' were a bit near the knuckle.

To prepare for live performances the group needed a new start: new name; new image; new repertoire. Group names were generally the lead singer's name followed by the group name: Cliff Richard and the Shadows, Marty Wilde and the Wild Cats, Vince Eager and the Vagabonds.

Kenneth Waterfield was a mouthful, so Kenny Waters was born. The Waders seemed to fit somehow; no-one remembers quite how. The image change was in the form not only of the electric guitars, amps and drums but new stage wear.

Linda's mum made each of the members a blue jacket with a white letter 'W' on the breast pocket and for Kenny, a red jacket. They wore white shirts with black and white spotted bow ties and black trousers. The first time out they drew screams from the on-looking girls and were nearly mobbed. Ken loved the new adoration.

To discover new songs, write down the words and establish the key and chord sequences, Gary would listen to Radio Luxembourg on a tiny transistor radio he had especially bought for the purpose. Also, he and Ken would rush home from school and meet at Gary's house to listen to AFN Stuttgart or 'Salut Les Copains', a French radio station on the Europe 1 wave band early evening to learn the latest American numbers. Gary thought the 'Station of the Stars' was great as it was mainly for teenagers, with its non-stop pop music. He, like millions of teenagers all over Britain, used to listen secretly each night under the bedclothes - a secret society. Often Gary fell asleep in the small hours with the radio still propped up on the pillow by his ear, the sheets over his head, his brother oblivious.

Gary was certainly the driving force behind the Waders, although it was Ken who got the plaudits. The fact that Ken was the front man, had his name up in lights, wore a different coloured jacket, and looked and sang so well, you could be forgiven in thinking Ken was the main man. The girls idolised Ken, and Ken flourished.

Although Ken was dating Val from his early teens, Gary had caught him more than once around the back of the hall or in the toilet with other girls for a bit of slap and tickle. Gary never said anything to Ken or Val but it was always apparent that Ken could sometimes be a loose cannon when it came to loyalty. 'If he ever as much as touches Linda, that will be our friendship finished,' Gary asserts to himself. 'I could never forgive him! I would smash him to a pulp.'

Gary feels assured that his best mate will never do the dirty on him and is certain that his Linda has more sense than to fall for Ken's transient charms.

Chapter Fifteen

10.00 am

Ken's frustration with his father has been building up for months - no, more like years - but it is getting worse: 'He'll learn soon what he's done. I'm off. Bye-bye; cheerio; auf wiedersehen!'

He parks up outside his old school. After locking the car he collects the New Musical Express that he has on weekly order from the newsagent's, crosses the Wellingborough Road and beelines for the red and white spiral-striped pole outside Wilson's Men's Hairdressers.

'Hello Ken, your dad said you'd be in. Take a seat. There's a couple before you.'

Fifteen minutes drift by. Ken has brought in with him his NME as Mr Wilson's magazine collection, provided by the proprietor for his customers, is dated and not contemporary. The NME headlines with the fifth anniversary of Cliff Richard and the Shadows since they started with 'Move It' and a short stint at Butlin's. He flicks through the other pages, having quickly found the new charts in the usual place near the back. No.1: 'Bad to Me' by Billy J Kramer & the Dakotas. No.'s 2, 3, 4, 5 are all British groups.

'Yeah, it could be me one day,' he asserts to himself. 'One day very soon! Not 'could be' but 'will be'! What's this? A new LP by Johnny Kidd and the Pirates live at the Hamburg Star Club? Wow! I wonder if it's in the shops yet? I must ask Linda.'

As he reads on, Mr Wilson has got 'Saturday Club' on his pale blue 'Bush 7 Transistor' radio, the one with the big round tuning dial on the front.

'Good, but could be louder!' Ken thinks.

As Mr Wilson snips away, Ken catches his attention and by his swivelling hand actions suggests that Mr Wilson turns up the volume; the barber needs to bear all his customers in mind, and shakes his head whilst silently mouthing the word, 'Sorry.'

The dulcet tones of Brian Matthew intervene after each track, with the unique style and warmth of voice that captures your attention but in a laid-back sort of way. Together with his detailed knowledge of seemingly everything 'pop', Ken is, as usual, suitably impressed.

'How does Kenny J. Waters and the Dominators sound, Brian? Direct from Hamburg and with their latest No 1 hit? Sounds not 'Bad to Me' - one day soon, very soon… '

Ken is lost in his thoughts about his future, going over the various scenarios, all of which end in a blazing row with his dad. He struggles to turn his mind to something more pleasing but it is not easy when your father is Charles Waterfield. Finally, he breaks free of his anticipations and, more happily, he recollects the first time he came here for a haircut, having had his mum cut his hair with kitchen scissors for the first four years of his life.

He had a big kiss curl, like Bill Haley has now, but then he was taken by his father to Mr Wilson. He was too small for the barber's chair, so they placed a wide and solid piece of wood across the chair arms, which hoisted him up to the right level. He cried all the way through that first encounter but Mr Wilson was very kind, in distinct contrast to his father who looked on in disgust and embarrassment.

It is now his turn again. Mr Wilson beckons him up as he brushes away the black and grey trimmings of the previous occupant on the worn black and white diamond-patterned lino floor surrounding the chair. Mr Wilson is married, middle-aged and a solid member of the community; everyone knows him. He establishes Ken's requirements to his preference, not his father's!

Mr Wilson shakes the grey nylon gown, which Ken notices is still warm from the previous customer and has it tucked into his collar. Mr Wilson then begins a story about a young lad, about Ken's age, who came in the salon the other day and wanted him to cut his hair like the Beatles. Mr Wilson had never even heard of the Beatles, let alone their hairstyle and he didn't have a clue what the lad was on about. Apparently he was then educated by this young whippersnapper that they are a pop group from up the North.

'Like this, Mr Wilson?' Ken points at a picture of John Lennon in his NME.

Mr Wilson's opinion is that they look like they'd had a pudding basin put on their head and the barber had cut round the bottom of it. He told the lad to forget it and sent him off, bound for a barber in the

Town Centre to see if he would do it for him. He had also pointed to the sign on the mirror in front of the customer which stated 'No styles, No trims, Cheap Rates for OAP's'.

Mr Wilson explains that he can do a DA for the Teddy boys, a quiff, a short back and sides for the likes of Ken's dad, or variations of each, but that's all.

'If the customers want anything fancy, they'll have to go elsewhere!'

'In my opinion, Mr Wilson, a haircut like the Beatles could be all the rage over the next few months. If you could master it and maybe even advertise it in the local paper then you could make a fortune.'

'I don't think so, Ken, but thanks for your opinion. I don't want hordes of teenagers in here. What would my regular customers think - people like your father?'

'Yes, but without extending your services to teenagers all you will be left with are the likes of short back and sides for people like him. Other barbers will steal this new market. Don't you want to move your business forward?'

'No, I'm happy with my current clientele. Thanks, all the same.'

Mr Wilson changes the subject and remarks that Ken's dad seemed in good form this morning and told him how Ken had passed his 'A' levels and that he is joining the company business. He congratulates Ken with a 'Well done, lad.'

Ken is slightly embarrassed to contradict Mr Wilson and his congratulations on joining his father's company, suggesting that it is not a done deal yet. Mr Wilson mentions that the head clerk at Waterfield's Accountant's, Jack Tyson, is long-established at the firm, having huge experience, as well as one of his customers, too, and how he'll look after Ken really well. As Ken's mum did earlier, Ken diffused the conversation by enquiring whether Mr Wilson always wanted to be a hairdresser when he was young.

Mr Wilson continues snipping away with his scissors as he thinks back. 'No, not exactly, Ken, but I only went to Secondary Modern School, not the posh Grammar School like you. I was no great shakes at school. I could have gone into a shoe factory, I suppose. My late father owned this business and he made it real easy for me to join him here. He trained me and the business is mine now. I get to meet people, the work is easy enough and I make about enough money to keep Mrs Wilson happy.

'Yes, sounds familiar,' Ken thinks to himself. 'Dad makes it easy, easy work, to take over the business in due course. Did you have any dreams as a lad that went unfulfilled?'

'Dreams? Let me think.' Mr Wilson stops snipping as he thinks back. 'Funnily enough, once I had trained to become a barber I always wanted to work on a liner.'

'As a barber?'

'Yes, Cunard or similar, cutting the hair of the rich and famous and seeing the world, too.'

'Sounds great, so why didn't you do it?'

'I was going steady with my wife-to-be, then we got engaged. She fell pregnant so that was that. Dreams of New York and the Caribbean all went out the window. If you are going to follow a dream, Ken, then you need to do it before you settle down. Afterwards is too late.' Ken understands this completely and nods in acknowledgement.

'Have you travelled abroad, Mr Wilson?'

'No, furthest me and the missus have been is a week in a B&B in Blackpool up North, and a few days in a small private hotel in Torquay down South. Skeggie and Hunstanton, of course, for the occasional Sundays. I do the most travelling when I listen to my customers when they are telling me where they have been on their holidays, as I cut their hair.'

'Do you envy them, Mr Wilson?'

'We could go on holidays now, I suppose, but when you've got a small business like this it's not that easy. People expect you to be here when they need a haircut. If you are closed for holidays and they go elsewhere, then maybe they'll never come back again.'

'Or maybe they will?' Ken's mood is back on track and he just wonders how this man could have just put aside any dreams that he may have and settle for second best. 'Well, not that Mrs Wilson is second best, but all these years cutting hair and making small talk with customers, and no holidays, either! Sounds worse than Waterfield's Accountants!'

Ken mulls over Mr Wilson's comments. His assessment, which he keeps to himself, is that Mr Wilson took the easy option, took his father's direction, got a girl pregnant and has been stuck ever since. He really feels sorry for him, although on the surface he seems content enough.

The more that Ken talks to Mr Wilson, the more he is convinced that he has made the right decision in that he needs to get out now, go to Hamburg and strive to make a career as a pop star. The alternative is stay, marry Val, have three kids, join the accountants' firm, play golf, become a mason and have two weeks' holiday each year at the seaside.

If he fails to make it as a pop star then he can surely come back and carry on where he left off: easy! That is his safety net. Not unreasonable, surely!

Mr Wilson spends a couple of minutes with his thinning-scissors and is happy with the result. But he needs Ken's approval. 'There you are, young Ken. How does that look?' He holds the mirror up at the back, then each side. 'A little dab of Brylcreem, Ken?'

'No, that's fine, thanks. Keep it for your OAPs!'

'Hairspray?'

'You're joking? Not for me, thanks.'

'Are you still going out with young Valerie Roberts?'

'Sure am.'

'Nice girl, Val. I know her dad. He's a customer here, too. Lovely family.'

Mr Wilson bends over Ken and whispers quietly in his ear: 'Would you be needing something for the weekend, Ken? We don't want any dream-shattering accidents do we?'

Ken blushes and looks around at those waiting to see who may have picked up Mr Wilson's question. 'No, I'm in good shape. I've all I need, thanks all the same.'

Ken declines all the product offers, especially the Sunsilk hairspray. He has his neck brushed to clear any hair cuttings that may have slipped onto his collar, has his gown removed, gets up, receives a brush down, pays Mr Wilson over at the cash register by the door and prepares to leave.

'Ken, it's been a pleasure. Are you playing tonight?'

'Yes, St Mary's. Are you coming down to see us, Mr Wilson? Bring Mrs Wilson for a night out.'

'No, we're far too old for that noisy music you play. Mrs Wilson and I will be sat in front of the tele as usual. Good night on the box, Saturday: 'Wells Fargo' and 'Sergeant Cork'. Have fun, Ken.'

'See ya, Mr Wilson.'

The radio and the NME have reconfirmed his thoughts that British pop music is leading the world. Mr Wilson has corroborated his thoughts that he needs to act now, not wait! There is more to life than 'Wells Fargo' and 'Sergeant Cork', that's for sure. If he is going to make it big, he has to start now. He has to leave Northampton. He has to go to Hamburg.

'I shan't half miss Val. How will I tell her, and when? Then there's the thorny issue of my dad!'

Chapter Sixteen

10.00 am

Back home, Colin finds the front door a-jar. He is sure that he had shut it, but in his haste and with an anxious heart, it is quite possible the latch had not caught. No-one in the street locks their doors between sunrise and sunset anyway, and keys are always left dangling on a string on the inside of letterboxes. He bundles in with his shopping and nips straight along to the kitchen. To his horror, yet not entirely to his amazement, and certainly not for the first time, there is his mum's leopard-skin purse lying open on the greasy top of the dresser. There is a pile of copper coins in the zip pocket. But all the silver and all the notes, some of which he gave her last night for housekeeping and placed in the wallet partition… gone!

Colin goes mad, then ups his anger when he glances across to where his mother's handbag is lying open on its side, with bus tickets, a hankie and a hairbrush in disarray. A quick inspection reveals that her powder compact, cigarette lighter and packet of twenty Consulate cigarettes are missing as well!

'Mum, what game are you playing? I worked my socks off for that pittance, and it's disappeared. Again! How many more times do I have to tell you? Put your handbag somewhere safe. Keep it out of view when you bring home these Toms, Dicks and Flash Harrys. Mum, this is driving me mad. I don't get it!'

There is no-one with him in the kitchen, of course, but at least he has begun to get it off his chest whilst kicking the new-fangled pedal bin around, slinging the note-less purse at the wall, and punching the back of his dad's favourite armchair, hurting his knuckles and bruising his plucking thumb.

'Jeannie, what are you up to?' asks Colin, as his sister creeps quietly into the room, looking scared, still in her love-heart pyjamas. 'Didn't I tell you to stay in bed until I called you?'

'How can I,' Jeanette snaps, 'with you shouting like that? How long do you expect me to lay there waiting? You've been half an hour, Col. I'm starving and you're taking me to the 'ABC Minors'. Or have you forgotten?'

Colin lobs a lump of lard in the frying pan and puts four rashers of streaky bacon in so that they can have a sandwich each. He fills the kettle, lights the gas and puts that on, too, before swilling yesterday's tea-leaves down the sink.

'You know how I like to put on a bit of Mum's eye shadow when I go to the pictures, Col, and a bit of lipstick. It upset me so much when I opened Mum's bedroom door to help myself. Colin! Mum's horrible. I hate her! She told me to get out!' Jeanette broke down, screaming, 'It's horrible!' again and banging up and down her clenched fist on the table.

'She'd left her make-up down here in her handbag, Jeannie, and it's gone, along with her fags and lighter. When I got back from the shop… ' he tries to continue.

'If you hadn't have been so long over there you might have stopped him,' butts in Jeanette. 'I peeped out and saw him through the glass. Tall bloke with bent shoulders.'

Colin goes over and gives her a hug. He can't speak, but for several minutes, which seem more like half an hour, he hugs and hugs her. She sobs and sobs and he weeps his heart out in the most tender moment either of them has ever known. They cling to each other for their very lives as the fat sizzles and the kettle whistles. Both these culinary intrusions prompt them to come to their senses: the bacon has frazzled and the water has begun to boil away before they let go.

Quickly they pull themselves together and polish off their sandwich. Their conversation lightens as they do the dish-washing and drying. 'Jen, come on, get dressed. We'll be late.'

Whilst Jeannette is slipping into her jeans and tee shirt, Colin puts his head into his mother's bedroom and breaks the news to her that she has been robbed yet again, and that it is obvious who the guilty party is. But she is in a right state, sitting dazed on her wicker chair in front of her dressing table mirror. She is in no condition to discuss anything. She never even looks around, so Colin merely says, 'Mum, we're off to the ABC. Come on, perk up. I'll see you at lunchtime and we'll have some fish and chips.'

Lil just sits there, staring into the mirror - mascara tears, blotchy eyes, blubbering almost, and Colin well knows that it is best to creep away and leave her. Jeanette pops out of her bedroom, but before she can ask how Mum is, Colin simply puts his hand over her opening lips, whispers 'Shush', and beckons her away and off to the cinema.

Colin waits until he sees Jeanette ushered in through the marble foyer and decides to nip into Lynn's Café for a coffee and to listen to the music for a while. Lynn's is a favourite haunt because of the great jukebox and the camaraderie of loyal Teddy boys who congregate around it.

Since the late-fifties, Colin has always wanted to be a Teddy boy and still wears a quiff and a DA. However, he stops short of wearing a drape coat, brothel creepers and bootlace tie. He follows the style as far as he can afford or dare. He cuts his ties down really thin, wears winkle picker shoes and a new line in chisel toes, and has his trousers tapered to twelve inches at the bottom.

Into Lynn's he walks, home from home for him. He orders a coffee and takes a seat along the side wall.The jukebox is blaring out as usual, though no longer with the Genes, Eddies and Jerry Lees that he loves so much. Mersey Beat is sweeping the country and Ken and Gary of the Waders are full of the Beatles and Gerry and the Pacemakers. Lynn's juke box is the best in town for staying faithful to the old rock 'n' roll whilst blending in the new beat group style.

Then Colin's day really takes off, when two Teddy Boys who he knows well push in the door and barge through the café. They are Johnny Archer and Mick Miller, slightly older than Colin. They often come to the Waders` shows, and always deal with any trouble if they do. They are also mates of a sort to Dave, the group's drummer, and Colin has often seen Dave with them in Lynn's.

Johnny and Mick push past Colin rather dismissively, merely saying, 'Hiya, Col,' as they nudge their way through to the jukebox. Their off-hand behaviour surprises Colin, as they usually move very slowly, looking cool, mean and aggressive. But today something has changed. They look downbeat, edgy and a bit distracted, in a way that Colin is hard-put to describe.

They make their way to the jukebox, picking up cokes on the way. Mick fumbles under his pocket flap for a shilling and shovels it straight into the slot, agitated, completely unlike the slow, deliberate way he usually does before flicking it in the air three times prior to the purchase This is not the 'Slick Mick' of the coffee bar world, the cool cat of the alleyways, the minder that Dave Bell has had looking over his shoulder all these years. Johnny just sits there and stares into his coke, with no menacing eye on the blokes nor suggestive eye on the birds.

You know they are in the place, though, when on comes a rockin' 'Shakin' all Over' by Johnny Kidd. But they are not standing there imitating their idol, tapping their feet or twanging their nasal guitars. They sit there, gazing down the straws of their coke bottles, looking as miserable as sin. Something is up. Colin averts his gaze, because he knows what will happen if a peek becomes a gape!

Unbelievably, as if there isn't enough to wonder about, over in the corner, stuffing his face with a sausage sandwich and puffing a fag from an open packet of 'Consulates', having lit up with a familiar-looking gas cigarette lighter, is a tall man with rounded shoulders whose image rocks Colin to the core.

'No. It can't be! Men don't smoke 'Consulates', or at least they don't buy them, do they?' muses Colin, as he stares at the outline of the man, an outline that had brushed past him somewhere before with an elbow that would tip you over in a bathroom if it dug into your ribs. He rubs his side. Yes, the bruise is coming out now, and it hurts when he touches it.

Colin wonders what he has let himself in for, and suddenly Lynn's Café, that most revered of hallowed grounds, turns into a place of doubt and suspicion. He wants to get out, like the time when the water was cut off and the Teds had to vacate to a club down town and sabotage the bingo session, but he also wants to see what is going to happen next.

There are a few leery looks as a couple of rival Teds in powder blue drapes slouch by outside, glaring through the window as they go past and awarding a certain two-fingered salute to all and sundry, yet nobody in particular. And that is about that.

Colin wants revenge on the thieving bastard, but knows that when push comes to shove, he hasn't got either the nerve or the muscle to follow it through. He stands up, looks over to Mick and Johnny, then slowly moves towards them. 'Are you two up for a bit of action?' Colin looks hopeful, his voice quieter than normal as he leans down and across. Mick is staring down at the table, Johnny is lost in his thoughts. They never reply.

'Mick, Johnny, I could do with a bit of help, a bit of muscle, are you up for it?' Johnny looks impassive, he looks deep in thought; Mick similar.

'Col, I don't know what you want, but it's not a good time. We're busy, right?'

As Colin is about to ask again: 'Colin, mate, we don't need any trouble right now. Sorry and all that, but leave it out!'

Colin returns to his table, sits down, looking dejected and feeling rejected. Mick and Johnny swig up after they have heard their three tracks, and move out. This is totally out of character, because they are past-masters of sitting there for at least two hours with one coke each, bopping and joshing, looking for a scrap and ridiculing café visitors and passers-by with wicked tongues and speedy wits. They totally ignore Colin, too, which is unprecedented as they always like to try and get out of him what the Waders would be playing in the evening and what Dave is getting up to.

Once they have gone, Colin's attention switches back to the gangly man who he has nicknamed 'Spike' in his mind. He is still downing his grub, and smoking to help it on its way down his gullet. Spike is a solemn man, a dodgy-looking character whose sour complexion and droopy eyes demand some sympathy, but who from Colin gets none.

'Yes, you dirty robber. I know who you are and what you've been up to. If I come and sit near you, I would be able to smell Mum on you as well.'

Colin cannot act alone, though. He would be pulverised, but he has got Spike's number and stores away the information for future reference. He thoughtfully chastises his mother for deserving to lose what she has had swiped from her handbag, and has to be content to dismiss the man with the contempt that he deserves. He stands up, glares at his adversary's neck, then leaves. He pops round the corner to the Post Office to pick up a 'Reveille', then it is time to nip down to the ABC and collect Jeannie.

Colin begins to wonder why he bothered to go into Lynn's Café in the first place. He had the brush-off from his mates, who look as though they are carrying the cares of the world on their shoulders, neither wanting to start a fight nor smash the place up in the usual manner.

Moreover, he had the dubious pleasure of catching more than a glimpse of the unwelcome guest from his home, and it made him feel physically sick to see the thief smoking what he guesses were his mother's cigarettes, lit with what looked like her lighter.

He browses through the girlie pics in his 'Reveille' as he waits outside the cinema. Soon the kids will be on the way out, and he has to get down to the foyer to meet Jeanette and take her home for lunch. He is very agitated, and is becoming edgy with things that are happening around him which he cannot put his finger on, and which are beyond his control.

This is becoming an impossible day for Colin Harris, with borderlines between hopes, fears and expectations getting more blurred by the minute.

Chapter Seventeen

11.30 am

Apart from serving and generally supervising the others, Linda needs to complete the 'Chart Returns' form which is communicated to the Record Industry and which contributes to the national compilation of the 'Top 50'. At least on Saturdays Linda knows that there will be no sales reps calling from the major record companies. These men (they are always men) insist on her undivided attention (especially Trevor from EMI who really fancies Linda and fancies himself even more) while they show off their companies' products, especially the very latest record releases, and set up in-store displays. They are well-dressed, generally well-mannered and always have a humorous story ready. Linda, although only eighteen, through her upbringing with numerous lodgers and extensive knowledge of pop music, can easily handle these hard-selling salesmen.

For the two weeks each year that Linda is on holiday, mysteriously no sales reps appear. There is no real point, as Mr Jones has a very limited pop music knowledge and never agrees to any purchases until Linda is back.

Unbeknown to Mr Jones, Linda is also able to secure for herself the occasional special promotion (given for hitting a particular order level) from a rep, which might be a bottle of wine or some record tokens. She would smuggle these from his briefcase into her shopping bag behind the counter. On one unforgettable occasion 'EMI Trev' offered her something that could only be described as 'suggestive' or 'seductive' provided she met up with him one evening at the local B&B he regularly used for his sales trips out of London. She took the offering, never turned up at the pre-arranged meeting and warned him if he ever came on strong again she would report him to both Mr Jones and his own boss at the record company with the evidence still in her possession.

Gary eventually became the sole recipient of a private viewing of this special promotion item in their chalet on their first night at Butlin's. He never dared to ask where it came from but was well pleased with the amazing effect it had on both his and her libido for the rest of the week.

'Thanks, Trev!' thought Linda. 'In future you are going to have to come up with some amazing sales promotion gifts to beat this one!'

Linda normally prepares the purchase orders on Monday or Tuesday, the slackest days of the week, so that they will be delivered on Thursday or Friday, ready for the Saturday rush. On Saturday, however, there is still a chance to receive a stock delivery and if time permits, one or both of the Saturday girls would open up the boxes, check the delivered goods against the order form, check for breakages or scratches and update the stock forms.

When prospective Saturday girls are interviewed by Linda and Mr Jones she always insists on selecting the ones with presence, providing they have some degree of mental aptitude. The test she applies to each of them is their ability to successfully reach to '4' on the '6/3d times table':1 x 6/3d is 6/3d, 2 x 6/3d is 12/6d, 3 x 6/3d is 18/9d, 4 x 6/3d is 25/-. She figures out through experience that the chances of any girls reaching '5' or more are about nil. But then again, who buys more than four singles in any one transaction? Nobody! Since their appointments, singles have gone up in price to 6/8d and a retraining plan might well be needed.

After hiring Saturday assistants, Linda then trains them and drills into them the importance of looking smart and being 'nice' to the customers, especially the teenage boys, who nowadays have more money to spend. She has even organised for Val to give new employees an hour's instruction on face make-up, which is particularly needed by Beverley, especially the concept of how 'less is sometimes more'.

This has all paid dividends as sales have surged ahead since Linda has been there. Its only drawback is that last year both the Saturday girls ended up getting pregnant, getting hurriedly married and leaving. Linda has since modified her definition of the word 'nice' and the two current Saturday girls have now been there for over six months which is 'nice' for all concerned. Linda has proved the falsehood of her English teacher's advice to avoid inappropriate descriptive words:'The dog's dinner is nice and nothing else!'

This morning the two Saturday girls, Wendy and Beverley, are arguing about the ownership of a piece of chewing gum that has been left stuck under the counter next to the till since last Saturday, each claiming it is their's. Wendy wins, retrieves it, checks it over quickly and pops it into her mouth.

Linda is not surprised to see two of her regular customers entering the store and heading straight for her. Norman and Paul, local beatniks-cum-art students are real music aficionados. Considering they cannot be more than seventeen or eighteen years old, this is remarkable. What these two don't know about popular music, especially American music, isn't worth knowing.

They have been regulars at the shop for the last year or so, since they realised that Linda knew as much about modern music as they did, and since they realised that she could obtain for them records that no other shop in the town is interested in even discussing, let alone ordering.

They are unremarkable-looking lads. Norman has dark, longish hair and wears Buddy Holly-style glasses. He has the beginning of a beard that is struggling to break free from his face and which looks like bum-fluff. He is dressed in a black beret, black turtle-necked shirt and blue jeans, which have been not very successfully dyed black.

Paul is wearing dark glasses and is dressed in a long thigh-length ragged jumper, velvet trousers and suede shoes.

'Mornin', Linda.'

'Hello, lads.'

'Paul wants a copy of The Rivingtons' new single, 'The Bird's the Word', on the Liberty label. We guess you won't have it in stock, Linda, perhaps you can order it? Remember, 'Papa-oom-mow-mow'? We got that here. This is the follow-up. Fantastic! Here's one to test you, Linda. You remember the Duane Eddy recording of 'Rebel Rouser'?'

'Remember it? How can I forget it? Gary plays it most nights either on his record player or on stage!'

'Well you know all the yells and whooping going on in the background? That's the Rivingtons before they became famous!'

'Before they became famous', she thought. 'No-one apart from these two have ever even heard of the Rivingtons! I wonder if anyone will be able to say the same about any of the Waders should any of them become famous?'

Linda selects the right trade catalogue and looks it up: nothing.

'Can you check for us in the week and we'll be back next Saturday. In the meantime, last week we ordered a copy of 'Twist and Shout' by the Isley Brothers on Stateside. Is it in?'

'I think it might be. Now let me see.' Linda steps to the back of the counter where around twenty singles are filed in a section marked 'Customer Orders'. She knows it is there because she had already taken it home yesterday and played it to Gary. This is a routine she has followed for all the lad's purchases over the past year and which has given Gary advanced notice of new music coming across the Atlantic from the 'Tamla' and 'Motown' catalogues, like Mary Wells, Martha and the Vandellas and the Contours, issued on 'Oriole' here in England. In some cases, Gary has introduced the songs into the Waders' repertoire having noted down the words and chord sequences. The boys jostle each other in excitement, then Paul nods approvingly at Linda's legs when her back is turned and smiles suggestively at his mate.

'Yep. Here it is.'

'Wow, look at that dark blue sleeve, Norman! Fabulous! That sleeve is worth the price, let alone the record. Can we hear it please?'

'Yes, listening booth No.1, over there,' points out Linda.

'Are you both coming to St Mary's Hall this evening? The Waders live and rocking!'

'No chance! Paul and I spend most weekends in London, don't we Paul? We're leaving by train late afternoon?'

'Yeah, we're down the Smoke. We've found a great music club in Ealing, in a really atmospheric cellar near the tube station.

'Yeah, it's a bit hot, damp and packed out, but there's a great buzz and terrific blues music. We met some guys at the Richmond Jazz Festival a few weeks back. They introduced us to it and we kip on their floor each Saturday night, don't we, Norm?'

'Come with us, Linda, it's amazing. We can also recommend a great music club in Soho called the Flamingo. It's an all-nighter, and they even have music on Sunday afternoons. Norman and I were there last Saturday. Great music. They call it rhythm and blues, black roots blues updated, electrified and with terrific 'Oomph'. We've seen Cyril Davies and Long John Baldry. I tell you, Linda, it could be the next big thing. Go on, come with us!'

'Sounds great, but you've caught me there. I've never heard of them!'

Linda dismisses the pleas of the two lads.

'Well, when you get fed up with a variation on a theme called 'Elvis', let us know. We'll educate you, won't we Norm?'

The lads pay up as Wendy looks on, smiling. Beverley places their purchase in a small paper bag, specially sized to hold a single or two. Paul and Norman look at Beverley and wonder if she has a boyfriend and whether she might fancy either of them. They wonder if she likes the Rivingtons, also if she might fancy a night at the pictures. If not, the other one ain't bad looking either. She'd do. Both want to ask; both think they would look a right berk in front of the other if she said 'No'. So they both smile at both girls, turn and start to slowly leave the shop with the usual 'See ya next week'.

Gary, dressed in a black polo neck shirt, blue jeans and a jean jacket, then enters Adnitts and sees his Linda in the Record Department, chatting to Beverley and Wendy. He waves, strides across to her, embraces her and gives her a little peck, no more. Although he loves her, displays of affection in public are not his style.

'Were they those weird art students I saw leaving?'

'They're not weird, Gary; a bit different, that's all.'

'Pseuds, you mean!'

Gary knows that Linda finds them stimulating, but he feels a little bit in awe of, even threatened by, their eclectic musical tastes. He bids farewell to the also-busy Linda, 'Can't stop. I'm off to Dad's. See ya later!'

As Gary leaves through the back door, Ken enters through one of the big glass doors at the front and makes a bee-line for Linda. He can see her serving a couple of blokes, also a queue of other prospective purchasers clamouring for her attention.

Ken locates the LP section and starts flicking through the rack. Johnny Kidd, where are you? One after the other, his thoughts dismiss the offerings with a 'Got it'; 'Had it and went off it'; 'Not interested'; 'Never heard of it'. He plucks the occasional LP from the rack, checks the front cover picture, turns it over, checks the song titles, reads the first sentence or two of the write-up, then replaces it. Two or three LP's he leaves sticking out an inch above the others, for later secondary reflection and possible final selection. He loves the atmosphere in the record shop, the feel and smell of the records, the sleeves, the vinyl.

In one of the two listening booths a potential customer carefully decides whether to invest his 6/8d as he listens to his musical choice. In the other booth, four teenagers, two of each gender, lark about and jostle each other as their selection plays, with probably little or no intention of making a purchase. 'Bloody timewasters!' as Ken's dad would say.

Wendy, Beverley and Linda gradually deal with the happy queue of customers. Linda sees Ken and comes over to where he is still flicking through the LP racks. 'Hello, gorgeous. How are you today?'

Linda brushes up to Ken and takes his arm. She pecks him on the cheek. Ken is always embarrassed by Linda's normal greeting. 'She looks gorgeous herself,' he thinks to himself, 'a real 'looker' is Linda and always with a 'come on' twinkle in her eye.'

'Hi Lin. Busy today are you?'

'Sure am! Everybody's coming in for the new Beatles' single, 'She Loves You'. It's unbelievable. Definitely number one next week! Have you heard it, Ken?'

'Yep, I like it more than their last single. They seem to get stronger with each release.'

'Are you going to buy it?'

'Probably, but not today. Maybe next week.'

'I'm collecting the holiday photos later, Ken. Should be able to show you them this evening.'

'Me and Val'll see you two down St Mary's 'bout seven?'

'Look forward to it. I want a nice smoochy dance off you this evening, Mr Waterfield!'

'Only one?'

She squeezes his arm.

Out of the corner of his eye, he notices a familiar poster on the wall, though there is something wrong with it. But what…? He scrutinises it closely. 'Lin, who designed that bloody poster on the wall?'

'Which poster?'

'That one for our gig tonight.'

'Why, what's wrong with it?'

'My bloody name's not on it. It says 'The Waders'. It should say

'Kenny Waters and the Waders'.'

'I don't know who designed it, but everyone knows that you are the vocalist for the Waders. Is it that important?'

'See ya tonight.' Ken gives Linda a soft peck on the cheek, ignoring her question, before turning and leaving. She has that fabulous perfume on again. Wow!

Ken heads off back to his car. He's going to miss Val; but it won't be forever. Short term pain for long term gain. He'll miss Linda, too!

Chapter Eighteen

12.30pm

'Hello, Colin, where have you been?' Mrs Harris asks her son from where she is standing near the sink as he shuffles into the kitchen with a heavy heart and a worried mind.

'Hi, Mum. You're up, then?' Colin states the obvious, without answering her question.

'Up? What do you mean, 'up'? I've been up for ages, and I thought you'd have been back from town ages ago. Where's the shopping? You said we were going to have a tasty bit of fish for dinner.'

'Did I? Mum, stop this! What are you asking about fish for when you've had your fags and lighter and purse nicked by that bloke you brought home last night?'

Silence.

'What's going on, Mum? This is getting beyond a joke, and Jeannie knows what you're up to. How long do you think she's going to swallow the line that she has a load of uncles of all shapes and sizes?'

Silence.

'Look, Mum, if you're not going to talk, that's up to you. You know we're hurting, and if you keep on back-sliding... well, I suppose it's a free world. Come on, get yourself dressed properly. I'll put on some eggs and bacon. I didn't go shopping and you know why? Yes, I saw that tosser you brought home, and so did Jeannie. How can I go shopping when I've got that poor kid to look after? How do you think I felt in the café, him smoking your fags, lit with your lighter, buying breakfast from your purse, feeding the jukebox from my wages?'

'Colin, stop it! Come and sit down with me at the table. I've got something to tell you. Let's have a nice cup of tea together,' Mrs Harris at last breaks her silence, but looks gaunt. Despite being conciliatory, there is a frightened look in her eye that Colin hasn't seen before. Very quickly his anger gives way to concern.

'Mum, what is it? I don't want any long drawn-out explanations. All I want is for us to be happy and enjoy ourselves again. We need to live a little. It's been too long… '

At this, Lil Harris lets out an awful wail that knocks Colin for six. She sobs and sobs and sobs - beside herself with grief. Colin sits there horrified, neither getting up to cuddle her, nor offering any words of comfort. He has never seen his mother like this. She rocks backwards and forwards, trying to mask out the anguish inside her mind and within the immediacy of her surroundings. If Colin would exclaim to himself, 'What a state to get in!' he would rationalise: 'At the end of her tether!'

The cup of tea clearly isn't going to materialise, so Colin does the honours and slips a nice cuppa with milk and two sugars in front of his mum, who neither sees it, nor touches it.

'Mum, you Ok?' He walks across to the cooker to put on the eggs and bacon.

'Colin. Come and sit down, I said. There's something I have to tell you.'

With an egg in one hand and a spatula in the other, Colin does as he is told. His mum wipes away a tear, sniffs, sobs a bit more, then continues. 'I wanted to be the best mother in the world, the best wife and the best cook. I had to pack up the typing pool when Jeannette came along. We got by, minding each other with Bert and Ethel keeping an eye out for you two, and me and your Dad watching over Barry and Rose. Jeannette was too much of a good thing, what with the big age difference, and a different…' She stops abruptly.

'Different what, Mum?' Colin queries.

'Uh, um, different interests, and, um, things,' she splutters. 'Anyway, your dad hit the bottle big time, started to gamble, stopped putting his money in our kitty and we just went to rack and ruin. I was totally skint. I needed money for my fags and booze.

'There was no money. So where do you think it came from? What else could I do? You needed two sets of rugger kit, a satchel, long trousers when you were fourteen, a guitar, winkle-picker shoes, if you don't mind!'

'And a decent guitar, Mum,' adds Colin, with a wry grin. 'So now you know where the money didn't come from, Colin!'

'Yes I do, and no I don't! We still didn't have any back in '59 and again, if it wasn't for Gary, I wouldn't have had that tea-chest bass with the Abington Skifflers. He made that, too, or don't you remember? Anyway, Mum, where do you think the money came from to get you those powder compacts for Mother's Day, and that 'Long Flake' for Father's Day, and all those 'Buntys' for Jeannie? Where on earth is this guessing game getting us?

'That lousy, rotten paper round, the longest bike ride in town! All those tight-fisted gits from the other side of the mill, using our newsagent's because we only charged a penny halfpenny a week for delivery. 'Muggins' here drew the short straw, soaked to the skin before school, soaked to the skin going to school, then delivering the local rag in the evenings, then doing my homework, then, then...

'Mum, what is it about this that you don't get? It wasn't only you who was struggling. It was all of us, all because Dad was a fool with his money!'

It is supposed to be Lil Harris getting things off her chest, but Colin poaches the moment in order to get things off his. She gets a word in edgeways... 'Do you remember when those Essex Street lads roughed you up on the way home from school and ripped the lining out of your cap? That was another tailor-made excuse for your dad to clout you and blame you for keeping us poor. I can hear him now...' In wiping the slate clean about Colin's dad, Lil appears to have completely forgotten what it is she wants to get off her chest in the first place.

'At least you can see why I took up skiffle, Mum. You kept pushing the Boys Brigade on me; they kept pushing more instruments on me to learn and pushing me to join the boxing team. Everyone kept pushing me to go to Sunday School. You can see why I got hacked off with it all and sat in my bedroom with my little amp practising the guitar Gary made for me, playing along with my records. Paradise!'

It dawns upon Colin that this is the first time they have spoken like this, ever, and he warms to the open manner they are talking. 'Anyway, Mum, what's all this about? At least you've got a smile on your face. What's going on?'

'Times have been much harder than they should have been. Look around the house. What have we got? Nothing. Where do you and Jeannie go? Nowhere. What did I want for you both? The world!' Lil breaks down again, and this time Colin gets up and gives her a hug. It has been years since he has cuddled his mum. Lil winces, tells him to be gentle, and Colin is horrified to find her ringing wet with sweat and trembling like a leaf.

'I`m so sorry, Colin,' she says, apologising for something or other. 'I've got a lump on my breast.'

'You've got a what? Where?'

Silence.

'Come on, Col. Let's have another cup of tea together. Everything will be alright.'

The tea is by now stone cold, so Colin goes over to the teapot, tops it up with a little hot water and pours them each another cup. He sits there staring at her, speechless, his brain and body numb.

Lil continues to tell Colin how she first discovered the lump some months ago, how scared she has been, how the fear that it might be spreading makes her panic, and how that has frightened her into smoking like a chimney and earning money in the way she does.

Silence.

'So now what, Mum?' asks her son, in shock, fighting back the tears and giving her an opportunity to clarify the situation.

'Well, Col, I went to the doctor's last week, and I'm going for tests and x-rays and things. I hope things haven't gone too far, but most of all I don't want you to worry because that will make matters worse.

'Please don't tell Jeannie yet. There's no rush, and we'll see what the results show. I've been putting up with the lump and the hurt for long enough now. I'm sure a few more days won't make any difference.'

Lil and her son never do get their fish lunch. Colin makes a pretty good job of knocking up a lovely fry-up for them both. They pass the time chatting about Dad and Jeannette, but say no more about the unwelcome overnight guest nor what he had stolen. Colin knows enough about his mum's deviance in looking after her property.

Once his mum has polished off her breakfast, and they share the washing up, it is time for Lil to get herself washed and dressed. Colin needs a break to get his head clear. With the clock spinning round to two o'clock, he gives his mum a peck on the cheek, tells her to keep her pecker up, and makes for the front door.

'Colin, please don't worry about me, will you?' Lil pleads, a strange request really, because that is exactly what Colin always does, day after day.

'I won't, Mum. You'll be alright. This lump'll be nothing. You see!'

'I hope so, love. You take care. It's a big night out for you and Kenny and the boys, isn't it?'

Colin shuts the front door and makes his way up the street. What a day! Town are away to City, so there won't be any fans clad in their claret and white bobble-hats and scarves, many carrying rattles and bells, streaming out of the rows of terraced houses and across the park to see the match. He fancies watching at least half an hour or so of a Town League match to clear his head. He hangs around where a few pitches have been chalked up with the goal nets erected. There is often a good scrap going on over there.

Chapter Nineteen

1.00 pm

Lunchtime soon comes around. Right on cue and out the corner of her eye Val can see Linda waving and beckoning her through Boots' side door. Val checks the wall clock, hangs up her smock, grabs her handbag and hurries off to join her best mate.

Linda and Val, like the best friends they are, leave together arm in arm. Over the road Val spots Roger on duty by the police pillar, but she doesn't wave, as they have no time to waste. Poor Roger never seems to be at the top of anybody's wish list. An hour for lunch is the bare minimum that the two girl friends need to catch up with all that has gone on since they last talked in the pub, a little over twelve hours ago!

As they stroll away from the outdoor market, which is all hustle and bustle, their shopping done, Linda pops in to Dollond's to collect the holiday snaps. The girls take their seat in Lynn's cafe for lunch. They start discussing Val's chat with her work-chum Jenny Wilson, who has just got engaged to Barry Price. 'Jenny was apparently worried about being left on the shelf. She said being engaged is a nice feeling. I've got my man!'

'How old is Jenny?'

'Twenty.' It hits Val that that's twice she has heard that today, and it is only lunchtime! Val tells Linda that she asked Jenny if they were having an official engagement picture in the newspaper.

'Ooh no,' Jenny had replied. 'That's just for posh people! Mum and Dad have invited Barry's parents around for tea later - corned beef sandwiches, some cake and a cup of tea. Nothing fancy. Then, after 'Thank Your Lucky Stars' and 'Cheyenne', we're all going out for a drink. There's a great bar at the hotel around the corner. I think they have a house trio on there at weekends. I suppose we'll be back for 'Dial 999', starring Mum's heart-throb, Robert Beatty.'

Linda chirps in, 'She's welcome to Barry Price. He always smells of machine-oil from that engineering factory.'

'You know, Linda, we're really lucky having Ken and Gary. They've got the looks, the smell and the style; they don't drink, they don't smoke...'

'But they do go out with women-us, and musically they're the best in town,' rejoins Val. 'You and me are good catches for them. Perfect, us four!'

'I don't know what you did to Ken at Butlins? Well, I guess I do, naughty girl! He's been grinning like a Cheshire cat since we got back.'

Looking a trifle embarrassed, Val only comes back with, 'Yes, best holiday of all time. It'll take some beating next year! Ken was wonderful! He was ecstatic to be away from his dad.'

'Being away with you lifted him even higher! Ken's dad's a bully: yes Dad, no Dad, three bags full, Dad. I don't how he puts up with it, day after day!'

'I suppose we've all got our crosses to bear, Lin. Look at you. You don't even have a dad.'

'Yes, but what you never have, you never miss, Val, always remember that!'

The assistant serves them doughnuts and coffee, and they both admire the sleeping face of the owner's baby lying in a Moses basket by the counter.

'Perhaps we should all get married, Val. What do you think? Hey, what about a double wedding? How groovy would that be?'

'Don't start! First Mum, then Jenny Wilson, now you! We're Ok as we are, aren't we?'

'Dunno, Val. They might well be right. It'd be good if you and Ken got engaged. You could have a great party with live music from the boys, and a diamond ring on your finger. Keep him under the thumb. Petticoat rule. Keep your mum and dad from worrying. It'd stop Ken from finding someone else. Where would you be without him?'

Being without Ken is beyond Val's comprehension. He is the love of her life, her whole life.

'Oh, by the way, here's the holiday snaps,' says Linda, unwittingly being right on cue for a major surprise.

Valerie flicks through them expectantly, but it dawns on her that there aren't many with her on: Gary and Ken, Gary and Linda, Ken and

Linda, another Ken and Linda, yet another Ken and Linda! Finally, Linda finds one with Ken and Val and she is quick to offer it with an imperceptible, beautifully-disguised sigh of relief! Then Linda finds another and she suggests she will give it to Ken this evening.

Linda rewinds the subject back to holidays: 'How about a foreign-holiday foursome next year? They say the booze is dirt cheap in Spain.'

'But you know I don't drink!'

'A-ha, not now you don't, Val. Once you see the price, you may as well hang in with us. Booze is cheaper than boring soft drinks.'

'Have you got a passport, Lin?'

'No, have you?'

'No, but Ken has. He went on a school trip abroad last year. Russia, wasn't it?'

'I'm not sure about Gary.'

'You'll need a new swimming costume and plenty of suntan oil, too. Sexy bikini? They're all the rage! Topless? Can you imagine?'

'No, I can't. I don't want all those playboys ogling me.' Val blushes and her heart flutters.

'Why not. If you've got it, flaunt it! Even the word cliché is a cliché, but that's what I say. When in Rome!'

'Well, we all know that you've got it, but I'm not sure that I have. Will we always be best mates, Lin?' Val is keen to change subject.

'I bloomin' well hope so.'

'Me, too. Even if you do steal my boyfriend on all your photographs! Do you fancy Ken?'

'What sort of question is that, Val?' asks Linda, having hoped that she had steered Val away from where the camera never lies.

'Well, do you? Be honest! Yes or no?'

Linda considers her answer, wanting to be completely honest but at the same time not wanting to upset her best friend.

'Let's put it like this. Is there any girl you know who doesn't fancy Ken?'

'So you do, then!' Valerie is stunned, and wonders why she asked this self-effacing question in the first place.

'Do you fancy Gary?' Linda hopes for a similar answer from her best mate but knows that Valerie will probably avoid a direct answer. She is not mistaken.

'I've never really thought about it. While I have Ken, I don't really think about other lads. Ken is all I need, all I think about.'

'I do; I like to check out all the runners and riders, Val.'

'What about Roger?' asks Val.

'Who, our Rog from the band?' Linda's tone turns more to slight ridicule. 'He's Ok, sexy-necks in his police uniform. He can lock me up with him and throw away the key anytime.' Linda's eyes are sparkling as she turns herself on at her own suggestion.

They both giggle, catch breath, then start chuckling. It takes a few seconds for both of them to regain enough composure to talk again. Valerie explains to Linda how she was busy talking to a young customer that morning when out of the corner of her eye she noticed a policeman approaching.

She had finished talking to the customer as none other than Roger himself arrived, looking a bit flustered, as he always was when he spoke to Val. Roger informed her about a burglary last night where a lot of stuff was taken - fags, booze, jewellery - explaining that if she should hear anything she should let him know immediately. He gave her a police circular whilst undressing her with his eyes.

It seemed clear to Val that Roger was wasting time with nothing of real interest to say. On the other hand, she was pleased to think that he dropped by to see her now and again and she was flattered. Roger always appeared as if he wanted to say something but couldn't quite spit it out. Strange!

'Well, he drops by because he fancies you, Val. Obvious isn't it?' Linda had cut to the chase.

'But he knows I'm with Ken.'

'Doesn't matter. He likes chatting to you and being seen with you. Sounds like he's obsessed. Got a crush on you, eh Val?'

Val blushes. 'He's wasting his time, then. I'm with Ken forever. Hasn't Roger got a girl-friend?'

'I don't think so but I don't really know. I've never had a proper chat with Rog. He's a bit shy, I think.'

'What about Colin and Dave?'

'Colin's a good lad. A bit shy with girls, but I like him. He needs someone to sort him out - tell him to get his hair cut, buy him some trendy clothes, smarten him up a bit. He's still trying to be a Teddy boy. He needs a good woman!' They both laugh.

'Like us!'

'I think his home life isn't the best, what with his dad and all.'

'Yeah, and his mum. I've heard rumours about her, too.' Linda seems to know an awful lot more than Val. She looks around to see if anyone is eaves-dropping. 'No, I better not say what I've heard. All I'll say is that she's not quite normal, either.' They giggle again.

'And Dave?'

'Dave is Dave. He's more interested in cart-horses than girlfriends. He's not my type at all. He's a bit rough and smelly, but his heart's in the right place. Dave would never do you any harm and he's always very helpful. If you need a favour, then Dave's your man.'

'And his drums are falling apart!' adds Val.

'So's his gammy leg, and it's a wonder he can play the drums at all. Poor Dave. Shame, i'n'it?'

'So all in all, the Waders aren't a bad bunch to hang out with? Ken and Gary are the main men, and with us at their side they can't go far wrong,' says Val, assuredly.

'Why don't we set up a Fan Club? Five bob a year to join and we send them a membership card, a signed photo and a half-yearly newsletter.' Linda looks excited by her own idea.

'I was a member of the Lenny the Lion Fan Club years ago,' retorts Val.

'Yes, I'll work on that with Gary.' Linda dismisses her best friend's comment.

'Linda, I really appreciate having you as a confidante. I feel really close to you. I don't know how things would ever work out without you.'

'It's the same for me, Val. You and me have been friends all our lives. I can be myself when you're around. You bring out the best in me.'

'I know that I'm never alone, cos' you're always there. It's great to have a friend who you can trust, Linda.'

'I'll drink to that.' Linda finishes her coffee, then replaces cup to saucer.

Linda's attention is drawn to a young chap looking in through the window, who is smiling in her direction. She smiles back then realises that Val has noticed this impromptu assignation and turns her back to the window.

'What are you wearing tonight, Lin?'

'Black swing skirt, white blouse and black bolero jacket, I think.'

'Right, in that case I'll wear my new white scoop neck blouse and black pleated skirt.'

'We can both wear black. Our outfits are quite different so we'll hardly look like the Beverley Sisters, will we?'

'I suppose not. Mine has some white piping, too.'

'So we'll both wear black. The idea of you as my sister would be great.'

'We're as good as sisters anyway. But we don't need to fight over bedrooms, the bathroom, stealing each other's clothes, boyfriends and make-up like normal sisters, do we?'

'You're right. I like it exactly the way it is!'

Chapter Twenty

1.30 pm

Gary enters his father's music shop. The place is normally busy on a Saturday and today it is chock-a-block. Gary's dad is pleased to see his son, particularly as he might be able to help serve.

Mr Hall points to a group of lads who have been patiently waiting to see him and he asks Gary if he would be able to help. Although only eighteen years old, Gary is not shy. He is used to dealing with customers and has recently helped out during school holidays. He knows the music game better than most and he loves musical instruments. Never happier than when he is discussing his pet subject, Gary gets stuck in!

'Hello, lads. I'm Gary, the owner's son. How can I help?'

An unusually lanky lad acts as spokesman for the five youngsters. 'We're desperate to start a beat group. Can you give us a few tips about what we need to know, especially the cost?'

This is music to the ears for Gary! He confirms to them that they have approached the right man for the job, as he set up a group some years ago which is still in its prime. He beckons them towards the legendary studio out the back. In the tempting atmosphere of that vaunted scenario, that's where he'll fill them in with the relevant information. As an added bonus for his dad, their disappearance from the shop will free up prime space for the afternoon's clientele.

Upon entering the studio, the lads gaze around with such awe and wonder that one would be forgiven for believing they had happened upon some mystical grotto! How their mouths drop open when their eyes land on the heavenly guitars languishing upon their trusty stands.

Gary brings them back to earth by pulling up some chairs and arranging them in a semi-circle. Preparing his head for his soliloquy, he invites them to sit down. 'Ok, lads, let's begin with the most important question of all. How old are you?'

'We're all fifteen or sixteen. We left school this summer.'

'Ok. Now, have any of you any musical skills or experience, maybe the Boys' Brigade or school choir?'

'I can play piano,' comes a tremulous voice from a wee lad with beer-glass spectacles.

'Good start. Ten out of ten! Anyone else? Come on now, don't all speak at once!' The poor kids shake their heads, furrow their brows and look as embarrassed as gigolos in a nunnery! 'No? Well there's a surprise - great credentials for wanting to start a beat group!'

'We want to be famous and make lots of dosh. We're sure we will!'

'Like the Beatles?' quips the host, beginning to take a bit of a shine to these likely opportunists.

'Where shall I begin? You need to hang out together. You'll be jamming together, practising together, travelling together, appearing in concert together and all being well, recording in a studio like this together. Musketeers - all for one, and one for all!

'If you can succeed in getting arrested together, you'll move onwards and upwards, become famous and make your spondulicks. Write your own songs. Get a good front man who is loyal and true. His style must be unique; his moves - sexy; your clothes - trendy; your manager - a smart opportunist. Sorry to say this, lads, but you may well have to leave Northampton and find another cemetery with electric light to make the big time!

'That's my opinion, for what it's worth! So who's the vocalist amongst you, your very own nightingale in Berkeley Square?'

'Yeah, Barry, here. You're good, ain't you, Bazzo? Ex-church chorister!'

'Sure was. They paid me 1/6d on Sundays, two bob for moveable feasts and half a crown for weddings. Tight buggers! Then my voice broke, so I switched to paper rounds!'

'Thank you, Barry, and good night! You need three guitarists - lead, rhythm and bass - and a drummer to aid and abet whichever one of you becomes the singer! You could also have a guitarist doubling as vocalist.'

'How do we decide who does what, Gary?'

'Easy question, not easy to answer. The lead and rhythm guitarists need to work well together, and it's no good the rhythm being a frustrated lead. The bass player and drummer have to be a great team, like Jet Harris and Tony Meehan. It's on the rhythm section's shoulders that the whole performance is underpinned.

'Your drummer must be confident to go for it and lay down the beat. The success of the whole sound depends entirely on the power and timing of the drummer, a bit like the conductor in an orchestra, the piggy bank for the others to make their fortunes on. Your drummer has to be as fit as a fiddler's elbow, the rosin for the bow. Drummers are in short supply, as parents in this town would see themselves as stark-raving bonkers if they were to purchase a set of drums.'

'Jimmy's bonkers, ain't you, Jim-lad?'

'Piss off!' comes a resonant reply, vocal cords rosined to perfection!

'The vocalist needs to have power and control, confidence and good looks and a tremendous camaraderie with the lead guitarist. They have to be like a married couple, think as one - act as one. In the Waders, Ken and me have been best mates all our lives and wild horses wouldn't tear us apart!'

'Well, that counts Bazzles out! You ain't ready to tie the knot with one of us, are you, Baz? You're a bit of a Prima Donna, ain't you?'

'I don't do ballet!' objects the ridicule-weary Barry when they suggest he should audition as a prima ballerina for 'Swan Lake'.

'The vocalist, which is unlikely to be you, Barry, will be the group's focal point. He will need broad shoulders because the whole band depends on him - the heart, the head, the swivel and the crotch. He'll need presence, confidence and, yes, a touch of arrogance. A showman with great sex appeal,' advises Gary, his second-love, wrestling, informing his allegories.

'Barry, sex appeal? You're joking, ain't you?' chimes in one of the others, sniggering, as his mates finally rule him out.

'Barry, have you or have you not got sex appeal?' asks Gary, warming to the sense of humour of these unlikely beat merchants. 'Have you got a bit of fluff on the side?'

'Not right now at this very moment in time as we so speak,' Barry admits, unconvincingly, 'but I'm working on it!'

'Nah, not right at any moment!' another chimes in, although they are well aware that he does have a secret admirer. 'Approximately who in her tiny mind would want to go out with you?'

'Anyhow, nonetheless, moreover… the vocalist will become your master of ceremonies. He will connect, control and bond with the audience. He'll be your guiding light. Your approval-rating will be down to him. So a bit of charisma, hey? Watch Cliff or Adam. Did any of you see 'Ready Steady Go' last night?'

'Yeah, we all watched it round Baz's house.'

'Good, here's your role model: Johnny Kidd leading the Pirates from the front with 'I'll Never Get Over You.' Us Waders have got Kenny Waters up front; he's got all the attributes apart from a eye-patch and a cutlass!

'There must be no passengers in the group. Everyone must play his part. It's a team game. You don't act as five individuals. You act as one, driving the beat, the energy, the lyrics, the key changes - in harmony or unison. Discipline. Pride. Professionalism. If you were a gang, who'd be leader?'

As one, they point to the strapping lad called John, even him pointing at himself. Gary thinks this is a good start. 'Can you sing, John?'

'Only in the bath and the school toilets. My voice is crap but the echo's fantastic!' he jokes, remembering how the school kids admired his double-tracking impression when rasping out U.S Bonds' 'Not Me'!

'Crap voice, great echo? Sign you up, you're the man! What's your surname?' Gary itemises John's serious credentials for the job!

'Jacobs.'

'Johnny Jacobs and the Cream Crackers?'

'No, Johnny Jacobs and the Boomerangs!' There you go. How's that sound?' enquires Gary.

'Boomerangs come back to bounce off your forehead, like Johnny Jacobs and the Echoes off the toilet walls,' chips in Barry, smartly. 'Like my girlfriend. She's a bit like a boomerang. Bet you lads wished you'd a boomerang, eh?' Barry gets his own back, laughing kitbags at his own joke!

'J.J. and the Cherry-pickers? How's that?'

'Johnny and the Durex?'

'That's the idea. You can go on all day thinking of names. J. Arthur Rank and the ......s! Great fun!'

'You may like to cough up your paper-round money for some

private guitar lessons, or you can learn from a teaching book like Bert Weedon's 'Play in a Day'. It won't break the bank at 4/6d a copy. Private lessons cost about 10/- an hour. I can recommend a great tutor in Jimmy's End.

'The kit you need comes in all combinations of makes, quality and price. With a little nudge from me I'm sure my dad could fix you up with a good deal, and maybe help you with your on-costs - strings, repairs, skins and stuff - at very little extra expense.'

Neither wanting to blow his own trumpet nor put them off the idea, Gary gives a run-down of the kit Kenny and the Waders use. This is what they have come to hear. If Gary hits the right timbre, Hall's music shop and recording studio could notch a new clientele. He speculates to accumulate.

'You need a PA System. You can get a good one for around £175. This will enable you to each have a microphone, so you backing vocalists better start flexing your larynxes. Your drummer will need an adjustable boom.

'You need guitars. Hank B. Marvin, lead guitarist of the Shadows, uses a Fender Stratocaster. For one like his you'll need 150 guineas, which is about £170. That's what I use. Your lead will need a good amplifier, typically a Vox AC30 which will cost about £110.

'Our bass guitarist, Colin, plays a Framus, which costs about 60 guineas. You'll need a similar amplifier.' Gary's mind is like a ready reckoner, and he convert pounds to guineas and back again with alacrity.

'Roger, our highly dependable rhythm guitarist, plays a Hofner Golden costing around £70, his amp going out at about 101 guineas.' Johnny Jacobs, proud owner of Lonnie Donegan's Golden Hits on Pye Golden Guinea, takes up the 'golden' theme. Remembering what he paid for the album, he begins to knock up some quick conversions with a biro on the inside of the lid of his Woodbine packet.

'Dave, our dynamic drummer, has an old, no ancient, no fossilised Olympic 60 budget model drum set. Such splendid gear would cost you about £60 in blue or red sparkle: snare drum, bass drum, rack tom and clamp, floor tom and stand, hi-hat cymbal, cow bell, floor cymbal and tilter - sounds a pretty good deal to me. Dave can't use the hi-hat because he's got a gammy leg.

'His set's now knackered, but if you got one similar then go for the main or de-luxe, double the price at about 125 guineas. If you buy from us, we'll throw in the sticks and brushes free of charge.

'For guitar and mike cables you could do a lot worse than purchase the special ones that we prepare here at Hall's Music.'

A couple of the lads are beginning to get fidgety and look at each other somewhat nonplussed. The cost is fast dampening their enthusiasm after this five minutes with Gary, though the others remain wide-eyed and entranced.

'To round things off you need 'spares': drum sticks and brushes, plectrums, guitar strings, bass and snare drum skins, guitar straps, plastic covers or specially-designed guitar cases. £1000 the whole kit and caboodle, 10% off, if purchased exclusively from Hall's, with a few extras thrown in.'

'I didn't know it'd be that much,' says Barry. 'A thousand quid!' It all goes very quiet as the dream of becoming the next Johnny Kidd and the Pirates begins to fade like ash on the tally-lid of John Jacobs' fag packet.

'Not necessarily lads,' Gary reassures. 'After the financial mess, the strategic miracle!'

'You have two options. Purchase second-hand from upgrading musicians, or, as I mentioned, Hall's also can supply a wide range of nearly-new second-hand instruments and quality accessories. To get started, avoid the top-of-the-range Fender guitars or Vox amps. Lower your sights.

'Otherwise, don't pay cash. Go for hire purchase at so much a week then you can pay it back from your revenue from the gigs: a kind of dock-as-you-rock plan like our Charles Waterfield's. He stumped up the cash; we pay him back at reasonable interest.

'Oh, nearly forgot. Big omission! How are you going to transport your kit to each dance-hall? Simple answer: a van and someone to drive it.

'That's about it really, lads. You better go away and think about it. I've got some practising to do, then I'll get back in the shop to help Dad. Talk amongst yourselves, and I'm always here to help should you have any other queries. It's easy to want to be a beat group. Everyone wanted to be the next Elvis, now all they want for Christmas is a

Beatle! Money, dedication, time, practice and the greatest blessing of all, support from your parents.

'If you want to see all this kit in action, why not come down to St Mary's Hall this evening and be blown away by Kenny Waters and the Waders, supported by the Spitfires?'

'Yeah, we can all come along, can't we lads?' J.J. and the Percolators nodded in agreement!

'When the big time comes and you secure a deal with a record pressed at Hall's, top the charts, travel the world and become millionaires, don't forget me!' Gary never ceases to enjoy talking about guitars (any instrument in fact) and the performers themselves. Right now, he gets a tremendous buzz and feels a genuine 'high': wonderful groundwork for this evening's show!

Chapter Twenty One

1.45pm

Archie Bell is the Albert Steptoe of Northampton. He is a third-generation rag 'n' bone man based in Far Cotton. His father, William, known throughout town as 'Big Bill Bell', died two years ago and Archie, a veteran of thirty years in the 'totting trade', has inherited the family business. This includes the scrap yard, the two horses, Mungo and Shoddy and an old Fordson van, but little money.

All his life, Archie's son, Dave, could remember his dad each day in all weathers, jauntily clad in white shirt, red and white spotted neckerchief, waistcoat and bowler hat, driving the horse and cart, in Seth Adams-like majesty. At weekends since the age of six, Dave has played the part of Flint McCullough, scouting around the local estates and helping his dad load up with scrap iron, rusted car and motor bike parts, batteries, copper and lead or any other metal that might be sold on for a few quid.

The family house and adjoining garden is adorned with interesting and valuable finds as well as carrying the overflow from the yard. There is no comfort here, only a frugal existence of drudgery. The house is always cold.

All the family members are well-used to being out and about irrespective of temperature. Dave's bedroom is draughty and damp. One window-pane has been broken by stone-throwing kids and stuck up with paper. The other gets ice-bound in winter as a result of which Dave, as a schoolboy, kept his clothes overnight under the blankets. He would dress himself under the covers before his feet would even touch the floor!

At junior school, Dave had been persistently bullied for the width of the long trousers he wore whilst the other kids were in shorts. His mum had cut them outrageously wide to cover up and muffle the clanking of the leg-iron that he struggled with as a result of the polio he contracted when he was three years old. The rest of Dave's clothes were also reclaimed from the sacks of cottons, worsteds and woollens which were brought into the yard. It was Dave's job to sort these out, weigh them on a big floor-scale and pay the provider in kind with either a balloon for the vendor's child or a cream or brown donkey stone.

At secondary-modern school, Dave was two-thirds the way down the bottom stream and struggled with all subjects. His parents had neither the knowledge nor the time to help him improve. He was, however, skilled with his hands and his bedroom was full of model aeroplanes. He also created all sorts of 'Meccano' models from discarded sets and part-sets brought home on the cart.

It was at the Boys' Brigade meetings that Dave bonded with a young somewhat truculent, yet stalwart, Colin Harris. Dave had been stigmatised by his affliction, and his mate Colin had been let down badly by his dad. Dave's and Colin's minds were still locked into the Teddy boy era, transfixed forever when they got to become 'sort-of mates' with two older lads. Their two role models became their pseudo-heroes: Johnny Archer and Mick Miller - rough-and-ready Teddy boys with kindly hearts. They protected Dave from being bullied into oblivion and stood by Colin in the wake of his dad's dastardly demise.

As can often happen, hard-cases like these can become righteous protectors and playground vigilantes. Johnny and Mick were no exceptions. Dave came into their life when he limped onto the scene with a left-leg iron after spending all his formative years in open air recovery schools. It was Johnny who had first teased him about his lurching swagger and Mick who had joined in with a few oblique references to spasticity and catching germs off him.

'Don't go anywhere near him, Mick; you'll catch the dreaded lurgy,' Johnny Archer warned.

'Oooer!' was all Mick could murmur, never having been in the same playground as an alien and fearful that he would catch a bug that would strike him down and render him an invalid.

Dave's nickname, 'Ding Dong', was ironic - 'leg-ironic', one might say - because as he lurched from side to side across the playground, the kids would chant at him in time with his strides. This was when Johnny and Mick flipped. Something must have touched them inside and in a light-bulb moment they switched to Dave's side. Whereas the teachers and parents completely failed to stem the bullying tide, these two ruffians succeeded.

'Why me?' Dave asked Johnny and Mick one playtime.

'Cos it weren't us,' they replied, not knowing what else to say. They bonded then and that loyal friendship has stood up through thick and thin, to endure forever.

Since he left school at fifteen he has worked full-time in the family business. The money is poor, the prospects daunting! Dave loves the noisy old BSA his granddad left him along with a dented little sidecar which, although well-maintained, is also suffering from geriatric groans and terminal rust.

He started in the skiffle group as a washboard player. This came about mostly through Colin's coercion, although he did seem relatively proficient with his mum's small metal thimbles. These he applied to the tips of the fingers of his right hand in order to kick up a sally racket with an old metal washboard, a cast-off from that part of town where twin-tubs had become all the rage.

Dave himself is desperate to break away from the family rag 'n' bone heritage and throw himself into motorcycle or car maintenance - a role for which he has had plenty of grounding. Crawling under oily vehicles in greasy overalls is therapy for Dave. Moreover, it gives his aching leg a rest, being supported by a concrete garage floor.

Spanner in hand, Dave is like a terrier with a bone! A career as a grease monkey seems far more preferable to Dave than one in scrap. Along with the ancient motor-bike, he loves tinkering with the family's pedigree Fordson van which is also on its last legs and is interminably being emptied of cast-offs and gadgets that the Bells have collected from the sheds, attics and cellars of the affluent areas of town.

As neither his mum nor dad can drive, he has commandeered the van for himself. He learned to drive by manoeuvring it around the yard with a block of wood strapped to the clutch pedal to compensate. He passed his test first time, despite never having gone more than thirty yards in a straight line, never having driven in third or fourth gears, and never faster than 20mph. The instructor was quoted as saying, 'For one so young, his three-point turn and reversing skills were impeccable and his emergency stop was second-to-none.'

Whilst his drumming expertise may be perceived as no better than average, his provision of van and driver keeps Dave locked into the group as a solid foundation propping up the group's pecking order.

It is now Dave's responsibility to store the kit at the yard and to load and unload it before and after each dance night and practice night. If both Colin and Roger need a lift he cunningly locates a tatty deck-chair behind the driver's seat. A bit like perching on the sand at Skegness beach, the occupant has to be careful not to topple over as a result of the rotting remnants of the van floor, which are covered by a carpet tile to keep out the draughts and the road-surface spray, the only things missing are the sea view, the whiff of ozone and a splash of sun-tan lotion.

It was only a few weeks ago that the Bells, and Dave in particular, suffered their greatest loss. Mungo, the dear old nag that for so many years had pulled his granddad's cart, crumpled in a heap and couldn't get back to his feet. The vet was called, and with tears streaming down his face Dave spent a heartbreaking half-hour laying with Mungo, stroking his ears and neck, blowing into his nose and talking quietly about old times - the halcyon days! Reluctantly, Dave kissed him twice, once a-piece on each faltering eyelid, before standing back to allow the stricken vet to administer merciful relief.

Since then, Shoddy, who had himself stood and stared impassively as his lifelong companion was despatched to that great Glue Factory in the Sky, has become the sole object of Dave's love. The hallowed ground of Mungo's little corner of the stable has become a shrine in the second stall: home from home for Dave; sanctuary for his motor bike; space to practise his drumming. The workshop behind Mungo's memorial ground is where Dave unloads and stores the group's equipment between times, as safe and secure a location as could be found in Far Cotton until last night...

*

...the Far Cotton milieu is ablaze with moist reflections of saloon bars and smoke rooms at every turn. Street corner society at its hottest! Lounging against pub walls or loitering near yard gates, prostitutes huddle and pout, sliding their forefingers and thumbs provocatively up and down the lengths of their lipstick-tipped fags; the more they suck and fondle, the quicker the fag-ends dwindle and droop!

Plunging necklines are the titillating order of the steamy night, along with short leather skirts, extra-high heels, bright blue eye shadow and pink face powder. If these girls went out to kill a circus, they would go straight for the juggler! What of the men who pay up front for the wares they ply? Well, the men with loads of money, naturally! Without itinerant labourers from the Semilong lodging houses, posh folks from Abington or self-made men from suburbia, there would be no flourishing vice ring down the engine-shed side of the tracks.

Inside the Clinton Arms, prospective clients prop up the bars, jostling and clamouring to be served quickly by the overworked 'I'll be right with you' landlords and landladies. They have given their excuses at home and mustn't be out too late or their wives will become suspicious.

The locals wave their emptied pint pots from a distance in one hand, a rolled up ten-bob note maybe, in the other. They plead for attention, eager to swill down the hardship of another day's grind on one of the town's factory floors or toiling in the claggy fields nearby.

A glance within any such watering-hole would show a wearing-thin lino floor crowded. Alongside the workers and punters, jivers' hips rock and their knees roll. Middle-aged women striving to hide with mascara, lipstick and garish make-up, the terrible lines which that grim artist 'Dissipation' loves to draw on such faces.

An assortment of 'Calamity Janes' and 'Diddlin' Doras' quaff their gins, suck their lemon slices and crunch their ice cubes, some gaining solace from a lively hand-jive, others joining in with the barely audible lyrics: 'But there ain't no cure for the Summertime Blues… '

Around the jukeboxes, boppin' Teddy boys hang around having donned their extra-velvety Edwardian chic, slicked back quiffs, brocade silk-patterned waistcoats and incongruous florid shirts. They snarl at passers-by belatedly heading for the toilet exit, their bladders hanging on for grim death! Not for one instant do they need to be waylaid by these impeding dissidents, threateningly blocking their desperate way.

The latest renditions of Eddie, Elvis and the Everlys struggle to compete with the noisy hubbub: feet stomp, fingers click, guitars strum and the 'Shadows' Walk' is walked. Around the side walls of the bars under a thick, choking, blue haze, groups of old men with roll-ups drop ash down their beer-stained cardigans and drip tar into brown-silver moustaches.

With dominoes precariously but professionally held single-handedly within nicotine-encrusted fingers, or cribbage cards held chest-close to avoid prying eyes, they 'tut' at the energetic boogieing, whilst themselves teetering on the very edge of their graves.

The Bells would normally be here: Archie, Elsie and Dave... all present and correct. They would be enjoying the news, gossip and atmosphere amongst their respective cohorts. But Archie and Elsie have gone on a much-needed short break. At 10.00pm on Friday, 30th August, 1963, Dave is alone, drowning in his beer the sad loss of Mungo. Then in walk Mick Miller and Johnny Archer with their proposition!

*

Saturday is Dave's favourite day. He only works in the morning, but more especially he plays drums in the evening. On Monday, Dave tinkers with his bike, the van and the cart. He mucks out, washes and brushes Shoddy and becomes a recluse in his workshop room listening to second-hand records on his third-hand record player, reading his fourth-hand collection of girlie magazines and daydreaming about what might be a fifth-hand girl.

But today is Saturday, and after lunch it is a time to get ready to make sure the space is available for Johnny and Mick and cherish the £25 they are going to slip into his hand towards the acquisition of a new drum set that seemed a million miles away until last evening...

*

...Johnny Archer and Mick Miller enter the Clinton Arms pub as usual. They do a bit of bopping around, have a brief altercation with two blokes they have never in their lives seen before but to whom they take an instant dislike. On their way out they corner Dave Bell, who is as good as anyone to corner, and usher him out into the pub yard.

'Davey-boy, you know how we have always liked to look after you? Well, it's your turn now to look after us!' Mick is appealing to the more compassionate, feminine side of Dave's brain.

'Yes, Dave. It's your lucky day, too, as well as ours! No need to waste your hard-earned cash on Zetters or tomorrow's 3.30 at Towcester. No indeed! How would you like to earn a few extra quid, Davey-lad? Easy money? Money for some of your old rope? A kosher deal!' Johnny slowly nods a few times to enhance the vocal persuasion of his dangling carrots. He winks at Dave as he is talking, then winks at Mick once he pauses.

'Easy? Like how?' Dave wasn't born yesterday. He was born the day before! He knows full well that there are only two ways to earn money - slog your guts out or do a dodgy deal!

'All we need is somewhere convenient to store some gear for a day or two. Now, how tasty is that? Davey-son, you are a great mate and we would love to share our good fortune with you. Are you up for it?' asks Mick with beseeching eyes, as doleful as any landlady's cocker spaniel.

'What gear are you on about?' is Dave's reasonable request for illumination.

'Ask no questions, tell no lies, Davey-nick-nack. Is there anywhere in your yard we could shoot some loot? It must be secure, dry, out-of-sight, out-of-mind. You know what we're saying, Davey-kins? Away from the beady eyes of your old man, hey?' questions Johnny.

Dave gets a bit interested. 'Mum and Dad are away for a week's holiday, the first break they've had away from the business since, well, since forever! I've been left holding the baby. My workshop is secure - only one key, and that's in my body belt. The Waders' guitars and amps and stuff go there. There's plenty of space, depending on what gear you're on about.'

'Interesting!' thought Mick. 'That piece of information could come in handy at some later date.'

'How very convenient,' says Johnny, with a guarded and very personal sigh of relief. 'The yard is normally closed on a Saturday afternoon, isn't it?'

'Hang on! I haven't said yet that I'll do it! It's the first time Dad's left me in charge. I can't let him down, can I? He'll have my guts for garters if you land me in trouble!'

'You'd be a twenty-four carat diamond-encrusted mug not to. We've knocked about with you long enough to know you're no mug, Davey-boy. We'll see you down the yard tomorrow about three o'clock. You be there, now. Don't let us down, David. We don't like to be let down, do we, Mick?'

'We don't like to be let down, David,' Mick agrees with Johnny. They both crack their knuckles in unison to seal the deal: Dave is in it up to his neck!

'We'll pap the hooter in the van, twice. You open the gate and let us in. Lock the gate behind us. We'll unload and be gone in half an hour. What's in it for you? £25! All you need to worry about is what to spend the money on!' Johnny's final words.

Chapter Twenty Two

2.30pm

Ken strolls through the Town Centre, the Saturday shoppers crowding the pavements and having to step off into the gutters to pass one another. He always feels better after seeing Linda, who has lifted his spirits after the bleak start to the day, courtesy of his dad.

Roger presses on with his daily duties and it isn't until early afternoon that he is spotted by Ken, who is walking across to Boots and who sees Roger looking pensive, standing by the police pillar outside All Saints church.

'Hi Rog. How's it going?'

'Hello, Ken. Yeah, pretty good, thanks. Steady old morning. Routine stuff.'

'Have you caught those train robbers yet?'

'Not yet, though I'm onto the case!'

'Three and a half weeks and you've caught nobody. I don't know why we pay you coppers. Money for old rope, seems to me,' Ken laughs. 'Hundreds of sacks of cash? Millions of quid? It can't be that difficult, can it?'

'If you think it's that simple, Ken, you solve it and claim the £10,000 reward.'

'£10,000, Rog! Not to be sniffed at, eh?'

'You know that we found their hideout at a farm not that far from here? While they've been holed up it seems they've been playing 'Monopoly' with real money. I tell ya!'

'Pass Go and collect £200, Rog? Hardly worth Old Kent Road either, when you've got millions.'

'We're launching some special operations in town next week. As it happened near here they could be laid low in the area, or stashed the loot under our noses until the heat is off. Who knows, Ken? I'm only a common or garden bluebottle. Anyway, I'm off up the Racecourse at two o'clock to play footie for Crusaders against Owens. We had a player sent off in this fixture last season, and another carried off on a stretcher.'

Before they go their separate ways, Roger asks Ken for a couple of minutes of his time for a subject that has been bothering him. As always, Ken is happy to oblige.

'Look, Ken. I'm twenty one now and I desperately need a regular girlfriend. I've been getting bloody depressed about it. I look at you and Val, I see Gary and Linda, and to be quite honest it makes me envious. Two beautiful girls, and here's me at my age with nobody! It's bloody frustrating. The lads in the mess room have started to take the piss and call me a queer. How on earth am I to get a bird like Val?'

Ken is taken aback, and wonders where to start without insulting him. He takes a stab. 'Rog, you've come straight from the army into the police force. Think about it. You need to 'get with it'. Get some decent chat-up lines. You're a good-looking bloke, fitness without fatness. Get yourself a decent haircut, try a new style. Go and see Mr Wilson and tell him I sent you.' Ken rises to the task.

'You're the second person to tell me to get a haircut.'

'Really, Rog? Who was the first?'

'Ringo, when the Beatles turned up in the spring before their concert at the ABC.'

'You're kidding! You met the Beatles?'

'Sure did. They turned up in their Austin Princess and pulled up at HQ before transferring to a CID car to go to the show. Sgt Jenks let me take a ten-minute pee break, so I guillotined some foolscap paper, grabbed a couple of pens and nipped out to get their autographs.

'Ringo sat at the front. He wound down his window and I passed him the paper and pens. I got their autographs eighteen times and flogged them off at the Nurses' Ball at the end of May. John sat behind the driver, George in the middle and Paul behind Ringo.

'Ringo asked me if I liked being a copper and John chipped in with a few quips about my short back and sides. As Ringo seemed to have the longest hair, I joked that he needed a haircut. Ringo joked that I should get mine cut, too. I mumbled some nonsense about mine being so long that I would need an estimate - a bit cheesy, but at least George shot me a grin.

'I told them I had tickets for the show and that I could understand why Ringo flicked his fringe from side to side whilst drumming, otherwise he would never be able to see his kit. Paul handed me a pile of autographs, and I made the handsome sum of five bob each from the nurses. I told Ringo that I envied them their freedom, and that the police forced me to keep my hair short. He smiled as he wound the window back up with his left hand and ran the fingers of his right through his fringe, asking me what I was going to do about it, then?'

'And what are you going to do about it, Roger?'

'Buy some decent aftershave, I suppose,' was all Roger could lamely joke.

'Then go and see Val at Boots. She'll make you smell nice. What about some new clothes? I know you told Ringo about what the police force expects, but come on, Rog, you'll be Ok in the sort of stuff Gary and me wear.

'Get some wheels. £250 for a Ford Anglia or a Triumph Herald - piece of cake on your pay. Roger, beauty is in the eye of the beholder. So find a young lady with character, not looks,' Ken concludes, with words straight out of his father's paternal parental portfolio.

'The minute I tell 'em I'm a copper, they'll run a mile.'

'No they won't. Nice uniform. Steady job. Promotion prospects. Sounds appealing, Rog. When I'm talking with Val about the group she never has a bad word to say about you, so don't be discouraged.'

Roger is dead chuffed to hear that Val thinks something of him and his eyes light up! So there's hope yet for the codger, the lodger, the sod! 'You're a good mate, Ken. Thanks. You won't tell the others that we've had this chinwag, will you? They'll take the piss.'

'Mum's the word, Rog.' Not perhaps the most convincing remark Ken has ever made, and by no means the most sensitive!

'Right, Ken. Nearly two o'clock. I better sign off and get to the match!' They make their separate ways.

After being intercepted and diverted twice by a neighbour and an old school mate, Ken enters Hall's. A doorbell quietly tinkles. The store is crowded with the usual suspects, mostly group members from local outfits, plus some older guys who play for dance bands. A couple of them acknowledge him. No surprises here!

Ken catches the proprietor's eye and says, 'Hello, Mr Hall.' All Mr Hall can do is wink back, because he has a pine-coloured Fender Telecaster hanging on a strap around his neck and a cherry-coloured Gibson in his hands. Ken hears him explaining to a young customer the difference between the two. He apologises on interrupting Mr Hall, to ask if Gary is on the premises and is pleased to hear that he is out the back, in the studio.

Ken pops through the internal door from the shop, along a small corridor and then through the studio door. The big red bulb over it isn't shining, which means that no recording is taking place. Ken walks straight in as the five wannabe musicians are leaving.

The studio is full of very expensive sound equipment which was bought by Mr Hall on hire purchase a couple of years ago: the very best condenser microphones, large and small booms, a master reel-to-reel tape-recorder, filters, a pre-amp. Additionally there is an echo chamber and an oscilloscope, all of which go to make this studio one of the best-equipped outside London. An intercom system allows the control-room technician to communicate with the main studio.

Separately, at the back, there is a record-cutter where record disks are created out of aluminium plate, covered in a vinyl-type material. The demo disk can then be sent away to a specialist company to have the normal 45 rpm records made.

Many local groups make recordings at the studio, for which they are charged around £4 per hour. Some of the recordings go on through the evening and night. Records are eventually released to the public and are marked in gold lettering, 'Studio Gold'. They are normally sold at local record shops. If all goes well for Kenny Waters and the Waders, this is where they will make their debut pressing; Ken and Gary have already got in mind the song they started writing at Butlin's - a top studio with top equipment for a top song by a top group.

Guitar sounds cut through the air. Gary sees Ken coming in and stops playing. 'Hello, mate. What's happening?'

'Hi, Gary. I was passing the store so I thought I'd drop by and discuss this evening's play list, especially what the order is. Did I hear you playing that song we wrote together at Butlin's, 'My First Love'?'

'Yeah, but it's still not quite right; I must admit that I'm running out of ideas. As soon as we've nailed it we can cut it while we're hot. I've come up with an interesting riff to kick it off, though… listen!'

After closing his eyes and absorbing the song, Ken says,'Ok. Not bad. Certainly different. Now we need to polish up the words and we can decide if it needs an instrumental interlude, though we don't necessarily have to have a guitar solo in it at all.' Ken always likes to keep the spotlight on the singer, not the guitarist.'Have you got the latest words written down, Gaz?'

'Yep, here you are.' Gary hands Ken a piece of lined paper on which the lyrics are written, with various crossings-out and words substituted.

'Thanks, I'll take a look sometime and see if I can come up with something. I'm sure it's not far off being a good song, and our first 'Hall & Waterfield' hit! Northampton's answer to McCartney and Lennon!'

Gary puts the red electric guitar back on its stand and picks up a folder from the floor, handing it to Ken.'Here, Ken, take a look at this. It's tonight's set list. 90% the same as usual.'

A full-size sheet of foolscap shows all the numbers they practise and which could be included in their repertoire. Written alongside some of the entries are the start key and playing order number for the evening. They both agree that although the group has to progress from Cliff numbers to Merseybeat numbers, for tonight's encores they will resurrect 'Bad Boy' and 'Will You Love Me Tomorrow', sure-fire showstoppers from their archives.

Gary then drops a potential bombshell!

'Ken, do you know a fella called 'Mick' from the Dominators?'

Ken's face drops like a lead balloon. Aghast! Snared! Hi-hatted! 'Mick James, their drummer?' he asks.

'Yeah, that's him. He dropped by the shop earlier this morning to get some stuff for his drum kit and some strings for their rhythm guitarist. He asked about you, Ken.'

'Oh yeah? Such as what?' Ken looks sheepish and feels nervous, panicky almost.

'Nothing specific. I think he recognised me as a Wader. Didn't we share the same bill on one of those 'Jiving by Candlelight' evenings down the YMCA?'

'Sounds familiar. Could have done, now you mention it.' Ken knows full well that the two groups played together but is playing dumb.

'Top outfit, aren't they? He asked after you in passing, just to make polite conversation I guess. Weren't they the group with that knackered old white van with the red flash along the side? We ended up pushing them out of the car park and down the road at midnight.'

'Yeah, that was it, Gary. Then once their van fired, they helped us push ours.' Ken knew right enough it was them, so changes the subject completely. 'Right, see you later and we'll go out afterwards as usual. Linda's picking up the holiday snaps today, so we'll get to look at them, too.'

'Great! It's all happening, eh Ken?'

Leaving Gary to practise in the studio, Ken silently folds the two sheets of paper and slips them into his back pocket alongside his comb.

Chapter Twenty Three

2.45pm

Girls have never appeared high on Dave's agenda. In fact they have never appeared on his agenda at all.The girl guides and brownies always seemed to avoid him, stuck out their tongues then turned their backs on him. Even worse, they would huddle together, point, whisper and giggle. His wonky leg seemed to be the main issue although his scrawny, scruffy, raggle-taggle appearance with long, greasy hair and his 'dull-as-ditch-water' complexion didn't help his cause with the opposite sex.

Rather than suffer the humiliation of their mockery, Dave preferred to avoid girls altogether until very recently when an unlikely find of 'girlie' magazines among a sack full of cast-off clothes gained his attention. Now these are secreted in his private workshop behind Mungo's stall at the yard. He has still never been out on a date but through reading the magazines and studying the pin-ups he now appreciates what delights a relationship is likely to offer and what relief it will ultimately bring.

Dave has developed at the flick of a page a lusty appetite for dream-girls of the ilk of Linda and Val, and he particularly appreciates the fact that these two treat Gary and Ken teasingly and pleasantly. He would like to be married one day and have kids but has no clue yet as to how this might come about.

Dave is in his den, contemplating the double-page centre-fold credentials of the 'Mayfair Playmate of the Month', the delectable Janine! It is a quarter to three and here he is, sexually distracted by the voluptuousness of her breasts and the glint in her eye; yet he is gripped in trepidation of Johnny and Mick's arrangement with him. So it is time to cover up Janine's charms and fold her away for another day, for another climax... for the Teds are coming!

When the 'Beatle Boom' burst briskly upon the unsuspecting world late the previous year, it was little wonder that the 'Pink and Black Days' were destined to become an anachronism. However, as in all revolutions, many loyal supporters of former regimes would continue to champion the cause and there were no greater aficionados of Teddy boy culture than Johnny and Mick. Rockabilly retribution and rock 'n' roll revival would live forever! Those determined to drag the past into the future had better stick together!

Dave and Colin's friendship with these two scallywags dates back three years to an insane night out at St Michael's Church Hall with the Abington Skiffle Group. Johnny ran amok at the front of the hall and tried to boo the support act off stage.

Davy Crotchet and the Quavers had been around since the time Elvis had first jammed in the Sun Recording Studios with 'The Million Dollar Quartet' in 1956. Unlike 'The King', the Quavers had neither the looks, the swivel nor the gimmicks to create a riot (no-one ever tripped up usherettes at their concerts and scrambled about for free tubs of ice cream that had gone tumbling down the aisle!).

The young church verger, Edgar Vickery, threw out Johnny for creating a disturbance with his boos and cat-calls. The ebullient Colin, the affable Dave, maestro Ken and the truculent Johnny himself clubbed together for two bob. The nervous verger did well to pocket this, for it was either this or for Johnny to have throttled him with his own dog collar in his own vestry, which would have been the least tidy and less remunerative of the two options on offer.

Edgar Vickery was thankful to escape with his life. Upon being let back in, Johnny refused to promise not to misbehave again. 'He was only giving his considered opinion that the Quavers' version of Santo and Johnny's 'Sleep Walk' was sending us all to…' Dave explained before Kenny completed the sentence with, '… wake up to the fact that this isn't a vicarage tea party, it's a church hall hop!'

'Yeah, we don't want to listen to all that graveyard stuff. We can get that down the Salon with Reg Burgess and his Moonlight Vocaliers. I done you a good turn, Mr Vickery. Any more of that music to commit suicide to and the kids'll go back down the 'Bunny Run' and you know what club that'll get 'em into!' advised Johnny, rather proud of his ecumenical expulsion in that he had martyred himself to the cause of local family planning.

Johnny's coffee-bar credibility is determined by deviant family genes and flagrant juvenile delinquency. He loves to kick people's heads in for a bit of a lark and does not baulk when he draws their blood. He continued to cause havoc unabated now that Mr Vickery had been 'bought-off'.

Davy Crotchet and the Quavers had become needful of a rumpus to raise their dirge-like performance. Chicken-wire to protect the stage had already been rolled up in the wings, all set to unravel if a riot broke out. Balancing on a rickety chair through the group's lamentably pretentious rendition of Conway Twitty's 'It's Only Make Believe', Johnny tore off his drape-coat to wear it inside out so that he looked like Gary Cooper in a Western shoot-out at High Noon. He insulted the group by screeching, 'It's Only Fake Belie-e-e-e-eve!'

By the time the half-filled coke bottles began to fly in the half-empty hall, Davy Crotchet and the Quavers were half-way up the A5. During the interval the verger discussed, with the voluntary help from the parochial council, the question of bringing the chicken wire into play to protect the Abington Skiffle Group. After a lengthy powwow it was agreed that as the skifflers were a much more polished act, this would be jumping the gun... a sort of pre-emptive strike which might backfire on them.

The church did not want to be implicated should the performers on stage and their equipment incur personal injury or incidental instrumental incursion. Church funds everywhere were tight and the last thing the parochial council needed was an increase in premiums should they lose their no claims bonus by paying out on a violent skiffle scuffle.

When the Abington Skiffle Group took the stage with a rip-roaring version of 'Gamblin' Man' the evening caught fire. Now it was Mick Miller's turn to send the fans wild, but unlike Johnny in confrontation with the warm-up group, this time in support of his favourite group. Off came Mick's leopard-skin drape jacket, only for him to wave it in circles inside-out around his head. Edgar Vickery's difficult evening was far from over. 'If I ask you politely, would you mind stopping doing that with your coat?' asked the nervous verger.

Mick replied by asking Mr Vickery to politely remove his hand from his arm lest he wanted to end up in intensive care. 'If I ask you politely never to lay your hand on me again, do you think you could refrain from thus doing? And it ain't a coat, mush! How would you like me to politely stitch you up, tosher?'

When the group skiffled into 'Don't You Rock Me Daddy-O' Mick couldn't contain himself any longer. Off came his leopard-skin jacket again! This time in a fit of pique and modicum of bravado the verger tried to grab the drape, only to end up in the hospital he had already been threatened with, so no surprises there:'For those of you sitting in the peace and quiet of your own home, or laying on a hospital trolley in the corridor of A&E, this song is just for you!'

The verger never pressed charges in fear of the church hall being razed to the ground in revenge. He did contemplate, however, that this had been two bob painfully earned! When asked by the police who the troublemakers were, he refused to name Mick Miller and Johnny Archer, for fear of his life. The parochial church council acceded to the demands of the nerve-wracked local community and closed down the venue for a while, much to the disappointment of the police who became hard-pressed to deal with the ensuing trouble on the streets and the dreaded 'Mustard-cress Wars'.

When the club started up again after six months' closure, the Abington Skiffle Group had been removed from the booking list because of their associations with Teddy boys and their uncontrollable laughter all the way through the rumpus on the very evening the vexed verger was verily stitched up.

Even after the verger had been obliterated, they continued to egg-on the rioters by playing 'Cumberland Gap' faster and faster whilst the St John's Ambulance crew patched up the verger and a random assortment of onlookers who had been pole-axed by Mick and Johnny, the bloodiest evening in the church's history since its sacred consecration.

Sweet memories for young Dave Bell and Colin Harris, to whom being banned from the church hall circuit amounted to a seal of approval for their aggressive posturing and loyal allegiances. Being kicked out was also a mark of respect. Furthermore, Colin's magnificent quiff was a dedicated badge of honour from Northampton's Teddy boys. In fact, in tune with their adolescent fervour, all of the Abington Skiffle Group members were quite happy to have a few scuffles at their performances. It was their natural challenge to authority and they revelled in it in the face of their parents' admonishments and the consternations of their manager. Whilst Charles Waterfield was happy enough to rake the money in, he was loathe to be paying increased insurance premiums - which were running high enough, anyway!

As Lonnie acceded to Cliff in the nation's affections, Dave's musical career also advanced by reluctantly discarding his veteran washboard for a contingency drum set. This initially consisted of a big bass drum, propped up by a chair, which he kicked seven bells out of with his good foot. His cymbal hung yearningly from the wooden roof-beam on a length of thick string and a side drum sat there, plonked unceremoniously on an old armchair. All of the instruments were provided courtesy of St Jude's Boys' Brigade, which was long defunct.

Dave used to practise in the stable at the scrap yard, so poor Mungo, the older of the two horses, was reluctantly led out into the yard where he patiently stood, come rain and shine. Poor Mungo was indeed the lucky one, as the unfortunate Shoddy became a captive audience, remaining in situ, standing seemingly impassively even though his eardrums pleaded, 'Neigh!' The young stable lad bashed, clanged and thudded his way through rehearsals like an epileptic Eric Delaney.

One day, all Dave's Christmases came at once when his dad knocked him for six with a proper drum kit. It was a no-longer-to-be-tolerated Christmas present that some semi-deafened mother, her nerves now teetering along a tortuous tightrope, was pleased to dump.

It can now be said in all honesty that the drum kit has seen better days. Over its short life it has been subjected to multiple abuses such as when gangs from rival villages spilled over onto the stage, the drum kit being hurriedly dismantled and thrown out through the nearest window to relative sanctuary.

Dave's drum-set also survived a severe scraping and dunking one late and icy winter night when he miscalculated a tight bend on a country road and ditched his motor bike, sidecar and drums a little short of a sturdy oak, which would have led to greater demise. For a time, Dave had to travel to dance nights by double-decker bus. It took him three trips to and from home to get it to the bus-stop. Then the conductor harrumphed and looked away as Dave struggled single-handedly to haul first his leg and then his kit on board. He stashed his instruments under the bus staircase, before twenty minutes later at his destination reversing the procedure - all this to earn a few shillings whilst his motor-bike was off the road being repaired. But he loved it!

There was the time when en-route to a dance, a newly-signed-on off-duty up-beat PC 280 Roger Edwards would squat in the side-car having been picked by the bike shed at the back of the police station near where he'd met the Beatles. He would remove his boots and trousers, then draw back the side-car hood so that he could stretch out his arms and remove his jacket, tie and shirt before donning his tee shirt, jeans and slip-ons ready to go straight on stage.

A quick splash of after-shave, a touch of Brylcreem, a couple of signet rings and his lucky registration book which never left any pocket he was ever adorned with, and the job was done. Watch out, girls, here we come!

Along with all the other things in Dave's life he feels guilty about his limp, his rag 'n' bone stigma and the family prefab home; his pride and joy beloved drum kit had become the latest in the series of mortifications. The more he became really embarrassed, the more the group increased its popularity and the tattier the drums became.

The more he chivvied a reluctant Ken to tap up his dad for the £100 it needed from the group's coffers to stump up for a decent Premier set, the more the chasm between Ken and his dad made this unlikelier by the day. Dave had toyed with the idea of funding a new set but was reluctant to get it on the never-never; the chance of raising enough cash was about as great as Davy Crotchet and the Quavers releasing a number one single.

When Johnny Archer and Mick Miller come calling, what choice does Dave really have but to answer their demands? As the ardour of imagining his hands cupping the succulence of Janine's curves diminishes, the clock ticks towards three o-clock and right on cue a van draws up with its hooter sounding twice. Dave steps out of the door and lurches over to the huge, rusty gates, glancing furtively to right and left as though he is breaking out of jail. He unlocks the strong, chunky padlock, draws back the long, black bolt and opens the gate to let the van in.

Johnny leaps out of the van. 'Right, Davy-boy. Let's see this room of yours. Mick, you start to unload.'

Mick flings open the van doors: many large cartons of cigarettes; a pile of smaller but much heavier boxes marked with branded names of whisky, gin, vodka, rum and brandy.

'Bloomin' 'eck! Booze and fags, bound to be a knock-off!' self-asserts Dave, his blood pressure rising, his ears ringing, a look of panic enveloping his face. He has already loaded up the group's kit into his van so there is plenty of room for the booty, and the whole transfer of goods is completed in less than twenty minutes.

'As soon as we've notched up a 'fence' we'll make arrangements with you to collect it. In the meantime, 'Mum's the word, hey Davy-boy?'

Johnny and Mick pull slow away, looking mightily relieved at last. Dave leaves shortly afterwards, the weight of their deep concern having been transferred onto his gullible shoulders.

PART THREE

AUGUST 31 1963

AFTERMATH

Chapter 24

10.30pm

St Mary's Hall is now nearly empty. Big Frank, the doorman, produces a mop and bucket of soapy water to sort out the sticky mix of Coke, Fanta, Tizer, tea, sweat, glass, saliva, urine and blood that oozes over the dance-floor at the site of the brawl. Flo snaffles Colin's redundant plectrum that she sees lying at the edge of the stage, thus enhancing her collection of memorabilia.

The drinks table that has serviced Colin's broken body as a makeshift support gantry is re-righted, as is one chair; another chair is broken beyond repair. Colin knows the feeling! Frank, in stating the obvious, finds a piece of paper and Sellotape from the cash desk drawer and writes 'BROKEN' in large letters and sticks the note onto what is left of it.

The rest of the group muck in to load up the van in double-quick time. A fragile Colin, already starting to throb all over and still bleeding profusely from the remains of his nose, is eased sympathetically and slowly by Roger and Dave into the passenger seat. He sits slightly forward but with his head tipping back, sheets of pink toilet paper quickly turning scarlet and protruding from each side of his battered nose. They all wish Colin well, congratulate him for putting up a magnificent show and for giving a good account of himself, close the van door and wave him and Dave away.

As the van disappears down St Leonard's Road, Roger reflects on what he has witnessed. He has seen hundreds of punch-ups like this, especially at weekends in town centre pubs. He was advised at police training school to, 'Proceed to a brawl at the pace of a dying snail on a sheet of sandpaper, Edwards!'

He has always frowned on the blood-letting stories the older local coppers told him about the heyday of skiffle. For reasons of an orphanage upbringing and a military brainwashing, Roger is now an arch-diplomat, a left-wing copper holding the cop-out middle ground in all circumstances.

Whilst Roger's calming influence would have dampened down the fervour of many a young rioter in those days, his damp-squib contribution this evening has been completely ineffectual, his lame plea failing to prevent Colin diving in head first then coming off second best. In trepidation of the consequences, Roger has always been nervous of upsetting any apple-cart, even if the apples have gone rotten.

'Well, what a sudden end to proceedings!' Ken comments in disappointment.'Better go and get a real drink and mull over what has happened. Colin, of all people. Amazing! Down the club, everyone!'

In total agreement, the band members don mufti and off they go. Roger, cadging a lift with Ken and Val as per usual, slings his holdall in the back of Ken's Anglia and jumps in after it.

He sits in the centre of the seat, slightly forward, looking intently over Val's shoulder, enjoying the hint of cleavage that her new blouse is revealing. He is desperate to see more, should she move in either direction. He takes in the aroma of her musky perfume and is totally intoxicated. Such an innocent and fresh fragrance - so different from the sweat and oppressive odours of the warring gladiators. No-one speaks, as each is engrossed in personal interpretation on what has been witnessed.

Mopped-up and swilled-out, Big Frank is now cashing up as a dozen or so dwindlers stand around, pointing and pronouncing judgement. Ebb and Flo hang about, on the lookout for more valuable residue to add to their burgeoning collection.'C'mon Flo, the party's over. Let's call it a day and go and get a drink. We've got half an hour before last orders are called.'

'Where're we going Ebb? We're banned from all the pubs round here; they won't serve us.'

'How about the off-licence? We can get a couple of bottles of IPA and bite the tops off. Thirsty work fighting with the boys!'

The two victorious Teddy boys return from the toilets with their drapes straightened, their ties reconstructed and fags drooping from their lips.

'Drink, Mick?'

'Yeah, a farewell drink to those three scruffs; we'll not see them again.'

'I hope we do. Soft as putty, those three. We never got a sweat on.'

'Even Colin put up a good fight, and he's hardly a scrapper. He did well for a banker!'

Ange and Karen move towards the back of the hall, having seen Colin and Dave leave. They are discussing intently, then Karen pushes Ange forward towards the Teds. She speaks softly and nervously. 'Erhm, excuse me. Can you help us?' The Teds are surprised by their question.

'We jus' did help you, darlin', or didn't you notice?' Johnny is razor-sharp with his reply.

'Of course we noticed and are grateful for your help.'

'You two need to be more careful who you mix with, don't you? It'd be a shame if your pretty faces got all messed up, like Colin's.'

'But we do need you to help us again, don't we Karen?'

'Again? This is getting a bit frequent, isn't it?' Johnny laughs.

'We need to catch the 11pm bus to town from Cotton End, and...'

'...And?'

'And we're worried that those yobbos'll be hanging around and waiting for us.'

'They'll be long gone, luv. No need to worry about them.'

'But we do!'

'You're scared?' Mick is similarly brisk on the uptake.

'Yep!'

'And you want us to ride shotgun?'

'What?'

'You want us to escort you to the bus stop and keep you safe?'

'Please, if that's not putting you to too much trouble.'

'That's protection, and protection costs, don't it, Mick?'

'What are you offering, girls?'

'Offering? What would you like?'

'What I would like, darlin', I don't think you'll be offering.' He looks her up and down and runs his tongue across his bottom lip, smirking to himself.

'A pint, erhm, each.' Karen makes the first offer.

'Two, each! That's seven bob. Take it or leave it!'

'We'll walk you to the bus stop then we can drop by the Old White Hart and drink to your continued good health.'

'Deal!' The girls look reassured. A smile of relief breaks out on Ange's face.

'But we're not walking alongside you. No. We can't be seen walking with you two tarts, can we Mick?'

'No, this is our manor; we've got our reputations to think about. We'll walk ten yards behind you.'

'Ok. Let's go.'

Before we do, how about you two?' Mick looks towards Ebb and Flo, who are hanging about and ear-wigging this most unlikely of conversations.

'Would you like to join our happy throng?'

Johnny is quick to add, 'Those yobs might be waiting for you, too. I saw what you did. Good moves, girls. Neat weapons, those shoes!'

'Like yours, eh?' Flo looks down at Mick's feet.

'I think they got the point, don't you?'

'We can take care of ourselves, can't we Ebb?'

'We're not scared, but if you want more company, safety in numbers, we'll walk with you, won't we Flo?'

'Cost you seven bob, cheap at twice the price, for the privilege.'

'No chance, but we'll buy you a pint each in the White Hart, won't we, Ebb?' Flo winks at her sister.

'But you'll have to order. We're banned! And we ain't ready to walk with Teds. We'll walk with the other girls, here.'

Mick is in a great mood now. A burglary that will net them beer and fags money for the foreseeable future, a right bundle at St Mary's, now the best looking girls at the dance want escorting and will even pay for the privilege. He makes an offer that even surprises Johnny. 'It's Ok, girls. None of you'll have to pay. We're messing with you. Big Frank is paying, ain't you Frank?'

'Yeah, sure am. Here you are, Mick. Two quid, wasn't it?'

'Two quid is randy dandy, Frank. Same time same place next week? Let's go, girls. Drinks are on Big Frank.'

Johnny grabs his mate by the arm. 'Did you take a blow on your bonce or are you going soft in your old age?"

'Let go of my arm, Johnny, or I'll have to sort you out next. No harm in buying the local totty a drink. Look, we've had a good day. Let's celebrate!'

'I suppose. Then perhaps you'd prefer to walk with the skirt, too. You can carry their handbags for 'em.'

'Piss off!'

As the six of them leave the hall door, Ken starts his engine and pulls away. 'Eyes right!' Roger points out of the side window. 'Archer and Miller with those dolly-birds! Blimey, Ebb and Flo, too; four for the price of two! Bloody hell. How did they accomplish that?'

'Made in heaven, eh, Rog?' Ken laughs.

'I hope Colin's going to be alright,' says Val, looking nervous and worried. 'He looked more dead than alive when he left. Do you think we should go the hospital and check that he's Ok?'

'He'll be alright, won't he Rog? No thanks to you!'

'What'd'ya mean, no thanks to me?' Roger feels edgy. Unknown to anyone but himself, he had his warrant card in his holdall all the time, tucked away with his police uniform and his soccer kit. He replies after an uneasy few seconds. 'I should think so. A few cuts and bruises. They'll soon patch him up down the General. They don't need us there.'

'He could have waited until I'd sung my encores, selfish git. I'd been practising them all day. Got the songs straight in my mind when 'Boom!' and Colin steals my thunder.'

Val, looking dismissively away, swallows hard, having lost her sense of humour. 'I don't think he'd too many options, Ken, do you? Nobody else was sticking up for those two girls.' She is appalled by Ken's comments.

'I was only joking, Val. Of course Roger could have stopped him, should have stopped him. Shouldn't you, Rog?'

'There was no stopping Col; the red mist had come down.'

'You're trained for this precise situation! Why didn't you arrest them?'

'Yes, Roger, you stood back and let Colin get hammered.' Val turns and looks Roger straight in the eye, wondering what sort of copper he really is.

Roger looks out of the window in silence. After a long pause he replies, 'Arrest? Arrest who?'

'Those three troublemakers!'

'For what? They caused a stir: they pawed the girls, but not much else. If I'd have arrested anyone then I would have arrested Colin.'

'Colin?' Ken and Val shout his name in unison.

'Yeah, Colin. He started the bloodbath: he landed the first punch; he's really to blame. Trust me!'

'Rog, what I saw was what everyone else saw: those troublemakers started it. Until they stuck their oars in, everything was fine. You must've seen that!'

'Val, I know it looks like that. Yes, they were being bloody obnoxious - provocative and trying to get a reaction! Nothing unusual in that. They're well-known around town. I repeat - Colin landed the first punch!'

Val was irritated by Roger's officious stance. 'If he hadn't, what would have happened then?'

'Most probably, nothing. It would all have blown over.'

'Huh. You reckon?'

*

The five of them (Ken and Val, Gary and Linda and Roger) have been at the club about an hour. The fight and the chaotic end to the evening has surprised them all and given them loads to talk about. Consequently, they are already in high spirits and on their third round of drinks, except Val, who is looking a little pale.

She pulls Ken away from the group for a private word: 'Ken, I don't want to be a drag, but all that blood and fighting seems to have upset me. Would you mind if we go home now?'

Ken is put out by Val's words. He is having a good time and is in fine form, but Val does look rather fragile. He grudgingly resigns himself to having to leave early.

'Of course we can, love. Hold on while I tell the others.'

'Sorry guys, we're off now. Val's not feeling too good.'

'No, don't you go, Ken,' interjects Gary, 'I can't afford to be home any later as I'll be up early for a private job that I've got to finish. Let me take Val. You stay and bring Linda home later - if that's Ok with Val, of course.'

Ken looks at Val with wide, appealing eyes and a slight nod, hoping she'll take up Gary's kind offer.

'Is that Ok, love?'

'Yeah, that's fine. Thanks, Gary.'

'Is that Ok with you, Lin, if I take Val home?'

Linda looks toward Ken, winks and says, 'Yeah. That's perfect. Ken'll take care of me, won't you, Ken?'

Ken then remembers that he was intending to tell Val about his planned departure to Hamburg tomorrow, but quickly figures out that he will have sufficient time to phone her in the morning. He kisses Val and confirms that he'll call her early in the morning. Linda and Gary kiss farewell.

Val and Gary wave as they leave the room and head for home.

As Val leaves, Roger looks on, frustrated. If he had owned a car he would have loved to have driven her home and spend fifteen minutes alone in her company, even if she was not feeling so good.

Ken, Linda and Roger pick up the threads of their discussion. Various local acquaintances, musicians and former school friends come up to the threesome, introduce themselves, chat and move on. The ambience is good, the club's vocalist is excellent, the backing trio adequate.

Ken introduces Roger to a mate who works in a local garage as a car salesman; following their earlier discussion in town, Roger gets into deep discussion about makes, models, years, mileages and prices. Ken is glad to get Roger off the scene for a few minutes; he does tend to be a bit of a hanger-on. He is doubly-pleased to now be alone with Linda, whose own facial expression of relief when Roger leaves them confirms Ken's thoughts. Ken and Linda grab a dance, then a slow smooch, as the cabaret singer seductively continues after her short break.

Linda is in fine form, like Ken. If you didn't know better you would think they themselves were a couple. They have known each other for years but the number of times they have been alone together you could count on one hand. Then suddenly… !

'Ok, Ken, you can drive me home now!' Linda's words surprise Ken in their directness and timing. It is barely half past midnight, but like the true gentleman that his parents have proudly nurtured, a lady's wish is his command.

They wave 'Goodbye' to Roger and squeeze their winding way through the clusters of dancers and drinkers that now fill the large, smoky room, being stopped once or twice for brief conversations with lads that Ken knows. A couple of local band members notice them leaving and pass a private comment, something to the extent of 'Lucky Bastard!' as Ken ushers Linda through with his arm draped around her shoulder.

It is a warm but clear evening now. They soon find Ken's car in St George's Street, jump in and begin their journey home.

'Ken, it's a beautiful evening. It would be a shame to finish it so soon. Can we stop off for a while, gaze at the moon and stars, have a chat and enjoy a bit of time on our own?' Linda's words come out exactly as she had rehearsed them in her head.

Chapter 25

Monday September 2nd 1963

10.30am

There are no collections for Dave to make today. He only has to attend to callers, clean and brush Shoddy the horse, and answer the phone in his father's absence. He can look forward to a restful day, or so he thinks. He is sitting in his chair in the office. It is an ex-typist's chair, its padded seat ripped at the side with the stuffing pushing out from the old, and now inadequate, restraining parcel tape.Additionally one of its three wheels is missing, which has been skilfully replaced by a small cube of wood. This fits perfectly for height, but means the chair can only operate effectively if the sitter does not need to change position. This is ironic in that Dave's gammy leg only allows him to operate at a similar diminished performance.

Over his eighteen years, Dave has come largely to terms with his disability. He can now drive, although his clutch-changing is a little jerky and heavy, as is his drumming with the band, which while lacking the use of a hi-hat cymbal is clearly outweighed by his extra enthusiasm and occasional unwarranted improvisation.

The big punch-up on Saturday at St. Mary's Hall was a shock that he had still not fully come to terms with. His best mate, Colin, had, totally out of character, not only started a fight with three ruffians but had got himself pulverised to within an inch of his life.

Dave, in his van, had rushed Colin down to the hospital, his nose oozing blood. Some teeth were clearly uprooted and sharp cries of anguish emanated every time he changed gear, braked, or even went round a corner too fast, with Colin tightly hugging his painful ribs. A one-hour wait in Accident and Emergency ensued, after which Colin re-emerged with his ribs bound up and his battered nose plastered. His loose teeth were still hanging on by a thread. His pen-pushing and plectrum-plucking right hand was badly swollen and could yet need an x-ray once the swelling subsides.

Dave had subsequently visited Colin yesterday afternoon at his home but his mum had answered the door, announcing that Colin was still in bed and in too much pain to see him. 'You can tell that group of yours that you can find a new bass player. He resigns!' she bellowed.

Dave was not sure whether that was Colin talking, or his mum. Either way, he then wanted to update the others. He drove round to Roger's digs. However, Roger was out looking at cars. Gary was out working somewhere, and Ken's mum unusually gave him short shrift, saying that Ken had gone away. Gone away? Strange!

Dave switches on the electric kettle. Meanwhile, at Police HQ Roger has been called back from his Semilong beat to work on what the desk-sergeant calls 'a special operation'.

'You drive Panda cars, don't you, Edwards? Are you any good?'

'Yes, sarge. I learned in the army.'

'Well, go into Traffic and get the keys for the one in the yard. It's the only one at base. It's got its blue roof light missing. Bloody out-of-town vandals! Drive it round the front and I'll join you in two minutes. Here's a tea towel to stuff in the hole. We've been promised rain later.'

'Yes, sarge. Erhm, where're we going sarge?'

'We're going on a raid, lad, to see if we can find ourselves some train robbers. First stop is Archie Bell's yard. Now go! Go on, go!'

Ten minutes later, the pale blue and white Morris Minor draws into Bell's Yard. The sergeant gets out. 'Hello. Anyone at home? Are you there, Arch?'

Dave is engrossed in his Playboy magazine, half way through the Lola Stromboli page, as hot as any volcano and boiling over inside! Before he reaches a similar climax, he hears some bellowing outside, gets up and walks into the yard.

Roger thoughtfully takes off his police helmet so that Dave might recognise him. 'Aye up, Rog.'

'Where's your dad, young Bell?' The Sergeant assumes control.

'Away, sir.'

'Away is he? When's he due back?'

'Next Saturday, sir.' Dave was always taught to be extra polite and helpful to the police.

'So, you presumably won't mind if we look around?'

'No, help yourselves. There's nothing to hide here.' At the split-second he says the word 'hide' he panics. His heart sinks, his pulse starts racing, his ears start buzzing, his face blushes and he starts to feel nauseous.

'Oh shit! The stuff Johnny and Mick brought! What the fuck shall I do?' Rhetorical question maybe, but Dave still needs to find a credible answer.

'Act cool, that's it.' Dave has found a credible answer.

'I'll be in the office. You can look anywhere you want. That'll fool 'em,' he thinks.

'Edwards, you check the yard. I'll check the buildings.'

'Sarge.'

The sergeant enters the office. 'What have we got here, Davey lad? Dirty mags, eh? Are you eighteen? Give them here, sunbeam, let me have a shufty.'

The sergeant takes his spectacles from his breast pocket. 'Does your dad know you've got these, lad? I may have to confiscate them.' The sergeant critically scrutinises Irma the Squirmer and lingers awhile in examining the inventive contortions of the alluring Roma from Cromer. Before Dave can give precise information as to the back of which lorry the soft porn fell, another car pulls into the yard - a Humber Super Snipe. Out steps Charles Waterfield. He sees the police car, then he spots the sergeant in the office.

'Hello Alec. Trouble here?'

'Good morning, Charles. No, no trouble. New weekly checks since the Great Train Robbery.' They shake hands masonically and gesture furtively.

'It's about time you found those blighters. That poor sod of a train driver is in a bad way. You're David Bell, aren't you?' Charles turns his attention to Dave, who stands in awe of these bastions of civic authority. 'Kenneth Waterfield is my son. Of course, you know that. I've come to collect the kit - guitars, amps, paraphernalia. Where do you keep it?'

'Why do you want the kit, sir?'

'Simple. I own the kit and my son has... (he briefly stops while thinking of the right words) left the country to work abroad for a short time. The group is now defunct.'

'Abroad, Charles? I thought you said at the last lodge meeting that he is joining your company?' The sergeant is quick to add his input.

'He is, Alec. He certainly is, but not until he has completed a special work assignment (he clears his throat), that, erhm, has been arranged for him.'

He quickly changes the subject. 'Where's the stuff, lad? I need it for safe keeping. I don't want any more of you lot buggering off and leaving me with the HP bill and no assets.' Charles Waterfield says exactly what he thinks, but not perhaps in the way he might mean. The sergeant looks at him quizzically.

Dave is now no more in panic. He is not thinking straight at all, his whole attention being diverted by Ken's dad saying the band is no more. 'It's in the back room, sir.' Charles Waterfield pushes open the storeroom door and there on the floor is the band's kit.

'Don't take the drums, sir. I own them.'

'Yes, I know that. About time you got a new set. These are a bloody disgrace!'

Charles starts to load up his boot, then the back seat: guitars, amps, mikes, wires, booms - the lot! Then he sees some more boxes, and not sure whether they are also part of the kit he opens one: whisky! So he opens another: cigarettes, hundreds of packets. He smiles to himself. 'Alec, take a look at this lot!' He beckons the sergeant through.

The Sergeant frustratingly puts down the girlie magazine at the same point of erotic limbo that Dave had reached a short while ago. He shuffles damply into the storeroom at the back. Charles flips open the lids on the two boxes and points to their contents.

'PC Edwards, come here, please!' He shouts at the top of his voice, then whistles in disbelief.

Charles recognises Roger. 'Aren't you the… ?'

'Yes, sir. The rhythm guitarist in the Waders.'

'Open all these boxes. I think we've unearthed Santa's grotto!' the sergeant barks.

'Charles, you've uncovered something very interesting… not that I wouldn't have found them anyway, but thank you all the same.'

'Always glad to be of assistance to our local constabulary. Look I must fly, Alec. See you in the lodge bar on Thursday. You can update me on what transpires here.'

The Sergeant returns his attention to the work in hand. Edwards, read him his rights. 'David Bell, I am arresting you for the possession of stolen property. You are not obliged to say anything unless you wish to do so, but whatever you do say will be taken down in writing and may be given in evidence against you.'

Dave looks crestfallen. His hands start to shake with apprehension and his legs turn to jelly. Someone is playing the cymbals in his ears and his heart launches into a drum roll.

'Take the car back to the station, Edwards, and arrange for a van to be sent down to pick up all these boxes. I'll detain the suspect here then take him back with the van. David Bell, you are likely to be detained in custody for a very long time.'

Roger looks at Dave, and gestures to him and mouths, 'Sorry, mate!' With the sergeant here, there is nothing he can do to help him. Compromised, Roger drives off, leaving Dave to contemplate the following: 'Suspect? Detained? Oh, Dad; oh, Mum; oh Shit!'

'Is that your van, Mr Bell?'

'Yes, sir.'

'Open it up. Let's take a look. See what else you've got stashed away!'

At that moment the phone rings and the sergeant motions to Dave that he should answer it.

'Hello, Bell's Yard.'

'Davey boy, don't say one word. Not one! Listen, then put the phone down. It's Johnny Archer. We're in the phone box over the road. We were just coming round to see you when we saw you've got the rozzers with you. Tell them nothing, not one word. If they find the stash then it's nothing to do with us. Right, Davey-boy? And Davy Crocket, if you don't want to end up propping up the M1 bridge at Rugby, and you value the good health of that nag of yours, you'll keep your trap shut. Understand?'

'Are you Ok, Mr Bell? You look like you've seen a ghost. Not more bad news is it? Anything I can do?'

'No, it's alright sir. Wrong number.'

'Wrong number, eh? Let's go and take a look at this van of yours.'

Dave collects his keys and opens up. There are drops of blood everywhere and bloody toilet tissue, too. The sergeant looks at Dave Bell and smiles. 'It isn't our lucky day, is it Mr Bell?'

'But this isn't my blood. It's C… !' He stops himself.

'It's who's? So, you had an accomplice, too?'

'No, sir. I had no accomplice.'

'Well, with the booze and fags nicked from the Crown on Friday night, your dad away on holiday and blood all over your van, you've done a pretty good job of not doing anything! We know the culprits may well have cut themselves when smashing their way into the pub. We can either analyse the blood and find your accomplice, or you can cough up to everything and take the rap yourself. How's that for a deal?'

'I'll take the rap!'

Chapter 26

Monday September 2nd 1963 - 8pm

Hamburg is West Germany's second biggest city, a port with a huge harbour and waterfront. It has beautiful tree-lined suburbs, some fabulous chic city centre shops and parks where the German middle-classes promenade on a Sunday morning and show-off their very expensive finery. Like most cities it has a pulsating orthodox night life, but Hamburg's 'deviant nocturnalism' is down by the docks and is plain manic. It is always thronged with the hustle and bustle of insatiable sailors craving a good time in the form of prostitutes, music, drugs and alcohol.

The St Pauli district, in the daytime, feels grimy; the narrow and mazy cobbled streets are crumbling. There is a pervading stench of dockland industry mixed with raw and spicy aromas emanating from the wharves and tall red brick warehouses. In the late evening it mutates into an epicentre of debauchery and lawlessness, a Roman orgy of a place where anything goes.

There are a few classic streets where all hell is let loose. The Reeperbahn and Grosse Freiheit are the nuclei, lined with night clubs, bars, cafes, cabaret cellars, music halls, saloons, clip joints, gaming rooms, massage parlours, tattooists, arcades, standing shoulder to shoulder - bathed in neon and vying for your attention and your money.

*

The Dominators have a contract to play at 'Planet Hamburg', a new music bar on Grosse Freiheit, only a few steps from the 'Star Club' and the 'Kaiserkeller'. These places come alive from 7pm to around 4am each night. Ken has been promised £40 per week immediately (more than he could have expected after five years' studying to be an accountant). When the Dominators arrive, an unknown Liverpool band called the Searchers is appearing at the 'Star Club'.

The five Dominators roll up at their hotel, the one booked by the club management. They are shown into the manager's office. It is tantamount to an SS interview in a Concentration Camp and they are brusquely shown to their two rooms at the top of the building, up endless flights of narrow and steep wooden, creaky stairs.

Each room is very basic: one wardrobe, one chair, a wooden table and three ex-Army single camp beds with lumpy mattresses and dirty pillows. There is cracked lino on the floor, no heating and a shared washroom - very sparse. A single, naked, dusty low-wattage light bulb hangs from the ceiling. There is barely a foot of space around the beds. The walls are painted dark-green to try to mask the signs of damp and mildew where the guttering must have been leaking. It is worse than a Third World youth hostel, much worse; the squalor is depressing.

'Ok, lads, it's not luxury, but it's home. Let's grit our teeth and get on with it. After all, it's only rock 'n' roll.' Mick is adamant.

Within days, the rooms are festooned with stinking socks and underpants, overflowing ashtrays, empty beer bottles and used coffee cups. The shared toilet is two floors below! With the warm weather changing towards the cold seasonal end of their blankets' effectiveness, the lads begin to sleep under their coats as well.

'It's not that bad. At least my dad isn't here!' Ken is trying to see the positive whilst surrounded by so much negative.

It also confirms to him beyond all shadow of doubt, that bringing Val with him to Hamburg would have been a total disaster. The digs are awful and judging by the group's weekly timetable, Ken would be either performing or asleep. He convinces himself that Val would have hated it and would have pleaded with him to take her home again. With none of the other guys having their girlfriends with them, Ken assures himself he has made the right decision.

The Dominators start work the next night, one day late. When they have finished all their sets, and once during 'eine kurze Pause' (a short break), they drop in to watch the Searchers next door, to be inspired by them, even to copy them. They soon conclude that whoever is on at the 'Star Club' is worth seeing and to play there or at the 'Top Ten' or 'Kaiserkeller' would become their first rung on the ladder of success.

'Planet Hamburg' is mainly one vast bar area with a low ceiling, flock wallpaper, heavy drapes, a sticky floor, brown corduroy settees positioned all around the walls and barrels converted into tables with red-shaded lamps. The dance floor has a stage about four feet high with a Manhattan skyline backdrop. The atmosphere is hot and smoky, with the pervading aroma of spilled beer. That is the downstairs.

Upstairs are a strip club in one half of the building and an erotic film club in the other. On show are strip films showing full frontal nudity which none of the group has ever seen the like of before in Britain.

One day, after a couple of weeks, there is a knock on the bedroom door and it is the hotel manager, Obersturmbannfuhrer (his new nickname) Brandt. He says that they have to scrub the floor and offers them a long-handled scrubbing brush and a bucket which he pushes into Mick's hand. He barks, 'You scrub die floor, English,' and leaves.

Mick grabs the brush, chases the manager down the stairs and shouts, 'Me no fuckin' fraulein, you scrub the fuckin' floor!'

It doesn't go down too well but they all find it hilarious at the time.

The manager ripostes, 'And remember, no fucking women in the room!'

It is Spartan and crowded, with a cacophony of snoring, farting, coughing and throwing up. Ken's aim is to spend as little time at the digs as possible. However, it means that there is nowhere for him to go for a bit of peace and privacy. It starts to grind him down.

In Northampton, the group would usually play a ninety-minute session or a two-hour session with a thirty-minute break during an evening booking. In Hamburg they play typically six or seven one-hour sessions, with fifteen- minute breaks between each. One evening, they even play ten sets.

House rules are that there is no talking to the audience through the microphone, no bad language and no eating or smoking on stage. No performer is allowed to leave the stage. Nor can they sit down - except the drummer - and after a few hours, he can hardly even stand up! This purgatory is six days per week with only Monday off.

They can even be fined for lateness, foul behaviour or other malpractices. There are lots of clubs vying for passing custom. The key decision on whether or not to go into a club is determined by the music blaring out from speakers positioned in the doorway on the street.

It has to be loud and hot, and that is the Dominators' job! To achieve this, they have in their repertoire rock 'n' roll for the first four hours then slower R&B/blues numbers late into the night as the mood mellows. Ken's singing, which initially is pretty good, becomes expansive as he sings more. The house provides a superb PA system, as well as amps and speakers for the rest of the guys. They work more hours than ever they could if they had regular jobs back home. Although the conditions are dire, it nevertheless doesn't seem like work. It is fun, like a long holiday, and there is tasty magic in the pungent air.

The Dominators gather more songs and they learn to develop some of them to last five, even more than ten minutes, with guitar breaks, drum solos and repeated verses. This allows time enough for a punter to go out of the club, cross the street, buy some cigarettes or tobacco and be back before the song finishes. Ken hones his stagecraft and they all learn to sing 'What'd I Say' with thirty minutes of 'Heys' and 'Yeahs'. Spontaneity and innovation is the name of the game for Kenny and the lads!

Apart from the miserable living accommodation, the natural spoil of the rock 'n' roll lifestyle is screwing their brains out with the free-spirited frauleins, and ace lead-singer Ken gets to play the field the most. Everything is free and easy. They do not need to chase sex, it comes to seek them out.

The girl fans ring the stage at every performance, a seething mass of female desire. Ken consequently has all of his dates lined-up before the end of the first session. In the break he finds it easier to get a 'knee-trembler' than a Schnitzel! 'Planet Hamburg' is a sexual paradise for randy young sods, and Ken gets sucked into the promiscuous void! Val and Linda whetted his appetite, now he is gorging in the trough like a pig!

The Dominators are naïve in initially thinking the girls who ring the stage at 'Planet Hamburg' are simply fans, groupies. In fact, they turn out to be prostitutes, but that fact takes them time to figure out. They are eventually recommended a walk down Herbertstrasse, a block or two away.

When the lads get there the narrow street is permanently barricaded by the local police department at both ends by a twelve-foot barrier which they can barely squeeze through. Once inside the barricades there is a cobbled street lined both sides by small terraced-houses. Picture windows and doorways are lined by prostitutes scantily clad in garters, black silk stockings, teddies and thigh-high boots. Under the make-up and costumes they identify themselves as their fans. In fact, not only their fans; they are everyman's fans.

Some are schoolgirls just out of uniform, some are schoolgirls still in. Some are barely teenagers, others older than your grandmother. They come in all shapes and sizes, from the primitive to the professional, from the good-looking to the deformed and downright odd! Once the group finds this out, then the thought that they might be the sixth person today to have sex with them, or indeed the fiftieth this week, dulls their ardour. Some of The Dominators came down with something they never bargained for, 'the clap'or 'the pox' for which they had to seek out help in the form of antibiotics from a local doctor.

Ken is just an innocent grammar school boy from Northampton, but he is reacting against everything that he wasn't allowed to do at home. The adrenaline created from performing in such an electric atmosphere for so many hours each night turns his head, makes sleep a habit of the past and as his energy wanes, so it becomes the norm to take 'speed' to give him energy and verve. These pills are supposed to be only available on prescription but in fact Ken, as and when, pops to the corner to get all he needs. He becomes a hedonist with an insatiable appetite. Every night is like Saturday night: there is no let up for him!

Customers buy the lads beer as they perform and send it up on stage - not a bottle, not a glass, but by the crate, generally beer, sometimes bottles of sekt or schnapps. 'Speed' lifts them but makes them thirsty; alcohol quenches that thirst. The more they drink, the better they feel; the better they feel, the more they drink. They all get hooked on the potent mix of adrenaline, drugs and alcohol all coursing through their bodies: 'Love Potion Number 9'.

After performing, some of the groups end up in a local café or pub where their high jinx and practical joking turns into personality clashes. Petty jealousies often develop in to horseplay and tantrums. Their antics are little more than a hyperactive chimps' tea party: fisticuffs, slanging matches, food and drink thrown about, crockery broken, joshing leading to fights breaking out, tablecloths slashed, wallpaper torn, carpets stained.

In absolute contrast to everything Charles Waterfield invested into Ken's nurturing, there is no discipline. They are running wild, resulting in bans from countless places. Yes, Ken is growing up fast!

One memorable night after the Dominators finish playing, they have a wild party - ten girls, five Dominators, a sexual swaparama. When the music stops, pass the prossie! Where now the furtive and seedy sex trade of Northampton? And where now the longing and faithful arms of Val? This decadent behaviour in St Pauli is plain debauchery, an erotic fairground rollercoaster of perfumed temptation, a helter-skelter which the Dominators access along with many other groups!

Ken is free, free as a bird, free of school, free of his father! He insatiates himself in this Life of Riley, going mildly berserk, gorging himself on forbidden fruit. He soon begins to spiral out of control. Within a few short months of deserting his small-town romance, he becomes a totally different person - someone Val would never recognise. This is Ken behaving like a crazy man, not the precocious boy she knew and loved.

In 'Planet Hamburg', the white-aproned waiters - ex-criminals or ex-boxers - are not only that, but also trained henchmen who enforce club law and order with rapier-like ruthlessness. They luxuriate in their power by using knuckledusters and rubber coshes, which are kept in the manager's office, whereas back in Far Cotton they were kept in Mick Miller's and Johnny Archer's inside pockets.

On one violent night after the Dominators had been resident for some weeks, during their fourth set the mood should be mellowing. Hamburg had struggled to a 1-0 win at home, and a group of Munich supporters is in the 'Planet'. Ken downs a few drinks and serenades them with a heartfelt version of Adam Faith's 'Don't That Beat All' when a Munich fan bashes a giggling waitress over the head with a bar stool.

The waiters batter the Bavarian infiltrators to a pulp with fist and boot, frog-marching them backwards out of the back door, raising them aloft weightlifter-style and dumping them bleeding in the alley with the garbage. In true Johnny and Mick tradition, they spit all over the unfortunate offenders before putting the boot into their ribs a few last times!

Ken is amused and rather nostalgic as he remembers one of the favourite songs he sang in the early days soon after the Abington Skifflers went electric, a song for the Teddy-boys: 'Don't Mess with my Ducktails' by Rudi 'Tutti' Grayzell. Nor do you mess with these waiters and waitresses! He chuckles at the ruckus, wondering how no-one gets killed, reflecting on his last night at St Mary's Hall.

The band bought new stage suits as soon as they arrived for their great adventure. Initially they looked well-groomed, very sharp with gold lame jackets, black shirts and trousers and black Beatle boots. Within weeks the jackets and trousers had become stretched and ripped; the seams simply rotted away as the fabric decomposed in the heat and sweat of performance.

After a typical session on stage, a pool of sweat would lay at Ken's feet, as though he had emptied a bottle of water on the stage. Soon their stage suits fray, with greasy collars, worn elbows and stained trousers - wear and tear you would expect of people obliged to use public baths, communal cold water sinks and indoor washing lines!

Ken is on a runaway train of lust and insanity and he can't get off! He can't find the brake and all signals on his track are up! He has gone from tea with two sugars, ham sandwiches and peaches and cream at a Sunday afternoon tea party with his grandparents to an endless 'Happy Hour' of booze and drugs and an 'eat as much as you can' buffet of sex.

After six sleepless months of self-gratification, Ken is absolutely exhausted, a shadow of his former self. He needs to change something but he is hooked. His mind is in a whirl. He is slowly going insane.

Then Fate intercedes in the form of a German girl: Carola Maier!

Chapter 27

Late-1963

In prison, Dave's first port of call is a cobbled courtyard surrounded by imposing high brick walls, topped with barbed wire. There is a stand-alone, single storey, tin-roofed reception area where the new inmates, transported together in a police van from town, are met by a stern and somewhat regimental prison officer. The lads are shown no sympathy, no empathy, nothing. The officer gets straight down to business, checking their paperwork. Hospitalities begin.

'Which one of you is Bell?'

'Me.'

'Me what?'

'Me, sir,' Dave whimpers, his eyes glazed with tears, his memory lapsed on the term of address which had been inbred as an emblem of subservience.

'Louder, Bell. We can't hear you!'

'Me, sir!' Dave looks around to see who else was there. 'We?'

'That's better, Bell. We are learning already.'

Dave again ponders... 'We?'

'Now, Mr Ding Dong Bell, pussy's-in-the-well-Bell. Cut the snivelling, stand in that circle marked 'CIRCLE' and strip off your clothes. All of 'em. Don't be shy, Mr Bell. We've seen it all before.'

Dave glances around... 'We?' He eases forward tentatively. Everyone seems to be looking. 'Ah, so there we all are!'

He takes off all his clothes as instructed, except his Aertex pants and Woolworths' socks, treasured possessions from the yard's pile of 'tat and shmatter'. 'We take off all our clothes, Mr Bell.'

Then he is strip-searched. He stands there as naked as Nature intended, destined for centrefold if only 'we' were adorned with tennis racquet and ball. 'We' is trembling and shrivelling, which does nothing for 'our' self-confidence. It is cold and damp on the stone floor, and with no Harrison Marks to photograph his Adonis pose, his manhood droops to the lowest point of his young life - lost liberty, lost underpants, lost prowess. He is now more naked and vulnerable than the day he was born.

The officer stares at Dave's gammy leg. 'What's up with your leg, Bell?'

'Polio, sir.'

'Polo hey? Fell off our horse did we?' He sniggers to a colleague, who also finds it funny, nay hilarious!'

'No... 'Polio', sir.'

'Polio, hey, the mint with the hole?' He makes a note. 'Well, we've got a pantomime at Christmas, Bell. Perhaps you could play Long John Silver. We'll fix you up with a parrot!'

Their humourlessness is cruel and juvenile. Dave already feels abused and bullied after merely five minutes here. 'Go into that cubicle and take a shower, Bell. We stink!' (He apparently says that to everyone.) 'Here's our welcome present.' He hands Dave a cardboard box, slightly bigger than a shoe-box, which contains a towel, soap, shampoo and toothbrush. Dry yourself thoroughly and wait there for the nurse!'

A trim young 'angel of mercy' with an hour-glass figure and a middle-aged miserable-looking doctor in white coat with a grubby stethoscope hanging round his neck, her golden tresses flowing, him as bald as a coot, arrive to take more details: height, weight and so on and so forth, etc, as they said. The doctor asks Dave about his general fitness and specifically about his leg.

The nurse runs her slender fingers through Dave's hair, along the gum line, behind his ears and between his fingers before checking both sides of his hands. Then the moment he dreads: memories of his school nurse come flooding back and his member reacts accordingly.

The nurse gently lifts his scrotum, squeezes his testicles and, asking him to cough, checks for a hernia. At the moment of the cough his penis quickly lifts towards erection, and he knows what's coming. The nurse eases her right hand provocatively into the left breast pocket of her uniform and slowly slips out a thermometer. Dave knows she isn't going to plonk it under his tongue. No, here it comes: 'Thwack!'

The nurse flicks the thermometer down onto the top end of his erect penis! No sooner has she squeaked, 'Naughty boy', than Dave droops to smarting flaccidity. The lecherous old doctor gives her a wink and hands her a tissue. No fear of cross-infection on his watch! She thoroughly wipes off Dave's germs by running this up and down the full length of the thermometer before slipping it provocatively back into her breast pocket, its little bulb peeping cheekily above the hemline, its duty performed.

As if things could get no worse, Dave has to turn around and lift each foot, on one of which he can wiggle the toes better than the other. Legs apart and poised above a mirror attached to the floor, Dave has to bend forward and spread his buttocks. (This is a visual search only, no touching or invasion, not a photo shoot for the girls.) Dave squats and coughs twice. He guesses they are presumably checking for concealed weapons, maybe files, jemmies, screwdrivers or the like; drugs such as purple hearts; other prohibited items such as his front door key, straw for Shoddy, perhaps a lucky horseshoe. He thanks his lucky stars that Sergeant Jenks and PC Edwards didn't subject him to this down at the yard, up to his rectum in puddles and horse muck.

Leg apart, chin on chest, scrotum in hand, Dave is given a clean bill of health. The first thing he does to celebrate this triumph is cross his legs, trapping his testicles between his thighs to stop his urine running as freely as he had seen happen at St Mary's Hall. He remembers the best advice Roger Edwards ever gave him on long journeys to gigs where no lay-bys or field-gates came along. 'Cross your legs and let it stew!'

At least Dave has some morsel of comfort to thank Roger Edwards for - at this desperate moment, the best advice he had ever been given. Sadly, it doesn't work!

Having mopped up Dave and dried him down, the clinicians despatch him back to Reception for his property to be logged, folded and placed neatly into another bigger cardboard box, which is then slung into a storage area. All Dave owns are the clothes he arrives in, two ten bob notes and a florin, and a small black and white photo of his two horses, one that still pulls the cart, one that doesn't - the loves of his life, Shoddy and Mungo. This is all he has to show for his eighteen years as a partially paid-up member of the Human Race.

'These thoroughbreds'll never win the National, Bell?' Witty as well as cruel! 'Why do we want a picture of two old nags like these? Best we can do is sell them to the glue factory, if we ask us,' he chuckles.

Dave at last gets angry, as Mungo is already there, neither sold nor given away.'He didn't even go of his own free will, sir. Poor sod had no choice!'

Dave is getting livid with the warden's vindictiveness and irritating use of the word 'we'! This reaction is presumably what the warden wants, being the arrogant, ignorant, malicious bastard he is. They take 'our' fingerprints and photo. Finally they give 'us' 'our' (plural) prison uniform (singular) and, with the photo of Dave's horses now in the shoe box, they escort 'us' to our allocated cell.

The harsh sound of steel-on-steel as his cell door is slammed and locked behind him for the first time is enough to send his already delicate nerves over, or at least close to, the edge. The vibrating hollow echoing sound which bounces off one steel wall to the other, then travels to the core of his brain and the axis of his spine.

Dave is completely alienated, alone to adjust to and take in his new surroundings. The first five minutes are the most terrifying in his life, as it dawns on him that he will only see daylight again if some other person comes along and turns the key. Psychologists call it 'depersonalization'; Dave calls it 'shit'!

For the first night, Dave is on suicide watch in a cell on his own but his luck is about to run out. The following day he is removed after breakfast to a slightly bigger cell which has a pair of steel bunk beds, a steel table, steel chair, steel washbasin and a window with four steel bars. His new cell-mate introduces himself with a grunt and a glare then barks his name: 'Jackson!'

He is mixed race, a tall lanky Scouser with a unique accent. He tells Dave that he is in for manslaughter. He killed his wife, beating her to death with a starting-handle after an argument when she went for him with a kitchen knife.

This useful information helps calm Dave's nerves as effectively as a Gatling gun at the Alamo. He walks straight over to within a couple of inches of Dave, looks him straight in the eyes, stands nose to nose and asks, 'Bell, are you a homo, or a nonce?'

His breath smells disgusting and his teeth are more yellow than white with the majority missing. 'Look at me whilst I am talking to you! Well, tell, Bell!'

Dave confirms he is neither, though not having the courage to declare that he doesn't particularly want to become one. He doesn't exactly know what a 'nonce' is, although he has heard the word 'punce' a few times used by market grafters in the Market Square land where ripe bananas grow. The renowned 'Grapefruit King', visiting Northampton from his warehouse in Seven Sisters Road, had once called Dave a 'punce' for not having enough cash for the grapefruit he fancied, but this was not the time or place for Dave to digress.

'Are you sure you are neither nonce nor homo? You look a bit queer to me!' Fifteen seconds pass by, neither prisoner speaking.

Dave tells him his name, and recounts his sorry tale. Rick Jackson chills a great deal and proves initially to be a half-decent cell mate. Half-decent is as good as it gets in here.

Dave finds 'the slammer' a more intense version of secondary school, of which he is a veteran, only having survived thanks to Archer and Miller. In all walks of life, Dave has got the general idea of cliques, wimps, bullies and weirdo's. He has learnt that providing you keep yourself to yourself, don't snitch and keep constant contact with your family and friends, the experience will go by much quicker and with least hassle. He prays that what he is about to endure will have light at the end of the tunnel.

He soon gets into a routine of slopping out, eating, education, work (because of his leg he is allocated the library), association with other prisoners and thirty-minutes' exercise in the yard. Boredom is an issue, especially at weekends when there are less warders and the prisoners are banged up almost all day. Dave reads old and well-thumbed car magazines, but sadly the limos are not draped with Janine, Irma or Roma.

Sometimes a good day comes and one such occasion is when Colin visits Dave, bringing with him his sister, Jeanette. He thinks this would be an outing for her, rather than leaving her prisoner in her own home. Jeanette is a few years younger than Colin, but as she instantly takes a shine to Dave she tags along for each subsequent visit.

A tentative friendship grows between Dave and her, and it would appear that the feeling is mutual. In prison, any visitor is a bonus, but to have a girl visit you is special. Jeanette finds Dave pleasant company and he finds her a breath of fresh air. She even starts to write to him but the letters are restricted, opened, read and checked for contraband. Dave also starts to write letters back, something he has never done before. These may also be read and must be placed unsealed in the post box. There is no privacy, but neither Dave nor Jeanette have any secrets to hide.

During the endless hours with nothing to do, Dave tells his cellmate, Rick, about his family and how Colin is giving him some extra money to pay for a few treats. One day when Dave is lying on his bed reading the newspaper during a 'unlocked hour', two thugs come in, close the door and threaten him with vile and perverse things.

While one keeps lookout on the door the other drops his trousers and invites Dave to suck his penis, or else! When he refuses he punches him in the breadbasket and forces him down on his knees to give him oral sex. Luckily, before the unthinkable happens, Rick shows up in the nick of time and fights off the attackers, who scram. There is a right commotion.

Dave is traumatised by the deepest fear he has ever imagined and is reduced to a helpless state of desperation. Later that evening, after the dust has settled, Rick suggests that Dave hire himself a bodyguard and after proposing some likely candidates, Rick, himself, volunteers for the job. So Dave uses all of Colin's money to pay Rick weekly for protection. In fact, it comes to light a few months later that Rick and his two accomplices had set the whole thing up and the fees went to a three-way split!

Rick had dreamed up this scheme and the other two inmates who shared in this plot completed the arrangement by taking their cut, from then on leaving Dave in peace. The old saying, 'Love of money is the root of all evil' is an understatement. In prison, money is power and respect; with centrifugal force, everything else revolves around it.

What Dave finds out later, much later, is that one of those attackers in his cell, the one who stood over him with his penis exposed, was in fact Colin's dad, Walt Harris. Although he had heard Colin talk about him, Dave had never met him previously, and never got to know it was him until after he was released.

Within a year Dave has one chance to get even with him and he takes that one chance. One chance, which gives Dave Bell the greatest satisfaction ever!

Chapter 28

February 1964

Ken always likes to spend his one day a week off alone, away from the other lads; he needs to try to clear his head. He often walks down to the local music store. He gets to know the owner, Freddie (Friedhelm), who is 'The Man' and knows everything about anything to do with bands and instruments.

After grabbing a bite at a café or at a Chinese restaurant, usually 'Bratwurst', 'Frikadelle' or 'Currywurst', he wanders around the fish market on the waterfront or down to Der Dom, the city park. He drops by the Seaman's Mission for a chat with the management and one really cold winter's day with a biting wind coming off the North Sea he is so very weary and feels so drained that he enters St Joseph's church, sits down in a pew and tries to clear his head. His tank is being fuelled by alcohol and drugs, his natural energy is almost spent; in short, he is 'running on empty'.

Then miraculously he hears, 'Allo, wie gehts?'

'Excuse me, my German is not good. Do you speak English?' Ken feels a bit foolish when he realises he has not even attempted to reply in German, even after more than six months in Hamburg. He doesn't have the energy to try.

'My name is Carola. What is your name?'

'Ken Waterfield.' mutters the dumb-struck Kenneth.

'Ken, you do not look very well. Are you Ok?'

'I don't think I know anymore what Ok is.'

Carola looks at Ken's pale, now blotchy face and greasy hair. She then notices his glazed, bloodshot eyes. He has a splitting headache and a raging thirst; his eyes are struggling to focus and he feels dizzy and panicky.

'Ken, you do not look in control. Can I help you some way?' She looks interested in his plight and willing to help. Ken's initial reaction is to ignore her, thank her for her concern, then leave. Something, though, has clicked between them. He's not sure what.

‘Carola, I know that we only met two minutes ago but I’m in a bit of a mess and I do need a friend to talk to, to listen to me and help me find the right way. Now you mention it, I am a little bit lost. Do you know someone who can help?’ A corny chat-up line, maybe, but reasonably subtle.

‘Ken, my English is not good, but I am improving. I would like to help you. You sit here for ten minutes while I finish my work in the church, and we will then go together to somewhere quiet where we can talk.’

Carola is in the last year at school prior to university and at holiday time she earns some money doing odd cleaning jobs around the church. When she returns, Ken is slumped asleep in the pew. He feels like death warmed-up when she wakes him.

‘Hi, remember me?’

‘Yes, Carola, I remember you. You are my guardian angel.’

‘Was ist ‘guardian’?

‘You have been sent to help me, to look after me, to save me.’

‘Carola looks at him a bit ‘old-fashioned’. He seems to be a bit off-the-wall. She is very ‘matter-of-fact’ and ‘to the point’, in fact ‘typisch Deutsch’. She is around his age but seems to have infinite patience; she knows exactly what he needs.

‘Come, Ken Waterfall, I take you for a coffee to see what needs to be doing with you.’ Perhaps Waterfool is more apt than Waterfall? He thinks to himself, enjoying the light relief that is in the air.

They walk and chat for a while, then stop off in a cosy coffee bar overlooking the harbour. They chat together in a hybrid language somewhere between German and English. They start to understand and get to know each other.

*

Ken starts to meet Carola once a week, then twice, then more. Their friendship flourishes abundantly and he starts to make an effort. He cleans and smartens himself up, and over time he totally gives up girls, drugs and rock ’n’ roll (except for one girl, Carola, and the rock ’n’ roll).

He cuts back on boozing to a couple of bottles a day during performances to lubricate his vocal cords, and starts to eat properly. This makes him wonder that if Val had come to Hamburg with him in the first place, despite what Mick had warned, then perhaps he wouldn't have landed in this mess in the first place.

Ken sees Carola for a boat tour of the harbour, a walk in the park and by Alster lake where they stroll hand in hand for the first time and watch the rowing boats and swans. They take a circular bus tour of Hamburg and Carola shows Ken sights which are new to him. They take quiet meals in German restaurants, where again Carola introduces him to the sort of food and drink that the Dominators would never in their lifetime learn about.

Ken even starts swimming and they have days out at Travemuende on the Baltic Sea with long walks on the beach. She improves his German in leaps and bounds and he helps improve her 'already-adequate' English. Life is becoming normalized. It is brilliant to talk in depth to a normal human-being of his own age and someone not tied into the night life madness.

One day, Carola ratchets up the relationship by notches when she suggests that he comes home to meet her family. They take a bus, not too far, but to a suburban area of Hamburg he has never seen and that he never even knew existed. In nearly a year he has never been more than a half mile in any direction. Until now, he has been totally engrossed in the band and in himself.

Carola's family house is solid-looking and detached in a very fashionable neighbourhood with lots of gardens, hedges and trees. It has big terracotta plant pots on the doorstep, tall shrubs in the garden, a perfectly manicured lawn, a big summerhouse at the back and an expensive Mercedes car on the driveway. Everything looks prim and ship-shape with white duvets half-hanging out of the bedroom windows airing in the breeze.

She invites him in. The house is warm and welcoming with the aroma of baking and freshly-brewed coffee. It feels like heaven, a worthy home for his angel! In a few minutes he has gone from Stalag Luft 3 (his name for his hotel) with Red Cross Parcels, pick-axes, miners' lamps and an escape committee, all the way to Paradise. From the ridiculous to the sublime. The house has wooden floors, thick rugs and curtains, and heavy wooden furniture.

'Mutti, Vati, hier ist Ken Waterfool, erhm Waterfield, mein Freund aus England, ein Musiker.'

'Guten Tag, Herr Waterfield wie gehts?' Herr Maier offers a strong, formal handshake with a slight bow and click of the heels. Her handshake is equally strong but much more inviting and friendly.

'Guten tag, Frau Maier, Herr Maier. Ich bin gut danke.' Ken's 'O' level German from grammar school is coming in handy at last.

Carola speaks to her mother and father in German to explain who he is and how they met. Then she invites him into the living room, closes the door and they chat and laugh together. After half an hour or so, it is 4pm and on the dot as the grandfather clock chimes, they are formally invited into the dining room where Ken is served Kaffee und Kuchen - fresh-brewed strong coffee and large wedges from two huge home-made gateaux, each bigger than a dinner-plate, both still warm from the oven and with a healthy dollop of Schlagsahne on the side. Ken feels that he must have indeed died and gone to heaven: right person, right place, right time and they met in church!

This is the first of many such visits to her home. Carola is not only an angel, she is slim and attractive and wears short leather skirts and thick black tights over her long shapely legs. She wears her glossy hair short and layered, has dark eyes and understated make-up, a captivating smile and smells delightful. She has intelligence and style, an intellectual aura and she has snapped Ken out of his nightmare. Now his runaway express train is slowing down, and occasionally stopping at stations for him to get off and look around.

Ken starts to call her 'meine svelte deutsche Schutzengel', a nickname he makes up. He likes to call her 'Schutti'; she calls him 'Beatle'. At her home, her parents get to know him more and grow to like him more. He improves his German. They appreciate his efforts with the language, even when he gets the genders mixed up, uses the wrong tense, or the verb in the wrong place puts. After a few months he starts to become a small part of their family. The boys in the group have no clue where he goes each day, only that he spends less and less free time with them. Carola is his secret.

For weeks and months they cherish each other. He sings to her. He starts to gradually temper his love for rock 'n' roll, but not music in general. Ken is now starting to grow up. Another dilemma is soon upon him. Is he falling in love?

The rest of the Dominators get bored, not bored stiff with nothing to do, but bored to tears with the excesses. They, too, are on a runaway train but they have no guardian angel to save them. They have run out of energy but there is nowhere to stop on the main line, nowhere to take on water and no-one to change the points or work the signals. It comes to a head when the bass-guitarist, John, picks up a girl at the Monika bar, takes her to a hotel, which you can rent by the hour, only to find himself undressing a transvestite.

He tells the others that he has never moved so quick in his life when his wandering hand reached a part that wasn't supposed to be there! Shortly after that, they tell Ken that they have wearied of the lunacy and are leaving at the end of the month. Is he staying in Hamburg or returning to Northampton with them?

His hardest decision being the one he made to come in the first place, his easiest decision is now the one to remain here. He is staying, not only for Carola, but his ambition remains unchanged and re-ignited in that he wants to be acknowledged as a great singing star. Now he needs to find work and another backing group. This is proving more difficult until the lead singer in a group from the north of England upsets the German Auslander police - something to do with residency permits - and is deported. This sees him put on an aeroplane with two hours notice and no chance for him to return to Germany for at least a year. So Ken joins the abandoned Alley Cats.

He can now earn his living purely on singing, and, with the help of Carola's coaching, common sense. Next year, though, she will leave for college and study to be a lawyer; the best he can hope is to see her at weekends or during term breaks.

The Maier family is not financially rich, but comfortable. They have hearts of gold and will do anything for anyone. They have a wealthy togetherness. At Christmas-tide Ken is invited to stay over for three nights in the spare room. On Christmas Eve, all together as a family, they dress the Christmas tree in the living room with real candles and small edible gifts. They stash presents (not expensive ones) under the tree then they go to church together 'dressed in their best' where they sing carols in German, 'Stille Nacht' being Ken's favourite. Upon returning home, all the lights in the house are switched off while they light the candles on the tree, open their gifts, and enjoy a simple but traditional meal of sausage and potato salad.

On Christmas Day they get stuck into a big meal of goose with potato dumplings, superb tasty stuffing and red cabbage (which is not to Ken's liking) followed by Apfelstruedel. It is the only time Ken sees Herr Maier drink anything stronger than coffee; they heartily swig back a generous toast to Christmas.

Outside, the snow is billowing and it is desperately cold (-10degrees C). The advent wreath hangs by the door, and the spruce in the front garden is adorned with white lights. Herr Maier lights a wood fire in the living room and they sit all together and enjoy each other's company. The Maier's sing in German, Ken sings in English and they all talk and laugh and get to know each other even better, even though sometimes they have to guess what each other intends! Music is the international language of love.

The Maiers start to treat Ken like a family member and begin to invest their trust in him. There is no bitter arguing, no television Christmas specials, no excesses, no 'me': the romantic ideal of Christmas! Only the wind is bitter, and even that caresses the woodland darkness, singing through the branches to morning light!

The fact that Herr Maier never had a son perhaps means that he sees Ken as the next best thing. Although their names are Jorg und Giessaler, Herr and Frau Maier are always addressed thus by Ken. There is deep respect for one's elders in Germany, an innate reverence, not one that is prescribed.

Ken respects Herr Maier, but unlike his own father, Herr Maier respects Ken. He treats him like an equal. He has elegant style, but he is worldly-wise and never lectures Ken or makes demands on him. He is non-judgemental and even though he has read enough about the antics of the English pop groups, he knows there is a concept gap between the printed broadsheet and the person who holds his daughter's hand.

The Maiers have brought Ken back from the brink. Now he is blooming again; he is their golden daffodil and is full of life and confidence. He, in turn, becomes a guiding light for the lost-in-the-Alley Cats! He is getting rave reviews in local and national music press. Unfortunately, all good things come to an end.

The contract with the Alley Cats soon runs out and they also return to England. Ah well, nothing lasts forever! The best he can arrange is to front a band that is about to tour on the Starpalast circuit through

Germany, then Italy. Yet again, it is 'make your mind up' time for Ken Waterfield; yet again this virtuoso has to consider abandoning his safety net in favour of leaping onto the trapeze!

One day he gets into deep discussion with Carola's father, another opportunity to practise his English on Ken. The story Herr Maier tells is mind-boggling! It is all about how Hamburg was bombed into oblivion during one week in July 1943 and the effect on him, his family and his lovely city. It is a long story told with passion and tears. All that Ken really remembers is that 42,000 Hamburg locals were killed by allied bombers.

It was horrific what happened, absolutely terrible. But Mr Maier, then sixteen years-old, luckily escaped and eventually married his wife, followed by the birth of Carola. His story is long and detailed and with many breaks whilst words are translated from German into English, but he concludes: 'Why did I tell you this story, Ken? Well, I lost my parents and my grandparents that night! I do not want to lose Carola! She is all I have. I have protected her all these years and I will continue to love and guard her until the day I die. She is so special to me and I hope this story will help explain exactly why.

'Carola is going to University soon. It has always been her dream. It has always been my dream for her, and out of respect for our family, I expect you to let her go. Please do not try and convince her otherwise. You left your family to pursue your dream; now Carola will do the same.'

Ken has never heard such emotion before. He is totally dumbfounded of something sensible to say. His brain is in shock and has shut down, such is the intensity of Mr Maier's story. Suddenly and unexpectedly from his heart come the words: 'Mr Maier, I am so, so sorry you lost your family. I do not have the words to say more but trust me I will never do anything but good in my relationship with Carola. You have my word and my handshake on that.'

He moves toward Mr Maier and offers his hand, which is warmly taken and shaken. Mr Maier then hugs him.

'It is a privilege to be part of your family. Thank you for all your help and support!'

*

Ken decides to leave Hamburg because he needs money and work and his mission is still unfulfilled. Herr Maier's story of Hamburg in 1943 makes him realize that perhaps he is not the right man for Carola, or, if he is the right man, then this is certainly not the right time. Mr Maier tells him in his own Germanic way to go, whereas Ken's dad only told him not to bother to come back.

Carola is to be away at university eight months of the year. It is not an easy decision for Ken, but it is discussed with the Maiers, not only Carola but her father, too. He gets their input, their perspective. It makes sense; it is logical but it hurts him and Carola like hell. He leaves Hamburg with their blessing, with their friendship intact, with tears in his eyes and with an offer to return as often as he wants.

Ken leaves with his new band, a bit less rock 'n' roll, a bit more middle of the road. The music industry is changing, and they tour: Hamburg, Berlin, Flensburg, Kiel, Koln, Bielefeld, Dortmund, Gelsenkirchen, Dusseldorf... up to twenty German cities with each venue holding hundreds of fans, an endless round of travelling and performing. Ken speaks with Carola on the phone daily, then weekly, then monthly then rarely.

Ken treated Carola initially like a best friend. Then she became more like a sister, but as the weeks went by he fell more and more for her. He slept with her once, the week before he left Hamburg for the circuits. Her parents were out of town for a family event. Carola and Ken had the place to themselves and he made love to her and rather than it being an end to their relationship, he hopes that it may have sealed their friendship forever. Again Ken falls in love, beds the girl once and is then off. Coincidence… or something more profound?

Ken is in love with Carola. When he leaves, he really misses her for weeks. His singing improves with its greater sense of feeling. He is so sad that he even writes some ballads and sings them on stage. Ken is mellowing and has fallen in love also with Germany.

A wise man could draw a parallel between Herr Maier and Ken. In July 1943, aged sixteen, Mr Maier lost his parents and grandparents in a firestorm. In August 1963, aged eighteen, Ken lost his parents and grandparents in a brainstorm. The big difference? Ken had a choice; Mr Maier had no choice!

Chapter 29

1982

'Thanks for meeting up, Val. I'm feeling a bit down and need my best friend and fellow mum to talk to.'

'What's up, Lin? When you call me for a chat, I get worried. Let's get the coffee on.'

'My Richard, like your Kevin, is coming on eighteen now. He's always at school, hanging with his mates, off for weekends away camping, Val. He's never at home except to sleep!'

'Amazing how time flies, Lin. At least my Kevin tends to be at home more, studying for his exams and playing football on Saturday afternoons. It doesn't seem five minutes ago that we were teenage mums: kids in pushchairs promenading around the park, around the boating lake, feeding the ducks, making daisy chains, chatting on the park benches by the aviary. We'd push the kids across to the swings, the slide and the roundabout. We'd have big debates on breast-feeding, nappy rash, teething, child-rearing, schools and husbands.'

'I know, Val. We were both always shattered, never time to sleep, no time for ourselves, our clothes always smelly with sick and grubby with stains. But they were wonderful times, and we enjoyed many rewards for the hard work we put in. We had picnics in summer, went swimming with the kids down the open air pool and leant upon each other for years. It was great to have a good friend who was in exactly the same boat as me.'

'My Gary has been a great father up to now, but I never get to see him anymore. As a husband he's a dead loss. Ever since he started his own building company he works six days a week, and often Sundays preparing quotes and contracts. If he's home then he's asleep in front of the tele. To put it bluntly, Val, he looks knackered and I feel lonely.'

'Yes, setting up the Party Plan business together was a good idea. It's been Ok, mixing with the local girls, having get-togethers in each other's houses. It is going better than I expected.'

'We are good together. We've got a good name. I'm glad we

expanded to clothing, lingerie and cosmetics. It is great.'

'It is a real challenge and we earn some good money. You are even Area Manager of the plastics house-ware company.'

'And you the same on the lingerie side.'

'It makes us feel appreciated. We get out and about, meet new people and develop ourselves. Right little business women we are!'

'This is why I need to talk to you, Val. As you know, I have to attend one-day Head Office seminars on new products, special promotions and debrief quarterly in London. I travel down by train early morning, then get back really late on the same day. Long days - lots of talking, lunch and dinner. It makes a nice change and I meet new faces.'

'So what, Lin?'

'Well, some of the people who travel to London from further a-field arrive the evening before and stay over in the hotel where the seminar is to take place so they are fresh in the morning. All expenses paid. One of the Head Office managers suggested that I did that. So I did, and guess what?'

'Linda Hall, you never… you ended up in bed together. Correct?'

'Spot on! You know me well, Val. In fact there is more than one guy; I put it about a bit, I am ashamed to say.'

'Linda! Linda, how do you look when you're ashamed?' she asked, shaking her head. 'You're incorrigible. You're a fabulous girl, but what the hell possesses you to behave like that? What about poor Gary?'

'I know! I'm an idiot, a complete bloody idiot! There's been a couple of other dalliances previous to this, moments of weakness. It's the fun aspect and Gary knows nothing about what I'm up to, which makes it more exciting. I've realised what I'd missed all these years. My twenties and thirties have been spent being Mum. This is my time, some freedom to be a bit wild. I'm now living out the rest of my youth. It's me, being me. I need a change; I need some fun; I need to be loved.'

'I feel like this, too, now and again,' says Val, 'but I don't leap into bed with guys from Head Office?'

'You could! I've seen blokes chat you up loads of times!'

'I could, but I've more sense! And more control!'

Linda lowers her voice and looks around the room. 'Sex is an activity for which I have innate talent. Moreover, I find it intensely enjoyable.

Out of the blue, I've had an opportunity to spread my wings and I meet guys who are similar to me - married, but a little mislaid by their partners. I'm not stealing them from their wives. I only borrow them for our joint pleasure. Providing we're discreet and if we're not discovered, then it's just passing fun and doesn't break anyone's marriage or cause any lasting harm.'

'It's bloody risky, Linda.'

'Also part of the fun, Val - top ingredient!'

'But Lin, you have Gary to consider!'

'Over the years, Gary has gradually forgotten that he has a wife. He has a house, a business and a son. I'm well down his pecking order. I've not fallen out of love with Gary, or in love with any of my weekend associates. I need fun and sex, company and affection. None has become serious enough to jeopardise my marriage. I've always come home to Gary.'

Val looks at Linda, but says nothing.

'Well, there is one particular bloke.'

'I knew it!'

'The single overnight stays are now set to become a long weekend - fortnightly. My head's got well and truly turned and I'm not thinking straight. You must remember that I've only ever dated Gary and I got pregnant at eighteen. Anyhow, this guy, Eric, wants me to go and live with him in London. But I haven't told Eric that I have a son and husband to look after, too. I hide my rings in my handbag.'

'All of this is unbeknown to Gary?'

'Gary's working like a Trojan. He sees me unhappy, then he sees me very happy. Who wouldn't be, with all the frolics in London? I know that he's beginning to feel that something isn't right. Our own relationship is going down the sewer, and we've become ships that pass in the night.'

'What I really need to tell you is that I'm going to London tomorrow for the day. I've told Gary that I'm going to be around your house again. Ok?'

'Linda, it's not fair to drag me into it!'

'It's the last time, Val. I'll tell Eric tomorrow that it's over, and I'm also going to resign from the business.'

'You are?'

'Yes, I certainly am.'

'You're going to return to drudgery and loneliness? Why don't you tell Gary that unless he eases up on work and takes you out more then you're leaving him. See how he reacts.'

'That's not a bad idea. How do you think he will?'

'I don't know. I'm not a bloke, but if I was him I'd do as you say.'

'He's addicted to work, Val. It's like a drug for him.'

'A bit like sex is for you.'

'Now, now, Val! I'll tell him this evening, but I need you to cover for me tomorrow. Ok? This once?'

'This once only, providing we can meet up on Sunday and you can update me on what happened. By the way, if you're going to quit, I think I'll pack in the business, too!'

*

The following afternoon is Saturday. Gary is not at work, but as usual he is working at home, upstairs in his office, preparing some plans and quotes. His mood is melancholy.The previous evening he had a strange conversation with Linda. It had come out of nowhere.

'Gary, we need to talk!' Gary is slumped in front of the tele in the dozing zone somewhere between awake and asleep.

Linda turns off the television. She is in a mood. Gary hates her moods, hates the confrontation, hates the scene, the tears, the accusations. All he wants is a simple and easy life. He doesn't need histrionics, they wear him out. He braces himself for the onslaught.

'I've told you endlessly that I'm unhappy, and I'm unhappy with you.'

'I know.'

'You know? You know? Yes, you know, Gary! I've told you enough times - but nothing ever changes. We talk, you agree - then nothing! Unless you give me more of your time then this marriage is over and I'm leaving you!'

'Linda, I've told you endlessly that if you want to live in a big house and you want the best clothes and the best and most expensive holidays, then I have to give everything to the business. What more do you want?'

'I want all weekends and two or three evenings each week of your time for myself. When did we last have a quiet night in? An early night - come to think of it, when did we last make love? Gary, I can't do this anymore. Can't you see what a lonely life I lead? No Richard, no you, no life!'

'You've got your business interests with Val.'

'It's not enough! I'm fed up with it! I'm chucking it in! You and I need to get back to how it used to be. I'm not even sure that you love me any more!'

'Of course I do, love.' Gary must have had this conversation at least seven or eight times over the last couple of years. It upsets him to see his wife like this, but without hiring extra staff which the business definitely cannot afford, his workload keeps increasing. The discussion lasts less than an hour, but the fallout from it, as it always does, lasts for the rest of the evening and night. Linda goes to bed at 11pm, still in a bad mood. Gary follows a little after midnight. By then Linda's asleep and he slips into bed beside her. An hour later, after much cogitation on what she has said, now with a dull headache, he falls asleep.

When he awakes at 8am, he is sleeping alone. The shower is running and Linda is singing. 'I'm off the hook,' he thinks, guessing that the coast is clear. Half an hour later he realises that he is very much not off the hook!

'Think about what I said last night, Gary. I'll see you later. I'm with Val all day.'

'What time will you be back?'

'Whenever. Bye.' Without feeling, she kisses him on the cheek as she picks up her car keys and makes for the door.

*

It is now the late afternoon; it is cold and getting dark outside. Gary is sitting snugly and warm at his drawing board, and actually thinking to himself, 'Ah, this is the life and no difficulties since this morning. It will all blow over as usual.'

He has a cup of coffee and a couple of chocolate biscuits. A music tape plays in the background. Then, out of the blue, with no warning, no prior exertion, no specific preceding emotional trauma that one would suspect might've brought it on, it happens! He feels a sudden, sharp and steady pain in the centre of his chest.

Analysing it, he doesn't have the well-known heart symptoms of arm- numbness or pain spreading away from the centre. It seems concentrated in one area. It's the sort of pain that you can still feel hours, even days, after it has gone, it is that bad. At first, he thinks it is perhaps a pocket of gas from his stomach, but he remembers that he hasn't eaten much that day, although he does tend to get a bit of indigestion or heartburn at times. He tries to burp the gas away, but there is no relief. The pain becomes more intense, and he begins to realize that it's not going away and he might be in serious trouble.

He now cannot think totally straight and begins to panic. He shouts for Linda. Is she back yet? He hasn't heard her return and she would normally call him or come upstairs when she returns home. The house is silent. Gary is alone and certainly in a bit of trouble. He curses Linda's absence when he desperately needs her here. She always seems to be out, nowadays.

He decides to look for some medication, painkillers or whatever might help. He struggles downstairs, slowly keeping a strong hold on the stair rail then staggering through to the kitchen cabinet. But all in vain, as there is nothing of any use there.

He goes back upstairs to the bathroom to look in his travel kit. He stoops down to get it from the vanity unit under the sink and realizes he isn't going to be able to stand and bend over. He sits down on the edge of the bath, feeling absolutely awful and searches in vain. He is now sweating very hard; his breathing seems a bit laboured and he has gone clammy. He goes back to the office to get to the phone to call Linda at Val's.

Val answers.

'Thank God you're there, Val. I need Linda to come home. I'm having really bad chest pains. She needs to come at once.'

Val is distraught. Linda is not with her and by now probably holed up in some sleazy flat in West London with a chancer called Eric. What should she say? Val is still considering.

'Val, are you still there?'

'She's out at the supermarket right now, Gary. How can I help? Have you called 999 for an ambulance? Should I call them?'

'Yes, please call them, Val, and get Linda back here pronto. God I feel awful!'

*

When Gary arrives at the hospital, he is wheeled in. He is intercepted by a nurse and a doctor who bend over him asking lots of questions, but it is clear that he can make no sense of what is being said, or form an answer. He is somewhere else, the same as his wife.

When he 'comes to' he is in Intensive Care hooked up to an ECG monitor, an oxygen mask over his face, a cannula in each arm, a drip already pumping life into him, his vital stats being checked and displayed on the monitor. He is scared, terrified!

He feels freezing cold. His blood pressure is low and his initial thoughts are, 'It can't end here. It can't end now after all we've been through. Surely not! How will Linda manage without me? The business will surely fail. Richard will be devastated. I can't leave him, and Mum and Dad; they're not too well themselves. I need to see them again.'

Everything Gary has worked for over all the years, all the late nights, all the sleepless nights, would be for nothing. The lights would go out and that would be the end of Gary Hall. It would be the proverbial red book and Eamonn Andrews - the long tunnel of brilliant white light, then nothing!

'I'm scared to death. I need to see Linda!'

The next thing Gary is aware of is again waking in a bed in Intensive Care. Soon they get him stabilised then they let Linda into the room. Gary is shocked. Linda's face seems to have aged ten years. Tears run down her face and her eye make-up is ruined; she looks distraught!

'Linda, if I don't survive this then I want you to know that I love you. I really love you, sweetheart!'

'Don't be silly, love, of course you'll survive it.' She is very reassuring.

Within days he is greatly improved and sent back into a normal ward for recuperation. Lots of people visit him, including Val and even Colin and Dave who he hasn't seen for ages, following on from which he starts to make regular contact again and go out for a beer (or in

Gary's case, an orange juice) or with their respective wives for a meal. Lots of family, friends and workmates phone or visit and send cards and flowers. Gary is amazed to learn that so many people care about what happens to him.

He is prescribed a mountain of multi-coloured pills and capsules, then spends the next couple of weeks taking follow-up tests and resting before he returns home.

The whole hospital experience he finds manic. There is no time to sleep. It is all eating, washing, medication, doctor visits, bed making, ward cleaning, blood tests, blood pressure tests, X-rays, results and visitors.

Gary is worn out when he gets home; he needs peace, quiet and sleep. Both Gary and Linda need time to reflect on what is happening to their marriage.

Chapter 30

1995

The Alitalia jet from Rome begins its descent into Malpensa.

'Ok, so where does our star couple live?' Arnaud Moretti, Italy's best known celebrity photographer, connects his seatbelt and prepares himself for the landing. 'Even though she is in her early-sixties, Signora Lombardi is still one of the best-looking and best-dressed women that I ever photographed. He is extremely fortunate!'

'A big estate on Lake Como. It is an hour's drive north. A car is waiting for us. We have a one-hour appointment at 11am.' Elmo Vega is the chief features writer with 'A-List Italia', the country's best-selling celebrity magazine.

'An hour with Italy's best-loved celebrity couple? Not bad. How did you manage that?'

'We normally get ten minutes, but there is an upcoming album and tour so he needs all the publicity he can get.'

At five minutes to eleven, the car pulls in front of the closed iron gates at 'Villa Pomona'. A security camera blinks then the gates clank open. The car purrs along the gravel drive and the two men are greeted at the side door by publicist to the stars, Gianni Giordano ('GG' to his friends) and invited in.

Ken arrives for the interview first; five minutes later Aniela Lombardi sweeps down the curved staircase and gracefully enters the room. Vega is taken aback. She is slender, five feet nine inches tall and meticulously groomed with her dark hair swept back. She has a slim waist and almost endless legs - a classic natural beauty. Her skin is porcelain-smooth. She wears little make-up with a hint of light lipstick.

Aniela is dressed in a simple ensemble, in perfect taste and harmony, with a youthful air, not adventurous but not conservative. Chic blue jeans with a crisp, white blouse and neck scarf, are her immaculately well-cut day clothes. Vega also knows from what Arnaud has told him that she has the ability to wear beautiful and elegant costumes at society cocktail parties. The simplest gown becomes distinguished when she wears it.

Ken looks cool in a dark, three-buttoned Armani, charcoal suit, with an open-necked cranberry-coloured shirt, sleek black Oxfords and wraparound shades. A silver Rolex adorns his hairy left wrist.

Moretti sets up his cameras, arc lights, white umbrellas and tripod as Vega opens up his pocket-sized tape recorder on the antique, rosewood coffee table. Ken and Aniela sit closely together on the settee.

'Shall we begin?' Vega looks to them for a nod of agreement. 'I will start at the beginning of your career, finishing with the forthcoming tour, if that's Ok.'

'February 25th 1995, Villa Pomona with Signor Ken Waite and Signora Aniela Lombardi are Elmo Vega and Arnaud Moretti.' Vega introduces the participants to his recorder.

'Mr Waite, you have been in the music industry a long time. Where did it all begin?'

'Northampton, a small town in central England in the early 60's. I fronted a local band - Kenny Waters and the Waders.'

'The UK led the 1960s' Music Revolution. Why did you not want to try and launch a career there?'

'In 1963, I was eighteen and inexperienced. I needed regular daily work. I decided to develop myself in Hamburg for a while. I then started a band which toured all over Europe for many years. If I had stayed in the UK I would have married young, had kids and never had a music career at all. I was destined to become an accountant; it was a tough decision to leave.'

'Was it the right decision?'

'Definitely!'

'I guess the early days were the hardest!'

'After leaving Hamburg I was on a relentless treadmill of road travel to lonely rooms of dingy back-street hotels, grabbing meals when I could. I had no settled lifestyle, no close friends, only the boys in the band for company. I was smoking and drinking far too much, partying and not sleeping long enough.'

'The rock 'n' roll lifestyle, eh?'

'You could say that, but it eventually caught up with me when my voice started to play up. Initially, I contracted bronchitis. I was coughing incessantly. My voice got hoarse and gravelly, then tender. I struggled to sing the high notes. This led to me becoming stressed. Something had to give. One evening I had to walk off stage mid-concert; my voice - my income - was a spent force.'

'Your voice was your life. You must have been terrified.'

'As it never seemed to improve, I paid 'top dollar' to a specialist in Zurich who attacked things holistically. I took one step at a time. I had to stop singing. I even had to stop talking for nearly a week, speaking only occasionally during the second week - imagine that!'

'What did the doctors find?'

'I had a couple of medical issues. Firstly polyps on my vocal cords, which needed surgery. I was getting acid reflux which was damaging my throat and causing inflammation. The doctor sorted out my sleep. I quit smoking and stopped drinking alcohol and caffeine. He improved my diet and my liquid intake. I practised relaxation and meditation techniques. I even exercised.'

'Were the polyps cancerous?'

'No, luckily they weren't, so I was confident enough to consult a vocal coach and move on. She helped me to control my breathing and taught me how best to train and protect my voice for the long haul.

'I guess by then your career had ground to a halt?'

'I thought I was finished. I had little money left and was depressed. It was a tough time. I needed some balance back in my life.'

'How did you get that?'

'What this period of rehabilitation did was enable me to take stock of where I had come from, what I had achieved, where I was heading and how I was going to fulfil my dreams.

'What were your dreams?'

'To make it to the top and to perform at the highest level.'

'How did you channel your career?'

'I needed to change my style for the various European club circuits, as much for the shows as for my own stimulation. I made music my best friend and found solace in it. I listened endlessly to other singers and learned to play guitar, read music and play the piano. I had daily singing practice to keep my voice in shape. I was a driven man. I knew that I wouldn't progress by touring endlessly, singing cover songs in the same style as the original.'

'You became a song-writer, too?'

'Yes, the years of singing covers gave me a good appreciation of song construction and writing provided a new string to my bow.'

'You continued touring?'

'My new band toured all over Europe. I mellowed the act and focused on love songs from all music idioms - pop, country, blues, soul, jazz. I had found my niche and exploited it. I wanted every stage appearance to be like it was the first. I got to understand that if you keep moving then you eventually reach nowhere. I was also lucky to be given two gifts: one, the ability to dream of a better life; the second, the ability to know that one day I could make it happen. Yet my goal remained frustratingly out of reach.

'Was it at this time you met Signora Lombardi?'

'Yes, we initially met in Zurich, at the hospital. It happened by chance. We got talking and we took a shine to each other. After a while, she became my manager. We fell in love and eventually got married and bought this house.

'Our readers would already be aware of the details of Signora Lombardi's unfortunate car crash in which her first husband was killed, her consequent desperate fight for life and long recovery from her bad internal injuries and, of course, her coming to terms with her loss.'

Ken looks sadly toward his wife and puts up his crossed finger sign to change the subject.

'You do not have any children. Is this by choice or… ?'

'Let me answer this please, Ken.' Aniela quickly intercedes. 'Mr Vega, I could not have children, due to my injuries. I made Ken aware of this before we started our relationship. We both accepted the situation.'

'Did you, Mr Waite, want any children?' Ken puts his hand softly on top of his wife's, which is resting on her lap.

'Let me answer, please, darling.' Aniela nods her approval.

Both Aniela and Vega look closely at his face for a reaction and listen intently to the words he would choose. 'At this time, my career was in full swing. I was fulfilling my potential. My mountain was about to be conquered. I had my passion back for singing. Maybe a few years previous or a few years later I would have been ready for kids, but fate deemed it was not to be.'

'Your wife became your manager. How does she help you in your career?'

'Aniela initially taught me Italian. She works with me on my songs and helps me with interviews for television, radio, the newspapers and music magazines. We have many things to organise: albums and tours to promote; fan-mail to answer; souvenir programmes, posters, and album covers to design; merchandising to manage; photos to autograph. Aniela has a lot of contacts and oversees all. We are both devoted to my career and like to be 'hands-on'.'

'And as a wife?'

'Invaluable! She steadied my ship; I could trust her. She developed our wonderful home and filled the garden with beautiful flowers and trees: a Garden of Eden; 'La dolce vita'.

'My wife also hosts amazing evenings with friends, cooks sumptuous local dishes and even taught me to cook.

'Is he any good, Signora?'

'Not bad - for an English boy!' She smiles then sticks her tongue out at Ken.

'How is the Signora at cooking?

'Aniela is a fabulous cook. She was taught by her mother that you need time, patience and focus, plus the magic ingredient!'

'The magic ingredient?'

Aniela intervenes: 'The magic ingredient, Mr Vega, is love. You must put all your love into your cooking. This indicates your joy of living. To cook for somebody is to really love them.'

Ken concludes the answer: 'Aniela cooks with tears in her eyes... tears of joy!'

They are now holding hands as Ken continues, 'Aniela is a very touchy-feely person. Lots of hand-holding, as you see, cuddling and kissing. A spell in her company will always leave you in better shape than before you met her. She manages me, she promotes me, she loves me, she adores me and I adore and love her. We will share everything until the end.'

A tear starts to form in Aniela's eye. She looks adoringly across to Ken.

'A tribute indeed, Signora. How is your life with an international singing star?'

'When we met, we both had major problems. We helped each other to overcome these. He's the yin to my yang. I wanted a companion. I wanted a passionate lover. I wanted a role and a role model. My husband and I still have to work at our marriage. Our relationship is about kindness and compromise and we constantly watch what we say and how we say it.'

'You certainly both seem easy together.'

'We are, most of the time.'

'Not all the time?' Vega is quick to seize upon a possible imperfection.

'We are together twenty-four seven; it is not always possible to be on top form, to agree on everything. It is normal for couples to have their differences.'

'If you disagree, who wins?' Vega is keen to know more. Perhaps a headline is evolving.

Ken is used to interviews and Vega is not the toughest by far. 'If we are discussing the house, the garden, relationships, Aniela wins.' He pauses. 'If we are discussing my career, then of course, she wins also!'

They all laugh. Ken has teased Vega, and the moment is lost. Vega changes the subject. 'How do you find Italy and the Italian people, Mr Waite?'

'The Italians are greedy people: greedy for life, greedy for love, and they live for their families. They express their feelings with real intensity. They can have the noisiest and most emotional argument. When it has ended it is forgotten completely. They love music in their ears, art in their eyes and good food and wine in their bellies. It is like starring in an Italian movie. Fantastico!'

'Do you have a daily routine or is each day unique?'

'No, if we are at home we need a routine. Whoever wakes first will make breakfast, which we usually take together on the terrace. No phone calls are made or answered before breakfast is over. At home, Aniela insists we speak in English; if we are out with friends, we speak Italian. The exceptions are my German friends, Carola and Peter Lehmann, with whom we speak English, too.

Once Aniela caught me talking in German with Carola. She was not happy and let me know it… in pure Italian! If Aniela gets angry, beware! An eruption of Vesuvian magnitude will ensue, but it has never happened above a half a dozen times in all our years together.'

Vega and his photographer are engrossing themselves in the interview, so much so that Moretti has suddenly remembered that he hasn't taken any photos. He intervenes: 'Perhaps we can take a ten-minute break for photographs. Maybe three shots of Mr Waite and two of Signora Lombardi?'

'You surely have sufficient of me, Arnaud?' Aniela knows him from her fashion shoots over many years.

'I can never have enough shots of you, Signora.'

'You are very kind, or maybe just a little naughty.' They smile at each other.

Moretti directs them to the various locations in the room best suited to his needs and gets to work. He knows how simple it is to get a great shot of Aniela. She is so beautiful that only a novice could fail to make her look stunning.

'Mr Waite, a few years ago the newspapers were accusing you of infidelity with a string of young ladies?' Vega goes on the offensive; he still feels that he has not uncovered anything shocking.

'The paparazzi started to chase me - looking for scandal, never found any, so they made it up. I was rich, drove fast cars and was linked with all sorts of beautiful and famous women. It was all fabrication. I was and still am dedicated to my wife. They soon got bored and moved on.' Ken crosses his two index fingers and pre-empts any further questions on this subject.

'Why do you think you made it big in Italy, where you had failed previously in other countries?'

'I never failed in other countries. It took a special country like Italy to recognize my voice and song-writing talents.'

'You have a tour starting next month. Do you still enjoy touring?'

'I am looking forward to the challenge. I prefer to sing before a full stadium or theatre rather than private parties and small venues; there I can escape into my own little world. Often, I sing to Aniela. She is my audience of one, coming to every show!'

'Do you read the reviews?'

'Aniela's critique enables me to polish the act day by day. That is the only review I need.'

'What can you, Signora, tell us about your husband that our readers will surely not know?'

'What your readers may not know is that when it comes to ladies fashion - dresses, handbags, shoes, jewellery - ask Ken anything and he probably knows as much as me. Chanel, Dior, Givenchy, Gucci, St Laurent, McQueen; he knows their stores, he knows their wares and he knows their designers.'

'Is that true, Mr Waite?'

'I love shopping with Aniela. If she is shopping with me alongside her, she is at her happiest. If she is happy, then I am happy.'

'How would you define your wife's fashion sense, Mr Waite?'

'Aniela believes that clothes should make a woman look like a woman - soft, feminine and graceful. She thinks that you should see the woman first and the clothes afterwards.'

'You are reaching, dare I say it, fifty years old. Will you continue performing and for how long?'

'When my voice goes or people stop buying tickets to see me on stage, then I will stop.'

'You are a very rich couple. How do you enjoy that wealth?'

'Aniela was very rich through her husband before I met her. Then her father, who was an industrial magnate, passed away and left her further wealth. I have earned a lot of money from my career.

'For our fashion trips, we bought an apartment overlooking the Jardins du Luxembourg in Paris and we have a studio apartment overlooking Central Park in New York. We like to rest up on our yacht in the Med.'

'Are there charities that you both support?'

'Of course. We have set up the Aniela Lombardi Foundation and each year set aside a significant sum. We sponsor a young person under eighteen to train in Bologna with a view to becoming a top opera singer. Aniela loves opera and whenever I hear it I think of her; it is a beautiful combination. The reason I am going back on the road is to donate to our foundation.'

‘Is there any other subject we can discuss before we finish?’

‘No, I think you’ve covered everything. Mr Arnaud and Mr Vega, have a safe trip back to Rome.’

Ken and Aniela leave the room and head back upstairs. Once out of ear-shot, Aniela stops and turns to Ken.

‘Ken, I’ve got a telecom with Paris scheduled for two o’clock. That gives us around two hours. Shall I make lunch or… ?’

He smiles adoringly and caresses her. ‘Better idea, my angel. Why don’t I open a bottle of vintage Burgundy and I’ll see you in bed in five minutes?’

‘No, Ken. I think not.’

PART FOUR

SEPTEMBER 15 2010

REUNION

Chapter 31

0900h

It is eight o'clock on a warm late-summer's day. The flight from Milan is a quarter of an hour early, giving Ken time for a quick phone call before transferring to the Northampton train. He stashes his bag in the overhead rack, then settles back and stretches out his long legs following the cramped conditions on the packed early morning flight, starts to relax, and closes his eyes. He is very tired having not slept very much last night. It has all happened so quickly following that most unexpected phone call yesterday.

*

It is midday in Northern Italy. The Lombardy air is bright and sharp, clean and clear. The sun is towering overhead, brilliant in the blue cloudless sky, and very warm. Alongside the many narrow stone paths in the long, winding garden, beds of flowers and flowering shrubs are in full show, vibrant with colour and oozing their perfume. Bees buzz, insects hover or scurry busily around. Frisky, patrolling male cicadas click and tymbalise their mating love songs as their female quarries flick their wings in a 'C'mon, then' sort of way.

Ken is standing under a huge, ivory-coloured sun-shade at a large, solid oak table on his terracotta-tiled terrace. The hot sun is drying his six-foot plus, lightly-tanned frame since completing his self-imposed, daily routine of swimming a hundred lengths of his outdoor pool.

Midway through his exercise he thinks he hears the phone ring more than once. Each time it disturbs his concentration but not his stroke, then it suddenly stops; his secretary must have picked it up at last. He straightens his hair with his left hand then from the table he picks up his sunglasses and the remaining half glass of ice-cold freshly-pressed orange juice that he has poured himself half an hour earlier. It is a perfect drink for a perfect day and today he feels particularly energised and decides that he deserves a little reward for his well-being.

He gazes out, down, then across the large expanse of the lake below, shimmering with a phosphorescent gleam, which merges perfectly on the horizon with the grey and green wooded hills and the deep blue sky. The magnificent unspoilt beauty of the scene occasionally is disturbed by a distant tourist steamer, a small wispy white cloud, or a glinting aeroplane high above the distant hills.

He moves the heavy crystal tumbler to his lips and as the fruity aroma starts to penetrate his nostrils, the phone rings again. He takes a taste, swallows, satisfyingly nods to himself then places the now-empty glass back down. He looks up as his attention moves to the large window overlooking the veranda where a woman with long chestnut hair, much younger than him, very attractive, tanned and well-dressed in a vivid multi-coloured silk blouse and deep blue cotton trouser suit, points and gestures to him with her hand, thumb and small finger spread apart to suggest there is a call he needs to take.

Ken slips on his canvas espadrilles, dons a lightweight, pale lemon-coloured cotton gown, and moves toward the phone which is through the wide open, sliding double doors in the large living room behind him.

In the hall of her three-bedroomed semi in Northampton's Spinney Hill, Val has picked up the receiver twice in the last fifteen minutes, dialled and then both times baulked and replaced it without speaking. She takes a deep breath, then, for the third time, she picks up the scribbled piece of torn-out address book paper and starts to key in the number. She looks apprehensive, but she feels hopeful. After a few moments the ringing tone cuts in but after ten seconds there is still no answer. She clears her throat and waits: nothing! 'Is it the right number? Did I copy it down correctly? Ah well, try again later.'

After ten minutes she decides to try once more, the last time. Right: she dials; it rings. Then: 'Buon giorno. Villa Pomona.'

It is a woman's voice, in a foreign tongue which she presumes is Italian. This surprises Val; she is not expecting a woman to answer, but if she is quite honest with herself, she is not really sure what she is expecting. In her best East Midlands English accent she asks for Ken Waterfield. Val speaks particularly slowly and correctly in polite recognition of the fact that the woman is obviously not English, and Val knows not one word of Italian.

'Hold the line, please. Mr erhm… Waterfield will be right with you.

Who is calling?' comes the reply in perfect English.

'I am an old friend with some news for him.'

After twenty nerve-racking seconds Val hears what, to her, are magical words: 'Hello, Ken speaking.'

'Ken, I don't know whether you remember me. It's Valerie, Valerie erhm...,' she stalls momentarily, 'Roberts, calling from Northampton, England.' Her voice is nervous, hesitant and totally lacking in self-confidence.

'Please remember me, Ken,' she thinks to herself. 'Please!'

A five-second pause ensues as Ken gets his brain in gear. To Val, it feels more like an hour! Her heart pounds and her breathing quickens as she waits for his response. Or will he just hang up without saying another word?

'Valerie Roberts? The Val Roberts? My Val Roberts? Crikey! Hello, Val. It's been a helluva long time! Wow! I'm sorry for the delay, but I'm so surprised, no, shocked, to hear from you. I wondered who it might be asking for Mr Waterfield. I haven't used that name in years. What are you doing calling me up after all this time? Where are you? Northampton, did you say?'

Val is too nervous to remember to exchange pleasantries; she gets right to the point. 'Ken, I know this is right out of the blue, but I've some important news for you. I don't know whether you realise that I've kept closer contact with your mother since both your father and my parents passed away; we've now become quite close. I've been to see her today. She's in hospital. Ken, she's extremely poorly. She gave me your phone number from her address book and asked me to call you. She would really, really like to see you, Ken.'

Ken's initial surprise, then enthusiasm, in hearing from Val is quickly tempered as he absorbs the information she has given him. He sits down in a big, white leather armchair, his reinvigorated well-being now compromised on the strength of the news from England.

'What's happening with her, Val? Is she going to be Ok?'

'She had a fall at home a week ago, serious stuff when you're eighty eight. She was lying on the kitchen floor and was luckily found quite quickly by a neighbour who was doing a bit of shopping for her. They rushed her to hospital in an ambulance, but she's not getting any better; my understanding is that she has heart failure. The ward sister won't tell me much as I'm not family, but your mum asked that I call you. The prognosis doesn't sound good, Ken.'

Ken's sharp brain quickly assesses the situation, and he has already decided that he is on his way to England. If his mum has asked him to come, then it must be serious. Time to drop everything. In almost fifty years she has never before asked him to come home, not once.

'Ok, Val. I'll need to rearrange a few appointments here. There's absolutely nothing that can't be delayed for Mum. I'll check the flights. What number can I get back to you on? Do you have a cell-phone, Val?'

Val reads out both of her phone numbers; Ken correctly repeats them back to her.

'Right! I'll call you back later today, and as at now I'll plan to be there tomorrow morning. If the scheduled flights are fully-booked, then I'll try and organise something privately. I appreciate your concern, Val. Thanks for the call, and Val - the strangest thing -when you said, 'Ken, I don't know if you remember me,' I knew it was you instantly. I immediately recognised your voice. I knew it was you. Isn't that weird after all these years? Hey Val, are you keeping Ok?'

'Yes, I'm fine Ken, thanks.' Val is still not chatty, but not stand-offish, more business-like and 'to-the-point'.

'Ok, you go and get things organised and I'll expect your call later.' Val replaces the receiver. Her heart is pumping like an old steam engine! Her blood pressure is temporarily off the blood pressure equivalent of the Richter scale!'

She thinks to herself, 'After all these years he can still have that effect on me… Crikey! I thought he might not even know who on earth I was. He did! He really did!' Val feels excited, in fact exhilarated. She is going to see her Ken again after all these years. 'I wonder what he looks like now, and I wonder how I'll look to him? After all, I wasn't even eighteen when I last saw him!'

Ken feels shell-shocked, too. 'Val Roberts calling after all these years. I knew it was her. Amazing! Good of her to call. A great girl, my Val. I can't wait to see her again. Poor old Mum! Please hang on, Mum! I'm on my way.'

A few hours later, Val's mobile phone rings, and they agree to meet at the Northampton Castle Station café by the main exit at eleven o'clock the next morning, which Val confirms isn't very far from its original location.

Val puts the receiver down and immediately goes into headless-chicken mode. 'What should I wear? I have nothing to wear! I better go and wash my hair. I hope he still likes me. He still sounds really nice. I better wash the car and Hoover the house!' It is like being a teenager again on a first date, needing to impress a boy that she really fancies, not the sixty four year-old that she is now.

*

The Euston to Birmingham train stops at Northampton, the door opens and a tall, distinguished, very well-dressed man steps off . He is wearing a beautifully tailored, mid-blue, lightweight, silk and linen suit, an ivory-white, open-necked, button-down-collared, silk shirt and tan brown, leather Oxfords.

His hair is immaculately groomed, collar-length, with golden brown streaks mingling among his mainly grey mane which has little signs of any receding. He is half-wearing a long, dark blue trench-style mackintosh across his shoulders and he is pulling a brown leather, two-wheeled, cabin-bag with a briefcase mounted above it.

His splendid looks belie his sixty-plus years. He has the air of a man with total self-control, though unusually he is extremely anxious. He looks all around to find a friendly face then moves confidently and gracefully away from the train door. He takes a deep breath of local air, the first he has breathed for well over forty years and crosses the bridge.

There at the back of the platform by a neon café sign he spots a lady smartly but conservatively dressed in a cream-coloured blouse, dark skirt, short jacket and brooch with short-heeled brown shoes who is adjusting her blonde-streaked grey hair in the reflection from the café window.

She turns round quickly and nervously and scans the less-than-a-dozen passengers who leave the train and start heading for the station exit. 'Let him be handsome and friendly, let him be exactly like he used to be when he was 'my Ken'.'

Ken heads straight for her. He smiles nervously at first, but cannot hold back and suddenly, without control, he beams from ear to ear.

'Ken, over here. Hello Ken, it is you, isn't it?' She is churned up inside, a kaleidoscope of butterflies are holding a knees-up in her stomach. It is a warmish September morning but she feels chilly, shivering with nerves and anticipation as ice-cold adrenaline courses through her veins; her voice sounds shaky. She has a startled, worried look which will only subside when she hears his voice.

Before he can say anything, she jabbers nervously on. Right in front of her now is his face. Yes, it has aged but it is the same one that she has spent years wanting to reach out and touch. They look at each other for a second, neither really sure it is the other, but then the mists of time clear and they are both transported back to a time when they were young and in love.

'I'm so glad we arranged to meet by the café, else I thought I'd maybe not recognise you or you might not recognise me. You're looking really well. How was the trip over?'

'Hello Val, before I say anything please give me a lovely 'welcome home' hug.' They amusingly struggle for hand holds like two novice sumo wrestlers, then warmly embrace. He squeezes her up off her feet until she is struggling to breathe, and neither wants to be the first to let go.

'Oh yes, that's so good! Thanks again. Great! You still feel and look so good after all these years. It's wonderful to see you again, absolutely wonderful!' Ken speaks with the confidence of a successful man who is used to dealing with all sorts of people but as ever he feels particularly confident talking to women. He, too, is overcome and very emotional.

To his amazement, tears start to trickle from Ken's eyes. To meet again the girl he fell in love with as a child, his first love, and to see her smile at him is a great feeling: the best! It brings it all back: 'Your first love you remember forever,' he thinks, confirming to himself that this is true.

'Now I am close to you, I truly see you, Val. Your eyes haven't changed; they're as beautiful as ever they were. Oh yes, I remember those eyes. You look great, Val. I admit that I'm nervous to see you again, even more to see Mum. It all feels very peculiar being back in England, in my home town, after nearly fifty years. It's more than half a lifetime!'

Val's breath catches in her throat; she almost chokes! 'Don't be nervous with me, Ken. Be the person you always were.'

'Here is me telling him not be nervous,' smiles Val to herself. 'I'm quaking in my boots!'

'It's a pity that your return happens to be under unhappy circumstances.' she tells him.

'Has Mum's condition changed at all since we spoke late on the phone yesterday?'

Before Val answers his question, they start to walk towards the exit. 'Let's get to the car. It's a fifty-yard walk to the car park; follow me. To be honest, she's fading fast. Since her collapse last week I've been to see her every day and it's not looking good. I don't like saying this but I think perhaps you should prepare yourself for the worst.'

'Before you drive off, Val, let me take another long look at you.'

They turn to each other. Their tearful eyes meet. They both smile - almost chuckle; there still seems to be a tremendous bond between them, even after all this time.

'Yes, you look pretty damned good; you must have had a good life!' Her eyes soften even more. The startled look of a rabbit in the headlights has now completely gone. Her feelings untouched and untarnished are still as they had been on that fateful day in 1963. She already feels more relaxed.

'Thank you. Lots of compliments as ever; keep them coming. I can never get enough. You sit back and enjoy the short journey. You may notice a few changes since you were last here.'

The ice is broken: 'Good-looking woman!' thinks Ken.

'Wow, what a hunk!' thinks Val.

'I booked you a room for a couple of nights at the best hotel in town. I hope that's Ok.'

'Yes, fine. I appreciate all your help. On the journey, I thought back and reckoned that the last time I saw you was at the night club after our infamous performance at St Mary's Hall that ended in a punch-up!'

'That was indeed the group's final performance, Ken. I've thought back, too. I reckon it was August 31st,1963. After you left on the Sunday the group tumbled like a pack of cards as event upon event overtook them. How long it took you all to build it up; how quickly it all fell apart!'

'Never! What happened to the others?'

'You don't need me to tell you, Ken. They'll tell you themselves, in person, this evening. After you called back yesterday, I arranged with Colin and his wife for us all to meet up at their house for supper; we'll meet them around 8 o'clock.'

'By the way, Roger died in '85, God bless him! I will tell you his part of the story, after all I married him! I'm officially Valerie Edwards now!'

Ken swallows hard as he recoils from Val's blockbusting statement! He is shocked, even taken aback, but chooses not to comment lest he should say something he might regret.

*

After three hours at the hospital, the nurse asks them to leave so that Mrs Waterfield can get some rest. 'She's not well, Val, not well at all. There's nothing any of us can do for her.'

'There is,' she assures him. 'Don't give up on her yet, Ken. We must keep her in our thoughts and pray for her. We'll soon visit her again.'

'Of course, you're right. Thanks.' He smiles lovingly at her. 'She seems to be in and out of consciousness all the time, Val. At first I didn't even know whether she realised who I was. That really shocked me, but after a while I think she recognised my voice. Then she looked into my eyes and in a flash I'm sure she knew who I was and why I was here. She smiled. For a few moments she looked really happy. She called me Ken alright, but did she know I was her son? I'm not totally sure.'

'She hasn't seen you for over forty years, Ken. Neither of us exactly look how we did back then. Even if she was well and in top health she might not have recognised you. 1963 is a long time ago! Eventually she knew, Ken. She knew it was you alright.

'Let's get you back home so you can relax a bit; you've been up early and not had a minute's peace since. The ward sister has my phone numbers so if anything changes she'll be in touch.'

'What was the date of the final performance of Kenny Waters and the Waders?' Ken thinks back, then Val reminds him:

'The last night was Saturday August 31st 1963.'

Chapter 32

1400hrs

After a short journey, Val pulls up with Ken at her house - a brick-built semi with a bay window, a short, concrete drive, and a front garden bordered by a privet hedge, which can only be described as 'small'. Ken has now regained his composure but he is deep in thought and feeling terribly sad; his demeanour is of a man about to lose his last living relative.

Ten minutes pass. The lounge door opens. Ken first sees a tray of sandwiches and two cups of tea and then Val, in some difficulty, trying to push the door open with her foot across the close-fitting shag-pile carpet.

He leaps off the sofa across the room and helps the door open as he hurriedly curtails his cell-phone conversation and completes his call: 'Ciao, tardi.'

'My secretary. I thought I should tell her I arrived Ok.'

'Is she the one who answered the phone when I called you yesterday?'

'Yes, Natalia. Good girl. She looks after me real well.'

Val is keen to know more about Natalia, but Ken moves the conversation on. 'So we have forty-seven years to catch up on? Shall I go first? How long have you got? Do you want all the details, or the twenty-minute summary?'

'Ken, you can give the other guys the twenty-minute summary this evening. I've waited years to see and hear from you. I need to hear it 'warts and all', in glorious Technicolor. Take us back to Saturday night at the club.'

'I think we both need to remember that in '63 we were young kids. I know that some things I did then make me cringe now. Anyhow, here goes, if you're sure - 'warts and all'! If I remember, it was around midnight at the club and you weren't feeling too well. You went off with Gary to be taken home. I gave Linda a lift home about an hour or so later. The next day…'

Val immediately interrupts. 'Hold on a minute, Ken, not so fast. Sorry to interrupt you so soon, but you took Linda home in your car? Right?'

'Right.'

'Did anything happen?'

Ken knows what is coming and tries to duck and dive. 'I didn't think you wanted a minute-by-minute account, Val. Crikey, it's years ago. I don't remember every detail!'

'I don't want every detail. I want to know if anything happened between you and Linda on the way home.'

'Why do you ask? What did she say happened?'

'She said nothing, but I know Linda and I know she really liked you. I know that Linda and blokes made, indeed 'make', a potent cocktail. Always have done; always will.'

'Give me a minute, Val, let me try and remember.'

*

'Ken, it's a beautiful evening; it would be a shame to finish it so soon. Can we stop off for a while, gaze at the moon and stars, have a chat and enjoy a bit of time on our own?' Linda's words are exactly as she had rehearsed them to herself in her head.

Ken readily agrees, 'Sure, anywhere in particular?'

'How about Weston Mill? That's not far from home and it's quiet and dark… ideal! Yes, Weston Mill.'

Ken looks at Linda. Linda looks straight back at Ken. He knows that look, like he knows that place! The look in her eyes is teasing, even mischievous. The place is known to him, known to locals, very well-known to courting couples. He drives on and starts to feel nervous and edgy, yet excited, a bit like a boy going to see his first FA Cup Final - you know it will be exciting, but you are not sure what will happen or what the final result will be!

Something deep inside him is beginning to react and Linda has only said two words: 'Weston Mill'. No, it's that look. It's that provocative look that has caused his reaction. Escorting Linda to Weston Mill is a bit like escorting Guy Fawkes to the Parliament cellars. 'Light the blue touch paper and stand well clear,' Ken thinks!

Linda is a gorgeous girl. All the boys are agreed on that. Yet she also has a spirit, an impulsiveness and a vivacity that cannot be resisted - not by the strongest-willed male, let alone by Ken, who has known her and loved her as a friend for most of his life.

'Of course if you don't want to, then say.' Linda is like a cobra preparing itself for the kill.

'No, I'd love to.' He trots out the words like the real sucker that he is. 'You don't say 'No' to Linda,' he thinks.

They soon leave the outskirts of town.

'Next right, isn't it? Linda suggests, an expert navigator.

'Sure is. Hold on, it's a bit bumpy on the track.'

They turn off the main road and drive down a rough track for maybe a quarter of a mile. In front of them looms a place of deep foreboding, a place not to be taken lightly, a place where lives have been changed forever... Weston Mill, a place whose reputation precedes it. It is early yet for a Saturday night. There is one other car there. It looks empty then a socked foot comes into view, brushing across the steamy window.

Linda looks around as Ken drives slowly over the bumpy terrain. 'Over there will be fine.' She points to an area off the beaten track and three quarters-surrounded by fifteen-foot high bushes.

'Been here before, have you?' teases Ken.

'Might have been, but I'm not saying who with,' she teases back, her eyes sparkling. 'How about you?'

'Same.'

'Two can play at that game,' he thinks.

Ken backs in, stops and turns off the engine and lights. It is indeed a beautiful moonlit night. It is quiet; they are alone: 'together alone'!

'What was it you wanted to talk about, Linda?'

'Talk, Mr Kenneth Waterfield? It has taken me ten years to get you here and you ask me what I want to talk about. No time for talk. You look nervous!'

'No, why should I be?'

'You shouldn't be nervous, not with me. Not with someone who fancies you as much as I do.'

Ken is cornered. Whatever is about to happen is totally out of his control. Mr Ice Cool is about to be melted by Miss Hot and Sexy.

She nuzzles in to his ear lobe and whispers sexily,'How much do you like me, Ken? As much as you like Val?'

Before he can answer, she turns to him, runs her tongue slowly along his lips and then kisses them softly, very softly but with so much longing. He responds, looks into her eyes and melts like he knows he would, like she knows he would.

'How's that, Mr Waterfield? I've waited a long time for that.'

'Lin, do you think this is wise? I'm not sure that Gary and Val…' He never finishes his sentence. She kisses him again, more of the same, but for longer. Then she opens his mouth with her tongue, which then searches for his and finds it raring for a party.

'I think you like that, Mr Kenneth. I think you like that more than you're letting on. More…?'

As Linda leans across, Ken notices that her skirt rears up showing more of her long slender legs above the knee. They lean in and clinch. The hand- brake is digging into Ken's groin. It is as hard as the erection gaining momentum inside his pants. It feels even better than it should have done. Ken is not resisting Linda; there is no point!

Linda snuggles in and tucks her head under Ken's chin. He sniffs quietly the aroma from her hair. It penetrates his brain and causes chemical reactions deep within him. She slowly flicks open the buttons on his shirt and slides her hand across his chest feeling and investigating his nipples with her wandering fingers. His trousers are now bulging under the zip. He is on the Yellow Brick Road to the Magic Kingdom; he is off to see the Wizard!

'Gee, you feel good!' Her hands slide down his chest, then he gets 'the old one-two'. She undoes his belt buckle with her right hand while her left hand moves slowly, oh so slowly, down to the waistband of his pants then further. Ken 'oohs' and 'aahs'. They are snogging madly. She unzips his fly then slides her hand down and under. He gasps.

'Oh, Linda. Oh, yes!' She has his whole world in her hand and that world is getting bigger and bigger.

'Big Boy, Mr Kenneth. Lovely big boy, is he coming out to play?'

His eyes are closed; he is getting close to entering a state of nirvana. His right hand slides under her skirt and along and up those gorgeous legs, which open on demand, like Tower Bridge when the fleet comes in. A whole new world is opening up for Ken.

'Naughty boy wants more?'

His hand slips under the waistband of her black knickers and he now knows what is at the end of the rainbow; he has found his crock of gold! She pushes her seat back to its full length and levers back the angle to a jaunty forty-five degrees.

'Right, Mr Kenny Waters. If you like the starters get yourself over here for the main course!'

She opens the passenger door and gets out. Ken quickly half-hoists up his underpants and trousers and manoeuvres his lanky frame over the hand brake and across and into the passenger seat. His shirt is undone, his trousers are undone, his defences are undone; he is ripe for the taking. Linda quickly pulls down her knickers, steps out of them, and moves back in for the kill. She closes the door, puts her knickers on his head and sits astride him.

She whispers in his ear instructing him to un-clip her blouse at the back, and free her bra. He does. She pulls down the front of her blouse.

'Love my big beauties, Mr Front Man, love them.'

Ken's brain is now being flooded with a potent mix of chemicals and hormones; he is now flying! He looks at her breasts, so big, so firm, so round. All of his Christmases have come at once! She tosses her long blonde hair back; they are both sweating - sweating sex. They kiss like they've never kissed before: lips, tongues, teeth. It is animal! It is primordial!

'Oh, my God! Oh, Linda!'

Her hands are on his shoulders, then the back of the seat. His hands are on her hips then her perfectly-formed bottom. He slides inside her. Oh, the glory! She rides him first very slowly, very tenderly, not to be hurried - then the pace quickens a little. They are at one. He is learning from the 'master'. At last, the sex lesson that she has always promised him. He clasps both her hands behind her back with one of his big hands while the other holds her face up while he kisses her - long lingering kisses. She is riding the buckin' bronco! 'Come on, Mr Big Deal singing star, do it, go on, do it. 'Now!' she screams.'

They climax together in a frenzy of orgasmic groans, semen, adrenaline, sweat and in Linda's, case tears. She is crying, really crying. Tears are flooding down her face. Her eye make-up is wrecked. Her whole face is wrecked. Both their entire bodies are lost in the moment.

Ken is satiated in a mix of emotions, desires and impulses, his face and body covered in sweat, his hands gently continuing to stroke her soft back, then her thighs. His lips carry on kissing her breasts all over. Linda maintains her position sitting astride him and they both continue to kiss lovingly.

Eventually the storm subsides and their brains clear. They laugh. They really, really laugh!

'That was amazing, Linda. Unbelievable!'

'Yes, not bad was it?' she ripostes. 'I couldn't have done it without you.'

'Not bad?'

'Only joking.'

'Do you want a cigarette, Ken?'

'But you don't smoke?'

'I do after sex. Here take one.'

Ken hadn't smoked for a couple of years, but he takes one, lights it, inhales slowly and waits for the nicotine to kick in. Linda is still astride him and she prepares to dismount as Ken's erection retreats from whence it came.

'No, don't move, Lin. I like you there. I can keep my eye on what you're getting up to.'

'You're some operator, Miss Murray.'

'So, it was a good idea of mine, then?'

'The sort of moonlit chat I like. I could get used to this.'

She reconnects her bra and slips on her blouse. She leans in and rests her head on his shoulder in between puffs. The car is full of smoke; the windows are steamed up. Ken winds his down an inch or two as another car snakes its way down the track before pulling up fifty yards away.

'You look like Julius Caesar with my knickers on your head!' She motions to remove them as she puffs a perfect smoke ring sexily into the air.

'No leave them. I like them. Can I keep them as a souvenir?'

'I don't think you need a souvenir, do you? You won't forget this evening in a hurry. First the punch-up, now your cock-up.' They both laugh. Ken tickles Linda's fancy.

'Now be honest. How long have you wanted me, Ken?'

'As long as I can remember.'

'Yet you've never really tried it on with me, which has always been a bit disappointing.'

'Look, I'm with Val; you're with Gary. If this gets out… !'

She interrupts him. 'Only a bit of fun, Ken, and I'm afraid it has rather got out, hasn't it!'

Linda continues to tease Ken. 'Am I better than Val?'

'You don't need to ask that!'

'I don't need to ask it, but I want you to answer it. Am I?'

'Yes, Lin, you're somethin' else! I'm getting cramp; I'm sorry but you better move now!'

They disentangle themselves. Linda gets out the car. Ken follows her, rubs and stretches his cramped thigh muscle, gives her a quick kiss then gets back in the driver's side. Linda gets back in and takes out her compact mirror. 'My face! What've you done to it?'

'Your face is as beautiful as ever. Needs a bit of … !'

'Needs more than a 'bit' of anything,' she interrupts. 'It looks as bad as Colin's! I better get myself together. I can't go home looking like I've been dragged through a hedge backwards.'

'Next time, Linda, next time. C'mon let's get home.'

'Mister, you'd better get all that lipstick off your face, too!'

*

'Sorry, Val, I'm thinking back… No, nothing special happened.' Ken starts rubbing his chin, nervously.

'Are you sure, Ken? You've a guilty look about you.'

'What are you suggesting?'

'I'm suggesting nothing. I only want the truth, Ken. I deserve the truth after all these years.'

'Ok, Ok, Ok, I'm sorry. You want 'All' the details with a capital 'A', in vivid detail?' Ken is very agitated. 'Let's lay all the cards on the table. Something did happen, but it was all over in a couple of minutes and it meant nothing. Linda asked me to drive her to Weston Mill. You know the place. She said that as we'd got a little time together we could talk.' Ken spoke quickly, subconsciously hoping that Val would not hear what he was saying.

'Is that what she called it - talk? At Weston Mill? I know why people went to Weston Mill and none of them went there to talk! Are you about to tell me now that my lifelong boyfriend, the love of my life, screwed my second-best friend, my life-long girl-friend, in the back of his car at Weston Mill? Then for forty-seven years she said nothing about it, having spent countless hours with me, talking together, counselling each other, sharing our lives and she said nothing? My God!'

'Look, Val, calm down. It's a long time ago. There's no point in raking it up now, is there?'

'It doesn't matter how long ago it was, Ken. My two greatest friends, the two people I loved most in my life, double-crossed me: I knew something had happened!'

'If I remember, Linda came on really, really strong. I'd downed a few beers and was high on adrenaline from the gig and the punch-up. I was too weak to resist. You know I always had a soft spot for Linda.'

'A soft spot in your pants, more like a hard spot, hey, Ken?' Always a show-off, always brazen is our Linda.'

'Will she be there this evening?'

'You bet she will, and you wait 'til I see her!'

'Look, Val, what happened all those years ago is gone in the mists of time and after this discussion it should be forgotten. Please don't attack Linda or I may well not come with you this evening.'

'It's not the mere fact that you and her… you know…! It's the fact that she's been my best friend all these years through thick and thin and she never ever gave me an inkling, not a bloody clue!'

'I'd guess that she never mentioned it because it meant nothing to her. Perhaps I was one of many… I don't know.'

'Don't you dare expect me to believe that! Stop defending her and at the same time dumping onto Lin your own guilt!'

'It was a moment in time. It meant nothing. No harm done. A bit of teenage fun on a teenage wasteland.'

Chapter 33

1500h

'During the whole of that evening, you never told me that you were going to Hamburg the next day. Did you tell Linda?'

'No. I told no-one. Until I got on that minibus on Sunday lunchtime and closed the door, I didn't even know myself if I would have the guts to go through with it. It was a huge decision. Look, Val, I was eighteen. I had a beautiful, steady girlfriend: you!'

'Obviously not beautiful enough!' Val interjects, bruised by his words. Ken continues undeterred. 'You were starting to pile on the pressure about getting engaged and us settling down together. My dad was determined for me to settle immediately into the firm, which meant being stuck with him and a maximum £40 a week for the rest of my life.

'Val, could you really see me in a desk job before taking over the company when I was old and grey and desperate to retire? All I wanted was to spend some time to see if I could make it in the music business, which is where my heart was leading me. I was cracking up under the pressure. I needed time away to think. Hamburg sounded ideal: miles away from my dad, miles away from the firm!'

'And miles away from me, Ken!'

'However ghastly it sounds - yes, miles away from you! Yet I hoped it would rationalise my thoughts for you. Absence makes the heart grow fonder!'

'Yes, but absence also makes the heart wander!'

'You know I loved you, Val. Always did, ever since we were kids. I wasn't ready to settle down; it was too soon.'

'Seeing the Beatles 'live' at the ABC in March was a revelation for me. We went along together, remember, to see Chris Montez and Tommy Roe? But as soon as I heard the Beatles sing 'I Saw Her Standing There' I knew that I would never be settled until I had my chance to emulate them.

That show was ordinary until the Fab 4 came on. They were young, bright, cocky and British, and everyone loved them! The girls in the audience went berserk. I knew that I was that good. Everyone said what a great singer I was, so why couldn't I make it big, too?'

'No reason at all, you're right again. I only wished you'd done it here, not abroad.'

'The Dominators had hassled me for a month or so about singing for them. They were an excellent band, as I'm sure you'll remember. Leaving Gary aside, the rest of their musicians were far superior to Colin, Dave and Rog.

'My musical career with the Waders had also reached its peak. Something needed to change. Playing once or twice a week in village halls and pubs was no way to make progress. Dave was driving that old van on which the starter motor kept jamming, or the bloody thing wouldn't start through dirty plugs, a flat battery or damp points. The nights we pushed it, or got towed! We were going nowhere with or without it!'

'You didn't call it a 'bloody van' at the time. It was your lifeline! The people of Northampton loved you!'

'It wasn't enough, Val.'

'Did you know that Gary had a similar offer from the Spitfires prior to that, but he turned it down? He chose Linda above all that.'

'How do you know about that?'

'Because he told me, later, and his offer was as good as yours. But he put Linda first!'

'Yes, but where did it get him? Northampton! Palookaville, in the words of Marlon Brando.'

'And where did your leaving me, get me?'

Ken absorbs her hurt look and feels her pain. 'Gary's dad was very supportive whereas my dad was driving me mad. I needed out! I wanted the best for me. I didn't want to be the best singer in town. I was lusting for more, not settling for less.'

'Well, thank you for reminding me that you weren't lusting after me!' Val is now thoroughly irritated. 'So it was all about 'you', wasn't it? No thoughts about anyone else!'

'I'm not talking about you, Val,' rejoins Ken. 'I'm talking about my singing career. Look, I did try to call you on the Sunday morning, but your mum said you weren't well, still in bed, and you couldn't take the call.'

'Did you call Linda?'

'No, I didn't! Can we leave Linda out of this?'

'Yes and no!'

Val wants Ken to tell his story unhindered by her interruptions but he touches a raw nerve immediately and quickly wants to skim over it. She is not prepared to allow him to breeze over that or anything else. While this heated exchange takes place Val has jumped up off the sofa and is standing directly in front of Ken and looking down on him. Ken is shocked by Val's aggressive attack and is unnerved by her hovering above him.

'Please sit down, Val. Look, I felt really, really bad that I never told you personally that I was going away. You must believe me on that.'

'You could have called me later.'

'I could have called you later, but I didn't! Why? Because...'

'Because I wasn't important!' Val interrupts.

'No! We were travelling - on the road to the docks, on a ship or on the Autobahn and it wasn't simple to call in those days. We didn't have mobile phones and you needed loads of local coins. In fact at that time you had to reserve an international call then wait some time while they found a line and connect it. Then there was all this discussion with the operator in a foreign language.'

'Poor excuse, Ken!'

'I knew I should have called but it was much easier not to. I was starting a new life but, sorry to say this, you were not part of it. I told the rest of the lads I was going to call you and they jeered at me and called me a wimp, a mummy's boy, so I didn't. I 'copped out'. Maybe I thought you might talk me out of it. I don't know.

'Here and now, forty seven years later, with you in front of me, I can truly say that I feel really, really sorry. I feel sick. I'm so ashamed. You deserved so much better. You must have been gutted?'

'Don't ask, Ken. Don't ask. Be assured that when I get my turn, I'll tell you! You feel bad now? You'll feel a hell of a lot worse than you do now. Hearing you waffle is bringing it all back like it was yesterday; God did I hurt! I couldn't sleep for days because I was scared of waking up again! In my heart even now there is a chasm that has been opened and has never healed. Maybe it never will!'

'But you got my letter?'

'What letter?'

'I sent you a letter from Hamburg a month or so after I'd got there.'

'No letter arrived here, Ken.'

'I definitely sent it. I remember writing it. I poured over it for days, trying to explain to you why I left.'

'Do you remember posting it as well? Ken, I never received it.'

'Believe me, Val, I wrote it and I posted it. Please believe me.'

'Why should I believe you, Ken. Why should I believe anything you say?'

'Because it's true.'

'The fact that I never received a letter doesn't alter the fact that you left me.'

'Maybe, but it does mean that I was still thinking of you and that I wanted you to know why. Over the next few hours I'll explain myself and maybe you'll forgive me.'

'Maybe.'

Ken's visit to the hospital is now all but forgotten. His total focus is on explaining his actions without upsetting Val too much. He has got off to a poor start.

'I had a blazing row with my dad. You remember what he was like. It was all about power, his power over first Mum, then me. He told me, 'If you walk out now, never come back again!' He said it more than once.

'Mum was crying. She hated arguments and tantrums. We were all upset. It was awful, but I was determined to go. I had magic dreams and I wanted to live for today not tomorrow, no thoughts of the big picture. My bag was packed, my mind was made up. So I left the house, met the guys, loaded up the van and off I went with a new band to a new land. It was a bit like going off to BB camp all over again!'

'But the difference was that this time you weren't planning on coming back were you, Ken?'

'If I was successful then you're right, I wasn't planning on coming back. If I failed I planned to be back in six months and carry on where I left off.'

Val shook her head and thought to herself: 'He thought he could breeze back after six months and pick up the pieces, cheeky sod. Some hope!' She soon realises that however angry she gets and however bad she can make Ken feel, nothing can change; the past is the past.

'The van was a bit of a wreck, with really uncomfortable wooden-slatted seats, chock-full of instruments and kit bags both inside and on the roof rack. With Mick driving, John sitting in the passenger seat holding the gear stick in fourth gear to try to stop it jumping out, and with twenty miles to the gallon of petrol and sixty miles to a pint of oil, we made Newhaven, just!

'The crossing was rough and our stomachs hung on until we made The Hook. Soon we were passing Arnhem en route to Hamburg, then the bloody van broke down in the middle of nowhere.'

'You'd swapped one lousy van for another! Smart move! Says it all, Ken!'

'We flagged down a lorry, eventually got a breakdown truck to tow us to the nearest village where we stood waiting while some Belgian mechanic poured over the engine, pulled out wires at random, scratched his head and swore incessantly, before eventually he had to order some spare parts which he fetched the next day. Overnight we kipped down in the van in his garage. It was cold, it was crowded, it was miserable, it was smelly. We had to have a whip round for the bill to be paid, then on we went under the advice that we should not exceed forty miles an hour or the van would develop kangaroo symptoms. Hamburg is a long way at forty miles an hour.'

'Hamburg is a mighty long way when you can't wait to see your boyfriend again!'

'The German border guards were Ok; we had work and residence permits.'

Val is now really mentally right back in that moment, in 1963. She needs to ask, 'Hang on, Ken. Hang on. You had work and residence permits?'

'Yep. When the Dominators asked me to go with them, they said I needed official documents from the Embassy. I gave them my passport a month prior and they applied for it and got it.'

'All before you finally decided to leave us all?'

'Yes. Although I got the documents, I could still drop out at the last moment, but without the documents I couldn't get into Germany.'

Val is about to explode again and is struggling with her emotions: 'Hang on. While all this document business is going on, we were at Butlin's and you know what happened there.'

'I know.'

'You badgered me incessantly to sleep with you, all the time knowing that you might be leaving me for Hamburg two weeks later. Then to top it all you had it away with Linda the night before you left, and you told her nothing, either?'

'Yes. I know it sounds bad.'

'Bad? Bad? It's worse than bad, it's diabolical! All I can say, Ken, is that you obviously cared nothing for any of us: nothing for me, nothing for Linda, nothing for the band, nothing for your mother and father. Absolutely nothing! You cared only for you!'

'I did care loads for all of you. I loved you, Val. How many times must I apologise? A million times sorry. I can't say it many more times, Val. It was something I had to do to get it out of my system. If I'd told any of you in advance, you would have made my life hell and tried to talk me out of it. I reckoned that only by keeping it secret could I go. Your anger now all these years later confirms how you would have reacted then and how you would have tried to get anyone to talk me out of going.'

'So how was Hamburg?'

Ken smiles to himself, raises his eyebrows and shakes his head a little.

'Incredible. I will tell you all the vivid details but prepare yourself for a few shocks.'

An hour passes, the mood has mellowed a little and the trauma of Weston Mill has subsided. After completing his description of his time in Hamburg, Ken shows Val a photograph of Carola, the girl who became more than a friend. As he puts it back into his wallet, she says, 'Tell me what happened after you left Hamburg.'

Ken draws breath, wipes his brow with a crisp white handkerchief, thinks back, then talks. Another hour shoots by, culminating in Ken showing Val a photograph of Aniela which he keeps in his wallet.

'When did you lose your wife?'

'Three years ago.'

'What's your situation now, Ken, in the time since your wife's death?'

'I took it very hard as you can imagine, and for a time became a bit of a recluse. I stopped performing and never went out much, merely loafed about at home and felt sorry for myself. I eventually sought some counselling in an effort to get myself back together again. I'm a director of some companies. I take an active interest in the foundation and I try to keep myself fit.'

'Is there any special woman in your life at the moment?'

'No. I'm right out of practice. Occasionally I might need a partner on my arm for formal or official dinners or a concert, in which case I invite my secretary, Natalia, which is nice for her and helps me out. Other than that I am pretty free to move in any direction I choose.'

'Are you lonely?'

'I'm alone but I'm not really lonely. I'm finally over Aniela and am now able to look back on fantastic memories with her. There are times that I wish...'

'Yes, what do you wish for, Ken?'

'I wish that I'd find another great woman to share the rest of my life with.'

Ken looks over at Val. Val looks down, choosing not to meet his eyes.

He breaches the silence. 'While we're looking at photos, let me show you the other photo in my wallet.'

'It's me!'

'Yes, it's you, taken at Butlin's. Linda gave me it on that Saturday evening. I've carried it with me every day for all these years. I loved you very much, Val; I could never forget you.'

'Oh, Ken. All these years I thought that you'd forgotten me.' Now Val is crying. They embrace. Ken kisses Val tenderly on the forehead and slowly burrows his nose in her long hair, taking a deep whiff of her unique aroma.

'Why did you never come back to see your mum and dad, not even once?'

'Dad made it clear that I was not welcome back. He gave me an initial chance to join the firm and when I rejected him he never had it in his heart to take me back merely as his son.

'Many times I offered to fly back and meet Mum somewhere convenient to us both, but she wouldn't go behind my father's back, so it never happened. All the years that I was away I rang Mum twice a year, once on her birthday and once on Mother's Day. I never missed.

'I tried to call at a time I thought my dad would be out at the office or playing golf. Only once or twice, in all those years when I rang, did my dad answer. I asked for Mum. He knew it was me. Not once did he offer a token hand of reconciliation, or even ask how I was.

'After he died, I did speak more often on the phone with Mum. I kept her informed as to my wellbeing and whereabouts. I invited Mum to visit me in Italy and stay as long as she liked, but for various reasons it never happened.'

'You never came back for his funeral?'

'No, for two reasons. Firstly, I was in South America on tour with fixed dates; to cancel would have been impossible.

'Secondly, I lost all respect for him on that Sunday that I left. I know he must have been upset. I understand that, but he could have said, 'Ok, Ken you go and do your thing. Try and become a top singer if that's what you want. If it doesn't work out for you, come back and we'll pick up the pieces. If you then feel right to join the firm then there will always be a place for you!

'That is what he could have said. That is what Mr Maier would have said. That would have been perfect. That is what you do if you love someone! Encourage them, let them fly away on eagle wings and let them fly back. Give them space to grow!

'My dad's reaction and attitude were all about him, his business, his colleagues, his father. Why he would want me in his business in an unhappy state I can't begin to comprehend other than he wanted control, like he controlled Mum. He was a bully, not in the alley but in the home.

'You contrast his reaction to that of Mum. She was upset, very upset to be losing her only son on some 'crackpot' (my dad's words) mission in Europe. Do you know that after he stormed out slamming doors in his wake, Mum slipped five £10 notes in my hand and unbeknown to me stashed a small tin of her home-made cake in my kit bag. In the tin she'd written a small note. It said, 'Be careful and eat properly'. I've always treasured that!'

'You made it as pop star, then. You made it as a husband, but you never made it as a father?'

'Seems not. I've a sister now. Carola is my soul sister. Without her I might still be lost. She found me. We talk regularly by phone. She keeps me on the straight and narrow. Val, I'm sixty five. I'm alive, in good health and ready for the next challenge, whatever it may be,' Ken says, starting to put the photos in his wallet.

'What's that other photo that I can see in your wallet?'

'This one? This is Mum. Four beautiful women in my life, how blessed am I? Please excuse me, Val, but I need the bathroom and I need another coffee.'

'Right, let's take five. But before we do I need to draw a final line under this encounter between you and Linda at Weston Mill. Will you allow me this one pleasure then I'll never mention it again.'

'Yes, if you must. what is it?'

Val moves toward Ken, then as he expects that she is going to kiss him, she draws back her right palm and wallops him mightily with every sinew of her burgeoning anger, slap bang across his left cheek with a resounding 'Thwack'!

Ken is totally dumbfounded and recoils in pain. He struggles to catch breath, let alone say anything. So he decides to say nothing. His cheek is smarting; his face temporarily reflects her anger and his ego gets its comeuppance. But his soul would permanently reflect that he is in no doubt whatsoever that the girl he loved and left behind had been crushed by his action. Ken has paid a very small price indeed for breaking Val's heart.

'Thank you for that, Kenneth. Now it's my turn!'

Chapter 34

1600h

Ken is quite relaxed, in fact, high, following the exhilaration of telling his story, a story that he had hoped would exonerate him from any blame following his hasty, unannounced departure from Val's life in 1963. What could she possibly say that would change anything for him? Even though he has taken a definitive swipe across his cheek, he remains completely unprepared for what is about to come.

'Ken, I've waited all these years to tell you what has happened in my life. I prayed that one day you'd hear it. Thankfully my prayers are now being answered. It's not an easy story, Ken. I patiently listened to you, I think, and I'm glad that I heard your story first. What I have to say now becomes so much more poignant. Please hear me out. It'll be such a weight off my mind to share it with someone, especially with you.

'More tea, Ken, or do you prefer a bottle of vodka; how about a line of coke? No, only joking! Here goes...'

Both are in a very sympathetic, respectful yet pragmatic mood now, a reflection perhaps of the real love they once had for each other.

'I sat by the phone all of the Sunday, still not feeling a whole lot better. There's nothing so lonely as a phone that doesn't ring. When you hadn't called back by mid-evening, I got worried. I rang your house and spoke with your mum, who was really upset about the big row you'd had with your dad about you clearing off with the Dominators. You'd apparently left around lunchtime.'

'Don't you worry, duck,' she said. 'I'm sure that he'll be fine and get homesick and be back before you've even missed him.'

'Don't worry,' she said. 'Don't worry!' Ken, I worried from that minute onwards. God, how I missed you. We'd been together since we were kids. I'd seen you most days. I thought we were joined together at the hip. Then you did a 'Lord Lucan' on me. I sobbed on and off for a couple of days. You were my everything and now you were gone. I listened out for the phone all week. It felt like someone had torn my heart out and stuck it on a spear. I was lonely; I was lost. It was horrible.'

'I never meant to hurt you, Val. I just needed to get away and search for my Holy Grail.'

Val wasn't going to be deflected. 'Gary and Linda came to see me later the next day to make sure I was alright and to see if there was any more news of you. Roger was a rock. His support was invaluable; his friendship got me through. He was extremely sympathetic about the fact that you'd left me. He tried to reason with me and to cut a long story short, he insisted on taking me out to cheer me up and help me put it behind me. He wouldn't take 'No' for an answer.'

'Good old Rog! I was hardly out of the country and he was making a play for my girl! Typical!'

'I asked him to take me to the same pub that we'd visited on our last Friday together. Bit selfish, but I felt closer to you there. He talked a lot. I felt sick and nodded and agreed with everything he said. I had one drink and it lasted all evening. I couldn't finish it. I'd lost my taste for it after one sip. Roger was really, really good to me, Ken. I was surprised how well he understood my needs, and he really wanted to help me.'

'I know he fancied you… and Linda! In fact he was getting so desperate he fancied almost anything in a skirt. I bet he couldn't believe his luck.'

'Ken, what a horrible thing to say!'

'Like most horrible things, horrible but true!'

'Roger always fancied me. I know that but he did come up trumps in my hour of need. He made himself available and turned out to be a good listener. My head was all over the place. I felt alone. You made me feel unwanted. You let me down. My stomach remained out of sorts, which made it even worse. Roger was very soft and kind and we hit it off right away, so much so that the following Saturday Roger drove us to Skegness in the new car he'd bought earlier that week.'

'All credit to Rog. I told him to get a car if he wanted to pull, and he did. But I never expected he'd pull you!'

Val smiled dismissively. 'We had a good day together so we agreed to stay overnight. I called home and told Mum that I would be staying out with Linda. Gary and her had gone away together so my story held water.

'In the evening Roger eventually found a guesthouse that had vacancies and he checked us in and paid. When we got to our room there was only one double bed. I'd specifically asked Roger to get us a room with two single beds, or better still, two single rooms. Anyhow, despite me stressing the point and following an exchange or two between us, it was his plea that we should share for one night. We unpacked and you can guess what happened. It was Butlin's all over again, this time with him not you.'

'He tried out his new car alright, even more he tried out his new girl… my girl!' Ken swallows, agitatedly.

'Your ex-girl, Ken!'

Ken is now feeling hurt and jealous even after all these years. He now fully understands how Val had felt when he told her about his session with Linda. It is becoming obvious to both of them that there were real feelings then, and there are still some real feelings between them now.

'Roger obviously had desired me for ages. When his chance came, he took it!'

'Meaning what? He didn't rape you, did he?'

'No, he didn't. But he certainly had his way with me! It was like years of frustration and longing was released in one ravishing night of passion! Looking back, I suppose it was more lust than love,' Val continues. It was almost like rape, but she can't say that to Ken or it would break him.

'I felt guilty for ages, thinking that I had betrayed you. If you'd have returned from Hamburg within a week or so you'd have found out what'd happened and you'd have flattened Roger. My parents would have found out what'd happened and my name would've been 'Common Slut'!'

'Spot on there, love.'

'Roger kept phoning me but I told him I was busy and couldn't see him. This went on for a couple of weeks until, well, my last period was late and a bit strange compared with normal. My breasts were a bit swollen and unusually very tender which I had initially put down to stress caused by your disappearing act! On that day it dawned on me that I wasn't to have a period at all, and it was confirmed by the clinic that I was pregnant.'

'Blimey! I bet that was a helluva shock!' Ken is now struggling to take in all what Val is telling him and is about to ask another question, when he thinks better of it.

'I summoned Roger to lunch in town and told him the news. Guess what? He was absolutely delighted. His first words were, 'So that's decided then. We must get married.' I was taken aback, I must admit.'

'Not surprised!'

'Within a few weeks, my steady boyfriend of many years had dumped me, another friend had taken me away for the weekend, got me pregnant and we were getting married. All I needed then was for you to return and it would have been like a Brian Rix farce at the Whitehall Theatre - one in the bed, one under the bed and one in the wardrobe!'

'And one in the oven!' quipped Ken.

'Not funny, Ken! You didn't come back, you didn't phone, you didn't write. To all intents and purposes you might well have been dead.'

'To put the record straight, Val, in my mind I didn't 'dump you'. I left you to pursue a musical career abroad. I did write to you. Remember?'

'It felt the same as being dumped, I can tell you, and to put the record completely straight, there was no letter! Anyway, I eventually plucked up the courage to tell Mum and Dad, with Roger in attendance. I thought that Dad was going to have a heart attack or kill Roger, or both. We kept talking, and the fact that Roger said he would stand by me and marry me, the fact that I said I wanted to keep the baby and bring it up normally, the fact that Roger was such a nice guy with a steady, responsible and well-paid job who Mum and Dad already knew of and the fact that I said that I was happy to marry Roger, all resulted in the four of us concluding that marriage made the best of a bad situation.

'A back-street abortion was out of the question. A stay at a Salvation Army home for unmarried mothers followed by adoption was completely unthinkable. A miscarriage by falling downstairs was contemplated for no more than thirty seconds. The hot bath, bottle of gin and wire coat hanger scenario seemed like a nightmare. Rather, I grew to like the idea of a baby to love and nurture. It was the least worst option.

'So within weeks we had a Registry Office wedding, a small

reception and Roger and I went off to Cliftonville for a few days' honeymoon.'

'Good job I never came back, then. I would have been distraught.'

'I did grow to love Roger, I suppose, in my own way. He was very kind and attentive, but I soon realised that I was not 'in love' with him. I was still in love with you. He was madly in love with me, and his self-confidence grew and grew.

'We got a mortgage on a small two-bedroom terraced house and I became the model mother. Over the years, Roger progressed well with the police and soon made sergeant. He eventually started studying to try to progress to inspector.

'The baby was born in April in the maternity home, a beautiful boy who we called Kevin - 8lbs 3ozs. I started my new role as mother, which was fine. Roger doted on Kevin and on me, and life was relatively rosy and believe it or not, the day I was checking out of the hospital with Kevin in my arms, Linda was rushed in! She may even have given birth in the same bed!'

'Blimey, what was she doing being pregnant, too?'

'Lin had Richard the next day. Gary had moved into the spare room at Linda's a few month's previous and there we were, both teenage mums. Soon baby Kevin took centre stage and I unconsciously began to shut out Roger and he likewise me. Our relationship hung by a thread.

'Young Kevin was the only glue that held our marriage together, and he flourished. He went to junior school at the bottom of the street, did extremely well, top of the class, popular with classmates and teachers - and the girls.'

'Like me!' Ken quips, but was about to hear something totally unexpected.

'At this time Roger proposed that perhaps we needed another baby to help our relationship and hopefully a baby girl would be a new challenge and breathe new life into our struggling seven year-old marriage. We also thought that a new brother or sister would enrich Kevin's life.

'We made a real effort to try to get our sex life back on track and both of us put our efforts in to me conceiving. It didn't happen. Month after month it didn't happen. Tempers got frayed, accusations flew around.

'Of course, by then the pill had come into general use and I had originally been using it as a matter of course. I stopped taking it when we tried for the second baby, but nothing happened. Roger accused me of still secretly taking the pill. I accused him of trying too hard. It was an awful, emotional time. The sex was horrible: little real love, no joy, routine baby-making - well, not even baby-making! I'd already given birth to one child, and he'd fathered it so it was a mystery as to why I couldn't conceive again.

'Eventually, after endless arguing and furore, Roger was first to be sent by the doctor for tests to the hospital, and guess what... ?'

'Go on...'

'Roger was declared sterile, infertile, however you want to put it. He always had been and there was no medical or surgical treatment in those days that would help him. Hospital practices and research were a lot more basic then than they are now.

'Now here's the rub, Ken. Listen to this very, very carefully...!'

Ken is fidgeting in his chair. He is starting to put the jigsaw pieces in place and the full picture that he is expecting is starting to emerge. He starts to swallow nervously and gnaw anxiously at his thumb nail. His head is beginning to throb, his temperature seems to be increasing; his leg uncontrollably jiggles.

'If Roger was incapable of having children, and Kevin was running around the garden, happy as Larry, then who was the father?'

Ken looks bewildered, but he knows what is coming. His heart-rate is rocketing. His clammy hands start a slight tremble.

'I know who the father is. Do you, Ken?'

'Are you saying what I think you're saying?' A strange, chilled feeling suddenly runs down the whole length of his back. Ken gets up and stands upright rubbing both hands time and time again through his hair and across his forehead, then his mouth. His face starts flushing; his brain starts misfiring.

'Butlin's? Are you telling me that Kevin was conceived at Butlin's?'

'Bull's-eye!'

Chapter 35

1700hrs

'You did make it as a father, Ken. You just didn't know it.'

'Are you sure? This isn't all a well-conceived and pre-rehearsed joke, is it, Val? This isn't something to joke about. This is damned serious!'

Both of them stand up; this melodrama cannot now be acted out sitting down. Val moves toward Ken and stands eyeball to eyeball with him, holding both of his arms. She looks deep into his eyes. She doesn't blink. He knows she is telling the truth.

'Shall I continue? No joke, Ken. This is reality; this is a secret that I've waited to tell someone for nearly forty years. Yes, I too can keep a secret.'

They sit down again.

'Let me get this straight. Before you even - hang on, hang on - I'm thinking this through.'

Val stops him. 'Let me help you here, Ken. When I finally gave in to your pleading doe eyes and we shared that single bunk bed in Butlin's what the hell did you do for contraception? You said, and I remember distinctly, you said, 'Don't worry, Val. I have a condom.'

Ken is alert, sitting forward in the armchair with his head resting between his hands. His left leg is now jiggling in unison with his right. He flushes as his mind recounts, and he hesitates as he fights for the right words to say. 'I did! I had a packet of three that I bought from the machine in the Beachcomber Bar toilets. I remember that night like no other.'

'You did?'

'I did, but now I'm gutted. We were both having our first real sexual encounter, right? It was our first time?'

'Right, so...?'

'So... I was so excited that you finally said 'Yes', and I'd never used a condom before, so in the excitement...'

'You just couldn't be bothered to use one!' Val completes his sentence.

'Not exactly. I was going to but then I was all fingers and thumbs and I panicked. I wanted to have you so much, before you changed your mind again. I didn't want it to turn into a fumbling disaster.'

'What a complete idiot you were, Ken. Your decision made on the spur of the moment without thinking of anyone but yourself, has changed the lives of quite a few people for a long, long time. In fact that single decision by you eventually indirectly led to Roger's death.'

'Good God, Val. What the hell are you saying? I'm devastated!'

'So you should be!'

With Ken's head in his hands, a few seconds pass and no-one speaks. Ken's brain is slowly getting back in synch. The mist is beginning to clear as tears form in his eyes. He takes out his handkerchief and tries to regain his composure.

'Are you absolutely sure that I'm the father?'

'Can I ask…?' He stops, then...

'If this question…?' He stops again.

He is struggling to find the right way to ask his next question without offending Val and getting thrown out the house and out of her life forever.

'Look, Val, I know that I shouldn't ask this but I'm going to anyway. I need to ask you whether you slept with anyone else except Roger after Butlin's and before you were declared pregnant?'

Val blows a gasket! 'You damned impudent arrogant bastard! This is Valerie that you're talking to Ken, not Linda or any cheap slut you've picked up in the stinking gutters of your lousy world. Your bloody stupid question stinks!'

'But I need to know, Val.'

'N and O spells 'no'! No-one, satisfied? What doesn't your nasty little mind get about those two extremely complicated letters?'

'Ok you've made your point. Sorry, but the question needed asking,' apologises Ken. Help me again here, Val. I'm trying to get my head around this. You believe that you were already pregnant when you had your dirty weekend with Rog.'

'Pregnant? Yes, I do believe I was pregnant when I had my dirty, sordid, grotty little bonking session with Randy Roger, if that makes you feel better!'

'So at that time, I presume that Rog didn't know that he was infertile,' Ken rationalises. 'He didn't know that you were up, erhm, pregnant, so he must have known that he didn't use any contraception, or did he?'

'I have thought about this endlessly over the years. I tried to discuss it with him but he refused to answer my questions. He clammed up and got aggressive if I brought up the subject - really nasty.

'My best guess, and it's only a guess, is that he wanted me so badly, and he thought a baby was one way in which to trap me into a relationship, so either he never used a condom, like you, or he used one that had split or he had one 'pre-punctured with a needle' before we set off for Skeggie. I don't remember exactly, I was being ravished at the time and it was a bloody long time ago, wasn't it, Ken?'

'Bastard! He wanted you to get pregnant as insurance so that you stayed with him, and if I came back then you would still stay with him.'

'That's no worse than what you did, Ken!'

'It's much worse. I did what I did out of over-excitement and naivety, and love for you. He planned it.'

'We don't know that for sure and he's not here to defend himself.'

'No, but it's a safe bet. Odds-on, I'd say.'

'Either way, it's absolutely certain that you and I have a son, Kevin, who is now himself a father to two teenage boys - Richard and Tim.'

'So when Rog found out he was infertile what happened?'

'World War Three broke out in our house, or so it felt! I talked through what you've heard in the last few minutes and told Roger. He went ballistic.'

'Did he hit you?'

'He smashed things up, he kicked a hole in the kitchen door and he slapped me about a bit then stormed out in a rage. Kevin was balling his eyes out and screaming. God knows what the neighbours must have thought.'

'I'm so, so sorry Val. Come here. Let me give you a big hug. Whatever happens in life there is no excuse to hit a woman, especially a good one like you. It wasn't your fault.'

'It wasn't,' she sobbed. 'All I wanted was you.'

They embrace for a good two minutes. Tears are flowing from both of them, whilst inside Ken is laughing, laughing with happiness. Neither of them can speak. They are totally overcome with emotion. They both expected a day of some soul-searching, but not this. They both cry, cry like babies, cry from the heart, cry from their soul, cry not as two but as one.

Eventually they sit down together on the sofa. They both use Ken's once- clean, now twice-damp, white handkerchief to mop up their tear-stained faces. They are entwined; they both need the closeness, they both get what they need. They have cleared the air and are back together. They both feel it, but neither comments. Eventually Val continues, 'It was awful, Ken, it was terrible! Oh, Ken, where were you when I needed you most?

'Roger and I eventually after a traumatic few days stopped arguing and threatening each other and we did manage to sit down together in the same room and have a discussion. It wasn't easy, as you can imagine, but we came to the conclusion that the onus was on him; he was the most affected, and what did he intend to do? I wasn't in love with him, never really had been. I had tried to love him but I couldn't. He loved me, now hated me at the same time. He had a son that he loved; now he discovered that he was not the real father and his love became compromised. He was in a right state.'

'Ok. Roger knew he wasn't the biological father, but he was the dad. Surely that was enough!'

'It could have been. Indeed it should have been, but for reasons only Roger knew, it wasn't. Roger had an awful upbringing. One day he told me all about it, then he broke down and sobbed. He sobbed like I sobbed when you left me, so I know how he hurt.

'Years before, he loved a girl called Mary from the home, and I could imagine how hurt he'd been. He had one day in Skegness on a coach trip from the school ten years previous in the summer of '53. That solitary day he had Mary all to himself and it was the only happy event in his miserable young life before he met us all in Northampton. He really loved that girl and he always hoped he might find her one day and continue their friendship like it was 1953 again.

'When we got married, I became his 'Mary'. When Kevin was born he then took over the mantle of Mary and when he found out that Kevin was not his son he couldn't handle it. When we eventually split up, it finished him.'

'Where did he take you for your first date? Skegness? Poor delusional sod!'

'Young Kevin knew something was up but not what. I clung to Kevin to give me the true unconditional love that I needed. Roger firstly decided that to save face at work, he would continue as was - married to me, father to Kevin - as long as he could. I must say he did Ok. On the surface he seemed to put it all behind him. He passed his inspector exams and in front of colleagues he played the perfect father and husband; he was a damned good actor, that's for sure!

'I think Roger had a few women on the side over the years, but it was in my own interest to keep my eyes wide shut, if you know what I mean? He never lovingly touched me again.

'Kevin was brilliant at school. He passed his 11-plus exams and went to the grammar school. He made the 'A' Language stream and got seven 'O' levels and three 'A' levels.'

'Better than his father, then?' Ken is now recovering his poise and starting to feel a little more confident, even smug. Within minutes he seems to be coming to terms with his new paternal status.

'Kevin even got a scholarship to Cambridge. This was about '82-ish. I can't remember exactly.'

Ken whistles: 'Wow, Cambridge! Top boys!'

'As Kevin was about to live away from home, Roger decided it was time that we split up and go our own ways; there was nothing left to keep us together. We had moved into separate bedrooms for the previous ten years and almost lived separate lives. Roger slept in the front room, which we converted into his bedroom. He was on shifts, studying for police exams, working as much overtime as he could so I never saw him that much. I met other mums and their kids and it became vaguely bearable, but only just.

'Ten years of misery?'

'Not exactly. Kevin was a joy and so intelligent. We sold the house and split the proceeds, which were quite substantial. I used part of my cut to help Kevin's university expenses - books and stuff. The rest I put down on a small house. Dad helped me with the mortgage.

'I never told Mum and Dad anything other than Roger and I had become incompatible and had gone our separate ways. They accepted this without too many questions. I never told your mum and dad anything, either, even though I saw them occasionally.

'After many months I had come to terms with everything, and two or three years had elapsed when something truly horrific happened. Hang on while I pop upstairs to fetch something.'

Ken is immediately discomfited again. No sooner has he been pronounced a father than something awful happens. He dreads to hear more.

'Here, read this!' A returning Val gives Ken a yellowing and now dog-eared cutting from the local newspaper. It is dated September 28th 1985.

Policeman found dead in suspected suicide

A police officer was found dead yesterday in a suspected suicide.

Police Sergeant Roger Edwards, who had served in all districts of Northampton, was discovered on the footpath alongside the new multi-storey car park in the centre of town.

In a statement, Northampton Police said - we can confirm that on September 27th, a 44 year-old serving police officer was found deceased. His death is not being treated as suspicious and the coroner has been informed. An inquiry has been opened into Sgt Edwards' death and a full inquest is due to be held next month.

Sgt Edwards had been on sick leave for six months and was being treated for acute depression. The 44 year-old was stopped by his colleagues in Moulton on the night of September 15th for driving under the influence of alcohol.

Yorkshire-born Sgt Edwards had taken up a role at Northampton Police in 1961 and was particularly well-known to the citizens of Semilong, where he worked as a beat officer for many years.

He leaves a wife and one son.

'Christ, poor old Rog! That's horrendous.'

'Months later, when all the emotion had died down, I analysed it and I felt so sorry for him - a decent bloke who'd a really rough deal from life. His police career had even stalled. Even after he passed his inspector's exams, he never got promotion due to his heavy drinking and dubious social life; they strung him along month after month until it was too late. The only remaining thing that could be taken from him was his life, so I guess he decided to take control of that. He chose the time, the means and the place. You can hardly blame him.'

The only thing Ken could say was, 'Did he leave a suicide note?'

'Well, yes he did. He had a deep, dark hole inside and neither Kevin nor I could fill it. As long as it was there, he couldn't move on. He was empty and had little to give, no matter how hard he tried. I pray that Roger will be happier dead than he ever was alive.

'We'd talked of divorce but never got round to instructing solicitors. So at the age of around forty, I was a widow with a beautiful grown-up son at university.'

'How did Kevin do?' Ken was relieved and happy to regain aloofness and to move on to a more pleasant subject.

'You don't really need to ask, do you, Ken? Passed with flying colours. BA Honours Degree in Modern Languages.'

'Wow, impressive!' Ken is beyond smug; now he is almost proud.

'Take a look at the photo there on top of the tele. That's Kevin and me on Graduation Day. I was so proud of him. Look at my smile.'

'He's a good-looking boy, Val, and it's a tribute to Rog and you that you got him through all this trouble and through college. You did bloody well, the two of you. So how did Kevin take Rog's death?'

'Firstly, he had to deal with our marital split then Roger's death. He still firmly believed that Roger was his father. He became very quiet and insular. He got even closer to me, and me to him. He became 'mummy's boy', but his education never suffered. He was determined to pass all his exams. All in all, he adapted remarkably well.'

'Does he still believe that Rog is his dad?'

'I consciously made the decision not to burden him with any more issues until he was grown up and able to comprehend it. This meant, in fact, that once he started courting his now wife, Christine, and marriage looked on the cards, I picked my moment and told him all. Everything you've now heard.'

'How did he take it?'

'He initially took it badly. He blamed me for Roger's death and said that he felt cheated. But Kevin is an intelligent person. He thought about it for a few days then came to see me, put his arms around me and said,'Mum, I have no right to judge you or blame you. Without your support and love I wouldn't be in the good position that I'm in today. I'm sorry I upset you when you told me about my dad. I love you, Mum.'

'Kevin met Christine at Cambridge. She got a 2.1 in Economics. She's a good level-headed girl and like Kevin, extremely intelligent. They got married in 1988 and now have two children - Jake, who is eighteen and James who is fifteen - both smashing kids.

'Kevin and Christine live in West London. Christine has just started back to work. They have good jobs, a great standard of living and lots of love in the house. I visit often, and enjoy them all no end.'

'Did you tell Kevin about Ken Waterfield, the villain of the peace?'

'I told him that you were my first love, my sweetest love, a fine man who went off in search of a dream. He asked me if you'd achieved your dream?'

'What did you say?'

'I said, 'Knowing Ken he will achieve his dream. He is a very determined man!'

'You knew me well!'

Chapter 36

1930hrs

Val is wearing a long plum-coloured, off-one-shoulder crepe de chine gown with a big bow across the waist, set at a jaunty angle. Ken approaches her and pecks her on the cheek. 'Wow, Val. You look gorgeous!'

'Thanks, Ken. I'm not on the scrap heap, yet! You look pretty good yourself.'

Ken is wearing a different suit now: German hand-made, navy, two-piece, two-buttons, wool and silk together with a white silk shirt, open-necked. He looks the epitome of 'cool'. 'Do I need to take anything to Colin's - flowers, champagne, gift of any sort? I must remember to take my briefcase.'

'All you need to take is yourself; that's the best present you could give them. Take yourself and be yourself. They won't expect any more or any less.'

'Oh, by the way, do you remember what day it is tomorrow?'

'No, should I?'

'My 65th birthday.'

'Oh my gosh, so it is. Happy birthday my darling. It feels like my birthday too, my re-birthday!'

Val and Ken already feel really comfortable together although it is only a few hours since they were reunited. The big issues are already discussed and there is now an ease that enables them to banter together.

The drive to Colin's house is about thirty minutes. They leave the town heading north, then branch off through two villages before bang on schedule drawing up at some big electric gates, overlooked by a CCTV camera attached high to a tree. A four-foot stone wall either side of the gates proudly shows the house name: 'Willington Hall'.

Val opens the car window and presses the button on the gate console. 'Ange, it's Val and Ken.'

'Come on in, Val.'

The huge gates click open and Val drives up a long, winding drive of crunchy gravel, edged by a six-foot wide grass verge. Tall, well-manicured shrubs and large mature trees peer down on them as they pass. A large, old stone-built house, its front covered with an ageing wisteria, comes into view.

'Colin lives here?' Ken whistles with incredulity. 'He's done well for himself, that's for sure.'

As they pull into the parking area at the side of the house, Ken spots two black Porsche cars, alongside them a Triumph TR4, a BMW 5 series and a van, with the words 'Hall of Music' proudly emblazoned on the side-panel. There is also a white van, with its tailgate wide open, advertising a local catering company.

'Looks like Ange has got the caterers in for us. That's excellent!'

As Val and Ken leave the car and approach the house, a stylish lady, tanned, blonde, with sparkly earrings and a ghost-long cerise gown with a pleated bust stands at the door to greet them.

'Hello, Val.'

'Ange, you remember Ken? Ken, this is Colin's wife, Ange.'

'Hello, Ken. Long time no see.'

'Ange, thanks for the invite. Do we know each other? Excuse me, my memory isn't what it used to be.'

'It's Ok, Ken. I'll explain later. Come on in, you two. Let's go through here.'

They enter a very large square room; three large triple-seater leather sofas are arranged around a large open fireplace. A Ray Charles CD is playing quietly in the background: 'Let the Good Times Roll' is the track; Ken knows it well. 'Count Basie backing? Sounds like it,' he thinks to himself. 'Dig this!'

'Right, let me introduce you.'

'Ken, you remember your drummer, Dave?'

'Dave Bell. Hello mate, good to see you again!'

'Ken, good to see you back in town. This is my wife, Jeanette.'

'This is Gary and Linda's son, Richard, and his wife, Louise. This is Ken, a really old friend of your mum and dad.'

'Hello. Not so much of the 'really old', Ange!'

'Linda has just popped upstairs. Colin and Gary are in the garage; they'll be back in a minute. Colin has just bought a new car and he's showing it off to Gary. You know, big boy's toys and all that.' She winks secretly at Val.

'Oh, and by the way, everybody; it's Val's birthday tomorrow.'

'Happy birthday,' rings around the room.

A minute later another woman confidently enters the room, smiling. She is more subtly-tanned, has long hair with the right mix of blonde and grey, wearing a long, cobalt blue, plunging Grecian-style dress made from a slinky stretch fabric with a 'V' neck and shoulder ties, oversized ear rings, multi-coloured necklace and gold bracelet, and with two rings on her wedding finger, one a sizeable diamond. She looks much younger than her sixty-five years.

'You remember, Linda, Ken?'

'How could I ever forget? Hello, Linda.'

The woman smiles warmly, her eyes making contact with Ken's. She is bubbling inside. She offers Ken her hand. Ken takes it softly then prefers to give her a warm embrace and a faint peck on both cheeks, then surprisingly a third.

'Ooh, thank you, kind sir. Three kisses - very European. Common practice here is six! That's three more, please!' Linda is rapier-sharp with her humour, as she always had been. Ken looks impressed. They both smile.

Linda turns to Val and kisses her twice on the cheek, then smothers her with a big, friendly hug. 'Happy Birthday, love. You certainly got yourself a birthday present never to forget: the man of your dreams! Did he turn up in shining armour on a white horse?' Linda's tone was now a little bit spiky.

'If you'll excuse me one minute I need to check out the caterers before they leave. Ken, there's wine, spirits, beer, soft drinks, mixers, ice, lemons, the lot - all over there. Please help yourself and see if anyone else wants anything.' With that, Ange leaves the room.

'Ken, please excuse Linda and me for two minutes. Linda has a present for me and I want to put it in the car before we get lost in the excitement later.'

Ken gives Val the stare, the look, that says, 'Please don't stir Linda up.

Don't rake up the dirt. Leave it, forget it, let it go!'

Val flicks her brow, then gives Ken the stare, the look, that says, 'It's Ok, Ken, I need to get this off my chest. Only then will I forget it.'

They all smile pleasantly, as the two ladies, arm-in-arm, each holding her dress slightly off the ground, turn and slightly hurry away out of the room back towards the car parking area.

'Let's get this present to you, Val.'

'Linda, get in the car and close the door. I need a minute with you.'

'Sounds intriguing. Ken looks dishier than ever. The long, greying hair really suits him. I think men get more sexy as they get older, don't you? He always had style, our Ken. Seems he's more debonair than ever. Lucky Val.'

'Linda. If I said to you 'Weston Mill, August 31st 1963' what would you say to me?'

After a pause of maybe five seconds and a deep in-drawing of breath, Linda's brain clicks into gear. She smiles inwardly, showing an impassive face to her best friend. Selecting her words very carefully she speaks slowly, I would say… that I'm glad he hasn't forgotten. I would say… that we were kids. I would say…… that I'm sorry, Val.'

Too quick for Val to respond, Linda continues: 'Before you say anything, Val, I would also say that you and me have been best mates, more so than even sisters would have been, for nigh on sixty years. Let's not have a row over something that happened all those years ago. You know what I was like, always have and always will have trouble keeping my knickers on when good-looking blokes are about. We shared everything in those days. I thought I'd share your bloke, too. I know I'm not perfect. Blokes are my weakness, Val.'

'Why didn't you tell me, Linda. In all these years, through all the chats, debates and heart-to-hearts we've had, and we've had plenty with all that's gone on… why did you never mention it?'

'Simply because I didn't want to hurt you.'

'If you hadn't wanted to hurt me, then you wouldn't have done it in the first place!'

'Maybe you're right, but it was an impulse, spur of the moment thing. You knew nothing and Ken had gone. So having done it, I didn't want to hurt you by mentioning it. You were already hurt enough by him leaving. Was I right? Tell me I was right, Val.'

'I was oblivious, so I wasn't hurt. But having forced the facts out of Ken today, I now feel betrayed by you, my best mate. Will you promise me something then we can put it behind us. Promise me that you'll never mention it again to anyone, not me, not Ken, not Gary, not anyone!'

'No problem, Val. I haven't thought about it for all those years, or mentioned it to anyone. My lips are sealed. Shake hands?'

'Shake hands? No! Give me a hug and a kiss!'

They hug. Val looks deep into Linda's eyes. She knows that she loves her like a sister but she can't be trusted with blokes ever. She hugs her again.

'Then you've never ever told Gary either?'

'No. As I said, it happened; it was forgotten. What Gary didn't know, Gary didn't worry about. You know what a whittle-bum he's always been. He's only one big panic away from another heart attack. You know that? Let's wipe the slate clean. What's happening with you and Ken? Come on, tell Linda all. You look radiant this evening, and happier than I've seen you for ages. Something's going on. What?'

'What's 'going on' is that Ken's mother is very ill. I mean, very ill. She's probably within days of passing away. We went to see her this morning and we're going to see her tomorrow.'

'How long is Ken back for?'

'As long as it takes. If his mum recovers then I would guess she'll need convalescence and maybe a Care Home organising. If she passes away, then I don't know.'

'And how is the great man?'

'He's very, very charming. He's how I hoped he'd be. No, he's even better than that. He's very gentle and kind with his mum and he's very understanding and pleasant with me.'

'Pleasant! Come on, Val. I've asked you to tell Linda all.'

'We've been chatting all day. We've got all the skeletons out of the cupboard, at least I think we have. We've laughed and cried. We've almost, in all honesty, continued where we left off all those years ago, unless any more startling revelations come out.

'All I can tell you is what he's told me. I don't know whether he's told me everything or whether there's anything else going on. He seems very close with his secretary, I know that. She's very young and good-looking, from what he tells me. I don't have the energy any more to fight for him with all this sexy opposition.

'Despite my doubts, my feelings for him have remained untouched and untarnished, as they were back in '63. He's taken knocks like we all have but he ploughed on and made it really big. He's been married, but his wife died a couple of years or so ago.'

'Very rich, very good-looking and very available!'

'If you want to put it in such a vulgar, direct way, yes, he is. Keep your claws out of him, Linda, else you're going to lose your best mate, and that's a promise. Are you listening?'

'Ok, Ok. I'm over all that now, believe me.'

'Ken is probably lonely and pretty scared. He's lost his wife of thirty years and he's stopped performing and writing. He's at a crossroads.'

'What about you, Val?'

'He shattered my heart into a thousand pieces and today, for the first time since then, I feel that the broken pieces are nudging back together again. You know that I've been at my own crossroads for twenty five years. I've been waiting for something to happen, or someone to come along, take me by the hand and show me the way. Not any old someone, someone special. I now know that the person I was waiting for is Ken, and he is here right now.'

'Slow down, Val. You don't know yet how he feels. He might be quite happy with his lot and not want another relationship. Be careful before you jump in at the deep end and get drowned.'

'All I know is that Ken is the man I always wanted to be with and that I would never want anyone else in the same way. I've always loved him and will always love him.' She pauses… 'Linda, if I tell you something now, will you promise never to mention it to anyone ever again?'

'You know I won't; I'm good with secrets, you now know that. I'm all ears. What is it?'

'You absolutely promise? Girl Guides Honour, cross your heart and hope to die?' pleads Val.

'Yes, yes, girl guides honour. Speak, woman!'

'It's my Kevin.'

'What about your Kevin?'

'Ken, not Roger, is the biological father of Kevin!'

'Oh, my gosh.' Linda is struggling to absorb Val's words.

'This has been my secret for forty years. I told Ken this afternoon. His reaction was just like yours: 'Oh, my gosh!'

'It must have rocked him to his boots. Has he got any other kids?'

'No, none. His wife couldn't have any. She'd been badly injured in a road smash before Ken met her and they always knew that kids were not an option.'

'Are you sure Kevin is Ken's?'

'Certain. Butlin's!'

'Butlin's, wow! Did Roger know this?'

'Not when I married him.'

'You mean you never told him?'

'We didn't know. I gave birth to Kevin in April '64; to all intents and purposes he was Roger's. But seven years later we found out that Roger was impotent and always had been. Kevin was conceived at Butlin's, no doubt.'

'I'm shocked, absolutely shocked! Can I tell Gary.'

'No, no-one. You promised.'

There is a knock on the car window.

'What are you two plotting now? 'Happy Birthday' for tomorrow, Val.'

Linda lowers the window. 'Hi Gary. Nothing, love, only a bit of girly gossip. We're coming right in. Is everything set in the garage?'

'Yep, see you in a minute.'

'Come on, Val. Ken'll be wondering where you are.'

The chums walk back into the house arm in arm, like the best mates they are. Linda has 'a cat that got the cream look' on her face.

'Ken, this is my Gary, and here comes Colin.

'Hi Gary, Colin, great to see you both! Fabulous place, Colin. They all shake hands warmly, half hug and slap each other on the back.'

Ken looks quizzically at Val as she returns to the room. The silent look which says, 'Are you Ok? What did you tell her?'

Val returns the silent look which says, 'Its all Ok. Don't worry, we've cleared the air. No big deal!'

Ken looks at Linda, who looks excited. Linda looks at Ken and lifts her eyebrows in a 'bet you didn't expect that, did you?' way.

Ange returns to the room. 'If everyone wants to come through to the dining room, there's a hot buffet; please help yourselves.'

As they file through, Linda takes Ken's arm and leads him back into the living room and shuts the door. 'Don't look so worried, Ken. I'm not going to attack you. Look, I've had a private few minutes with Val. She brought up Weston Mill. Remember, Ken? I think there's a chance you might!'

Before Ken can say anything, Linda is straight back in. 'Ken, we were kids. We had a bit of fun, that's all. I apologised to Val. You were her bloke at the time. I shouldn't have lead you on, should I? We've put it behind us. It's the last time it will ever be mentioned. Ok?'

'Ok.'

'How about you, Ken? Val told me that you lost your wife a few years back. I'm sorry to hear that. I know you've been successful, you're rich and as good-looking as ever.'

'Linda, you're still a stunner yourself. I love that dress. Expensive? Gary must have looked after you well?'

'That's another whole story, Ken. Let's say that Gary and I each know where we stand and we tolerate each other's foibles. Gary's basically a good man and I appreciate that. And Val?'

'Val and I met up again this morning. I was worried about today, how each of us would react. But we've spent all day together, and I've enjoyed nearly every moment. So much emotion, so much love! She's a fine woman, Lin.'

'She is, and don't ever forget it. Today isn't over yet; in some ways it hasn't even started. Let's go and join the others.' They move towards the door then Linda stops.

'Ken, you won't hurt Val again, will you? She's burned a candle for you for too long. She eventually got over you. She eventually got over Roger's death, she's had enough 'eventually getting over stuff' to last a lifetime. Now you're back. Handle her with kid gloves. She's not tough, like me!'

'Val is tougher than you think. However, be assured that I'll treat her like the lady that she is. Linda, it's good to see you looking so well, too.'

'C'mon Ken, let me take your arm. Let's join the others.'

Chapter 37

2100h

Val's ears are burning. She sees Gary and Ken chatting and goes over to them. 'Hi, boys. Are you talking about me again?'

'You should be so lucky! No, Gary's telling me about his heart attack.' Ken puts his arm around Val's waist. Gary excuses himself as his eye catches Linda beckoning him from across the room.

'Val, Gary was a lucky sod by the sound of it.'

'Luckier than even he knows.' Val whispers, 'Who do you think let the ambulance men into the house as he lay upstairs unconscious?'

'Linda, of course.'

Val smiles, gets close to Ken and whispers in his ear, 'No Ken, it was me.'

'You? Where the hell was Linda?'

'Linda wasn't at my house as Gary thinks she was. She was in London or somewhere with one of her fancy men. Sometimes she used to tell Gary she was with me. After he called me in an absolute panic, I drove to their house, and thank God I did, as I found the ambulance men on the doorstep and the door locked.

'I let them in with a key Linda had given me years previously in case she ever lost hers. It was me who went in the ambulance with Gary. I held his hand, I comforted him but he doesn't remember any of that. By the time he came-to after his op, Linda had turned up at the hospital and the story was hatched between us. He thinks she saved his life. In fact, it was me.'

'Blimey!'

'We had only one sticky moment with our story when the doctor addressed me as Mrs Hall. Linda and I were sitting at Gary's bedside after he'd woken up and Gary put them right. The doctor looked suitably confused before Linda ushered him away and set him right.'

'Linda caught with her knickers down again?'

'Yes, and by a stroke of luck, it was all smoothed over and the true series of events never came to light. Not to this day, so don't you go and enlighten him!'

'Secret upon secret! Oh what a tangled web we weave when first we practise to deceive!' Ken shakes his head slowly, raises his eyebrows and half-sniggers to himself. He is envious that Linda has this amazing ability to survive the most embarrassing situations and in this case she even comes out as the heroine.

'Gary's business started to go down the tubes in his absence. He lost contracts, missed deadlines and was hit by penalty clauses. Two of his key staff left the business at a minute's notice as they saw the writing on the wall. He never lost the house, but the business went bust.'

'Poor Gary.'

'He'd worked his socks off for years for nothing. It had all gone. The only good thing coming out of it was that Linda became the model wife and mother again, dedicating herself to Gary. She nursed him back to health and he got stronger. Eventually he became more confident in his health and wanted to get going again. It turned their lives and marriage around; they were together twenty four hours each day.

'They joined the Health Club at Colin's place. Linda started cooking properly at home again (no more takeaways, less eating out) and they ate the right stuff. Colin had decided that the Squash Club boom was over, business was diminishing and he drew up plans to convert it all into a Country Club. There was some internal building and electrical work needed and he gave Gary the contract, providing he could get a team of contractors together.

'Gary project-managed and completed the work on time and within budget. It got him back in the work ethic. He enjoyed it again. He was back to his old, bold self, thanks to Linda, then Colin.

'It wasn't long before Gary's dad passed away and Les Hall's Music Shop became part of his inheritance. The business, which he renamed 'Hall of Music', is still in its original location.'

Ange walks over and joins Ken as Val gets talking to Richard and his wife. 'Ange, you suggested that you knew me all those years ago.'

'Let me paint you a picture, Ken. The Waders played local pubs, church halls and night clubs dozens of times in 1962 and '63. Do you remember two girls who followed the band to almost every gig.

Always there near the stage?'

Ken casts his mind back. 'Hang on, I think so. One blonde, one brunette?'

'Spot on! I was the blonde - Angela White.'

'Angela White?' Ken squints his eyes as he thinks back all those years. 'Angela, are you that girl who was having the dust up with those three yobbos when Colin launched himself off the stage and got nine bells kicked out of him?'

'That was me.'

'If I remember, you and your mate, what was her name…?'

'Karen Mitchell.'

'Karen and you were real lookers. Not that you aren't now, of course. I mean you were head-turners. Very attractive, well-dressed, you were diamonds in a sea of mediocrity, Val and Linda excluded!'

'Diamonds in a sea of mediocrity, eh? Beautifully put, Ken. Very poetic. I appreciate your description. I'll try and remember that.'

'We all used to fancy you two and it was only because Val and Linda were our regular girlfriends that Gary and I never did anything about it. Blimey, Angela White. You had great legs if I remember correctly,' says Ken, looking down.

Ange lifts her long gown above her knee. 'These two, were they?'

'Wow, still great, Ange. I better watch what I say with your husband about.'

'Thanks for the compliment. We fancied you guys like hell, especially you. Kenny Waters and the Waders was a great band, our favourite.'

'Who were those yobbos giving you hassle on that infamous evening?'

'They liked to think they knew us. They hung around us and made suggestive remarks, but they were always tanked up and obnoxious. Colin couldn't stand by while they pushed us around. He leapt off the stage and 'waded' in. He was the only true 'wader', wasn't he, Ken? He took a bit of a beating but it wasn't in vain. He got his reward. Here he comes now. My hero!'

Colin walks across the room, a pint glass of beer in one hand, the other extended to shake hands with Ken.

'Who's your hero?'

'You are, the way you leapt to my rescue during that final Waders' gig!'

'Are you dragging that up again?'

'Ken wants to know why you did it? Over to you; I need to check how the food's going.'

'Ken, it's great to see you after all these years. Each of us in the group knew not to get involved in fights in the audience but (and it's a big 'but') those girls were regulars at our gigs. Those yobs were scum - pawing them, using appalling language and (again a big 'and') my dad was in prison.'

'So?'

Moving Ken towards the corner of the room and lowering his voice: 'What you didn't know, Ken, was that my old man regularly abused my young sister, Jeanette, and hit Mum more than once. When I saw those yobs behaving similarly something snapped inside me. I boiled over. No thought of consequence but a reaction to their action.'

'Is Jeanette, over there, your sister, who's married to Dave?'

'It sure is.'

'Well, your reaction was totally out of character with the Colin we all knew and loved.'

'Totally, but I'd had a bloody lousy day. Mum had told me she had cancer; her Friday night fancy man had robbed us; I'd heard that Jeanette was getting bullied by the local kids; the yobs at the dance kicking-off: I was totally wound up. I've done nothing remotely similar since. A pure one-off.'

'The last time I saw you, we bundled all the kit plus you into Dave's van with blood all over the place and heading off to the hospital.'

'Two things quickly changed my life: that young man there, David Bell esquire, got banged up in prison; Miss Angela White came to thank me for being her super hero.

'On the following Monday there was a knock at the door. As I opened it, with a face full of bruises, grazes, plasters, a bent nose stuffed full of cotton wool, arm in a sling, ribs paining me with each breath, in front of me stood a vision of loveliness.'

'Angela?'

'The very same. Bloody good name for an angel, eh? I always fancied her, Ken. I knew she loved the band but I was too shy to do anything about it.'

'But you did. You told me you became her super hero.'

'I invited her in. She wanted to thank me for saving her skin. She sat me down and dressed my wounds afresh. She had the gentle touch of an angel.'

'I know that touch, Colin.'

'Before she left, she asked me out.'

'She asked you?'

'She did. It was more a formal 'Thank you' on the following Saturday. She gave me a few days to recover. I was so dumbfounded, I said 'Yes'. How could I say 'No?' She was a cracker. We had a meal at the Chinese in Sheep Street and she paid the bill as a thank-you gift. My disfiguration and overall condition were the talk of the restaurant. It was quite embarrassing but I felt proud, proud to have helped Angela and proud to be with her, sharing a meal. It was a great feeling!'

'You deserved it, mate.'

'We got along like a house on fire. She was not only gorgeous to look at and talk to but I was always a 'legs-man'. Ange had great legs.'

'Has, Col! She showed me them a few minutes ago.'

'Ange enjoyed our evening and wanted to go out again with me. To top it all I found out that her dad was Joe White, who owned that big building company in Kingsthorpe. He was loaded!'

'Ah, I see now. You'd hit the proverbial jackpot.'

'I'd already decided to pack in the group. I'd had enough of playing in front of yobs like those and in any case Mum was seriously ill and died only a few months later. We also found out on the Monday that Dave was in trouble with the Law.

'As Mum went slowly downhill I looked after Jeanette and became more than a brother, also a mother and father to her. Angela was a big help, too. She and I grew closer by the week, and after a few months I plucked up the courage to let her invite me back to her house to meet her folks!'

'And?'

'And they were terrific. It helped that Angela introduced me as the man who'd saved her life. The story of that evening did tend to get exaggerated as the months went by.'

'As stories do,' interjects Ken.

'Incidentally, Angela's elder brother, Pete, was killed in a motorbike crash in 1961, so Angela became an only child. Joe White took to me and was happy for me to date his 'Treasure'. I couldn't settle at the Building Society with all that was going on at home, so Angela asked her dad to find me a job at White's. I made good progress there and they sent me on management courses. Working there enabled Joe White to check me out and satisfy himself that I was good enough for his daughter.'

'A perfect arrangement.'

'I'd imagine that Joe was alerted to the fact that my old man was in prison and this would have rung alarm bells for him. To his credit he gave me a chance. He gave me enough rope to hang myself, but I played a straight bat. I did everything by the book and he got to like me. I won my girl over those many months. Interestingly, I found out years later that Joe White's dad, Angela's granddad, went to prison for some minor receiving offences. Unbeknown to me at the time I had more in common with Joe than I thought.'

'An amazing sequence of events.'

'I told you that my dad was in prison, and by coincidence he was in Bedford at the same time as Dave. A nasty piece of work he was; a big mouth and a bully boy. Do anything for money.

'Dave got out of prison early with good behaviour. After a further couple of years he started dating Jeanette. We used to go out as a foursome with Angela.'

'So our Dave and your Jeanette became an item?'

Colin beckons Dave back over, who excuses himself from Jeannette again.

'All was going Ok until my dad turned up one day, fresh out of prison, commandeered the house and started bringing all sorts of women home; real slags. Things were a bit like that with Mum at the end, but everything had improved since her death and Jeanette and I had raised our standards and were living well. The old man started messing Jeanette about again and it was beginning to get to me. I told

Dave what was happening and he said 'Ok, leave your dad to me. I'll get him sorted!'

'Dave, you also became a battered super-hero?'

'Not exactly, Ken. Johnny Archer and Mick Miller owed me a favour for not shopping them for their burglary that I got banged up for. I called it in, pointed out Colin's dad to them in the Criterion pub one Friday evening and the following evening Colin's dad was set upon, bundled into a dark alley, kicked and punched into oblivion: broken ribs, broken jaw, broken teeth: a real hospital job! According to my sources, the perpetrators put £25 in his pocket and told him to leave town and never come back. He was never seen or heard of again.'

'The same £25 they gave you and put you in prison?'

'Not exactly, but I know what you mean. That was when I finally got my revenge on Walt Harris for what he did to me in the nick.'

'Being an ex-con, Dave was having trouble getting work, so I got him a labouring job at White's as a subby, no questions asked. He worked hard, earned good money and got back into the work routine. He extended his car maintenance education at Tech and soon got a decent job in the motor trade.'

'Yeah, Ken. I always liked tinkering with my motor bike and the van. Soon Colin and I started to buy old cars and restore them to their original glory, selling some, keeping others; it's our passion, isn't it Col?'

'It's our passion and now our business. That's Dave's old 1963 British racing green Triumph TR4 out the back, which he rescued from a derelict old barn and restored.

'Angela and I finally got engaged and we set a wedding date a few months later. In the meantime, Joe bought an old country house and land in the country and started to convert it into a Squash Club. For a wedding present he made us joint-managers on a salary-plus-profit-sharing basis with a promise: if we made a go of it, he'd give us the club in due course.'

'Give you it?' Whistle from Ken. 'Nice father-in-law!'

'He wanted to see how we worked together and how we reacted to pressure. We agreed that I would look after the Squash Club and gym and Angela would manage the bars and catering. It took off and we made big money. Joe was a happy man, and we loved it.

'As Joe got older and richer he gradually phased himself out of the business. Before he did, he separated off the Squash Club and handed it over to Angela and me - lock, stock and barrel. Then he floated the business on the Stock Exchange and made a boot-full of money'

'You fell on your feet with Angela, mate.'

'We got married. Dave was best man and Jeanette was maid-of-honour. She remained living in our old family home. Soon, Dave moved in with her. From what I remember one day Jeanette popped into the yard and found him reading Playboy. Dave told me that she plucked it out of his hand saying that she could perform better than that, and the rest is history.

'Joe passed away in '95 and Angela inherited everything. We sold his place and bought this. I built the garage block for somewhere to pursue my weakness: cars. I gave our old house to Dave and Jeanette as a Silver Wedding present. They sold their house, which gave them a few bob to enjoy life more.'

'So that rush of blood to your head, followed by a two-minute beating that you took at the dance, subsequently brought you untold wealth and a beautiful wife.'

'Crazy, but true. Instant Kharma, I guess!'

'Dave and Jeanette got married : reciprocal arrangement - I was best man, Ange was maid of honour. They had their problems, Ken, well Jeanette had, but they are through them now, and doing well.'

'I set up a Classic Sports Cars company fifteen years ago and installed Dave as General Manager. He has a workforce of four and Jeanette helps out on the accounts, phone and web site. If you want to hire a car we always have four or five available to choose from.'

'I might well need a car, Col. I'll bear that in mind.'

'Gary and I restarted the band about fifteen to twenty years ago. We recouped the guitars from your dad. Dave got some new drums.......at last! Gary's son, Richard, joined and it's like old times but without our star vocalist: you!'

Gary re-joins them and addresses Ken. 'Your dad had stored all the band's kit in a spare junk room since the day after you left. We forgot all about it. Then, years later when Colin opened the Country Club, he needed a house band for Saturday evenings. Rather than hire one he suggested that we did it. Rog had snuffed it, so Richard took his place on the Yamaha keyboard instead of guitar. I did the vocals. Rather than buy new kit, I went round to see your dad and after a tedious negotiation he released it for £500. Tight bugger!

'I made sure it was still in one piece, so I loaded it up and it was now ours to own. Here's the interesting bit: what your dad didn't know was that the original guitars from the early '60s were starting to be worth big money. Other groups in town from those days had sold their old instruments for nominal amounts and upgraded to new shiny ones. My Fiesta Red Fender Strat was a 1962 original and is worth around £15,000, maybe more. It's increasing in value as each year passes and is well insured. That's perhaps my pension pot there, although I would be loathe ever to sell it!'

'Wow!'

'Colin bought his Framus Star bass from me and chipped in £150 for it. It's now worth £1500-£2000. Rog's Hofner Golden I sold a couple of years ago for £1500. I bought the Yamaha Keyboard for Richard, and he's become quite accomplished. You'll remember that Dave's Olympic drums weren't the best. He's since bought some new ones from the shop.

'Louise, Richard's wife, is a good singer; she shares the vocals in between rearing children. We've kept the name 'The Waders' as we had good local street cred from the '60s. We play at the Country Club for two hours each Friday and Saturday evening. Our style is more 'middle of the road', with the occasional rock song thrown in on party nights.

'We play covers, nothing original: '50's, '60's, '70's pop, R&B, country… usual stuff. We enjoy performing even after all these years. I also like to throw in the occasional Shadows instrumental for old time's sake and to show off a bit!

'That doesn't surprise me.'

'It keeps us all together and it keeps us all friends, an extended family 'par excellence'.'

Chapter 38

2200h

Everyone continues to tuck into the delicious hot food and excellent wine, and chat about the last forty plus years: wives, husbands, children, grand- children, houses, cars, business, holidays, investments: the subjects that fill a successful person's life.

Covertly Colin, Dave, Gary and Richard individually leave the room while Ken, in line with a pre-arranged plan, gets cornered in the kitchen by Val, Linda and Ange, where he begins to entertain them with episodes of his life and loves over the years. Twenty minutes elapse and gradually music can be heard coming from somewhere. But where?

'Ken, the boys have a little surprise for you. Follow me.' Ange leads the way.

It is almost dark outside as they all file out of the kitchen to the other side of the building where the security arc lights flick on as they approach and bathe the courtyard in bright white light. As they approach the garage block, the music gets louder. Ange presses the remote control, secreted in her hand. One of the three double garage doors electronically starts to open and there inside Ken can first hear and then see a 'live' group hammering out a song he knows well.

The group is Gary on lead guitar, Colin on bass guitar, Richard on keyboards and Dave on drums. The song is 'It's Funny How Time Just Slips Away', an old favourite of Ken's, written by Willie Nelson.

Gazing around the huge fifty-foot square garage block Ken is amazed to see four vehicles: a Mini Cooper S convertible, what looks like a racing car, an old 1970's Ford Escort Mk 1 RS2000 and a really old van which looks the 'spit' of the old group van, the 1950's Fordson, same colours, red top, white bottom, and yes, on the side, it reads 'Kenny Waters and the Waders Tel 4640'. It can't be the original group van, can it?

Two big wall industrial size heaters cosy up the building and two big coloured stage lights on tripod feet add glitz and atmosphere. The five girls take the plastic chairs neatly laid out for them in front of the group. Ken points to three banners that drape across the ceiling.

In bold red and blue letters one reads 'CONGRATULATIONS, KENNY WATERS & THE WADERS - 50 YEARS' ANNIVERSARY' from your girls'.

The second reads 'HAPPY BIRTHDAY, VAL' and the third one, which appears to have been home-made at the last minute, not professionally like the other two, reads 'WELCOME HOME, KEN. IT'S BEEN TOO LONG!' Balloons and streamers festoon the whole area.

Ken remains standing, shakes his head and cups his chin in his right palm in awe of what he is seeing. He is bubbling inside and suddenly can't wait to get involved. The group breaks into 'I Live the Life I love, and I Love the Life I Live', the old Willie Dixon blues number given a great new jazzy feel by Gary and the Boys. Gary has lost none of his zip on lead guitar, and the sound he's getting from his original Fender Strat belies its years.

As the song ends and the applause kicks in, Gary chips in with, 'Ladies and gentleman, I would like to welcome you to Kenny Waters and the Waders' 50th Anniversary Bash. I invite onto the stage to do a couple of numbers, our original vocalist and leader and still our great friend - Mr Kenny Waters. Kenny please come and join us.'

Ken, very excited, heads on to the large, patterned carpet square which acts as the stage, having taken off his suit jacket, folded it neatly and handed it to Val. Kenny and Gary go into a huddle and after a few exchanges, Kenny takes the mike. 'I'd completely forgotten the Waders had indeed first come together in 1960, so in honour of that fact we would like to play two numbers from that era. These two songs were the two destined to be encores on that tumultuous night of August 31st 1963. I think it is now time to finish that gig!

'The first is from Marty Wilde and the Wild Cats. Maestro, please…'

Gary times the musicians in: 'uh 1, uh 2, uh 1-2-3..'

'All the people down the street, whoever you meet

say I'm a bad boy, say I'm a bad boy, say I'm a bad boy;

Even dear old Dad when he gets mad

says I'm a bad boy, says I'm a bad boy, says I'm a bad boy…'

Ken completes the song and bows to the girls, who applaud enthusiastically.

'Hey Colin, is that our old group van over there?

'It certainly is. It's Dave's original which I looked after for him when he was inside. Over the years it started to rust badly, so I decided to spend a few grand and Dave and I stripped it down and refurbished it. We replaced most of it and there it is, almost sixty years-old.'

'Amazing! I'll take a look in it later. Ok, let me just have a quick discussion with Gary and Louise. Val could you pop out to the car and fetch me my briefcase, please? We won't start the next number without you, I promise.'

Ken, Gary, and Louise chat with lots of nods and chuckles. Val returns and hands Ken his slim, brown leather briefcase for which he thanks her. He pops it down on the floor while Gary is updating the other band members and the microphones are repositioned.

'Ready? Yep? Right. I'd now just like to invite Louise onto the stage to help me with this one, and also all you other girls (yes, you lot), Val, Linda, Jeanette (he beckons them up). Please get together and use Gary's 'mike' Gary will share with Colin.'

'Us? You want us to sing? We can't sing!'

'Yes, you can do it. Don't be afraid. This will be a united effort and I need you all to help, Ok? This is the first ever performance of the new British super-group, 'The Waders Family.'

Louise has a quick discussion with the girls, who look dumbfounded to be asked to perform.

'I dedicate this to you beautiful girls, our special girls, to Jeanette, Louise, Ange, Linda and Val. Without them, where would we all be?'

'A bloody sight richer!' comes the retort from Gary. Linda sticks her tongue out at him. Colin chuckles, but cannot agree with Gary's sentiment.

'It's a Shirelles' number and for our backing vocalists over there I need you to help me with the refrain, even the verses if you remember them. Watch Louise as she'll give you the cue each time.'

The girls look generally excited, maybe a little nervous. After all they've never been on stage and they've never sung. Louise gives them a quick team brief and soon gets them organised alongside the mike stand.

'Ok, Louise, are you ready? Fine. Gary, when you're ready...'

'On 1... 1-2, uh 1-2

'Tonight you're mine completely
You give your love so sweetly
Tonight the light of love is in your eyes
But will still love me tomorrow?

Tonight with words unspoken
You said that I'm the only one
But will my heart be broken
When the night meets the morning sun...'

More verses follow, then tumultuous applause rings out from everyone - the girls, the band, and Ken clapping the band, too: so much love in the air. Ken shakes hands with each of the band members and a kiss for each of the backing vocalists and Louise. Ken's professionalism, voice and style just lifts everyone to participate and give their absolute best.

'For those of you who haven't performed live with a band before, how good does that feel? Wow! What a performance, no practice, straight in. Perfect. Well done!'

'For my final number, I've chosen a very special song. Richard, may I please commandeer your keyboards for just this one song. The rest of you can all sit down and relax; I'll perform this one alone.'

Richard is happy to accommodate, stands up and moves into the audience. Ken drags on another chair and positions it alongside his behind the keyboards. He invites Val to come and take the spare chair alongside him.

'It's Ok, Val. I'm not going to ask you to sing again. This song is special for me and special for Gary.'

Gary looks quizzical, wondering what Ken is going to sing.

'This song was written by Gary Hall and Ken Waterfield at Butlin's in August 1963 and is dedicated to our wonderful girls, Linda and Val.'

Gary moves behind Linda and stands with his arms around her. She looks over her shoulder, smiles at him and gives him a peck on the cheek. Ken repositions the height of the microphone, looks straight at Valerie and begins:

'I've been waiting so very long

To let you know how I really feel

I've always wanted to let you know

I've always cared for you

I am in love with you

You're the only one in this world

I consider my first true love

And if you ever go away

I'll always be waiting

Today, tomorrow and forever

Chorus:

My first true love is the one I'm thinking of

It's because it's my first true love

And baby it's you

There are two more verses and choruses. Ken sings the final chorus in Italian. A huge embrace is followed by a soft, gentle kiss on the lips for Valerie from Ken. 'So that's all from me for now. Let's take five as I need a few words with Gary and Linda.'

Everyone applauds.

'Remember that song, Gary?'

'Sure do. Well, some of it.'

'I took the handwritten lyrics from you at your dad's shop on that last Saturday afternoon in '63, remember?'

'Yep, we were both struggling to complete the song.'

'I took that tatty piece of paper with me to Germany, then on my travels around Europe. Twenty years later, I still had it and I finally discovered what was missing. I inserted a new melody line, did a neat chord change, played around with the words and slowed the tempo a little. In 1985, I finally completed it to my satisfaction.

'I recorded it in Italy, added some Italian verses and in 1987 it reached number one!'

'Blimey, number one?' Gary and Linda look at each other, totally amazed and excited.

'The song was copyrighted as a Hall-Waterfield composition. Ken takes out of his briefcase, a vinyl 45 in gold, in a presentation frame. This is for you Gary, mate.'

'And there's more. He hands Gary a file of papers. Each year since 1987 I've received a statement from the Italian recording company, in fact the one I owned, of the royalties earned on that record. Those royalties are for record sales and for air plays. They were split 50:50 between you and me. I opened a special bank account in Italy and your share of the money has accumulated in the account and even gained interest. The royalties initially were very substantial, but obviously have tailed off over the years.'

Hearing all of this, the rest of the group move in and circle Ken and Gary. 'Gary, I have a cheque for you here in Euros. Here you are, mate. Well done and congratulations!'

Gary, totally dazed by all of this, looks at the cheque and completely breaks down: '58,187 Euros. This is all mine?'

'Sure is.'

Linda grabs Gary by the hand in which he is holding the cheque and begs, 'Let me see, Gary. Oh my ....!'

Ken hugs Gary. 'So you made it big, too! You just didn't know it!

'I'm sure that you can put this to good use in the Studio or for your retirement, mate.'

Everyone is shaking hands and hugging.

Ken breaks the round of congratulations. 'I would finally like to thank you all for your warm welcome today. It's far more than I ever envisaged. You are all fine people. It's so good to be back amongst you all, my family!'

Val's mobile phone unexpectedly rings, breaking the adulatory throng as Val quickly finds her phone in her handbag and moves aside and away to somewhere more private.

'Hello, yes this is Mrs Edwards, who is this please? Yes, sister. Yes, Mr Waterfield is here, hold on.'

'Ken, it's the hospital on the phone for you.' Ken's mood does a 180; now he looks worried. Val passes the phone to him and stays close. She even links her arm with his, to try to comfort him in case.

'Ken Waterfield speaking.'

'Mr Waterfield, this is Sister Taylor on Grafton Ward. I'm sorry to have to report that your mother has taken a turn for the worse. She's a lot frailer. She's in and out of consciousness; her pulse is very weak. If you can get down here as soon as possible, I think you should. Mr Waterfield, I would suggest that someone comes with you, if that's possible.'

'Ok, thank you sister. I'll be there within (he looks to Val who mimes the words) twenty minutes.' He hands the phone back to Val.

'We need to go, Val. Sorry, love.'

'Ken, you don't even need to ask. I'll go and start the car and turn it round. You say a quick 'Goodbye' to everyone.'

He interrupts the others who are salivating at the size of Gary's cheque.

'Excuse me, everyone. I'm going to have to love you and leave you. The hospital has called. Mum isn't doing well at all; I need to be there immediately.'

Linda (a hug and a big kiss on the lips); Gary (a warm handshake and a back slap). 'I'm sorry to leave so early.'

Colin, Ange (likewise): 'Thanks for your hospitality; I'll maybe speak to you tomorrow.'

Dave, Richard (warm handshakes), the girls (quick embraces). 'See you guys, stay in touch, perhaps see you sooner rather than later, then I'll finish telling you what I started.'

They all wave as Ken gets in Val's car and they pull away. After ten minutes buried in his thoughts of his mother and how she might be, Ken awakens his consciousness. 'How was it on stage, Val?'

She smiles broadly: 'Wonderful. You're a real showman, Ken Waterfall! I mean Waterfield.'

'Do you now understand a bit more why I left to follow my dream? Would you ever get that feeling sat behind a desk juggling with taxes, depreciation and trial balances? Think what it would be like performing in front of an appreciative audience of five hundred, a thousand, five thousand or sometimes more. It's one hell of a buzz.'

'I hear you, Ken.' She squeezes his arm in recognition.

The roads are quite empty; they soon reach the hospital.

'Ken, I'll drop you at the double doors. You go in. I'll park up, get a ticket and join you in a minute or two.'

'Ok, and thanks, Val.'

*

'Sister Taylor, how is she?'

'Not good, Mr Waterfield. We've got the screens around her and please be aware that she's hooked into a few machines. Try to ignore them. She was about awake last time I looked in.'

'Sister, Mrs Edwards will be here in a few minutes. Please send her in, too.'

Ken takes his mum's hand. It is bony, it is slightly yellow in colour, wrinkly and bruised, but it is warm. He kisses it gently.

'Mum, it's Ken.'

After a few seconds she opens her eyes slowly. 'Hello Ken, are you here again? You're spoiling me now with your visits. Twice in one day, is it?'

'Mum, I need to say sorry, sorry for leaving you and Dad, sorry for going away, sorry for not coming to see you more often.'

'But you're here now, Ken, that's the main thing. Ken, would you promise me something? Would you promise me that you will look after Valerie and not leave her again. She is a really good girl. I think she is still very, very fond of you, Ken. Will you promise me that you'll do that?'

Ken takes his mother up from the pillow and gives her a gentle, gentle hug, then the softest kiss on the forehead.

'Yes, I promise, Mum.'

'Thank you, Ken.' She smiles then her eyes go glazed.

At that very moment the machines flicker and bleep. Mrs Waterfield, in the arms of her son, gradually eases her way into death and tranquillity. Sister Taylor rushes in with Valerie right behind her. 'It's Ok, sister. No rush, she's gone.' Ken's face is now a true waterfall... of tears. He slowly eases his mother back onto the pillow and kisses her again. 'Good night, Mum. Oh, and Mum, give my love to Dad. Mum, thanks for the cake.'

Val takes Ken into her arms and tears are now rolling down both their faces. 'Take my hankie, Val.'

'No, Ken. You take mine.'

'Will you look after her now, Sister?'

'She's in a safe place now, Mr Waterfield. Please take as long as you want before you leave but please drop by tomorrow; there will be some paperwork and your mother's belongings for you to take.'

'Val, I think I would like to pop into the hospital chapel before we leave, if that's Ok. C'mon then, let's go and find it.'

Ken and Val spend ten minutes in the chapel. It is quiet. He regains his composure, blows his nose, wipes his eyes and starts to feel a bit more together and ready to leave.

'Ken, can I say that when I came to see your mother a few days ago, she gave me your number and asked me to call you. She was very lucid that day and we had quite a chat considering, as it turned out, she was only days away from death.

'We talked about you, we talked about your father, we talked about Roger, we talked about me; in fact, I said a lot of stuff to your mum that I probably wouldn't have said to my own mum if she was still alive. I even told her about Kevin, that he was your boy.'

'How did she react to that?'

'Absolutely fine, a big smile. She said that she had an inkling all those years ago, especially as Kevin grew up; he does have some physical similarities to you.

'Anyway, as I was about to leave, she asked me to promise that if you came back to see her, would I look after you and never allow you to leave me again.'

'And what did you say?'

'I gave her my promise, Ken.'

Ken smiled.

'Well you better do it, then.'

They linked arms.

'By the way, I called the hotel at teatime and told them you wouldn't be needing your room after all.'

ABOUT THE AUTHOR

Martin Thompson is the pseudonym for the writing partnership between Derrick A. Thompson and William (Bill) Martin.

Either sitting at his workstation or pondering thoughtfully at a table in his local café, Bill can usually be found contemplating dialogue or phraseology toward the next writing milestone in his prolific partnership with his lifelong chum, Derrick. In 'Last Night' he can see parts of himself in all characters, their ups and downs, their hopes and fears, their strengths and weaknesses and between its covers, he reveals his love for cutting edge music within a context of social realism.

It should be noted that in Chapter 22, the discussion with the Beatles is a factual discourse between Bill and The Fab Four which took place at Campbell Square Police Station on November 6th 1963.

Derrick is a former European IT Manager for a large multi-national, who in 2002 retired after 37 years service. It left him well-travelled and with a project mentality of tasks, milestones, budgets and completion dates. His left hemisphere was overdue a rest then soon relishing a new challenge. At last he had time on his hands. In 2008 he produced 'A Whole Scene Going' an account of Northampton Town FC in 1965-66. In 2009 along with his lifelong friend Bill they produced 'Have Guitars Will Travel' a journey though the Beat music scene in Northampton 1957-66. His life-long loves are Northampton, football and 50s and 60s popular music. He yearned to exercise the right side of his brain, to create something new, fresh, fictional, but still complete it on time and within budget, the best of all worlds. He embraced the challenge. He longs to share it with you.

Here it is. Enjoy.